TWO KINDS OF COLOR

By Deborah Kennedy

Copyright 2009 Deborah Kennedy

License Notes

This book is licensed for your personal enjoyment only. This book may not be re-sold or given away to other people.If you would like to share this book with another person, please purchase an additional copy for each person you share it with. If you're reading this book and did not purchase it, or it was not purchased for your use only, then you should purchase your own copy. Thank you for respecting the hard work of this author.

June 23, 1970

CHAPTER ONE

Jimmy Tate stood at the bar. If one wanted to figure him out his clothes did the talking. To step back and take a good look at him he may have been fifty-five or fifty-six. He lied about his age so much he forgot the truth of it. In actuality no one knew his real age. To put forth his picture of vanity, his race to wipe out time while warding off creases, and wrinkles, he used Noxzema Medicated Skin Cream and avoided smiling too broadly. A red cosmetic sponge was always handy in his breast pocket. He used it to mop the shine off his face, decreasing the glare of moisture that bathed his dark skin. To maintain his weight of one-hundred and fifty-nine pounds he took two laxatives twice a day and ate more vegetables than meat. Where style of dress was of great importance he ignored current fashions. He dressed according to the look of black hustlers in their prime during the late 1950's.

Where call of crime demanded center stage, the color of skin being of great importance, Jimmy had no women who were darker than himself. To sum up the rest of Jimmy Tate besides his ownership of illegal gaming and whore houses in Chicago, Terra Haute, and Gary Indiana, and the extortion of a few black owned businesses, he made most of his money off the backs of women. Overall he was known as a malicious, vain, and nefarious bastard that lived by the mirror.

Jimmy was on his third whiskey. On this night his suit chosen over many of his expensive styles, and textures for the summer season, was a light brown silk. It was a perfect match to the light brown silk tie and white silk shirt. Reminiscent of the time when suits and hats, complimented the other, his hat was perfectly boxed and cocked to tilt down low on the right side of his head. He took off his hat and sat it on the bar next to his drink. In a poorly lit bar like 229, he appeared as a wealthy businessman out for an evening of fun.

He swayed slightly to the rhythm of the jazz music that came from the juke box. For the third time he gave Reggie the two-finger signal to move his ass and pour him another whiskey.

Reggie, a black man in his early sixties, owner of 229, took his time going to Jimmy. The bar was packed with a new model of noisy hustler shimmering in gold, demanding his attention. "I ain't pourin you more whiskey," Reggie told Jimmy. "When did you start drinkin' anyhow?"

Jimmy was not a drinker. He indulged when his mind was weighted with the type of trouble threatening his money. "Don't you have a fuckin' business establishment to run?" said Jimmy. "Why don't you mind it for a nice fuckin' change?"

Reggie blew off the comment and poured Jimmy another whiskey. "You knew you would never keep a woman like that. You dumb son-of-a bitch, puttin' all your money on one goddamn horse runnin' faster than all the rest. Freddie was too young when you caught her. She'll be young when you're old and dead."

"Women like her make a winner like me, old man."

"Not on the fuckin' day they decide to keep runnin' away from home."

"She's mine until I say she ain't. It ain't her decision."

"The word around here is you gave her permission to leave you."

Jimmy sipped his whiskey. "Yeah, well, I changed my mind."

"Nobody expected you to keep it."

"Somethin' ain't right, man." His voice took on a serious tone. "The way the motherfuckin' police is shuttin' me down. They're shuttin' me down, man. They won't take my money. I know who's behind the shit."

"You two-bit track-dirty pimps are all alike. When it all falls down you go lookin' to put the blame on somebody else. When the goddamn police don't take your money they're tellin' you somethin'. They're sendin' you a good clean signal. It's over."

"Go on," said Jimmy, smiling over the truth of the conversation. "Let me hear what you gotta say. I feel hot enough to listen to your shit. Come on with it."

"Yeah, you gettin' exactly what you deserve," said Reggie, wiping the bar around Jimmy, emptying ashtrays and putting them back on top of the bar. "You bastards make all the money in the world. When the well dries up you wanna kill some whore, because you ain't got shit to show for all the money you made off their efforts. If Freddie is smart, like everybody say she is, she's probably got more money than you ever had in your fucked-up life."

"So I heard." He drank the full shot of whiskey.

"Her and Ruby own that house, don't they? I heard it was paid for. Is your name on it, Negro?"

"Tilt the bottle motherfucker."

"I feel like a blessed king when you sweet daddy bastards get down to sellin' all your fancy shit. I can tell when you're ready to get a job sweepin' floors. Just don't come here lookin' for work. I ain't hirin' your black ass. Go on and get the fuck out of my business establishment. You drank your courage."

Jimmy tossed down the rest of his whiskey. "It's time to go anyway." He put on his hat, cocking it to the famous tilt. He reached inside his suit pocket and removed a hundred dollars from a gold money-clip. He threw the money on the bar at Reggie. "I'll talk to you later, old man. Take it easy."

"You do the same."

A lot had been said between the lines. Reggie hoped Jimmy heard him, and didn't take the conversation as just another pissing contest.

Jimmy exited 229 and stepped onto 55th Street's main drag on the South Side of Chicago. He had given Reggie part of the last eight-hundred dollars in his pocket. He thought Reggie was right. His time was over. His desperation of what to do with a life on the verge of losing everything colored him completely.

SPITS & ANGELA

Across an alley adjacent to the Walker house was a garage apartment that came with the property. It was a greasy and musty one-room hole. Spits, Jimmy's sidekick of support and flunkeyism, lived there. He was a tall black man in his early thirties. Because he was too thin for his height he had a crooked lean to an unsteady gait. The most noticeable and sustaining impression about his character was his intense call for life to recognize him as a man.

To step back and take a look inside the room, where Spits lived, the alley grime that came from shoes gave the once shaggy-red carpet the color of charcoal burgundy. There was an overused and ragged sofa that opened out into a full-sized bed. Most of the time it stayed in an upright position and Spits slept on it that way.

A handy man's make-shift table sat next to the sofa. A radio, edges broken and chipped, sat on the table. Sitting next to it was a black telephone with no dial. Spits could only receive calls. All of them were from Jimmy telling him what to do.

Overall Spits was a loyal, clean, man who had to live clean in a dirty place. He was not a complainer. Having grown up in Alabama, he was used to living in poorer than poor conditions.

On this same evening Jimmy instructed Spits to go to the Walker house and pick up his eight-year old daughter, Angela Walker. She sat on the far end of the sofa and Spits sat at the other. A sledgehammer divided the space between them. It sat with its iron head on the floor and its wooden handle leaned up against the sofa.

Though Angela was a pretty child, to get under the skin of others, she deliberately made herself ugly, creepy, and frightening to look at. Her face was always compacted into its most common form of poked out lips. An angry and tight brow swelled up high over shifting, narrow, cat-brown eyes. The way she wore her braids made her look like a puffed up baby bull. The three braids stuck out like horns ready to gore open anybody that got in her way. She loved and adored her braids. They assisted her with intimidating those who became her victim.

Jimmy believed nothing bad about his little girl. He admired her. When they were together he subtly trained her to idolize him. She exemplified his disregard and hatred for human life; in particular, her mother, Freddie Walker, and her mother's best friend, Ruby Johnson.

Angela swung and kicked her feet back and forth, banging them on the sofa, pretending they were heavy as lead. The dead thudding sound of her black brogans bothered Spits, making him anxious. He didn't like the girl. He wanted whatever crazy thing Jimmy had planned done and over with. He could feel how vindictive Angela's thoughts were against the adult she believed caused her new raid of terror.

Angela ended the awkward silence. She looked at Spits. "Your radio is all messed up. It stinks in here like dirty underwear. I'll be glad when my daddy calls. I'm ready to leave."

Spits smiled at her. "You like all this. I know you lied on the Jew just to get your daddy back here to hurt somebody."

"You don't know what you're talkin' about." She rolled her eyes at him. "That Jew did what I said he did. On top of that my mama had that goin' away party without evenin' tellin' my daddy. He's gonna beat her up real good. On top of that my daddy, my daddy, say nobody can come in our room."

"Now, I get it," Spits laughed.

"What you laughin' at showin' them old-crooked teeth. Your mouth looks like it's in jail."

"One day that's where you're goin' because you just that mean. You lied on that man because you know your daddy hates him.   He's your mama's friend and not her customer."

"I ain't movin' with my mama. My daddy said I can come and live with him."

"You don't know where your daddy lives. Nobody knows that."

"I do know where he lives. I do know. Mr. Ugly."

"I still say you lyin' about all that stuff you told your daddy.

"So what if I did tell a lie. You ain't nobody. You ain't the lyin' police. My daddy say you just his flunky and doormat."

"Yeah, I guess there's some truth to that."

She swung and kicked her feet harder against the sofa. She wanted to break something but the old sofa was tough.

"I'm through workin' for your daddy. I'm all fed up with the both of you."

"Good. We all fed up with you, Mr. Ugly. You just mad because my daddy always believe what I say and not what somebody like you want him to. I'm his little girl and nobody is but me." She lifted her arm and flashed her silver-identification bracelet in Spit's face. She pointed to the inscription. "See, it says 'Jimmy Tate's little girl.' My daddy bought it for me before he went out of town."

Spits laughed. He knew he had to do it. He leaned closer to her. Through his handicap of spraying spit, when he talked too fast, he told her, "Yeah, that's what it says alright but that don't mean it's true."

"It is true," she yelled. "I ain't like my brother and sisters. I know who my daddy is." She wiped her face with her hand. "You spit on me. I'm tellin' my daddy on you."

The phone rang. Spits answered it. "Yeah," he said into the receiver. It was Jimmy on the line. After a few seconds of listening Spits hung up the phone, rose to his feet, and picked up the sledgehammer. "Come on." He extended his hand for Angela to take it.

"Don't touch me. You dirty. You spit on people when you talk. I hate you." She stuck her hands into her jacket pocket, stood up, walked to the door and waited for him to open it.

After they stepped onto the alley's ground, and the door was closed and locked, Spits grabbed Angela by the collar of her jacket. He pulled her up on the balls of her feet. "You need to see all of what happens tonight. This is your work. I hope you remember it for the rest of your life. You hear me you evil monster?"

Angela jerked away from him. "Shut up. You spitin' on me again." She wiped her face with her hand and then wiped her hand on her jacket. "I'm tellin' my daddy everything you said to me."

Jimmy crossed the midway of 55th Street's heavy car traffic. When he got to the other side he was near the mouth of the alley that led out and onto the main drag. He went around the corner toward a black convertible, Ford, Galaxie 500. Spits and Angela were inside.

Jimmy drove onto 55th Street. Two young hustlers waved at his car before it passed them. Jimmy despised the young men who were taking on the same profession. To him they had no class or gentlemen manners. They wore big afros instead of processed hair. Colorful and flowering polyester blouses took the place of silk shirts. Gold chains were more impressive than silk ties. Bell bottomed jeans or tight polyester pants took the place of a silk suit. Their hats were big, floppy, and furry. Sunglasses, rimmed with rhinestones, were worn and never taken off until they went to sleep. Everything about the new and modernized Jimmy Tate was big and overdone. The men looked more feminine than masculine. Some even grew their nails long and painted them with color. To Jimmy this new look had no truth to it. Everything about the men taking his place was a lie. A lie to convince young women they were emotionally sensitive, kind, men with a young girl's feeling of feeling sweet compassion.

White women, those considered beautiful and ugly, were not a novelty anymore. Where there had been only one, maybe two, in the entire neighboring ghettos of 55th Street, there were now too many. From the old hustler's point of view they had no class or self

10

respect. Most were runaway flower children addicted to the worst kind of drug.

FAMILY SHOES

7:05 P.M.

Mr. Straub finished restocking his shelves and taking inventory. He was a shy, young, and quiet man with an affectionate and trusting smile. Though the store was closed he waited for Ruby Johnson to pick up four pair of shoes. They were going away gifts for Freddie's children.

His clientele, the same as all the shops on 55th Street, was black and ninety percent were women. Mr. Straub's best sales were made throughout the rush of an oncoming holiday, party, or special event. And within the panicky anticipation, surrounding such times, the women sent him running back and forth inside a war of shoes. Many wanted the same shoes Freddie wore with handbag to match. But not to appear as copy cats they wanted the items in a different color.

When the war was over, and the women satisfied with the dazzle of their handbags and shoes, Mr. Straub was exhausted. He had to close up, lie on the sofa, and take a nap. He was proud of his popularity with the black women. Their persistent, stubborn, aggressive ways, and precise knowing of what they wanted, pushed his business into being successful.

Some of his most loyal customers pretending not to like him, kept an eye on shoes and handbags behind the store-front glass. They told him when his merchandise was on its way out of style. He liked that the women thought enough of him to keep an eye on him.

His mind drifted to last night's going-away party and how much fun it brought. He was under the impression that the five who attended were special friends that Ruby and Freddie liked. It pleased him to find himself as one of them.

He pushed the party out of his thoughts and started his bookkeeping. A few seconds later the crashing sound of shattering glass stunned him to full attention. The door to the main entrance of the showroom had gone beyond its normal point of stopping. It slammed and kept banging against a wall of shelves that displayed Children's shoes. All the shoes were shaken loose from their balance. They fell in clutters, spreading out over most of the floor. Jimmy walked in. There was a sledgehammer in his hand.

Fear took hold of Mr. Straub and controlled him. It began its dissent from the pit of his stomach, climbed to his chest, and rested there to pound his heart.

The door swayed to and fro while hanging lopsided from its bent hinges and loose nails. The people passing by glanced briefly inside, but kept on walking. It was too dangerous to take on the role of witness regarding Jimmy Tate's tirade against a Jew.

Jimmy raised and flung the sledgehammer with quick precision onto every shelf and wall displaying high heel shoes and handbags to match. The core of his battering was directed toward the showroom's blue-pastel chairs. With the devastation of each one, Jimmy showed obvious hatred for the chairs as if they were despised people. Mr. Straub was aware that Jimmy must have known Freddie chose the chairs during the remolding of his showroom.

Finished with the destruction of chairs, Jimmy walked and stood in front of Mr. Straub who was petrified and stuck where he stood.

Jimmy wielded the sledgehammer over his shoulder, in back of his self, and to the other side of his self. With his feet planted firm, and with a swing of braced motion, he raised the sledgehammer as high as he could, over his head, and then sailed it to come down crashing upon the cash register. The blow of such violent force sounded as if a world of customers were being totaled and rang up all at the same time.

Thin splits and big pieces of metal as dangerous as shrapnel from a gun were air born and landed everywhere inside the store. A piece of metal lodged into Mr. Straub's shoulder. From the corner of his eye he saw his shoulder had begun to bleed.

Jimmy took a deep breath and looked around at the disaster. He wanted to see the result of his insane madness. It wasn't enough. He was only relieved of a small amount of frustration. His erratic and lethal adrenalin had wiped out all traces of Reggie's whiskey. He was his normal self again with a new upsurge of psychotic behavior. All of his violent tendencies were free flowing and deadly.

Mr. Straub's showroom had been destroyed within a little over sixty seconds. It took him and Freddie a long time to decorate the room to what looks and feels comforting to women not easy to get along with.

Jimmy picked up where he left off. He continued to destroy the place with his sledgehammer.

Mr. Straub found his feet. He eased closer to the telephone that hung on a wall near the register.

"Touch the phone," Jimmy told him, "I'll bash your head in."

Mr. Straub tried to steady his nerves to calm. "Take the money, Jimmy. Take it and get out of my shop."

Jimmy laughed. "You think this is about money? I don't want your money, motherfucker. Do I even look like I need your money?"

Those who didn't know Jimmy had begun to form a crowd in front of the store. Spits, holding Angela's hand, worked his way through the crowd. They walked inside purposely late. Spits lifted the loose door and straightened it good enough to close it and lock it. The door's shade had no window to support it. Spits pulled it down anyway. Angela slipped her hand back into his.

Spit's silent language with Mr. Straub conveyed the expression of no responsibility. Earlier, he had given Jimmy the sledgehammer telling him to do his own dirt. He told Jimmy he was terminating his employment and moving back to Alabama.

Mr. Straub read Spit's message clear and clean. Spit's fate would be taken under consideration when retaliation was being decided. Mr. Straub was street savvy. Every Jewish shop owner had to be that way to survive within an all black environment. Violent trouble that came upon one of them came upon all of them. What to do about it was decided inside their own court of law.

Jimmy laid down the sledgehammer. He held his hand out to Angela. "Come here baby," he told her.

Angela squeezed Spit's hand. He could feel the girl trembling and seemingly, in slow motion, urine began to trickle down her legs. A puddle formed and spread into the carpet under her feet. The smell of urine, plaster, and metal permeated throughout the showroom.

For Spits, seeing Angela like that brought about heart-felt sympathy. He reminded himself Angela was just an eight-year-old child. She was a victim of her father's insane, regimental, brutality.

"Come here baby," said Jimmy.

She tightened her legs together and tried to hold it back, but the last of her urine came spilling faster down her legs.

"Stop pissin' on the goddamn floor. What the fuck is wrong with you? Get over here. This motherfucker can't hurt you. Come here."

Spits loosened Angela's tight grip. He stepped out of the puddle of urine spreading under his feet. Angela went to Jimmy and squeezed her hand onto his.

"Is this the man, baby?"

"Yeah," Angela replied, looking at the floor.

"Look at him. Dammit!"

"I don't want to, daddy. Don't make me."

"I said look at him."

Angela raised her head, avoiding eye contact with Mr. Straub. She looked at his chin.

"What did he do?"

"He came into our room last night."

"What else did he do?"

"He closed the door and sat on my bed. I told him I was gonna tell my daddy on him if he didn't leave."

"What did he say?"

"He begged me not to tell you and then he got up and left. He was at Mama and Miss Ruby's goin' away party. Mama is leavin' you. I swear it daddy. You can ask Betty Jean and Neda."

Mr. Straub was in a place of stunned. "The girl is lying. She's lying. I did not go inside the room. I made the mistake of opening the wrong door. I was looking for the toilet."

"Shut the fuck up," Jimmy told him.

Mr. Straub didn't know what to expect next. He looked over at Spits. "I'm giving you a chance to get out of my store. If you do not leave, I will call the police. You will not go unpunished for this." Mr. Straub turned and attempted to walk to his phone. He had no intention of calling the police, but he did know who to call.

Jimmy pushed Angela aside with more force than intended. She fell to the floor and began screams of crying.

"What did you say, motherfucker?" Jimmy asked.

There was no more fear. Mr. Straub was just livid. "You know what I said, Jimmy. You will not go unpunished for this. The girl is lying."

Jimmy erupted. He reached out and grabbed Mr. Straub by the front of his shirt. He twisted and locked his hands into the material and flung Mr. Straub into the wall.

Spits unlocked the door and opened it. He yelled at Angela, "Go get in the car." She did not hear the order. She lifted her head and watched Jimmy drive his fist into Mr. Straub's face several times. When Mr. Straub fell to the floor, she stood up and ran out.

"Come on, man," said Spits. He went to Jimmy and grabbed his arm.

Jimmy pulled out of his grip. He reached inside his breast pocket, removed his red-cosmetic sponge, and mopped the sweat off his face.

Spits picked up the sledgehammer and walked out with Jimmy behind him. The sound of police sirens could be heard.

On their way out three men entered the shop. They were considered peculiar by those who saw them. The suits they wore were black. All had beards, mustaches, and side hair with curls. They were older than Mr. Straub. One of the men, similar in size, coloring, and height, could have been Mr. Straub's father.

The men were shocked when they saw the catastrophic damage. They silently agreed that Jimmy Tate had signed his own death warrant. Something so horribly violent happened and was now kin to revenge, justice. It was understood between both races that all forms of ramifications were fair and just. And even though their religious beliefs were not the same, all of them believed in the evenhandedness of one God.

MR. CLARK'S GROCERY STORE

Mr. Clark had a calloused and off centered face. Though his outer self was one of a hard, serious, middle-aged-black man to some others he was considered shy and bashful. From the young female perspective, where thoughts of an older man come up out of discontent, Mr. Clark had a sweet and reliable way about his character that sometimes, when comfortable enough, made its self known.

The business establishment in which he was sole proprietor was inside the heart of the 55th Street ghettos. Two blocks from the main drag. It was a fat and wide one level shack made of brick and tar. The ass of the store, same as the back porches of three story tenements, on either side, sat inside a long and narrow strip of alley. Overhead, because of an unstable patch of track, trains pushed forward careful and slow.

To help Mr. Clark conceal merchandise he could go back to prison for selling the store was a confined and disorganized wreck on purpose. There were many rows of shelves behind the counter that covered all four walls. They began at the base of the floor and rose seven stories to the height of the ceiling. There was no even, straight, or flowing harmony about their position. To assure an assortment of merchandise Mr. Clark sold only small items like canned goods, junk food, cigarettes, playing cards, dice, bullets and illegal half pints of whatever kind of liquor was popular at the time.

Where the satisfaction of a child's taste is concerned, before the last ring of the morning's school bell, children crowded into Mr. Clark's store to point and choose from the extensive variety of candies underneath a glass-counter top. For them his store was a place of mystery and anticipation.

On this night Mr. Clark was behind the counter. He had Ruby Johnson's grocery list in his hand. He was a short man who used a step ladder to reach for things on the last three top shelves. He was slow and methodical picking up the items he needed to put inside the brown-paper bag sitting on the register's counter. He thought about Ruby and Freddie, and of last night's going-away party. Most everybody knew private things about Ruby Johnson and her best friend, Freddie Walker. They knew and feared Jimmy Tate. Freddie had four children. Two of them were white, two of them black, and none of the children had the same father. For those aware of this it was negative-religious testament revealing what Freddie did for a living. For religious destroyers of the Achilles Heel, kicking those underneath their blind and hypocritical points of view, it was okay to subject spoken cruelty to Ruby, Freddie, and the children whenever an occasion arrived. If Mr. Clark was present on such occasions he always defended the family.

Half done with the most important items of the order there was a jingle of the bell at the store's back-alley door. Young Ruby Johnson had arrived. She was a quick stepping, pretty, slender, black woman in her mid twenties. She was average in height and weighed a hundred and fifteen pounds. To step back and take a good look at Ruby one immediately suspected she was raised in that place. Her brown eyes sparkled with an overflow of interest, and showed the kind of feeling that said she could fight just as hard as she loved.

Once a person heard her speaking voice they were given confirmation. She was indeed from that place of shame and fear … Mississippi.

She went to the counter. "Hi, Mr. Clark. You got me ready to go?"

Mr. Clark had sincere affection for young Ruby. He picked up another item and came down from his step ladder. "I'm almost there, Miss Ruby. How are Freddie and the kid's?"

"Oh, everybody's fine. We're lookin' forward to the big move."

Ruby looked inside the brown paper bag. She shifted around what was inside. Seeing that most everything was there, she looked at the clock on the wall above the counter. It was 7:45 P.M. The last shadows under daylight had left the store. She wished Mr. Clark would move faster. A bad sign crept near, beading her skin. The snaking of phlegm had begun draining from her nose and into her throat. Like a nasty, imaginary, cold coming on the taste made her stomach queasy. She believed it was one of her familiar spells—a warning of undeniable intuition. She thought something was going wrong somewhere, something bad was coming.

The jingle of the bell at the back-alley door had broken her thoughts. Thelma Brown, a black woman, in her mid thirties, a neighborhood grade-school teacher walked in.

Ruby took Thelma's presence as part of the sign of something bad coming. Because of a previous incident over the schooling of Freddie's children, Thelma had become Ruby's fine harassment. Each time Ruby came into contact with Thelma she treated her like a repulsive insect with the determination of more than a pest.

Cowering at Thelma's feet, sniffing, and wagging his upturned tail was her dog Chi Chi. He was a white-toy poodle but no longer recognized as being one. Thelma tugged him on a short leash to Mr. Clark's store three times a day. Because of the daily march, and dragging of his resistance, Chi Chi was a dirty hairball of black-alley soot.

"I told you not to bring that damn dog in my store to shit and piss everywhere," said Mr. Clark. "I told you to tie him up in the alley."

"Humph!" said Thelma, "My Chi Chi has never toileted on your floor, Mr. Clark. You must be talking about some other dog. Humph!"

Thelma picked up Chi Chi. In the way a mother carries a small child, easing the weight, she positioned the dog to rest on the bone of her hip. She walked and stood behind Ruby. The sour smell of whiskey had trailed in with her. The foul odors, including the dog's chicken breath, relaxed on Ruby's back.

Ruby turned and looked at Thelma. Her eyes were lifeless with no remains of sheen and the whites had switched colors to fading yellow. It was clear to Ruby that Thelma's liver and kidneys were not working together anymore. They had gone their separate ways in search of relief. Regardless, Ruby felt no pity for her fine harassment.

Thelma cleared her throat and readied it up for the correct enunciation of a teacher's proper English. She moved closer to Ruby who felt more of the heat of whiskey breathing down her neck. Thelma cocked and craned her head high. She looked over Ruby's shoulder and inside her bag. After seeing all she needed. "Why, in God's name are you buying a box of bullets, Ruby Johnson? The Lord only knows what you need them for. You might as well tell me too."

Ruby gave a bit of laughter. It had that infamous, unique, and well-stated ring of Mississippi sarcasm. She turned and looked at Thelma. "Well, Thelma, I was thinkin' about killin' Jimmy Tate. Then I got to thinkin' and talkin' to myself. I say killin' him may not be enough to satisfy my murderin' appetite. Maybe I should march down the alley, creep up the back steps to Thelma Brown's apartment, and knock on the door. When she opens it I'll shoot her in her proper-talkin' head."

Thelma took two steps backward, and four steps to the side, placing herself at the end of the counter.

Ruby turned her attention back to her groceries. She tilted her head sideways and watched Mr. Clark. She liked the way he was in love with his store. There was an ample amount of pride and dignity walking around it with him. She wondered if she would miss him.

Mr. Clark pushed aside what was in his way, covering up boxes of bullets, hiding them quickly. "How many cartons of cigarettes do you want?"

"Three."

He pushed, moved, and shoved around more items until cartons of cigarettes shown themselves. He walked to the counter and placed the cigarettes inside Ruby's bag.

"Don't forget Freddie's Wall Street Journal," said Ruby.

He reached underneath the top rack of newspapers and picked up a Wall Street Journal. He put the paper into Ruby's bag and began ringing up her items. His face was sad and his head low. "I'll miss you around here, Miss Ruby." Be careful walkin' down that alley."

"Don't worry about me, Mr. Clark. I got the Lord with me every step of the way." Knowing she would never see him again, she leaned over the counter and gave him a warm and brief hug. She touched his cheek and brought tears to his eyes. All she could do was smile at his sentimentality.

24

She picked up her bag of groceries and went to the back alley door. The bag was heavy and needed both her arms to cradle it. She turned and looked at Thelma, stroking the bleary-eyed old-poodle. The sudden tenderness of pity she felt for her, and the poodle, had softened her heart. She was happy Thelma had something to love even if it was just a dog.

"You take care now, Mr. Clark," Ruby said, leaving, back-alley door closing behind her.

It took forced effort for Mr. Clark to gain the composure that stops a man from crying. He was glad Ruby, Freddie, and the children were moving on the good side of town. He was pleased Freddie was dumping Jimmy Tate, and changing her life for the sake of her children. He punched the keys of his register, flushing out the rest of Ruby's sale.

Thelma stumbled up to the counter. "Did you hear that? I'm thrilled those women are moving out of this neighborhood. Humph! The Lord is not with Ruby Johnson in any step of the way. Humph! All of that whoring and gambling inside the Walker house, in front of those despicable children. I tell you, Mr. Clark. Ruby Johnson, Jimmy Tate, and Freddie Walker, are going straight to hell. If God doesn't intervene, with expediency, those ignorant colored and white children will follow right behind them. You remember my words, Mr. Clark. Remember what I said."

"You don't know what the hell you're talkin' about," said Mr. Clark. "Get your ugly-mean ass outta my store and go home. I ain't sellin' you no whiskey. You're drunk enough. Get out of here before I pick you up and throw you out."

On her way to 55th Street's main drag, walking down the alley, Ruby's thoughts were about last night's going-away dinner. The room available for the gathering was the kitchen. Five close friends had been invited. Mr. Straub was among them. Iris and Candy Thomas were there. They were two black sisters, twenty-year old identical twins, that lived in the last tenement closest to the Walker house. Both were single mothers. Mr. Clark was there. He left his young wife at home because she wasn't too fond of white people. To Freddie's pretended disappointment, Ruby had invited Parker Bishop.

To step back and take a good look at Parker he was twenty-seven and stood just over six feet. He was not a charismatic man, but good looking in an odd way that causes a woman to wonder which parent he favored. He had the kind of physique that could only come from playing tennis. One of the main physical attractions was his hair. It was blond, thick, layered, and heavy. It lapped about his head and stayed in waves where he wanted when he ran his fingers through it. It was more golden than yellow and had highlights of silver that glistened under dim lights and candles.

Though his features appeared spatially perfect they were not. His jaws were a bit uneven and the left side of his face jutted out more than the right. Ruby thought his eyes, the permanent color of dark blue during the sunniest part of the day, were set too deep in their sockets. Overall she thought he was handsome. She liked that Parker smiled a lot and laughed out loud. His upbeat personality made it easy to accept him.

For the twins Parker was like an exotic bird. He had landed onto their laps of intrigue and drama. As the night wore on, Ruby, Iris, and Candy drank too much champagne. They began whispering, giggling, and looking suspiciously at Parker. When the nerve was there Iris leaned and whispered something to Candy. Candy whispered what she said to Ruby.

Ruby was embarrassed. "You can't ask him somethin' like that," she whispered to Candy.

"Yes I can. He doesn't care."

The deep stare Candy gave Parker could have been taken for lustful desire, or just playing around. Candy narrowed her eyes, smiled at Parker, and asked him straight out. "Parker, have you ever been to bed with a black woman?"

Ruby nearly fell out of her chair. Iris and Freddie hid behind giggles while Mr. Clark and Mr. Straub laughed out loud.

Parker sat up straighter. He was not laughing and his look was serious and thinking. He kept his eyes staring into Candy's.

Candy kept her eyes staring into his. He moved his head slowly up and down and tilted it from side to side. He pretended to contemplate giving her more than just an answer. Candy didn't back down. The table was quiet and waiting for the answer.

Parker reached out and put his hand on top of Candy's. "Candy, I have to truthfully say no. I have never been to bed with a black woman, but," he squeezed her hand, "I'm ready anytime you want to give it a try." After the laughter had settled down Parker looked at Iris and then Candy, "Twins would be nice." The table's laughter didn't calm back down for almost a minute.

More wine and champagne was poured. Ruby studied Parker and looked closely for his faults. She saw how much he was in love with Freddie.

THE WALKER HOUSE

Freddie Walker, white, mid-twenties, was a vivacious woman with an unparalleled splendor of natural grace, class, and beauty. She stepped out of her bedroom and into the corridor. She was dressed comfortably in black slacks and a plain white shirt. How elegant she was shone through without the usual distraction of makeup and expensive clothing. To step back and take a good look at her, from a short distance, her hair looked like gathers of black velvet flowing heavy onto her shoulders and down the crease of her back. Most of the time she brought it up, pulled out the waves, piled it high, braided it firm and wrapped the braid in neat circles. She then pinned it into a flawless bun. One could see that her slow-blinking eyes were not hazel as believed. They were deep green, and the color of the ocean when there was no sun.

Besides the light of a small lamp, on the corner of her dresser, the rest of the house was dark. She picked up Angela's doll from the floor and put it inside an opened suitcase. Before locking it, and stacking it on top of the others, she took a moment to gaze at the face of the doll. Angela wanted a white doll. Because she was angry at the child she refused to buy it. "You're a little Negro girl," she told Angela. "Little Negro girls should have little Negro dolls." Now she believed she should have bought Angela the white doll. She had forced her own child to look at a plastic doll's representation concerning the difference in color of skin. For Angela the black doll had reiterated a negative fact instead of a positive one.

Freddie walked back inside her bedroom and stood in front of the picture window. While looking out from behind the white nylon curtains she could see the four corners of 55th Street and the parade of neon lights. Three of her children were with her. After years of not wanting them close enough, to feel their breath, she couldn't get an adequate amount of their presence. She had unexpectedly fallen in love with her children.

29

There was plenty of space in her bedroom for all them to visit when they wanted. Where decorations of beddings and curtains were billowing parts of the room, Freddie favored the faintest of pastel colors. The room was sparse of furniture. One dresser stood at the back wall. The top of it displayed bottles of expensive perfumes, powders, and makeup. Behind the dresser was a mirrored wall. It ran the length of the back of the room. Jimmy favored mirrors when mirrors favored him. After his reflection began aging, he stopped looking into mirrors with loving admiration for his self. One night table stood beside a full-sized bed. On the bottom shelf were library books about finances and next to them were several Wall Street Journal's. A small television on a gold-plated metal-stand was easily rolled out of the way. All the floors in the house, except for the kitchen, were made of oak and shellacked to a high shine.

Freddie turned away from the window and leaned against the edges of it. She wanted to look at two of her children. Danny was twelve and Neda was ten. Both were sitting in the easy chair with their feet up on the foot stool. While Danny watched a western on television, Neda flipped through the pages of a picture book about Puerto Rico.

Out of the four children Neda was her most delightful child. The unparalleled splendor of beauty and grace had been passed on to her. She had a perfect inheritance of her mother's long and shapely

30

legs, confident stride of her walk, and radiant smile. Though Neda's eyes were the same color, of the ocean when there was no sun, they were more vibrant with longer and thicker lashes. Her skin had the most intense hues of deep brown and red walnut. The bone structure of her mother's face, and high-cheek bones, were under a crown bursting with the waviest and blackest ropes of hair that stopped at the middle of her back.

Freddie remembered a terrible night when Neda was seven years old. She climbed onto Freddie's bed while she was sleeping. Neda pulled and tugged her arm until she was awake. Freddie rose up on her elbows and looked at Neda. "What is it baby?"

Neda shoved the photograph of a man in her face. "Is that him, Mama?" she asked.

Freddie took the photograph, looked at it, and asked Neda, "Is that who, baby?"

"Look at him real good," Neda told her. "Is he my father? Huh? Is he a Puerto Rican? Jimmy said I was a Puerto Rican."

Freddie sat all the way up. Photographs were strewn from head to toe all over her bed. The eyes of so many men were gazing up at her. It made her sick, disgusted, to see the mess of men. Neda had dug up the history from the beginning.

Coming out of her memories, Freddie looked with love and concern at Danny and Neda. The chair was close enough for her to reach out and touch them.

Neda turned to the next page of her picture book. She nudged her brother. "Look, Danny," she said, "it's a doggone miracle. I look just like her, don't I? I really am a damn Puerto Rican."

Freddie tried not to laugh but sometimes the two were as comical as they were inseparable.

Danny glanced at the picture. "You're nuts," he told Neda. "You don't look like that. I don't wanna here anymore about the damn Puerto Ricans."

Freddie laughed. She leaned and ran her fingers through Danny's straight-blond hair. It was beginning to mature into a sandy color, getting thicker. The boy was becoming tall and gangly. She thought him all arms and legs. She swept her fingers through his hair again, using them like scissors.

Danny moved his head away from under her hand. "Stop that, Ma. I don't need a hair cut yet." He hated the cutting of his bangs. He didn't like people looking into his blue eyes, trying to figure out what he was thinking. From behind the security of his bangs he could look through them and hate Jimmy Tate without him knowing it.

Freddie remembered the time Danny asked her, "Mama, do you know who my father is?" When she didn't answer him he accepted the silence to mean his father was a nameless blank. He never asked her again.

Six year-old Betty Jean was Freddie's youngest child. She had been born frail and premature. One leg was slightly shorter than the other. Starting at the age of three, in an attempt to stretch Betty Jean's right leg to meet the toes of the left, cruel methods were done with awkward braces. This did not work and gave Betty Jean great pain. The sound of the child's voice, even with laughter, was never without pain. To keep her from constantly falling down another heavy and stomp-around steel-brace had to be worn until she could keep herself balanced. On certain days when she was happy, playing like a whole child without the brace, her limp was not noticeable unless one was looking for her flaws.

Freddie looked at six-year old Betty Jean. She was asleep, curled up like a red cat in the middle of the bed. She remembered the face of a boy that had become a man where his age was concerned. The boy's skin was pasty white and every inch of his body freckled. He had the bluest of green eyes that were sunny and smart. What she remembered most about him was his shimmering-red hair.

Looking at Betty Jean, she saw the boy's red hair flowing on top of the white pillow case. She even had a fair amount of the boy's freckles. Just the same as the boy's, her eyes were the bluest of green and sunny and smart. Still, Freddie could not remember the boy's name or anything else he told her about his self.

For Freddie, threatening to change was no longer just a threat. She made the final decision for the sake of her children. Someway, somehow, they had crawled back up inside her; securing an immovable stay inside her heart. Everyday there was something about her beautiful black and white children to marvel at.

Freddie walked away from the window, sat on the bed, and covered Betty Jean. Outside a familiar car horn sounded three times through the room.

Danny stood and went to the window. He looked and saw Parker Bishop standing outside of his car. Parker smiled and waved at Danny. Danny smiled and waved back. It was the first time he had done that.

"It's your friend, Mama," Danny said.

Betty Jean stirred awake. She opened her eyes and rose up on her elbows. She looked at Freddie. "Is it time to leave, Mama? Don't we have to go before Jimmy catches us?"

"Go back to sleep, honey," Freddie told her. "I'll wake you when it's time to go."

"Promise, Mama," said Betty Jean, "this time we're really leavin'?"

"Promise, this time we're really leavin."

Betty Jean relaxed back into the comfort of the soft bed and closed her eyes. Freddie took a moment to look at her three children. She would not move without all four of them. As she turned to leave, a strong gust of wind came in through all the opened windows.

"Close the windows," she told Danny. "It looks like a storm is comin'."

After their mother left Danny and Neda became concerned. Seemingly out of nowhere a powerful, isolated, forceful wind stirred outside and inside. It was elastic, rigid, pushing against its own energy, suctioning to the house like an inflexible glove. A straight hum of the strange wind was heard under the guts of the house. It made the floorboards creak and whistle in tune with the rattle of window panes.

Danny remembered what Miss Ruby said about the wind: *"When a strong wind comes up from the ground and down from the sky, at the same time, and goes no place but one place, he's called Winder. Winder's weather means God is upset and worried over the salvation of something innocent."*

KEYS TO THE HIGH WAY
FREEDOM

Parker Bishop's 1969 Impala was parked in front of the Walker House. He was behind the wheel and Freddie sat next to him. Though it was the third year of their friendship, and he knew all about her, she was still extraordinary. She made him sweat with the worst passionate hunger a man can have for a woman …the shoving kind that can rip the insides of a woman apart. She was the kind of woman weighed down with all the right ingredients a man needs to fall deeply in love for the rest of his life. He thought if she didn't get out of the car soon the heat, and natural fragrance that comes from the earth, attaching its self to the hidden places belonging to a beautiful woman, would cause him to do something stupid. He did not want to lose the war he was winning against Jimmy Tate by making the mistake of groping and slobbering all over her. Though he loved her the rules they shared were those that promised them as friends and never lovers. He thought those rules temporary and believed she did too.

He shifted away from her and put his back against the car's door. He wanted to look at all of her. He liked the clean and innocent look she brought to sit beside him. She looked like a rich man's wife.

"I can't leave without all my kids, said Freddie."

"I don't expect you to." He sat up straighter. "I would never ask you to do such a thing." He removed a set of keys from his pocket. "Here," he said, urging her to take them.

"No." She pushed his hand away. "I don't want those keys if it means leavin' Angela behind."

"I wasn't thinking of leaving the girl behind."

"Sure you were. The way my kids are ain't anybody's fault but mine. Don't be ashamed of not likin' Angela. Nobody likes her. She's a mean and hateful girl. But I know she can change."

Parker did not want to think about the eight-year old that derailed their plans. "I've got an idea."

"I'm listenin'."

"She's still with this guy, Spits, right?"

"I think they're in the garage apartment. I told you he won't answer the door."

"I'll make a phone call. I can have a police escort here in ten minutes, before the sick son-of-a bitch follows through with Jimmy's plans."

"Don't blame Spits. He's just doin' his job. He does whatever Jimmy tells him to do. He's still a decent guy."

"Decent guys don't go around the neighborhood breaking arms and legs with crowbars, baseball bats, and sledgehammers. The worst shit is right in front of you, but the only thing you see is a fucking ice-cream cone. After all you've been through, how can you be so naïve?"

"He's caught up in Jimmy's crap like the rest of us. Involving the police is like begging for more trouble. I can't put my kids through that."

"You're not being reasonable. If you don't leave with me, now, you're putting yourself and your children in harm's way. Jimmy is out of control. He's losing everything."

"What do you know about him losing everything? Did you have anything to do with something, Parker? Don't lie. Look at me."

"No. I heard about it."

She didn't know if he was lying. He was perfect at blending the smoothness of truth and lies until they disappeared. "Are you telling me the truth?"

"Yes. Jimmy is responsible for his own demise. He doesn't need any help. This whole neighborhood is better off without him."

"You know nothin' about this neighborhood or these people. It's just strange. All his places are closing down, one after the other. That's why he's so worked up. He doesn't want me to leave him with nothin'. He's afraid of bein' an old black man with nothin'."

"Oh! Do you owe him some kind of retirement fund? I thought you and Ruby agreed to give him the house."

"I have to have the papers drawn up."

"I had nothing to do with his situation. I promised I wouldn't interfere in your personal life." He looked up at the window. He could see Danny looking down at them. From the way the boy moved near the curtains, fidgeting, showed how anxious he was and probably afraid.

Danny walked away from the window and back to Neda. He turned off the television.

"What did you do that for," asked Neda. "I was watchin' somethin'."

"We gotta make a plan."

"A plan for what?"

"Just in case somethin' goes crazy."

"Mama and Miss Ruby planned everything right. Mama's friend is nice. Miss Ruby thinks Mama might marry him. He don't care what color we are."

"Neda, you ain't listenin' to me. We gotta do somethin' if it doesn't work out. I mean if …"

"Huh, you mean about Jimmy. He knows Mama's leavin' him. Miss Ruby said he just don't know when."

"Snakes like Jimmy have got more than a million heads, Neda. He's got millions of snake eyes everywhere. Everybody is always tellin' him what mama is doin' when he ain't around. They even tell him what we doin'. Angela tells him everything."

"This is the right time to go, while he's out of town."

"What if he comes back before we leave? What if he is back? He's gonna be mad enough to kill mama for tryin' to sneak off. We have to help her if he tries somethin'."

39

"Help her how?" She reached and moved her brother's bangs away from his face, looking into his eyes. They were cold and serious.

"I mean it, Neda. I'll do anything to keep him from hurtin' her. I ain't kiddin'."

The look in her brother's eyes frightened her. "Miss Ruby will be back soon. We won't have to do anything crazy."

Parker pushed the keys at Freddie. "Take them." He put the keys in her hand and covered her hand with his. "The house is all yours for as long as you need it. Just hurry up and get the hell out of there. Okay?"

"I will." Her eyes pooled with tears and fell onto her lap without touching a cheek. "If you stripped Jimmy Tate down to the bare nakedness of nothing, underneath is just a frightened and useless-old bully."

"Yeah, sure, some useless old bully. The guy throws temper tantrums that border on psychotic episodes. That's what concerns me." Parker touched her cheek.

She lifted her head and looked into his eyes. "I have to go." She pulled away until she was out of the heat of him.

He grabbed hold of her hand and squeezed it. "This is scaring the hell out of me. I won't leave you. Just tell me to stay. I'll park around the block, out of the way. I won't come up unless ..."

"Don't be silly. If he tries anything, I'll call the cops. I'm not afraid."

The way she smiled, so reassuringly, had almost calmed him.

She opened the car door and got out. She bent down low and leaned halfway inside the car's open window. "I'll see you later, Parker Bishop."

He hoped his sensation of doom was just something passing by quickly, unnoticed by fate. He thought he had a chance of being the only man in her life. If he could win her for himself they would move out of the State of Illinois. Everybody would have a fresh new start.

TERRORIZING THE INNOCENT

Danny remembered what Miss Ruby said about ferocious lightning and thunder: *"Thunder is God's voice. He's growling at an evil monster causing his good children a lot of trouble. Thunder is the voice that comes up from God's stomach. Lightning is God's eyes blinking, helping Him see better in the dark, helping Him see what the evil thing is up to. When God is stirring up His thunder, and lightning in an unexpected way, it's best to run and hide under something."*

Jimmy was there, quiet, and seemingly depressed. He sat on the foot of the bed with his elbows resting on the tip of his knee caps. His head was down and his face cupped inside the palm of his hands. All three windows were open and the strong wind from the pending storm blew the sheer-nylon curtains to billow up high and close to the ceiling.

Danny and Neda were hiding under Freddie's bed listening to the thunder and feeling the swoop of the wind. They saw flashes of lightning bounce off walls and reflect on the floor around them. Still, there was no sight or sound of the rain Miss Ruby called God's tears. Betty Jean was still asleep and out of sight, buried underneath the white-satin sheets and comforter. Angela, her legs crossed, as though watching an entertainment show on television, was sitting on the floor near the dresser with her back against the wall. The strong smell of urine emanated from her clothes.

Freddie, appearing relaxed and free of fear, stood leaning against the window's sill. Her arms were folded defensively while her eyes were fixed on Jimmy. No matter how unafraid she looked she was terrified. She knew his sorrowful emotion was a manipulated-phony act for sympathy that would soon vanish and turn into terror. And no matter the fear, no matter what kind of weeping and pleading was done, none of it stopped Jimmy from beating a woman senseless. Female-scared emotions egged him on until the fever of his violence mingled with a woman's blood.

Jimmy saw Danny's bare foot sticking out from under the bed. A feeling told Danny his foot had been seen. He dragged it slowly out of view. He pushed his body up further, near the left poster of the headboard.

"I know you under there, white boy," said Jimmy.

"Leave him alone," said Freddie. "Or so help me God, Jimmy…"

"So help you God. God ain't in this. Tonight is the first time you'll meet the devil baby, the real thing."

Jimmy's voice awakened Betty Jean. She raised herself up on her elbows and peeked out from under the covers. She saw Jimmy sitting on the foot of the bed and began to cry. Freddie took a step toward her.

"Let her cry. That's what she should be doin'. Everybody in this goddamn room should be cryin.'"

Neda wanted Betty Jean under the bed. To get Betty Jean's attention, she hit the box springs several times as hard as she could.

"Hit this bed one more time," said Jimmy, "I'll drag both your asses from under there and break your fuckin' necks."

Neda looked at Danny and whispered, "Do something."

Danny thought he had no other choice than to be bold, but before he attempted to be that way something strange happened. Miss Ruby would have said it was God's intervention.

Danny looked toward the right side of the bed and saw the foot of Betty Jean's bad leg hanging over the edge of the mattress. He slid over to it and raised himself halfway up from under the bed.

His eyes were searching for his mother but he couldn't see her face. After he went back under he saw Freddie's foot quietly tapping the floor, signaling him.

Without any hesitation Danny reached up, grabbed Betty Jean's bad leg, and pulled her as hard as he could. She screamed when she fell to the floor. At the exact same moment there was the loudest clap of thunder and the most spectacular flashes of lightning any of them had ever seen or heard. Entire blocks of street lights, and the room's lamp, went out for a few seconds and then came back on.

Danny sandwiched Betty Jean's frail body between him and Neda. She felt like a long stick wedged underneath him. The look in Danny's eyes, and from the way he smiled at her, made Betty Jean stop her crying. She buried her head under her brother's arm and fell into another run-away sleep.

Jimmy took off his hat. He caressed the brim and then laid the hat on the bed. He slipped off his suit jacket and folded it. He laid it neatly beside his hat. He loosened his tie, took it off, and tossed it onto his jacket. He unbuttoned his shirt, took it off, and laid it onto his jacket. With care and concern, not to ruin the copper-penny shine, he took off his shoes and then his socks. He wanted his bare feet to have a firm grip on the cold-wooden floor. After stuffing his socks, inside his shoes, he purposely positioned the shoes on the floor and pushed them under the bed. He wanted

44

Danny to see the big size of them. It was his way of showing Danny who the man was.

Jimmy stood and went to the dresser, putting his hands on top of it. To stop his trembling, fueled with the remains of his terror against Mr. Straub, he raised his hands and shifted the weight of his body onto the tips of his fingers and spread them out wide.

He looked up and at his reflection in the wall-length mirror. His expression appeared disgusted with the aging man he saw looking back at him. He saw her reflection standing there against the window's sill. To his disappointment, and jealousy, she was still so young and beautiful. He thought about the times he had beaten her. He was always cautious, preserving her beauty. This time there would be no precautions.

"Where is it?" Jimmy asked her.

"Where is what?"

He turned and walked up close to her. "That metal box, the one you keep hidden. Where is it?"

"That has nothing to do with you."

Pretending to hit her, he raised his hand to her face and kept doing it until she flinched more than once. "Everything you do has got something to do with me," he said, stroking her hair away from her eyes.

She lowered her head and moved from under his hand. She took a step back. "I have nothin' left to give you, Jimmy."

45

"What about this fuckin' house? You and Mississippi Ruby own it, don't you? Where the fuck is Aunt Jamima, and Betty Crocker, all rolled up into one black bitch. You think she can help save you from me? She's too busy lookin' out for her own black ass. You two of a kind, baby. Rip the skin off both you bitches and nobody can tell who is who."

"You want this house I told you you can have it. Do whatever you want with it. Sell it. Burn it down. We don't care what you do with it. The transfer is only a matter of paper work."

"Only a matter of paper work," he said with sarcasm. Listen to you soundin' like a real businesswoman. Am I supposed to admire you now?" He turned away from her. The urge to kill her was too strong. He wanted to ease into it and enjoy his self.

He went inside her closet, ripping his way through her clothes. "You want all your shit torn up," he said. "That's all right with me, baby."

Freddie raised the covers of the bedspread. She looked under the bed and into the worry of Danny's eyes. "Now, Danny," she whispered. "Get out of here. Daniel, take your sisters and get out. Go find Ruby."

"No," Danny whispered. "We ain't leavin' you."

"Danny, please."

"No. I'm not leavin' you, Ma."

"We ain't leavin' you," Neda whispered. "We changin' our minds just like you."

"What?" She looked at her children as if they had lost their minds.

"We care about you too," said Neda, "just like you care about us now. We ain't leavin' you. We love you too."

"We've got a plan," said Danny. "I'm gonna kill the crazy bastard."

"Oh, Danny," said Freddie. "You don't know what you're doin'." She turned away from them and stood. She looked at Angela, sitting on the floor in plain sight, glaring hatred at her.

"You gettin' what you deserve," Angela told her. "And I don't even care if you cry." She spit on the floor and stuck her tongue out at Freddie.

Jimmy tore up the dresses that felt good to the touch of a man's hands. He snatched the fine-expensive suits, off their wooden hangers, and threw them onto the closet's floor. He used his arm to wipe all the shoes on the shelves, above her clothes, onto the floor.

Freddie went into the closet and came up behind him. She was thinking about the safety of her children. "I'm not goin' to leave you," she told him.

He paused. He wanted to hear the words that would bring him calm and relief. He turned and looked into her eyes. At the accurate snap of a second he flung his arm out and struck her as hard as he could with the back of his hand. She slammed into the side wall of the closet, bounced off it, and landed on the floor. She rolled over on her back.

"You're lyin'," he said. He went back to searching for the metal box.

She lifted her hand to feel the wetness on her chin. Her mouth had begun to bleed and the side of her head throbbed. He had almost knocked her out cold.

He pulled down the last of her things and threw the clothes on top of her. He saw the metal box. "That's what I'm looking for."

He reached up and removed it from the hole beaten into the wall to hide it. When he turned to leave the closet, he changed his mind about stepping over her. He pressed his foot down as hard as he could and ground it deeply into the pit of her stomach. She held her muscles taunt, forcing herself not to wail. He didn't stop grinding his foot until she screamed and begged.

He looked down at her and lifted his foot. "Oh, excuse me, Miss Wall Street Journal."

He left the closet like a child with a new toy. He tossed the box on top of the bed, reached inside his pant pocket, and removed his red-cosmetic sponge. After mopping the sweat off his face he sat back down on the foot of the bed and picked up the box. He shook it around and listened to its contents, but nothing inside had a jingle so he ruled out jewelry.

Angela was enjoying herself and her expressions were smirking, curious, unafraid. She was used to being witness to her father's violence against women.

Freddie pulled herself up on her feet and went out of the closet clutching her stomach. She balanced herself to stand and lean against the closet door.

"Where's the key?" he asked.

"Find it your damn self," she said, wincing from the pain in her belly.

"You still in here, baby?"

"I'm right here, Daddy," said Angela.

"Go get your daddy somethin' to open this here box."

"You mean like a screw driver or somethin'?"

"Yeah."

Angela scrambled up off the floor and hurried out of the room.

"Before you sneak off with your punk-ass rich-boyfriend, we've got business to settle."

"It was never like that between Parker and me. He's a friend, a decent and …"

"If that motherfucker is decent and honest I must be something like a priest or a saint."

"This is about my kids. I'm doin' this for them."

"You seem to forget one of them is mine. She stays with me."

Angela came back into the room and went to Jimmy. She showed him the screwdriver in her hand. "Is this okay, Daddy?"

"That'll work."

Angela did not sit on the floor in the same place. She sat on the floor in the opposite corner. She wanted to be closer to them.

Jimmy pried into the box, popping it open. He stuck his hand inside and removed the stack of papers that were in envelopes. He threw the box onto the floor and opened one of the papers. To him the papers looked like oversized fancy dollars.

"Come here and sit beside me, baby," he told Freddie.

"No."

"I'm staying with you, daddy," Angela blurted out.

"Angela," Freddie screamed.

"Shut up." Angela yelled. "I ain't goin' with you. I'm stayin' with my daddy."

"All my children are comin' with me."

"It's okay, baby," said Jimmy. "You're my baby, my flesh, my blood. You're stayin' right here with your daddy. I'm movin' in."

Angela looked at Freddie and stuck her tongue out.

Jimmy glanced through the papers. "What is Leland?" He couldn't pronounce the second word.

"Electronics," Freddie said, finishing the sentence.

"Does this have anything to do with you?"

"Yeah, it does."

"Give a bitch control and she think she owns the world. Again, what is it?"

"Read the papers, Jimmy. Oh! I forgot you can't read." She wanted to show him, tell him how much she hated him. She knew it would be the night he would kill her.

"I'm askin' you politely Miss Wall Street Journal. What is Leland Electronics?"

"Telephones."

"Telephones …"

"Yeah. They make telephones."

"What?"

"Telephones damn you," she screamed. "They make mobile telephones. It means you can take it with you. Got it?"

"Mobile telephones," Jimmy said quietly. "They make mobile telephones. That means you can take it with you." He grabbed the pink-princess phone off her nightstand and wrapped the cord around his right hand, yanking it out of the wall. He stood and glared at her. "How about I kill your ass with this here mobile telephone?"

Freddie went into her closet. She tried to kick the clothes on the floor out of her way so she could lock herself inside. It was a futile attempt.

Danny felt helpless and Neda cried. Danny reached over Neda and stuck his hand under one of the planks of the box springs. He found what he was looking for.

Angela did not like her full premiere. Her eyes were shut and her arms and hands were wrapped around her ears and head. She had urinated again.

Jimmy kicked Freddie in the ribs until the crack of a bone breaking could be heard. He kneeled and stroked her hair away from her face and lifted her chin, looking into her eyes. "I'm sorry," he said, smiling. "I know it hurts. I'm takin' a break."

He was breathing rapidly, sweating profusely. He walked out of the closet and over to the dresser. He opened the bottom drawer and found a half pint of Mr. Clark's whiskey. He thought about Ruby, wanting her to come back soon. He wanted to kill her too.

Ruby had finished her shopping. She hoped Mr. Straub was still waiting for her. The closer she went in the direction of his shop the more she realized that the red and blue lights of police cars were in front of Family Shoes. When she arrived it was impossible to mesh herself into the thickness of the crowd.

"Miss Ruby. Miss Ruby."

It was Candy, one of the twins. She always wore something orange. A small child was positioned on her hip, playing with the string of African beads around her neck.

"Miss Ruby you need to go home."

"Why? What happened?"

"Jimmy and Spits tried to kill Mr. Straub. He's all beat up. They tore up his store."

"No, that can't be right. Jimmy is out of town."

"No he ain't. I saw all three of them."

"Three of them?"

"Spits, Jimmy, and Angela."

PAINT THE PICTURE OF TERROR

Blackened eyes swollen shut, busted bleeding lips, cracked nose, knots on the head, ears ringing, eardrum busted, clumps of hair pulled out, length of hair cut off, maybe a broken leg, maybe a broken arm. During the progression of the beating brilliant flashes of lightning went all over the sky. The electrical show of force was magnificent and at certain intervals the full making of nighttime daylight lasted for more than five seconds. Still, it had not rained.

The crazy wind wanted to go about its own way of doing things. It spun away from the pending storm and like hundreds of mini tornadoes it stirred up all flyable trashes of paper and loose grit it could find.

When the wind, thunder, and lightning was not there the children worried that God was no longer alarmed about what was happening to their mother. To help drive away his thoughts, of God's non- existence, Danny remembered one of their bible studies and what Miss Ruby told them:

"When God's tears finally rain down all the bad stuff is over. The evil thing has been eliminated, ripped from the face of the earth. And if you look around at shadows, and the movement of strange things not really there, God is making His presence known. Sometimes God takes the shape of the devil just to throw an evil bastard off his balance."

Danny's prayers for God to rain his tears, step into the room, and show his presence as anything were silent and constant.

Neda's mumbled prayers were a series of begging lamentations. She was trying to make God employ the creation and consequence of one of His most impressive miracles.

Angela did not believe in God. She thought herself special enough to talk telepathically to Miss Ruby. She told her to hurry up and come home. Her beloved father had gone completely mad.

Jimmy had dragged Freddie out of the closet. She lay in the center of the floor of the bedroom. At specific times Jimmy called out, "You still in here, baby?" When Angela didn't answer he screamed at her. "Didn't you hear me?"

"I'm in here, Daddy," she cried. "I'm right over here."

"Look up," he would tell her. When Angela raised her head to see what her beloved father was about to do it was another brutal slap to her mother's face. If not that it was a kick to her legs or stomach.

Betty Jean was still asleep and snoring sweetly, wedged under her brother. Danny admired his little sister's ability to disappear into a world where only dolls and princesses were loyal best friends.

For the duration of Jimmy's third break time Danny could see his bare feet standing at the dresser in front of the walled mirror. He was gazing lovingly at his reflection while using the red sponge to mop the sweat off his face.

The skin on his face and chest was streaked with red traces of blood where she had scratched, clawed, and dug her fingernails into him. To stop the sharp nails from attacking him he bit down onto the tips of her fingers and bit off the long nails with his teeth.

During his breaks he looked into the mirror and saw an eccentric painter, an uncompromising writer, an emotionally-stricken musician. He felt his self to be a scandalous and gifted artist in the zone of creating and plotting while being self destructive. What he did to Mr. Straub had given him an outbreak of exhilarating rushes.

55

They were like incomplete orgasms that pacify a man until he has the real one. Every time he lifted the sledgehammer, bringing it down, the new feelings coursed their way up and down his inner thighs. When the thrilling rushes were gone the entrails of them settled down, heating up what was between his legs. He was having those same rushes again.

Break time was over and Jimmy came out of his daze. He grabbed Freddie's arm and pulled her near the edge of the bed, close to where he knew Danny was. He wanted the boy to see how badly his beautiful mother had been beaten to be so ugly. He wanted him to see the bloody-bald patches where he used his switchblade to scalp some of her skin when he cut off her hair.

Danny looked at Freddie. Her swollen and bloodied face was so near to his that he could feel the agonized warmth of her breath. When he put her hand into his most of his fear turned into hope. Their beautiful mother was still very much alive.

Besides his comic books, and Swiss Army Pocket Knife, Danny knew of other things between the planks of the bed. He raised his head and looked at Neda. "This is like a battle," he whispered. "It's like a crazy goddamn stinkin' war. Shut up with that cryin'. You can't think straight. I can't think straight hearin' it. You've got to shut up, Neda. You've got to do what I say. You hear me?" He reached over Betty Jean and shook Neda hard. "Shut up and listen to me. This knife ain't good enough to do nothin'."

56

"What if she's already dead?"

"She ain't dead. Look at her. Go on and look at her. She's breathin'. I can feel it. The heart in her hand is beatin' fast." Danny reached out and shook Freddie's shoulder.

"Ruby," Freddie mumbled, "Get out of here."

"See, she ain't dead."

The wind had picked up again. To Danny it sounded like the voices of a million old witches, screaming, chanting something bad at the same time.

Jimmy came toward the bed. They watched his hand reach down and grab their mother's arm. He dragged her away from them, walked back over to the bed, and kneeled down to look under it.

"What's all the whispering about?" he asked Danny and Neda.

Danny pushed his self hard against the floor, sliding Betty Jean and Neda to the other side.

"If I wanted to hurt you and your sisters all I've got to do is turn this fuckin' bed over."

"Please, Jimmy," cried Danny. "Don't beat her no more. We wasn't movin' no place without you."

"Is that true, Miss Puerto Rico?"

"Yeah. It's true Jimmy, honest."

"Well, if you wasn't movin' away without me then why is all those suitcases stacked up in the hallway? I don't see any of my stuff sittin' there."

"You don't have a lot of stuff here," said Danny.

"What about my tables? What was your mama goin' to do with them? Don't lie to me."

"Mama was tryin' to call you. She wanted to tell you to get a truck to move your gamblin' tables to the new house. Everything was gonna be a big surprise."

"Why is that?"

"We movin' on the good side of town," said Danny, "where more white people live. Mama said you always wanted to live around rich-white people."

"Oh," said Jimmy, "that kind of surprise."

"Yeah," said Neda.

"You ain't lyin' to me?"

"No." said Danny. "It's the truth. I swear it."

"You mean I beat your mama up for no reason?"

"Yeah," cried Neda. "You gotta stop before you kill her. Please, Jimmy."

"Okay, I'll pick your mama up and put on her the bed. All she needs is a good night's sleep. When Ruby gets back she knows how to doctor your mama up real good."

"I don't believe you," Danny told him.

"How about I prove it to you, right now?"

"I believe you," cried Neda.

"Good girl. I don't wanna hear no more talk about movin'. We don't need to live around rich white people. We got enough white people right here in this house. This is our home and we all one family."

"Okay," said Danny.

"I'm the only daddy you ever had. Ain't that right, white boy?"

"Yeah."

They watched his bare feet walk to Freddie. He gathered her from the floor and positioned her to sit up.

"Come on, baby. I'm done."

He pulled her onto her feet and reached under her legs, picking her up. She was laid across his arms. He took a few steps backward and toward the bed. But instead of placing her onto the bed, he pushed her limp body high above his head. As if to sacrifice his offering to something evil, unseen, he threw Freddie like a sack of potatoes across the room and into the mirrored wall.

Pieces of mirror became unglued and flew out everywhere, breaking, falling, shattering. Freddie landed on top of her dresser. When she rolled off perfume bottles and makeup crashed to the floor with her, breaking around Angela. The girl did not budge. She was silent, in a state of shock. Her eyes were fixed and staring at nothing.

The room was saturated with the sickening smell of urine, perfume, and whiskey. As if to finalize something the lamp, sitting on the corner of the dresser, fell to the floor and the bulb blew out. The room was dark except for the dim streaks of light that came through the windows from the corner street lamp.

Danny's scream was a war cry. When he scrambled out from under the bed the .38 revolver, hidden between one of the planks, was in his hand. He leaped and climbed up on Jimmy's back. He wrapped his arm around his neck and pushed the muzzle of the gun to the back of Jimmy's head.

Jimmy laughed because he could feel the heavy gun had no stability in the boy's weak hand. Danny didn't have the strength to hold onto him and pull the trigger at the same time.

Neda followed through with her part of their plan. She slid halfway out from under the bed. When she was all the way out she raised her arm as high as she could and rammed the blade of the Swiss Army Knife into Jimmy's bare foot.

"You fucked up pieces of shit," screamed Jimmy.

Jimmy tried to pull the knife out of his foot but it was impossible to do it with Danny riding his back. Jimmy swayed off balance, steadied himself, and then bucked his body hard. The gun fell out of Danny's hand, onto the floor, and tumbled to some place unseen. Jimmy bucked hard again, using his body like a whip until Danny was flipped onto the bed. He pulled the knife out of his foot and tossed it on the floor. He grabbed hold of Danny, picked him up, and held him high over his head the same way he had done Freddie. Like a smaller sack of potatoes, he threw Danny out of the room's entrance and into the corridor.

Danny hit the wall and bounced off it. The stacked suitcases became unbalanced, spilling to the floor. Danny felt no pain and his adrenalin was still pumping. He was unbroken and crawling fast on the floor, going back inside the room.

Jimmy pulled Neda by the hair and onto her feet. While he slapped her he did not feel or see the quickness of the boy's movement.

Danny grabbed him by the ankle. He remembered how Freddie screamed when Jimmy ripped off her fingernails. Danny opened his mouth as wide as he could and bit down into the muscled calf of Jimmy's leg. He sunk his teeth in to stay and could taste the salt of Jimmy's blood in his mouth.

"Son-of-a bitch," Jimmy screamed, letting go of Neda.

"Run, Neda," said Danny.

Neda did not run down the back-alley steps. The wind, thunder, and lightning pushed her to fly down them. When her feet hit the ground her running speed was so fast that the colorful flowers on the pink dress she wore were a blur.

Mid-point, she saw someone running toward her. It was Miss Ruby.

She picked up her speed. "Miss Ruby. Miss Ruby." Within seconds her arms were wrapped around the waist of Ruby so tightly that Ruby found it hard to breath.

"He's killin' mama, Miss Ruby. He's gonna kill all of us. Where've you been? You gotta do somethin'. Please don't let him kill us. Please, Miss Ruby."

Ruby grabbed Neda's arms. She shoved the girl away from her. "Go to Candy and Iris. Stay there till I come and get you. Go."

"Danny said I should call the cops."

"No!" said Ruby, running toward the house. "Do what I say!"

The hard blows of Jimmy's fist pounding him did not stop Danny from searching the floor for the gun or the knife. He found his pocket knife and rammed it into Jimmy's foot. It went in deeper than what Neda had done. Jimmy cried out and stumbled. Danny scrambled back under the bed.

The childish plot of attack had gotten the best of Jimmy Tate. He limped over to where Freddie lay. He wanted to kill what he could while he could.

He picked the telephone up off the floor and wrapped some of the cord around his hands. He straddled his legs across Freddie and sat on her. He lifted her head up gently and when he laid it back

62

down he had placed the phone's cord to lay behind the back of her head. He wrapped the cord around her neck and pulled as hard as he could.

The light in the gaming room switched on and Danny heard the sound of Ruby's feet. After a few seconds she was there. She stood in the doorway, her eyes adjusting to the dark room. She saw Jimmy sitting on Freddie, strangling her.

"Jimmy," Ruby cried. She went to where they were and attempted to pull him off Freddie. Jimmy stood up calmly and, as brief as an interruption in a conversation, he punched Ruby in the face.

She flew into the back of the room near the dresser and landed on the floor next to Angela. The blow to her face was damaging. She almost lost consciousness. Coming out of her daze, she saw Danny and Betty Jean under the bed.

Jimmy sat on Freddie. He continued to pull and tighten the cord around her neck. "I know this feels good to you, baby."

Freddie's thoughts were of her children, Ruby, and the happiness that came with loving Parker Bishop. When she let go and drifted willingly toward the light, toward death, there was the deafening sound of a gunshot.

Jimmy's body stiffened. Thick blood tried to ooze out of the hole in the back of his head. When he slumped over, on top of Freddie, his red cosmetic sponge came out his pant pocket. And like a small red wheel, as if the sponge had a mind of its own and knew where it was going, it rolled, fell over, and relaxed like a quiet dime at the tip of Angela's foot. The girl's scream was heart wrenching.

At that exact same moment with no supporting sounds of thunder or lightning it had begun to rain. It came down fast and hard.

Those who knew the story of what happened told their children this:

"In a matter of seconds the onslaught of God's crying flooded the alley, the sidewalks of 55th Street, and all her neighboring ghettos. The strange lightning of the storm compressed itself into large red orbs that hovered above the rooftops of the tenements. And when the lightning struck outward, and down, it busted and shattered the heads of all the street lamps and exploded hot wires.

When everyone was without electricity the independent wind came up tall from the ground, and opened itself up to join the rest of the storm. The neighboring ghettos were sent their own personal tornado. Upon the roaring arrival, of the twisting activity, windows were blown clean out of their panes. Doors were pounded on, knocked flat down, making room for the wild entrance of the wind. And when it rushed inside, encircling, up heaving everything from its place, some of the walls collapsed and eliminated the separation of neighbors. Some attempted to escape out of back doors but there

64

*were no back alley steps going down. The crazy tornados tore away
their back porches, freeing them from the root of the alley's ground.
God was furious at those who ignored the cries of help that came
from mere lambs.*

June 25, 1970

CHAPTER TWO
TOO LATE

8:00 A.M.

Cold water pushed out from the shower's head onto Parker Bishop's face. The combined bath, shower, and steam room was on the third floor of the house. It was an extensive and round enclosure of windows and skylights. He stood for a long time, letting the hard spray of the water beat down on his neck and shoulders. His personal bathing quarters were his refuge to let everything go, his favorite place to cleanse it all off.

On the night he arrived home it was the last time he saw Freddie. His father, Robert Bishop, mid fifties, had been waiting to confront him. He was a cold, strict, attractive man of average height and slender weight. His once blond and heavy hair was now completely gray and thinning.

Robert stood near one of the four pillars inside a foyer that revealed a considerable amount of rooms on either side. He was a bold and outspoken man who needed to stand face to face while getting a worry of points across. He walked and stood that way in front of Parker. "You will not move that whore and those bastards into your mother's house. Have you completely lost your mind?"

"The house belongs to me," Parker told him. "You have no say in anything I decide to do with it. Good night, father."

There was no one woman in his father's life. Robert's respect for women in general was low. He detested what he considered the slurping and hanging on of a constant, troublesome, and needless woman spending too much money while trying to boss his very existence.

Parker's mother had been a shy and reclusive woman. To his regret, at the age of nine, she died of an unexplained illness. He was a single child. After her death he became the sole heir of one of the world's largest rubber manufacturers. His father, a successful corporate attorney, was only left a considerable amount of cash.

At the age of twenty-one all of the inheritance was turned over to Parker. This included the house of twenty-seven rooms his mother had been raised in. It was not far from where he lived with his father. He offered it to Freddie for as long as she needed it.

After his shower, he entered the dining room and took his seat at the table. It was a rigid, dreary, and unfriendly room with dark heavy drapes that blacked out the brightest of sunlight. Where he loved light his father preferred dimly lit. It was a man's eating place of solitude. There was no hint of feminine existence except for the expert and spotless cleaning.

A housekeeper in her early sixties came in and went to Parker.

"Good morning, Joanie," said Parker.

"Good morning, Mr. Parker." She picked up the coffee pot and poured him a cup. She sat the pot down in front of him and left the room. She had worked for the family for over twenty years and the doldrums of her job made her smooth, unnoticeable, and respectfully boring.

He finished his breakfast quickly. Freddie, Ruby, and the children were on his mind. He had not called her. He kept his word and was waiting for her to call him.

He picked up the daily newspaper that sat on the table at the side of his plate. There was nothing special in the headlines. He thumbed to the metro section and when he read something his face riddled with shock.

The newspaper headline boasted: *Two women arrested on charges of homicide, child abuse, and possession of narcotics.* Below the heading were pictures of Ruby in handcuffs, and one of Freddie on a stretcher being carried down the front steps of the Walker house. There were pictures of the kids sitting in back of a police car.

"Joanie," he called out. "I need you."

He did not read any of the paper. He stood up from the table and left the dining room with Joanie scurring behind him. He made several phone calls to try and find out where they were. The most important calls were for the preparation of what needed to be done to get them out.

After shaving he asked Joanie to cut his long hair short and high above the ears. It was a wanting thing for her to do. She had not cut his hair since he was a boy. The sweetness that came with the scared and nervous way he asked her to do it made her feel needed again. She felt his sorrow over something and it saddened her.

They chose the dark brown suit that hung among the many others he had never worn. It was one of his most impressive. Joanie polished his dark brown shoes and when he put them on they gave him the needed lilt of confidence. Although it was empty of legal documents, and any other kind of necessary papers, besides a legal pad, he carried an expensive-leather briefcase. Even though he just started working for his father's firm, he needed to make the appearance of a young and successful attorney.

Whatever his son's motives were Robert Bishop knew all about it. By the time Parker rushed out of their home he knew all the details. The expedient calls to inform him included information about his son's attempt to involve his self from a legal perspective with the whore, her bastards, and the Negro. Every call Parker made traveled a full and private loop back to Robert. He thought if his son tried to use a penny of his inheritance for any back-door pursuit to help the whore it would be wasted effort.

Parker arrived inside the corridor of intensive care at Cook County Hospital. The Hospital was a diversified incubator where medicine and the desire to create God-like miracles rose above racism. The young and eager medical staff was from every country in the world. If it could not be diagnosed, or cured, behind the walls of Cook County Hospital then whatever the sickness was needed a new name.

He saw the uniformed-police officer seated outside of Freddie's room. The outer wall of the room was made of glass. He thought about approaching the officer. He wanted to take the bold opportunity to look through the glass and inside the room, but instead he went to the nurse's station. A petite and pretty black nurse was seated behind the counter.

He handed her his business card. "Attorney Parker Bishop to see Freddie Walker."

She looked at the card, stood, and walked away from him. When she returned she had a clipboard of papers in her hand. She looked at the first page and read down the next. "I'm sorry, Mr. Bishop. I don't see your name here. Miss Walker hasn't been out of surgery long enough to have visitors. She's also being held in police custody."

Parker swallowed hard. "What kind of surgery?" He tried not to show his personal and emotional concern but it was evident.

"I'm sorry. I can't give you that information."

"I'm her attorney," said Parker, raising his voice. Heads turned to look in his direction. The guard moved about in his seat. "That's as close to family as you can get."

The young nurse walked away and into an administrative office. She came back with her supervisor. The supervisor was alarming to look at and almost taller than his self. It was evident that the whole of the supervisor's physical self and acerbic attitude was there to block and stop him.

She snatched Parker's business card out of the young nurse's hand and looked at it. She looked down at the top of his slouching head, lost of its height. "What did you say your name was?"

"Bishop, Parker Bishop. Freddie Walker is my client."

"Uh Huh," said the Supervisor. "This card looks like it used to say Robert Bishop until somebody scratched his name out."

"What's in a card? Robert Bishop is my father."

"Yeah, everybody in Chicago knows who he is but that makes no difference around here. That woman is in no condition to see you. She may not make it. Besides me you got yourself another problem." She pointed to the police officer sitting and reading his newspaper.

It took Parker all his strength to hold his composure. He wanted to force his way in there and give her reason not to die on him.

71

"I suggest," said the supervisor, "you come back when Ms. Walker is able to put you on the list as her attorney … if she's still alive."

He wanted to sag into something low and deep and under the ground; to disappear like something useless, never allowed to exist as anything resembling a man. With all of his own personal wealth he was not skilled at using money to bribe people. He had no clue of who or what needed to be bought. He had no real knowledge of using cunning deceit on a professional level. He waited too long to pick up his briefcase.

He stepped off the elevator. Someone was coming up behind him, calling his name. It was Jack Connelly. Jack was not born into wealth. He worked his way through Harvard Law.

"Hey! Well I'll be damned," said Jack, "if it ain't Parker Bishop. What the hell are you doing down here, ole buddy?"

"Jack," said Parker, smiling, shaking the strong grip of his hand. "I'm visiting a client. It's been a long time. Where are you now?"

"Klein and Harper."

"It's a good firm," said Parker. "A great place to be. What are you doing here?"

"What else, chasing ambulances. You look a little washed out, ole buddy."

"It's this case I'm working on. Things don't look good for my client."

"Sorry to hear it. It was good to see you." Jack extended his hand and Parker shook it.

"Hey," said Parker, "before you go let me ask you something."

"Sure."

"What do you know about the case in today's papers, metro section?"

"You mean the one with the kids?"

"Yeah."

"A lot of heavy-duty drugs involved. They took the maid downtown. I believe the other one is critical. Before the guy was killed he beat the shit out of both of them. Who gives uh damn about some Negro chick? As far as the white chick is concerned, maybe it's time to hand over the little-black book if you know what I mean."

"It doesn't sound too good for them." He was getting desperate, searching for signs of hope from anyone.

"Hey, you're not thinking about getting involved with people like that?"

"No," said Parker. "I'm checking into some things. Just making sure the right names don't show up in the wrong place."

"A sort of look out for your ole man, huh?"

"Something like that."

"I've really got to go, buddy." He extended another handshake to Parker who took it. "Give me a call sometime."

He watched Jack hustle his way through the crowd and out of the building. Parker stepped onto the sidewalk. He held his head up and pushed his face into the pouring rain. He wanted to wash off the smell of sickness and dying. When he got into his car he drove toward no place. His thoughts were about Ruby. He had to find a way to get to her. He took a sharp left turn. The NAACP had come to mind. He knew someone who worked at their headquarters.

TELL US WHAT YOU KNOW

The narrow coffin of a room was hot, suffocating, and hellish. The three hideous shadows caused by a single overhead light swayed and hesitated in slow motion across the four walls. They gave the impression of six people sitting in the room instead of three. Above the bare bulb was a wide hat of loose and patched metal attached to an extension cord. The cord had been untangled so that the bulb could hang low and over a wide oak table. When the hot bulb was bumped into it felt like a small sun, swinging, looking for something to burn like the top of Ruby's head.

In addition to the heated discomfort sharp fits of pain were cutting into the meat of Ruby's nose and into the bone. Her face felt twisted, disfigured. She could move two loose teeth with her tongue. Jimmy had punched her harder than she thought and when the pain was more than great she had become so delirious she could have sworn, on stacks of bibles, the two rolling reels of the tape recorder were asking her questions too.

The two Narcotic Detectives had read her the Miranda Act. They even told her their names but she did not remember them. They wore no name tags. In her mind she referred to them as Detective's Stop, and Go.

Detective Stop, the pretending-bad cop, was white and in his mid twenties. He was an oncoming train of trained questions. When he stopped to think of something even more bizarre to ask her Detective Go, the pretending-good cop, picked up and continued on.

Detective Go was a mixture of black and white. Because he was mixed up with two kinds of color she thought it was the reason he had been assigned to her. As if that kind of reference to a kind of color would make a big difference regarding the outcome of their shocking interrogation.

What made the session appear authentic, when compared to the old black and white movies about fast talking jittery cops, the stained and moldy smelling detectives were chain coffee drinkers and chain smokers. For Ruby, watching them pace and pacify their addictions, at the same time, brought out the cartoon aspect of the hour. They were that animated and nervous.

On the table close to her face she could smell the chemicals in the brick of brown powder. It was wrapped in clear plastic and held together with grey-masking tape. It supposedly weighed over two pounds. She had never seen any such drugs hidden in the basement where the detective duo claimed it had been found.

Next to the heroin sat three bricks of marijuana wrapped up the same way. She had no knowledge of seeing that in the basement either. She knew every inch of the basement and everything inside of it.

Detective Go drank his coffee, put out his cigarette and lit another. "Where's the gun, Ruby?"

Detective Stop jumped up from his chair. "To hell with the goddamn gun. Who gives a fuck about a gun? What about all this dope sittin' on this fuckin' table?"

"Everybody just calm down," said Detective Go. "Bring it down low. Bring it down real low." He lifted and slowly lowered his hands onto the table, like he was using magic to soothe his partner.

"You're right. The gun is important. You know why it's important, Ruby?"

"I don't know," Ruby said.

"From our perspective, and every cop in the City of Chicago, there should be an award ceremony just for you."

"Now that's a brilliant idea."

"That beautiful gun should be dipped in gold and put in a museum so everybody can worship it.

"Trash like Jimmy Tate, the judge will give you a medal for murderin' that piece of shit.

"Ain't I got the right to talk to a lawyer?" asked Ruby. "Ain't I got the right to see a doctor?"

"We ain't got no lawyers. We ain't got no doctors."

"Like we said, Ruby, what we have is award ceremonies for bad Negroes who kill other bad Negroes."

"What we also have is nothin'."

"That's right, Ruby," said Detective Go. "We have nothin' for Negroes who don't tell us nothin'."

"What bastard in this city can put that much dope on the street without us knowin' about it?"

"It must be you Ruby."

"Seems every question you ask me you answer it yourself," she told them. "Don't that mean you got all the answers?"

"Okay," said Detective Stop. "You think you got the right to be a smart mouthed bitch? Maybe I need to break the rest of your face."

When he drew back his arm, and sent his fist speeding toward her face, he stopped just short of punching her. She flinched, closed her eyes, and turned her head. He had scared her badly.

"Bring it down low," said Detective Go. "Let's bring it down real low ... nice and easy." Again, like magically soothing his partner, he lifted and slowly lowered his hands until they touched the table.

"Let me ask you something, Ruby," said Detective Stop, "just to satisfy my curiosity. What kind of slave shit was you doin' for Freddie Walker, huh? Was you fuckin' Jimmy, or, fuckin' for him?"

She looked at the young detective and smiled. "Would you believe me if I told you I was still a virgin?"

Her thoughts had gone elsewhere. She wanted to cry over the children. Where were they and how were they being treated? She wanted to cry at the thought of Freddie being beaten so badly. Was she dead or alive?

When she started to cry, a beautiful young-black woman with a neatly cropped afro opened the door and came into the room. She appeared tall and straight and her head was held high. Ruby thought she stood refreshingly proud and militant. A wooden spoon, an earring, hung from one ear and a wooden fork from the other. Red, green, and yellow wooden beads were draped around her neck and this added more of an African style to the latest fashion of black leather mini skirt and matching jacket.

The woman was the blackest person Ruby had ever seen in person. There was no mix of any other color in her blood and her pureness, of being purely African, radiated all around them and intimidated the two detectives.

Where was the woman from Ruby asked herself? What was inside the black-leather bag? She carried it as if it were a representation of her accomplishments. The bag meant more to her than anything else in the world. Whatever she was, thought Ruby, she was snobbish and proud to be it.

Detective Stop switched on more light. Ruby got her best look at the two Narcotic Detectives. They were stained and dirty to look it. She thought they looked like they stink and the room was not as small as she thought. She forgot her pain and need to cry, for she was more interested in the female increase of drama standing up to Stop and Go.

The woman flicked her eyes at the detectives. Her lips were clipped tightly together and showed how angry she was at what she saw. It was obvious that the two detectives knew her and she knew them. The young doctor, from Africa, was one of the NAACP'S most valuable spies.

"Aren't you forgetting something," the doctor told them.

Detective Go reached his hand out and turned off the tape recorder.

The doctor then greeted the two men coldly. She walked to where Ruby was sitting and smiled down at her. "Hello, Miss

Johnson," she said. "I'm Doctor Crane. My friends call me Jah, short for Jahintia"

"Yeah," said Detective Stop, "like you was God or somethin'. Ain't that what Jah means?"

"I'm here on the behalf of God," she told Ruby, loud enough for the detectives to hear, "and the NAACP. You must be in quite a bit of pain." The doctor kneeled down to Ruby's sitting level and her eyes watered at the sight of her punched and swollen face.

Feeling the doctor's sympathy, Ruby could not stop her flow of tears. She examined Ruby's face and with the slightest touch the pain was so impressive Ruby nearly jumped out of her chair.

"You have a broken nose. And maybe some other fractures," she told Ruby. "Have you seen a doctor?"

"No," said Ruby. "I ain't seen anybody but them." Ruby felt that pity was a weakness the doctor had. "Where are you from talkin' with an accent like that?" She wanted the young doctor to keep standing her tough and bitching ground.

"I was born and raised in South African," she told Ruby.

"Jah, now that's a real pretty name. Does it mean God like he say?"

"Yes," said the doctor. "How long have you been in here?"

"I don't know. I don't even know what time it is."

"A little past 9:00 P.M." The doctor reached inside her bag and came out of it with a syringe and a vile of medicine. She stuck the syringe inside the rubber tip of the bottle and withdrew the liquid. "Parker Bishop said tell them nothing," she whispered. "Ignore."

"What the fuck was that?" said Detective Stop. "What did you say? What are you giving her?"

"This woman has serious medical issues," she told the two detectives. "You do your job. Shut up so I can do mine." She turned her attention back to Ruby. "Can you make a fist for me?" After finding a good vein she gave Ruby the shot and in seconds the pain was gone. Ruby could sleep anywhere and on anything.

"The woman's nose is broken," said the doctor, rising to her feet. "She's got a good shot of morphine in her. Any kind of confession won't be worth two dead flies, mashed up in shit, in Africa. It's best you wait and do it right."

"Bullshit, God," said Detective Go, "a broken nose can wait."

"You've got one hour to get her to the Hospital. "You were supposed to take her there after you arrested her. You don't think I know that?"

The young doctor walked out and slammed the door behind her, shaking the room up to show Ruby how flimsy it was.

"Fuck you God." Yelled Detective Stop. "Fuck the NAACP. Fuck Africa."

81

Both detectives were grieving. This was the type of case that sold newspapers and made careers. It made people think twice about screwing around outside their race. Innocence was involved, child abuse, murder and drugs. Two kids were black and two kids were white. The whole damn case was hot and ready to burst into flames.

While one cursed the other Ruby smiled. She looked at the block of heroin sitting on the table and imagined it as something soft like a pillow. She laid her head on it and in a matter of seconds she was asleep and snoring. The morphine sparked, played, and cursed through her veins. She dreamed of being a child again. She was running and laughing while her brothers chased her along the edges of a barren cotton field. Instead of Mississippi being the best place to run away from it was the most beautiful place in the world to be free, to be a child again.

The next time she opened her eyes her hands were cuffed behind her back. It was dark outside when two uniformed-police officers escorted her out of the heavy wooden doors. She lifted her head and the soft rain on her face was friendly and tasted sweet. She thought God was being gentle with his tears.

July 7, 1970

A FATHER'S CONCERN

12:35 P.M.

The clouds that hid the ball of the sun were vast, blackened, and wide masses of individuals. Two weeks of strong rain and damaging winds had finally stopped. It was colder than normal, as if the last days of summer had traded places with the front of October.

For those living in the neighboring ghettos of 55th Street the day was more than just depressing. The sky's offering were frightening to look at. Those aware of all that happened believed God was still showing his broken heart over the wrong women and children.

Robert Bishop was in his study. The books that lined every shelf concerned the law. His favorites were a collection of more than a century's worth of case histories. Most were on the subject of crimes committed by the most gifted corporate criminals.

Sitting across his desk was the snot eating Meaty Man. He wore the black suit and had grown out of it. The shoulders, noticed more than the rest of the disheveled suit, were slicked white because of dandruff. The Meaty Man was an advisor—a sort of intermediary between the rich and poor. Young and bored wealth often went searching for pleasure within the pit of those who were poor. When their sparks were ignited the fire consisted of black mail, drugs, unwanted women, children, and sometimes murder. After their parents or guardians had instant knowledge of the underlying threat that was hovering, calculating ways of how to ruin the reputation of their ultra clean lives, the Meaty Man was called in. It was his job to get rid of the mistake, or help turn it into the acceptability of rich kids being young and foolish. His price was not cheap.

Robert Bishop wanted him to get on with it, to quit stalling. He wanted him to quit using his bloated fingers to pick lint off his clothing. If he wasn't doing that he was busy wiggling his fingers through balding-grey hair. His hands worked consistently to keep his immediate self presentable for someone like Robert Bishop to stomach his unwanted presence. It didn't work.

Robert Bishop looked disgustingly at the man's face. He watched the snot ooze from his nostrils and down to the tip of his upper lip, snaking its way through his mustache and into his mouth. Like some type of reptile, catching a fly, with his tongue, the Meaty Man licked at the snot and removed most of it from his mustache and swallowed it. He enjoyed the taste of his mucus and the game he played with it. It was like he was trapping something, eating what was rich and envied. He would soon blow his nose with a soiled handkerchief. It was part of his nasty habit.

"The whore is a beautiful woman," he told Robert for the third time.

"I wouldn't know," Robert replied, "I've never met her."

"You can't fault your son for being bewitched by her. What man in his right mind could resist that kind of woman."

"Yes. I'm sure you know a great deal about women like that."

"You believe in witchcraft?"

"No." Robert's schedule was a critical one. He wanted the man to tell him what he needed to know. Stealing time was the Meaty Man's way of stalling, putting off what needed to be told. He wanted to stay longer within the comfort surrounding him.

"That type of whore is hard to stay away from. They use mighty powerful potions and spells to get what they want. A man has to bury himself in his work to keep his mind occupied. If he was my boy I'd give him a break based on the devil's work."

"Yes. I'm sure you would. Do you have any children?"

"Uh, no."

Robert cringed at the thought of the reject giving him advice about how to handle his own son. He wanted to open his desk drawer, remove his revolver, and shoot the nasty man where he sat. The house had a deep underground and he could bury the bastard down there. No one would ever smell him and no one would miss him.

"How much?" Robert asked.

"A pound of smack, and two kilos of pot. You can buy more if that's not enough. It's a big old house with lots of places to hide things."

"Yes. So I've been told."

The Meaty Man removed his soiled handkerchief and as predicted blew his clotted nose. "A house like that," he said, wiping his nose, "with all those rooms … you never know what kind of stash you might find. I can make it a hell of a lot worse for them. Just give me the okay."

"Where did they put her?"

"She's not in jail, yet. She's in Cook County Hospital … pretty banged up … a few broken ribs and a collapsed lung. It was touch and go for awhile but I think she'll make it. Whores are strong witches, powerful."

"The children?"

"Auden Home for Juvenile Delinquents, I can …"

"I see," said Robert, cutting him off. He was having visuals again. He wanted to pick up the silver-letter opener. Like killing a vampire, he wanted to throw it into the Meaty Man's heart. He opened his top drawer. He took out the envelope of cash and shoved it forcefully at him.

The Meaty Man took the envelope and the hint to leave. He stood quickly and stepped away from the chair. Robert's rude

86

behavior and the way he looked at him made him nervous and frightened him. "Anything else I can do?" he asked.

"I can handle it from here. Thank you for offering. If you don't mind, I have a very busy schedule. I'll show you out."

"Sure."

Robert ignored the handshake gesture. He did not want to spend an hour washing his hands. He walked away from the man and opened the door. When he looked into the corridor he saw Joanie nearby cleaning something insignificant. He knew she had been eaves dropping.

"Joanie, can you show this gentleman out?"

After the Meaty Man walked out of the study the door was closed crudely. Robert went back to his desk and sat behind it. He wondered if the whore had something rare like a heart and did she love her children? He wanted her to love them more than she loved to spread her legs.

Freddie had been moved to another unit but was still in intensive care. She was still under guard. It would be the first time Parker had been allowed to visit her. He had been told it would be awhile before she could speak. When he opened the door and walked in he saw a beat up, pitiful, mess hooked up to an array of machines keeping her alive.

He hardly recognized her. Her face was a swollen mass. There were circling indentations of the telephone cord around a neck heaving with welts and blisters. She had three broken ribs, broken collar bone, and a collapsed lung. He saw that patches of her hair had been pulled out and cut off far too close to her scalp.

He pulled the chair up close to her bed, sat down, and took her hand into his. "Hey, you," he said. She jolted awake, squeezed his hand and tried to manage a smile. "You're going to be okay. Do you hear me?" She squeezed his hand and pretended to write inside the palm of his hand with her finger. "You want to tell me something? Write something?"

She squeezed his hand again and her lips moved without sound. "Yes," she answered.

He unlocked his brief case and reached inside it. He took out a pencil and legal pad. He placed the pad underneath her hand and gave her the pencil. When she finished writing it read: "My kids. Where are they? How is Ruby?"

"Ruby has been arrested," he told her. "I don't know where they've taken the kids. I'll find out as soon as I can, promise. You have to concentrate on getting well." He knew where the kids were. He did not want to tell her. He raised her hand to his mouth and kissed it. "I love you, Freddie Walker. Do you hear me? I love you."

She held his hand tight and pretended to write with her finger. He gave her back the pencil and steadied the pad underneath her hand. She wrote: "Me too."

It was the first time she admitted it. For what comes up and stays caught in a man's throat causing his heart to drop, and slow its beating, was happening to him. He loosened her hand from his. "I have to go. I'll be back as soon as I can." He stood up and kissed her gently. Why, he thought, did it take all this to happen before she recognized she loved him too? He desperately needed his father's help. It was time to tell him what he did.

10:00 P.M., same day.

Jack Santo's Bar and Grill was crowded with legal personnel. It was an attorney's haven for discussing cases while surrounded with loud voices, laughter, and kitchen noises.

Parker sat at a private table across from his father. Their meeting was not going well. Robert was in a vicious state of mind. The three deliveries of more scotch than soda did nothing to loosen him up to the idea of helping his son. Robert never surrendered to the conquest of artificial warmth. Even the air around him was alert, cold, stiff, standing guard like a protective shield that had no emotion and received none.

"Who are the people you bribed to shut down the whore's pimp? Who are they, damn you?" Robert asked.

"That's not important. I can't undo what's been done," said Parker. "I need a straight answer from you."

"Do you realize you played a role in that man's death? What is it you would have me do?"

89

"Use your influence. Show me how powerful you are."

"This is not a contest, you idiot. I have nothing to prove to my own son. Have those women even agreed to take you on as their attorney?"

"No. But they will. I'm sure of it."

"You know nothing about the lowness of that kind of criminal law. You'll look like an idiot. Don't be ridiculous."

"I'm asking for your help."

"Since you believe I have the power of God at my fingertips, what do you suppose I do about the drug charges? What do I do concerning the charges of child abuse? White children are involved."

"There have been no allegations made by her children about being abused. The drugs belonged to Jimmy Tate. That can be easily proven. If you don't help me …"

"Don't you dare threaten me, boy, or give me any kind of ultimatums. You sound like a desperate fool."

"I'm not threatening you, father. I will go around you to get it done. You have your people, I have mine."

"Do you honestly think that your mother's old entourage of idiots can help you? Most of those ridiculous fools are senile, on their death bed, or dying from sticking their rotting dicks into the wrong hole. They are useless to you. They have no power to change the mind of important people in this city?"

"I know what goes on in the place where you congregate with your so-called club."

"I don't know what the hell you're talking about."

"The men, father," said Parker, "those who run the almighty machine. I know who they are. They're some of the men that really run this city. We followed you many times. We saw who came in and out of the back door of your club."

"Which back door are you referring to? There are many clubs with many back doors."

"The club on Wabash, downtown. The one you visit every Thursday evening before you pick up Sally. The whore you've been dating for the last four years."

"I hope you haven't gotten your friends involved in your disaster."

"Being able to do what you do is power, father. You're one of the men at the center of all the power in this city. I respect that now. I'm asking you to use it to help me. Use your power to help your son save someone worth saving."

"I've heard enough." He rose to his feet. "You're insane." Parker grabbed his arm, forcing him to stay where he sat. "Let go of me. Don't make a public spectacle of yourself. This is about sin isn't it, strange sex, the unusual?" He tried to reason with Parker. "Son, it doesn't last. Men grow tired of whores like her when there's no girl left in them."

"I've never slept with her. We don't have that kind of relationship."

"You'll meet someone else, someone suitable."

"I don't want what's suitable."

"I will not help you ruin your life. The woman is worthless, incapable of love. She's a beaten-down whore who, thank God, is on her way to prison for the rest of her life." He leaned across the table and lowered his voice. "Some of the men that whore has bedded are friends of mine."

"That can work in our favor?"

"What?" he was stunned. "Are you asking me to blackmail my friends?"

"I am your son. Don't make me hate you for the rest of my life."

"I want you out of my home. If you do not move out one of us will do something worth regretting." He stood up and backed away from the table. "One more thing, I will personally escort that whore to the front gates of lock and key if I have to."

"Father," Parker called out. "Please, father, don't walk out on me."

Robert Bishop worked his way quickly through the people standing in back of the stools at the crowded bar. His son was calling out at him, crying like a girl, begging him for the kind of addictive candy he should have never tasted.

July 23, 1970

CHAPTER THREE
AUDEN HOME FOR JEUVENILE DELINQUENTS

Betty Jean stopped talking. During the day inside a playground surrounded with red-brick, hooded on top with bob wire fence, she played games with friends who were invisible. When she was inside, no matter the place, she sat on the floor with her two dolls close at hand and cuddled with them as if they were newborn babies. She sometimes cried while rocking and squeezing the dolls tightly.

The first attempt to take the dolls away brought about biting, wild kicking, scratching, and hollering screams. At the end of the altercation, as if she was a noisy wind-up doll with a broken key in its back, she was given a sleep medication. Even though there were solid reasons for her traumatic fits they treated her the same callous way as other crying children. The staff that ruled was cold that way.

Caring members of the medical staff worried over ambitious employees damaging Betty Jean further. Oddly enough the entire story had begun its death away from the public eye. But there were still smaller newspapers interested in buying anyone's first-hand account about what happened that night inside a house of ill repute. To eliminate unnecessary access the medical staff formed a quick diagnosis about Betty Jean. The special report was sent by speeding courier to investigative officials involved in the tragedy. It declared that Betty Jean Walker was in an impenetrable state of shock. Questioning the child would prove meaningless. No person bearing gifts of cookies, candies, or sweet talk, with attachments to any authority, would be allowed to visit any of the walker siblings.

Angela kept her mind busy with bringing her father back to life. She imagined his polished shoes high stepping down the institution's corridors, looking for her. He was dressed fine for the enticement of women … his hat tilted and perfectly boxed. And like always he was playing with the wooden toothpick, positioning it with his tongue, settling it between his lips, leaving half of it sticking out at the corner of his mouth.

When his shoes found her and his eyes saw her he said, "Hey, baby girl. How's my baby girl? I'm here to take you home." He held out his arms, urging her to run to him. In one scoop, same as always, she was picked up and her head was laid on his shoulders and her arms were around his neck.

"I love you, Daddy," she said.

He replied, "I love you too, baby girl."

After that they left the Auden Home. Everything was fine until she opened her eyes and saw the black steel bars of the dormitory's doors. She wondered why her bunk was closest to the ugly gate of lock and key. It worked against helping her pretend to be with her beloved father.

Most of the boys living in the same dorm as Danny were black. They called him malicious names like dirty-bleached blond, cracker-boy, white-as salt, sissy-like and stupid. Danny ignored their cruelty and laughed openly at it. When feeling particularly brave he deliberately placed himself among them. He sauntered near and pretended to talk to air, behaving like a revolutionary bad boy tipping the scale of insanity. He said strange and crazy things, using maddening tones that included discreet seconds of giggling when there was nothing to laugh at. Through menacing looks of exhausted depression, pacing, and fearless body language, it was made frighteningly clear to all bullies that Danny Walker was capable of hurting them.

No matter their heartlessness they failed to shove him out of their presence and deeper into his self. If trouble found him in a kid's place, a near match to an adult prison, he made up his mind to set up plans of surprise attack. For the lead bully it would be one that came hovering quietly, face to face, over his bunk just before daybreak. It was a brutal plan and worse than what he did to Jimmy Tate.

Danny liked that his bunk was closest to the only window, for no night spent at the Auden Home was without restlessness. When lying in the right position he had a clear view of a sometimes sparkling sky. Talking to God and praying for His mercy was easier when looking up at the stars and moon. The longest flooding of his prayers were over his beautiful mother. He could not stop remembering his last look at her battered face.

On this morning the smell of toast, eggs, sausages, and bacon was everywhere inside the building. Grief stricken children from age four to early teens who were girls, and boys, of all races, walked in a single-file line that led down a wide and long corridor with meticulous black glossy floors. They were on their way to the cafeteria. It was time for breakfast. There was no playing among them. Their freedom of unchallenged and spirited chattering had been down-graded to listlessness, confused mumbling, and whispering.

For the eyes of those children not following their feet to food they found it comforting to look up at the childish drawings, and paintings, hanging along the deep purple and pink walls. The artwork, tables, lamps, and some of the plastic furniture was molded into imitations of popular cartoon fixtures. The work had been done by professional artists. Their talented use of brilliant color appeased a child's hyperactivity and wounded disposition. It was an artistic, psychological, contribution of encouragement to the bright and happy illusion of a child being in a happy place. Many of the children were in Auden for committing crimes and many were not. Regardless, like the donation of a toy, they were given away to the youth-jailing system. No matter where a child resided on the property, or reason for being there, they were all locked away against their own free will.

The breakfast line separated to make an entrance for a robust-young black-woman. She went to a guard monitoring the line. She whispered something to him. He pointed to Neda who was near the end of the line. Neda preferred being last. It gave her a better overview of the children. She was always searching for her brother and sisters, but for some reason they were never fed at the same time. They had not seen the other since their arrival. She knew they were in the same building, but her anticipation of seeing one of them always gave way to the forming of tears.

The click and clack of the woman's shoes came and stopped near the tip of Neda's feet. "Neda Walker," the woman said. "My name is Mrs. Adams. You have to come with me."

Neda did not look at her. She lowered her eyes onto Mrs. Adams's shoes.

"Neda step out of the line, please. You have to come with me."

"I'm not goin' anywhere with you."

"Sweetheart, you haven't much choice."

"Don't call me sweetheart. Everybody around here is always sayin' that. I'm not your sweetheart."

"Please, dear."

"I could give you a good run," said Neda. "You can't catch me with those shoes on. You might fall and break your neck. Another thing, don't call me dear. You said my name already." She raised her head, looked at Mrs. Adams, and then lowered her eyes back onto her shoes.

"Wouldn't you like to visit with your brother and sisters?"

"How do I know you're not lyin'? I think you're a liar like every grown person around here."

"There's only one way to find out. You'll have to come with me." Mrs. Adams extended her hand to Neda. "Be a nice-pretty girl."

Neda ignored the gesture of hand holding and stepped out of the line. While following slowly behind Mrs. Adams, she blocked out her surroundings. She wanted to remember a night spent with Miss Ruby. Danny and Angela were with her. The three of them were inside Ruby's bedroom. They sat on the floor around the legs of her chair. It was their bible study time. The discussion was about good children and bad children.

"When born all children are good children," Miss Ruby told them. "All children are God's children."

"Are we damaged children, Miss Ruby?" asked Neda.

She looked down at the four of them. "Yes," she admitted, "but not too much. You're the kind of children God likes to hold hands with."

"How do you know that?" asked Angela.

"He told me."

"I don't believe a word of it," said Angela.

"Miss Ruby," said Danny, "are you sayin' you can talk to God?"

"Sometimes," she said, "but not lately."

"Why?" asked Neda.

"I don't know. I guess he's mad at me for somethin' I can't recall. You just remember what I say. When the time is right don't be afraid to take God's hand. Let Him pull you up on your feet. Let Him lead you toward the plan He has for you in this life. Don't ever forget, He has never failed to give special attention to His good damaged children. When you don't need to hold His hand, he'll go on about His business."

"How will we know," asked Danny, "when God is holdin' our hand?"

"It won't be easy. We can't see Him. We can only feel His presence around us. If there ever comes a time when you hold your breath, and you can hear someone else breathin' like they're right inside of you, it's Him. It ain't no spirit. It ain't the devil. It's Him alright."

"You mean we can feel Him breathin' the way we do?" Neda asked.

"Yes," Ruby said. "God ain't no different from us. We made up in His image. The only difference is He can make miracles happen at the blink of an eye." She looked up at the ceiling. "That is if He ain't too lazy to whip up one of His damn miracles."

"He's gonna get you, Miss Ruby," said Danny. "You can't go around callin' God lazy."

"The hell I can't!" she said, looking up at the ceiling. "We ain't on good terms. I can say whatever I want. He knows what I need to set things straight in this house. He's been too busy eatin' His grapes and readin' His damn books."

Ruby stood and stomped her foot on the floor. Angela got up and eased her way out of the room. Danny and Neda had never seen Ruby angry with God. They wanted to hear more of what she had to say to Him.

"You remember that time in Mississippi," she asked, pointing her finger at the ceiling, looking up at it, "when I didn't believe you even existed? Remember when I was sleepin' and You sent that funny lookin' Angel, the one with a wing shorter than the other, to come and get me. I thought I was dreamin'. I stood up there in heaven with You lookin' down on me. You promised me that someday all I loved would be alright in this world. You ain't nothin' but a liar." She stomped her foot, crossed her arms, and started pacing back and forth.

100

Look at what's goin' on in this house," Ruby told God. "The devil showin' His self clear as night and day, infectin' everything I love with his disease of evil. All you do Mr. Grapes, Mr. Books, Mr. God, is lay around doin' nothin' to help us get out of this mess. You are a lazy, uncaring, old fool!" Suddenly out of the nowhere there was a loud boom that shook the house. Danny and Neda jumped up off the floor and ran out of the room. "Go on," Ruby shouted at God. "Tear this ole house of sin apart. Need some help?" She picked up the bowl of fruit on the nightstand and sent it crashing onto the floor. "You ain't the only one that's got the right to be pissed off. You hear me Mr. Grapes, Mr. Books, Mr. God?"

That night they stayed awake and listened to Ruby having it out with God. There were two more big booms that shook the house and rattled all the windows. After each one, Ruby screamed and cursed at God and then threw something else crashing to the floor. Neda and Danny looked out the window. They believed the big booming noises had nothing to do with thunder.

After the fight was over, and they had gone to bed, and the rain had come, their belief in God had been strengthened. Their respect and love for Miss Ruby was more profound. She was a woman that could talk to God and make Him talk back. She wasn't afraid to tell Him off. She wasn't afraid of God striking her down where she stood. To them her fearless standup to Mr. Grapes, Mr. Books, and Mr. God meant they loved each other very much.

The next morning it was Danny that answered the doorbell. A man was standing there with a bouquet of yellow roses in his hand. He asked for Ruby Johnson. Danny called out to Ruby and she came down the stairs.

"Who are these for?" asked Ruby. She took the flowers from the man and looked for a card. "There ain't no card with these flowers," she told the man. The man left without saying anything. Ruby closed the door. She stood smelling and looking at the roses, squinting curiously at them. She said softly, as if talking to herself while feeling the petals, "I guess I know who they're from."

"Who?" Danny asked, climbing the stairs behind her.

"Somebody with a softer heart. She's tellin' me I don't have much choice. I have to see it all through."

When Miss Ruby was busy in the kitchen Danny and Neda stuck their heads inside her room to look at the beautiful roses. They thought it odd the flowers had not died. Two weeks went by and the water inside the glass vase was never murky. It was always crystal clear, like the flowers were not sitting in any water that could be seen. Neda had to stick her finger inside the vase to feel something wet. Danny questioned Miss Ruby about the longevity of the flowers.

"Those flowers are so pretty," she told him, "I keep on throwin' the dead ones away and buyin' new ones. They make my room smell so nice, just like perfume. Yellow is my favorite color."

Acceptance of the answer was an honest deception that came out of their respect for Miss Ruby's privacy. Notwithstanding, they were certain that something God like was involved with the longevity of the flowers.

To prove their theory Neda marked the top of the stem, of each bud, with a spot of pink nail polish. Every day they were sneaking around the house like detectives close to solving a big crime. They slipped inside Miss Ruby's room when she was out shopping to examine the roses. The same spots of pink polish were on the buds of what they believed to be the same yellow roses. It was exciting to wait patiently for the roses to die. They wanted to evaluate the day after the end of something extraordinary.

On the last day of the fourth week the roses began to wilt. Later that same evening they died slowly. The two of them watched it happen. What they waited so patiently for saddened them to tears. It was as if they lost a friend of more value than any they ever cared for.

They never told Miss Ruby why they cried so vulnerably. She thought they were crying over something she read to them inside her bible. It pleased her to know that her teachings about having faith, and belief in God, had gotten through to them.

Besides the strange time, of acknowledging God's true existence, it was a time Danny discovered he had a way with words.

103

He wrote a short story titled: *Mr. Grapes, Mr. Books, Mr. God, Miss Ruby and the Roses that would not die.*

Neda had come out of thinking about Miss Ruby and God. When she entered the east wing with Miss Adams, the childish drawings had been replaced with portraits of rigid men dressed in suits and ties. The smell of disinfectant was replaced with the smell of shaving lotion and perfume. It was eerily quiet.

They turned down the last corridor and at the end of it was a single door. The glass plate read Child Services. Vibrant photographs of children were pinned to bulletin boards on either side of the door, and most were posing with their parents or adults in charge. While Neda looked at the photographs, Mrs. Adams stood at the door searching for the right key. It was among many on a bronze ring.

"What are those pictures about?" asked Neda. "Everybody looks so happy?"

"Oh, them, you mean our wonderful success stories."

"What kind of success?"

She walked and stood beside Neda and looked at the photographs. "Those are very happy children. They've found good homes with good people to take care of them. We hope the same for you and—we better go inside." She knew she had made a mistake with her words.

104

"We have a mother and a home," yelled Neda. "It's paid for. We don't owe a penny on it. We have Miss Ruby too. All of us are happy bein' together."

Mrs. Adams had not learned how to handle her mistakes said to incarcerated children. Her employment was a new position.

She walked back to the door and continued searching for the right key. Neda was crying, making it more difficult to concentrate. "You're right," she told Neda. Please accept my apology. I forgot that you have a home and a mother and a very good friend. It was stupid of me to forget such a thing."

"Nobody is goin' to take anything away from us, nobody. Nobody is goin' to separate us."

There was banging on the other side of the door. Neda heard the calling of her name. It was Danny's voice.

"Danny!" She grabbed the sleeve of Mrs. Adam's blouse, tugging it. "Open the door. Please open the door."

She found the right key and opened the door, letting Neda inside to face more tragedy. The day was over for Mrs. Adams.

Ella Partridge, the director of the Auden Home, was a bad-tempered stark-white woman in her late forties. She had an overworked face etched with deep lines and creases. Patches of tiny busted veins, always lost of their cover of makeup, could be seen through the bags of skin under her eyes. To others she gave the impression of being malnourished and cold, looking as if she were standing dead in deep snow. Her speed of aging had come from her selfish worry and lack of sleep over her selfish worry.

To make matters worse Ella had not received her most desired, yearly, invitation to the governor's mansion—a party gathering for liberals, societal women of good means and ambitious political figures. By not receiving her important invitation she took it as the right message. Her position was at stake.

Until Robert Bishop came along she had even considered suicide over the possibility of losing her loved position. He was her savior—a man she thought charming, handsome, and dangerously wicked had saved her from self destruction.

When their decided date to dine arrived she was taken to brief heights of fairy-tale awe. She was surprised to step outside her apartment building and discover a driver and limousine waiting for her. It was like being uplifted to her previous value. Unlike being invited to dine under the roofs of state given luxuries, Robert had invited her to a quiet dinner at his home. She was surrounded by the luxury of his personal wealth and it was just the two of them. A housekeeper waited on her as though she were royalty.

During their dinner, in between sips of wine, Robert overloaded her with hope and encouragement. Through his carefully chosen words, the kind used by a good-looking man to get what he wants, he gave her exhilarating expectations of picking up her success story where it should have never left off. He praised her and touched her hand, ever so slightly, causing her skin to tingle with desires long past dead. They discussed her needs and she nearly broke down when telling him of how the state had neglected her. Her request for the construction of sufficient office space and expansion of the east wing had been denied.

Before the night was over he told her about his son. His only child had been bewitched by a whore, her bastards, and a Negro maid. He told her that the whore's children were in Auden. She saw tears and shame in his eyes. The important legal figure had landed on her lap. He confided in her like a normal man, and loving father, in need of motherly assistance to help him save his son from dark seductions.

Throughout the drive back to her apartment her thoughts were about his requests. He wanted the Walker children separated with a lot of distance between them. In comparison to what she wanted from him the requests were small. He simply wanted her to do her job faster. She believed he could help her get what she wanted out of the State of Illinois, especially more money. Based on all he said, if available, she would find the despicable children homes at the end of the North Pole.

The four children were in the reception room under lock and key. Danny and Neda sat with Betty Jean. Across the room Angela sat alone. She avoided eye contact with them and her head was down. She swung her feet back and forth while playing a game of twirling one thumb around the other.

"Stop that cryin'," Danny told Neda. "You're makin' my ears wet."

"What's wrong with Betty Jean, Danny?" cried Neda. "She's not talkin'.

"I don't know. It's this damn place."

She's not eatin'. Look how skinny she is. Where's her leg brace? When we came to this place she had it on."

"She probably took it off. She's always takin' the damn thing off. It's too darn heavy."

"What are they gonna do to us, Danny?"

"See that door," he said, pointing to it. "There's a man and a woman in that office. They're talkin' about separatin' us. They wanna put us with people we don't know. I can hear some of the stuff they're sayin'."

"Nobody is gonna separate us," said Neda.

"Yeah," said Angela. "How are you gonna stop them? They'll beat you. I know they beat people in here."

"They don't beat people," Danny told her. "I ain't seen nobody gettin' beat."

"What did you hear them say Danny?" Neda asked.

"They said those children. Better do it now and get it over with. All the families have agreed any time would be okay. Why not now? No good reason for it. They said stuff like that."

"So," said Neda, "that doesn't mean we're goin' anywhere without each other."

"Sure it does," said Danny. They even talked about Betty Jean. They said where the youngest girl is concerned medical attention can be arranged. The state will pick up the bill. I'm tellin' you we're done for."

The office door opened out into the reception area and a clean shaven young-white man with dark hair stepped out. His hands were shoved inside his pockets. He did not look at the Walker siblings because he felt sympathetic. Ella's plan to pull them apart at the foot of his office was cruel. She ordered him to stand before the children with his arms crossed and told him not to smile because of the seriousness of the situation. He wondered why she had not called security to help her scare the children.

Ella, with four manila folders in her hand, exited the office and closed the door. She wore her red suit with the wide and boxy shoulders.

She looked at Angela. "You must be, Angela."

"What of it," Angela said, avoiding eye contact.

"I want you to get up and sit over here with your brother and sisters."

Angela ignored the request.

"Dear," said Ella. "Please take a seat next to your brother and sisters. Do it now."

Angela took her time standing up and going to them. She sat next to Danny. Ella pulled up a chair and sat down before them.

"Do you know who I am?"

"Yeah," said Danny, "you're the one that runs this shit hole. You're the one they want to shoot with a shotgun. They say you look like a long-neck crane with a broken back. They say you go flyin' around eatin' kids."

Angela giggled at Danny's comment. She was pleased he chose to be cruel.

Ella heard about their nasty and abusive tongues. However, she did not expect to be spoken to in such a way. "Who says that? Which employees have you heard say that?

"I ain't no snitch," said Danny. "Keep your skirt on."

"Maybe it was him," said Neda, pointing to the young man standing beside Ella's chair.

"It's true," said Angela. "You look like a bad photocopy of a dead person."

Ella dismissed the fact that they were children. It was time to hurt back. "I've brought you here to say your final goodbyes. This is the last time any of you will ever see the other for the rest of your lives."

110

"You can't do that," cried Neda. "They said we wasn't gonna be separated. We have a mother. We have Miss Ruby."

"Yes," said Ella. "Both of them will spend the rest of their lives in prison. So ..."

"You ain't nobody's judge and jury," Danny told her.

"Shut your filthy mouth you stupid boy. Do I make myself clear?" Ella had made up her mind not be threatened by the white and black mistakes. She looked at the three of them. "Daniel. You and Betty will be leaving here this afternoon."

"The two of you," she said, looking at Neda, then Angela, "will also be leaving the care of this wonderful institution. The four of you should consider yourselves lucky. You could have stayed behind these walls until the age of eighteen."

"When are we leavin'?" asked Neda.

"Are you looking for a specific date?" Ella replied. "I don't have one. Trust me ..."

"Trust is for fools," said Danny.

"You didn't have to make a big show," Angela told Ella. "I don't care where I go."

"Well, then, you can say your goodbyes quickly and go back to your dorm. This decision is what's best for all of you."

Ella rose to her feet. "You ole-skinny crane," said Neda. How do you know what's best for us? You ain't kin to us."

"You're right," she told, Neda. "I'm not. Thank God."

"Where are you takin' my brother and sister?" asked Neda. "They said we wasn't gonna be separated."

"Who is they?" Ella asked. "My decision is final." She stood to leave.

Neda stood and the movement made Ella nervous. She looked over at the young man. "Call security," she told him. "Now, please."

He hesitated before walking back inside the office, closing the door behind him.

"Why you doin' this to us, lady?" asked Neda. "You ain't sendin' my brother and sister no place. I can kill people. I can kill you. We ain't bein' separated."

"Kill her," screamed Angela. "Pick up a chair and beat her dead with it. Kill her."

"Shut up, Angela," said Danny.

"Kill her, Neda."

Ella walked to the office door, and with her back to the children she turned the knob. The door was locked.

"Kill her before she gets away," Angela shouted.

Neda leaped onto Ella's back and pulled her hair, trying to shake her brains out. Ella screamed as if she were being killed. Neda did not see the two security guards, but she felt their hands trying to pull her off Ella.

"Run, Danny!" Neda yelled. "Run!"

He ran past the guards, out the door, and down the first corridor. For the hell of it he jumped up high, using the palm of his hand to dislodge portraits of the distinguished looking men. Some fell to the floor.

The second corridor was wet, slippery, children were coming out of the playrooms and their dorms watching him run. Along the way he grabbed cartoon fixtures off tables and threw them as far as he could. When they shattered the sound reminded him of his mother's perfume bottles crashing to the floor, taking her with them.

The third corridor had a door straight ahead and a woman opened it. Sunlight poured in and the woman walked outside. Danny was almost behind her. God fixed it all he thought. Mr. Grapes and Mr. Books had opened a door just for him. It was like a miracle. It was like the roses that wouldn't die.

Outside, he ran around the first corner and made another right turn. The guard's fist slamming into his stomach knocked all of the wind out of him. It took a long time for the pain to go away and a longer time to catch his breath. After he could walk he was taken back to Child Services.

He went to Betty Jean. She was busy serving her dolls an imaginary cup of tea. He knelt, pulled her close, and cried. She felt so frail in his arms. He thought if she wasn't separated from him she would be easy to look after. She said nothing and didn't eat much. She just smiled and played and slept. He wondered if he would ever

113

see his crazy Puerto Rican, or the meanest sister a brother still loved just the same.

August 3, 1970

CHAPTER FOUR
A FATHER'S VISIT

It was around midnight and every bed in the dimly lit ward was taken by common women. Robert walked down the aisle, separating the beds, looking for the whore. Bile rose into his throat and then settled at the top of his stomach. His nose and pallet had never been exposed to a gathering of runny bowels and weak bladders. The smell was so repulsive he was sure some of the women were dead or very close to it. The ward was empty of medical personnel because he paid to have it that way. No one of any reputable or valid means could declare they saw Robert Bishop visiting the whore's sickbed.

He approached the far end of the ward and there she was with a single arm handcuffed to the rail of her bed. She snored and the sound was innocent, pitiful. He watched her for a while before he touched her foot gently, shaking it a little.

"Miss Walker." There was no response. "Miss Walker." After a few moments she moaned and stirred awake.

The swelling of her eyes and face had gone down. A few remaining bruises were seen. She raised her head and glanced at the good-looking man with strict-white hair. He stood at the foot of her bed smiling as if he knew her. She recognized him from somewhere

115

and thought that maybe she knew him too. It was the way he held his posture and tilted his head that reminded her of someone.

He went and stood at the side of her bed and looked down at her. "Do you know who I am?"

"No," answered Freddie.

"I'm Robert Bishop. Parker's ..."

"Yeah," she said, cutting him off, "I know who you are. I recognize the resemblance." His disgust and hatred of her was seen immediately and understood. "What do you want?" She was completely awake and alert like a cat.

"I can only hope you listen and take under consideration what I have to say."

"Parker said I should expect a visit from you. He knew you would do this." She lied and couldn't think of any reason why she told it.

"You can choose to tell my son about my visit or you can choose to say nothing. It makes no difference. The wedge you've driven between me and my son can be removed."

"Go on. Say what you have to." The way of a woman had emerged and sat up to meet the confrontation. She had to forget about the man he was. She would treat the visit as one from a customer—a man not pleased with her performance, threatening to take back his money and thinking about hurting her. She had to show no fear and make him believe it.

"My son is a young man with a good heart and a kind soul. Under certain conditions he's easily influenced. Under normal circumstances, I would never interfere in my son's private life. However, his relationship with you has left me no choice. Do you realize he believes he cares for you?"

"He loves me," she said.

"He's twenty-seven years of age, same as yourself. He's rather naïve and foolish?"

"What do you want from me?"

"I'm curious. What kind of woman is it he claims to love? Women like you are beautiful, fascinating, and so much fun to be with. But no matter how pleasant and loving you pretend to be most whores, of your caliber, are greedy for the destruction of everything good in a man. Women like you don't realize such truths about themselves. Do they?"

I'm listenin'. She sat up straighter and picked up her pack of cigarettes from the bed table. She removed one and lit it.

"Yes," he said, as if reading her mind, "I should get to the point. The reason I'm here is to promise you something. I'm here to give you a good balance of choice."

"Sounds conceived," she said, "sort of pre-planned. No … that's not the word, sounds premeditated. That's the word I'm looking for."

117

"If you try to escape your fate your children will to grow up in the worst conditions imaginable. Do you love your children, Miss Walker?"

She wanted to shrink and die inside the grooves of the overused bed. "No. Not like a mother should." She had to say that.

"I think you're lying. They are still children. They can be saved. I'm giving you an opportunity to do that."

"Saved from what?"

"You of course. Do you honestly believe that you and your maid deserve freedom after exposing them to that way of life … child abuse, murder, drugs?"

"The law says we deserve a fair trial."

"There are narcotics involved. Your children have given statements to the court about the life they've lived … the child abuse. Social Workers, the best in Chicago, are appalled and coming after you and your maid."

"You're borin' me. You sound badly rehearsed. I'm waitin' for act three."

"I can offer you this. No. I can promise you something."

"In exchange for what?"

"The welfare of your children. They can be adopted and raised in decent God fearing homes. I will personally see to it."

"Get the hell out of here." The vulnerable side of her that loved her children emerged. He saw it.

"You can get off with second degree murder, or, maybe even manslaughter, a slap on the wrist for being a bad girl. For those other mistakes involving drugs, prostitution, child abuse …"

"How much time are we looking at?"

"You mean you and the maid?"

"Yeah, sure, me and the maid."

"If you accept the offer the district attorney proposes …"

"How would you know about it?" she said, taking a drag from her cigarette, exhaling. "What offer is it?"

"Your fate in the hands of a judge," he told her. "I would say you'll receive twenty, maybe thirty years. Your maid …"

"She is not my maid, Robert Bishop. Ruby Johnson is my closest and dearest friend."

"Whatever she is she's also a Negro. There is no deal. She did the actual murder, didn't she? She did pull the trigger?"

"Are you lookin' for a confession?"

"If you agree to throw yourselves onto the mercy of the court there will be no newspapers. No cameras." He moved in closer to the bed. "Can you prove it, Miss Walker?"

"Prove what?"

"Prove that you care for my son," he said. "Do you love him?" Prove that you love your four children. Their fate is in your hands."

10:00 P.M.

Ruby had been released from the Jail's Infirmary and had taken her observation shower. Her vagina and rectum were inspected and she was sprayed from head to toe with a chemical that smelled like three-alarm roach-spray. All of it had been done by a malicious guard. She was a young and thin black woman of dark complexion.

To step back and take a look at the guard, reading her ways, Ruby concluded that she harbored many personal complexes and total lack of heartfelt sympathy for those in desperate need of it. Though it wasn't part of the guard's duty, she volunteered to walk Ruby down the tier to her new home.

Ruby carried a roll of toilet paper, a package of toiletries, one blanket, one sheet, and one towel. Her skin and hair were still wet. She was cold under the blue-shift dress that was too big and too thin. She walked barefoot on the concrete floor because they were out of the white-cotton slippers.

"I don't like your kind of yellow-negro trash," the guard told Ruby, while walking the way. "You think you better than every other colored woman … spendin' your life sniffin' the asses of white people … thinkin' you'll have a good life for doin' it. This place is only a taste of what you got comin'. You might as well take it all in and get used to it."

"I'm sorry you feel that way about a woman you don't know." Her broken nose had begun to heal, but she could hardly talk without pain.

"I know you," said the guard. "I read all about you in the newspaper. Looks like you and that white woman will spend the rest of your life in prison. You're gettin' what you deserve because of what you did to those kids. God only knows what happened to them inside that house. I hope you rot where they're sendin' you. I think I know where that is but I'm not tellin' you a damn thing so don't ask."

"Well, that's okay. I don't care to know. To tell the truth, the way I see it, I don't like your kind of too-black hearted-negro." The guard stopped walking, turned, and looked at Ruby. Ruby stood her ground with conviction. "You got a chip on your shoulder because you three shades darker than what you think you should be. You too ignorant to realize that anything that ain't white has a hard way to go. Life ain't better because a colored woman is a shade lighter than the next. Anybody that ain't white is at the bottom of the heap of shit."

The guard was stunned. "I think you better shut your trap before I shut it for you."

"No," Ruby said. She was clam. "You don' scare me. You said your piece. I feel sorry for women like you. You hate yourself more than you could ever hate anybody else. I know you don't have a man or children. You too damn evil. The only real physical pleasure, you'll ever know, is the kind you give yourself. It's the only kind that satisfies you. Evil women like you are easy to read. You put yourself up under the brightest light. You enjoy being recognized as a bully."

"You're in my house now. Say somethin' else like that to me and see what happens." The guard rolled her eyes at Ruby, turned, and walked the short steps to the front of a cell. "Open me up number fifteen," she shouted. After a few moments the door to cell fifteen slid open.

The sound reminded Ruby of the clanking steel of the neighborhood's big garbage trucks when they drove down the alley, picking up trash and dumping it into the compacter. Ruby stepped inside the cell.

The guard said, apologetically, "Hey you."

Ruby turned and faced her. Not to her surprise the guard spat a wad of spit in her face. At the closing of the cell's door the guard smiled at Ruby and walked away.

Ruby was not hurt by the spitting. If she had to spend the rest of her life behind bars, she made up her mind not to do it as a cry baby.

She was not alone inside the shoe box meant for two. There was a woman asleep on the top bunk. Ruby put her things down on the bare mattress of the lower bunk, unrolled a piece of toilet paper, and wiped the guard's spit off her face. She made the bed and crawled in under the itchy-gray blanket, resting her head on a bare-stained pillow with black stripes. Seeping from the pillow, like small amounts of tolerable gas, was the nauseating and sweet fragrance of tears and drool. The pickled smell of a thousand heads of unwashed hair tickled her nose. Sleep came easy.

The next morning Ruby met the middle-aged white-woman that shared the cell. She had short dark hair and roaming black-watery eyes.

Ruby lay on her bunk while the woman sat on the floor facing her. The woman talked incessantly fast with her hands and tiny hole of a mouth. She had been arrested for stealing six tubes of flaming-red lipstick from Goldsmith's Department Store. She bragged of being rich. When she smiled, flashing her perfect-white teeth, and from the way she held her posture, Ruby knew she was telling the truth. She thought of the woman as a troubled kleptomaniac with quick-flashing eyes searching for something to steal, something easy to fit inside a pocket. The woman bragged on and on about her petty crimes. To her they were some kind of heroic and remarkable feat.

"I've got a knife with me," she told Ruby. "It's wrapped up in plastic tape. I shoved it up there nice and deep. My fucking hole is still tight as a virgin dog's pussy, deeper than the black hole. I only fucked ten men in my life and that wasn't for too long. Those bitches didn't find a damn thing when they made me bend over and spread myself open. How about that?" she asked Ruby. "What do you think of that?"

Ruby smiled, appeasing the woman, "I think that's real fine, damn smart if you ask me."

"You're alright for a Negro. When I get out of this place, I'm going to send you something nice."

Two days after the woman had been released a package arrived and was delivered to Ruby. She lifted the lid and looked inside at the thoroughly inspected mess. She saw expensive soaps, shampoos, conditioners and lotions. There were ten tubes of flaming-red lipstick and tubes of different colored face makeup and face powders. There was no note. Ruby knew it was from the woman. She took what she wanted and gave the rest of it to the women on the tier.

On the fourth day Ruby was still alone inside her cell. Early that morning there was a lot of excitement, movement, and anticipated commotion up and down the tier. A wedding was about to take place between two women. They had collected rolls of toilet paper from the cells of those willing to give it to them, and with it they made wedding veils and bouquets.

As the wedding progressed and those that attended sang, Here Comes the Bride, Ruby saw the two women with their arms linked, walking past her cell. They were dressed up in their toilet paper veils and holding their toilet paper bouquets. She laughed quietly to herself.

A short time after the wedding Ruby's new cell mate walked in. She did not feel like greeting her. She hid under her blanket with her body facing the wall.

The new arrival threw her plastic bag of toiletries onto the top bunk, "This is a real shit hole of a place if I've ever seen one," said the woman.

Ruby swung around and her heart was beating fast. She saw the knees and legs of the woman and when she looked up at the woman's face her eyes watered and tears spilled down her cheeks, "Freddie."

MORAL OBLIGATIONS

10:00 P.M., same day.

It was a cold night. A lost gust of wind roamed the tier like it was trapped and looking for a way out—looking for the door it came in. It visited all the cells and the women complained of being too cold.

The lights were out except for the lamp of an old guard who sat behind a desk reading a book about vacationing in picturesque Virginia. The desk was outside the black-gated bars that were at the head of the tier's entrance. The guard had been told, by those higher up, to listen to Freddie and Ruby's conversation without interruption. For the sake and love of children she was told to remember what she could.

For the second time Freddie sat on the toilet's stool and the rank medicine smell of her soft bowel movement dominated the cell's air space and made Ruby gag.

"Whatever whore that is, takin another shit," a woman yelled out, "I wish you'd hurry it up. Smell worse than a dead rat. Jesus Christ."

Freddie had not heard the comment or laughter behind it. She stared at the floor. Her thoughts were deep and expressions worried. For Ruby, seeing her like that was almost new. She took it as a sign of something between them not being said. Freddie wiped herself, stood, pulled up her panties and flushed the toilet.

"It's about got-damn time," the same woman yelled.

Freddie stepped onto the edge of Ruby's bunk and hoisted herself on top. The distance between them was cold. The underhanded and invisible creature that derives its pleasure from breaking up friendship was present, and who they were as friends was about to be tested. What kind of relationship did they really have? Who they were as women was on its way of shinning through and nothing could stop it.

"We ain't said two words to each other," said Ruby. "It's bad enough with us bein' locked up."

126

"I'm just tired," said Freddie, "worried about the kids."

"Somethin' else is messin' with you. What is it?"

"I don't know, Ruby. When I look at everything, I know what I have to do. I don't have any choices. What I need is a strong dose of courage."

"You talkin' about the both of us, or just yourself?"

"It's not about us," said Freddie. "Nothin' is about us anymore. The kids, Ruby, it's about them. I had an unexpected visitor."

"Who was it?"

"Parker's father. He came to see me when I was in the hospital.

Ruby raised herself on her elbows. "That's not a bad thing. We need a good lawyer, why not the best money can buy? We got enough money to pay him."

"That's not why he came. A man like Robert Bishop—a man that important and powerful knows all the Judges in this city. You know what he can do to the kids?"

"Since you got here I've had to smell your shit closer than I ever had to. I'm smellin' more of your shit comin' out of your mouth. Quit stallin'. Tell me what you know."

"Robert Bishop is an evil man. He said the kids would be sent to live with the worst people. He said he would see to it personally. He wants us to plead guilty. He said the drug and child abuse charges is enough to keep us locked up for the rest of our lives. Killin' Jimmy is not as bad. He said the district attorney is willin' to make a deal. We'll still have to do some time."

Ruby uncovered herself from the blanket, swung her legs over the edge of the bunk, and stood up with her arms folded.

"I'm sorry, Ruby."

Ruby wanted to run until she was dog tired and half dead. The only thing she could do was pace back and forth, chasing her own frustration, trying to catch it and put it to rest. "I don't give a good goddamn what Robert Bishop say he can or cannot do. He ain't the only lawyer in the City of Chicago. You forgot his son is one too. Parker will help us."

"I can't let that happen."

"What?" She walked to the edge of Freddie's bunk and shoved her. "Look at me, Freddie Walker. What did you say?"

"We can't win. Anyway you look at it we're goin' to prison. If we go through with a public trial the kids and Parker will be dragged into it. We'll be in the papers and all over the news, on television. The kids will have to testify. They'll hate us for it. A trial that nasty and that dirty will follow them for the rest of their lives. I can't drag Parker into this. I can't do that to him. It would ruin his life."

"His life. What about our life, my goddamn life?"

"Either way you look at it," said Freddie, "we're doomed. We have to think of what's best for the kids."

"You tell me why should I give up my life because you realize you love your flesh and blood?"

"Maybe," Freddie said, switching subjects, "a long vacation is what I need."

"Prison ain't no vacation. You goddamn fool."

"I didn't mean it the way it sounded."

"Your kids are not mine. I ain't makin' that kind of sacrifice. I want to have my own children. I won't let you take every dream I've ever had, for myself, away from me because of your children.

"The dope charges ..."

"Those drugs don't belong to us. A good lawyer can help us prove that. No drugs were ever hidden in that house."

"We should have signed the house over to him before all this happened."

"What the hell does that mean?"

"It's our house. We bought it. It's in our name, and what's in it is ours."

Ruby lost her balance and fell into a heap on the floor. The way a silent scream takes away a child's breath happened to her. When the scream found her mouth, giving her breath, it sounded as if a thousand women had screamed for feeling the same pain. God was no longer Mr. Grapes and Mr. Books. He was God. She gave

Him the respect of saying His name, yelling it over and over again like He was walking away and she was trying to stop Him.

Freddie lifted herself to rest on both elbows, looking at Ruby. She had never heard her cry like that. All the women on the tier were awake and listening. They knew the women crying and screaming at the other were the ones accused of murder, narcotics, and child abuse.

NO GOODBYE

The Auden Home cafeteria was vast as any inside government institutions. It was overcrowded with colorless tables and connecting steel benches. Most of the children sat elbow to elbow. To bring it closer to the ring of truth, of the resemblance of prison lifestyle, guards were overseeing the children from designated areas.

It was Sunday night dinner and the first dinner hour. The children were not their adapted, quiet, and depressive selves. The sound of the line could have been mistaken for one inside an elementary school during lunch time. They ignored the line monitor's command to keep the line in straight order and be silent. Their bellies were infected with the aroma of roasted chicken, corn, mashed potatoes and apples cooking in brown sugar. The homey atmosphere brought about their need to play and socialize in ways accustomed to children being held in large numbers.

Sharita Brian, Angela's new best friend, stood in the middle of the line. She was an eleven-year old, black, muscular girl with a snarling face. And for looking the way she did, rejected by family members for looking that way, she developed an array of psychiatric complexes. This helped to make Sharita an unwanted-jealous child. She was quick to strike out and do physical harm to pretty girls and pretty women. Where children commit crimes to get attention from adults, Sharita was at the Auden Home for slaughtering stray cats and dogs. Her favorite was to beat them to death with a heavy-steel rod. Two days after she and Angela met, they cut their fingers, mingled their blood, and swore themselves as sisters and best friends.

Angela bullied her way up the line. "Here I am," she said, tapping Sharita on her shoulder. "I saw you lookin' for me."

"Hey girl!" said Sharita, "where you been?"

"Girl, I was way at the end of the line. I had to bump my way up here. I almost had to beat up and kill somebody."

"Good," Sharita told her, "They probably need it."

Neda was in the line. It was the first time she shared the same dinner hour with her sister. Whenever they came in contact through the exchange of one group for another, Angela avoided discussing what happened to Danny and Betty Jean. She gave insignificant reasons that roll easily off the tip of a liar's tongue.

To get closer to Angela, and Sharita, Neda bumped her way up the line. She stood next to Angela. "Why are you avoidin' me?"

Angela treated the confrontation like a ghost talking. It was her turn to be served. She put her tray on the rail and smiled sweetly at the food handler.

"What you want to drink?" The food handler asked.

"Milk, please," said Angela. The food handler put a carton of milk on her tray.

"What you want?"

"Juice," said Neda, turning her attention back to Angela. "I asked you somethin'. Why are you always avoidin' me?"

"I ain't avoidin' you."

"You're lyin'."

"She ain't avoidin' you," said Sharita.

"You shut up," Neda said to Sharita. "Ain't nobody talkin' to your ugly face." Sharita saw the mean streak in Neda. She turned her attention back to moving along the rail.

"You just mad cause you ain't got no friends and I do," said Angela. She picked up her tray, followed behind Sharita, and sat at a table next to her.

Neda took her tray from the rail. She went and sat down in the middle of them. "Move over," she told Sharita.

132

Sharita cared nothing about Angela's confrontation with her sister. Her eyes roamed over the trays of the other children. She wanted their apple cobbler.

"Did you hear anything about where they took Danny and Betty Jean? Asked Neda."

"No," answered Angela. "I already told you, I don't care. Leave me alone."

"What about grownups, did they say anything about mama and Miss Ruby?"

Angela's voice was loud. "I ain't heard nothin'. I don't care if I ever hear anything. "Go sit someplace else."

"When they separate us then see how you feel."

"I'll be glad you're gone."

"I ain't never gonna stop lovin' them," said Neda.

"You ain't lovin' much of nothin'."

Neda stood up. She had not touched her food. She picked up her tray and slammed it on top of Sharita's. "You can eat mine too. You fat cow."

Those children not afraid of Angela, or Sharita, laughed.

Get away from here," Angela whispered, looking up at Neda. "You're gettin' us in trouble."

"Before I go. I want you to look at me, Angela. Tell me you hate me. Tell me you hate me so I won't feel bad about leavin' you behind."

133

"Get away from me. I'm tryin to eat my food. I ain't tellin' you nothin'."

A guard approached the table. She grabbed Neda by the arm and pulled her toward the exit.

"Tell me you hate me, Angela, tell me."

"I hate you," Angela screamed. "We were never a family. "I hate you. I hate them too."

CHAPTER FIVE
SOMETHING GOOD FROM BAD ENDINGS

On a rainy afternoon a white sedan with the seal of the State of Illinois, printed on the doors, arrived and parked in front of the Auden Home and Mrs. Adams was the driver. During most of the drive Neda said nothing. She sat with her head down and when her head felt too heavy she stared out the window at the sheets of rain that fell around the car.

"I've seen your room, Neda," said Miss Adams. "It's really nice and sunny. There's a lot of space for all your things."

"I don't have lots of things anymore."

"Neda, by the time you're eighteen, if you're smart enough to continue getting an education, you'll find a good job and take care of yourself. Maybe you'll marry a nice young man and start a family of your own."

"Why can't I live with you? You're nice enough."

"Just about every child I drive to their new home, afraid like you, has asked me the same thing?"

"I'm not like every kid."

"If you stay out of trouble you'll be fine."

"When I turn eighteen I'm movin' to Puerto Rico."

"I see," said Mrs. Adams. "I heard it's a beautiful place to live."

"What do you know about it?"

"Not much."

"What are they like?"

"Who?" asked Mrs. Adams, "The Brown's, your new family?"

"Yeah, if you wanna call them that."

"They're very nice and very clean. Reginald Brown is the Reverend of a local Church."

"Great! That's all I need is some preacher tellin' me what to do all the time. Does he have a real job?"

"Yes. I believe it's a new position. I'm not sure what the details are."

"You sure know a lot about my new family."

"Do you want me to continue, or not? Mrs. Brown is a homemaker and very active with the church. There will be lots to keep you busy before you start school."

"What are they?"

"As in what?"

"What color are they?"

"Oh, a nice colored couple. They were children from Mixed marriages."

"What kind?"

"Colored and Caucasian."

"I guess that means everything is supposed to work out. Why can't you tell me about my brother and sister?"

"You know I can't do that. I told you it's against the rules."

"I won't tell nobody. I swear. Please, Mrs. Adams, tell me."

"I don't know, Neda."

"Will you tell me when I'm eighteen … when I knock on your door with a gun, and a knife, ready to kill you if you don't tell me?"

"Not even then. It's my …"

"Yeah," said Neda, "I know. It's your job whatever that is."

"I hope you don't behave this way with the Brown's. If you do you'll find yourself back at Auden.

Mr. and Mrs. Reginald Brown were in their mid twenties. Though of light complexion it was not to the point one couldn't tell they were of black blood.

To step back and take a look at the Brown's, Mrs. Brown was the perfection of pretty. She was a feminine woman with an oval face and thin lips that bunched up under a pug nose with lots of freckles. Her hair was light brown and she wore it with bangs. Flips of curls stopped just below her ears and the curls bounced in rhythm when she walked on the balls of her feet.

She reminded Neda of the cute mom in the Betty Crocker commercial. The only thing missing, thought Neda, was an apron around her slender waist line.

Mr. Brown was an athletic and tall man with a wide trusting face. The streaks of scaring along the left side of his cheek, and down his neck were responsible for his fixed expression. If it hadn't been for the permanent scarring, of burns, he would have been handsome instead of just attractive. Though he was different to look at, Neda thought him kind when he smiled and shook her hand. For some reason she felt comfortable about living with the Brown's.

Danny and Betty Jean were on the North Side of Chicago and under the care of Evelyn Newman who was white. She was a quiet widow in her late sixties. To step back and take a good look at her, she was over the edge of being just overweight. It appeared that the meat of her body had transformed itself into a transparent sac of rosy flesh, and moved about like another person with a mind of its own. Evelyn insisted they call her Mama Eve.

When Danny responded to her request he told her, "Mam, I don't mind callin' you that. It's my sister. She ain't talkin' no more. She ain't said a word since we all went to jail. If she don't answer

137

you I hope she don't get in any trouble for it. She can't help how she is right now."

"Well," said Mama Eve. "You are not in jail anymore you're in my home. There are no locks on any doors you can't get out of. There are no bars on any windows you can't crawl out of. No child gets in trouble while in my care. This home has the Lord's blessing."

"Yes, Mam."

It was easy for Danny to recognize that Evelyn was completely done with life outdoors. Her grocery shopping was done per telephone and delivered to her door every Friday afternoon. The only time Evelyn Newman would ever leave her home, thought Danny, would be for a medical reason that was too close to killing her or had killed her. He assumed she had no friends. No one came to visit her and her phone hardly ever rang. When it did someone dialed a wrong number.

She didn't say much to them. She fed them well, tucked them in after their baths, kissed them goodnight and told them everything would work out just fine. If they were not ready for bed she let them watch as much television as they wanted. If they fell asleep in front of the television the next day they were in their room, in their beds, and the remains of having been tucked in tightly was still there.

The aggravating question that shadowed Danny with anxious uncertainty concerned a young white couple, Wilfred and June Montana. Would they seek the opportunity to adopt them?

The first time the Montana's arrived in front of Mama Eve's home, and had stepped outside of their green-dodge pickup, to Danny they did not look like the drippy farmers he pictured. They looked more like western movie stars.

June Montana was a straight and curvy-slender woman with a head of golden sun-bleached hair and blue eyes. Her hair was pulled neatly away from a playful, girlish, face and braided into one long braid that fell down the middle of her back, stopping just short of her waistline. She wore a powder-blue shirt, blue jeans, and brown cowboy boots. Danny thought her to be somewhere around his mother's age.

When he shook June's hand it was not soft. It was hard and calloused. He wondered what she did to make her hands so rough. He thought maybe she was good at roping cows or riding horses.

Wilfred Montana wore a black hat, black shirt, blue jeans and black-cowboy boots. He was a sun-burned man who stood up confident and powerful, as if the ground had to ask his permission to touch the sole of his boots. When he greeted Danny and Betty Jean he took off his hat and a head full of thick hair, the color of chestnut, fell out around his ears and almost his eyes. Danny knew

139

immediately he was a man that didn't like haircuts, the same as his self.

Danny liked the goodness he saw in the young couple, and in a boy's way he liked that Wilfred Montana had those significant qualities that make a man a man. Everything about him said he was straight forward, determined, and sure of himself. The gentle side of him treated June Montana with tender and intimate affection, like she was a fragile thing to love and always pay attention to.

On the day of their first meeting the Montana's took them to a county fair outside the city. There were all kinds of animals like cows, pigs, chickens and horses. The larger animals scared Betty Jean. She held onto June Montana's hand and hid behind her legs much of the time.

Danny was in awe of seeing such a variety of animals and Wilfred let him get close to the horses. He encouraged Danny to stroke the flanks of a black colt that had a blue ribbon pinned on the long hairs of its neck.

"He sure is pretty," said Danny.

"Yeah," said Wilfred. "He's a beauty alright—a real looker. I guess that's why he won that ribbon."

As dusk began to settle the colored-flashing lights of the Ferris wheel took over the bright of the sky. They were walking the path that led to all the rides.

Danny looked back to see where June Montana was. He saw Betty Jean holding a roll of pink-cotton candy and she was smiling.

June saw that the boy was worried about his sister's limping. "You two go on ahead," she yelled out. "We'll sit here and rest for awhile." She sat down on a bench and Betty Jean sat beside her.

"What do you think about wheat, boy?" asked Wilfred.

Danny looked up at the powerful looking man. "I know the cereal we eat comes from it. Don't it?"

"Sure does. You think you and your sister might take to livin' on a farm?"

"I don't know, sir," Danny replied. "I ain't never been on no farm. I ain't never seen one except on television."

"You took to liking those animals you saw back there, didn't you?"

"Yes, sir. You got horses too?"

"Sure. I got a few horses. Matter fact, I got a young pretty thing due to give me a colt in a few weeks."

"Wow!" Danny turned to look for June and Betty Jean. They were coming up behind them. Thinking about Betty Jean's condition, Danny looked at Wilfred. "Maybe, livin' on a farm ain't so bad."

"Well," said Wilfred. "It's lots of hard work. Farm ain't no place for a boy that don't like hard work."

141

"Never had to work, sir. But I ain't scared of it. I ain't scared of too much of nothin'.""

"From what I've been told, if I was a boy walkin' in your shoes, I wouldn't be scared of nothin' either. I guess you can't afford to be afraid of anything."

"That's right, sir. Are you going to adopt me and Betty Jean?"

Wilfred turned his head and looked at June. She heard the question. "I don't know yet," he said. "If we come back we came to take you home."

A week went by and no calls came for Mama Eve. On the next Monday, after breakfast, Mama Eve's phone rang. Danny followed her into the kitchen.

She answered the phone, "Oh, hello Mrs. Adams." Disappointed, Danny left the kitchen.

The next day it was after 4:00 A.M. when Mama Eve woke them up and turned on the overhead light. She had packed their small suitcases.

"Where we goin'?" asked Danny. He could tell that she was upset and sad.

"Come on, young man, up at um. Go take your bath and get dressed."

"Are you comin' with us?" asked Danny.

"No."

142

After they ate their cereal they sat quietly on the sofa next to Mama Eve. She said nothing to them. Danny thought it best not to say anything to her. After fifteen minutes, or so, there was the sound of a horn.

Mama Eve hurried them into the hallway of her front door. She tossed Danny's hair and smiled at Betty Jean. "Take care of your sister, young man. Remember it was Mama Eve that told you one day everything would work out just fine."

"Yes, mam," said Danny.

"Go on," said Mama Eve, opening the front door, sitting their suitcases outside of it. When Danny looked up he saw Wilfred and June Montana smiling down at him and Betty Jean.

"You ready to go home, boy?" Wilfred asked, picking up their suitcases.

Danny smiled. His eyes watered and his voice trembled. "Yes sir."

"Have a safe trip," Mama Eve told them.

"Wait, Mama Eve," said Danny. "I forgot something."

"Well, hurry up. Go get it."

Danny ran past her and into the room he shared with Betty Jean. He hurried to his bed and lifted the pillow. Under it was a family picture of his beautiful mother, Miss Ruby, him and his sisters. He put the picture in his back pocket and ran out of the room.

143

"Thank you, Mama Eve," said Danny. She smiled, nodded her head, and closed the door. He knew why she had the sadness. She liked them and would miss them.

Betty Jean was in the truck sitting on June's lap. Wilfred started the ignition and let Danny climb in on his side.

"Can you drive?" asked Wilfred.

"No, sir," said Danny. "But I'd sure like to learn. Where are we goin'?"

"Kansas," said Wilfred. "I call it God's Country."

It was almost after sunset when they arrived at the edge of the road that led to the Montana's farm. They were six, maybe seven, miles outside of Ottawa County in North Central Kansas. Danny was asleep and his head rested on Will's shoulder. He had taken the drive inside his self and it heightened his senses to see the big city merge into small town life, into acres of farm land.

Will nudged him. "Wakeup son this is home." Danny rose up and looked out of the window. "Go on," said Will, "you don't weigh much more than a pea. Lean out over me and look out if you want. I can drive just the same."

Danny crossed eagerly over Will's lap. He pushed his body halfway out of the window, swaying to the movement of the quick breezes. For the first time in his life he saw the beauty of nature and nothing concrete was sitting on it.

144

He looked up at the sky and became short winded. It was as if Mr. Grapes and Mr. Books had picked up His paint brush. Rays of sharp sunbeams were holding steady and shooting out from the sun's center, piercing through layers of red and light purple clouds, trailing off into unending swirls of soft orange and golden yellows. All the colors hung low over the tops of the Montana's wheat fields. White clouds to the left and right of the sun were unmoving, like they were ordered to get out of God's way, giving Him room to go wild and crazy with His paint brush. Danny had never seen the sun reach out so far away from itself. It was like Miss Ruby said: *"God can be a show off when He wants to get His point across; especially, in ways that can take the breath away."*

Half of his body still out of the window, he closed his eyes and spread his arms out wide. He was pretending to fly. The warmth of a different kind of wind he never felt, or smelled, fluttered and tickled him like the soft wings of angels. The rich smell of wheat smelled like he had stuck his whole head inside a box of sugared cornflakes.

He opened his eyes and looked up at the sky. He leaned further out the window, looking up and into the sun. The black edges made the whole of the orange ball plain to see without turning away from it. It was sliding behind what looked like the end of the earth. And before it took all that color with it, it threw what was left onto the ground. The Montana's wheat flickered with an array of orange, golden yellows, dark reds, and shimmering violets.

Danny was shaken up with fear and feelings of things being too good to be true. He pulled back inside the truck and sat quietly close to Will.

At the end of the dirt road he could see the Montana's brown and white three-story farmhouse rising up out of the wheat.

"You all right, son?" Will asked.

"Yes, sir," said Danny. "Just don't seem real."

"I know what you mean," said Will. He didn't want to say too much else. He let the seriousness of the moment rest quietly with Danny. He knew the boy was on the edge of more than just tears. He was a dam ready to bust wide open.

Betty Jean awakened. She looked out the window and pointed at the long grains of wheat. "Look at all the red and purple flowers," she said.

Danny, Will, and June erupted with laughter.

"Why that's wheat baby," said June.

Betty Jean said simply, "Oh." And the way she said it sounded as if she had never stopped talking.

Wilfred felt the boy release his worry over his sister's silence. When they arrived at the end of the road, and parked in front of the house, Danny liked everything he was able to see under the last golden light of a sun almost finished setting.

146

He saw June's vegetable garden and all the flowers and bushes of roses that ran along the side of the house. He then knew why June's hands were so rough. He figured a woman didn't get a garden like that while wearing gloves. In the distance, left and right of the house, there was a barn and some other structures. He could hear the sound and stirring of the animals inside them.

June went out of the truck and was on her way inside the house with Betty Jean in her arms. Will gathered the two suitcases from the bed of the truck. He looked at Danny. The boy was standing with his feet planted firm, eyes looking out at the land.

"I'll leave the door open for you," said Will.

Danny did not hear him. He was thinking about his sister, his crazy Puerto Rican. She would have loved to have seen such a violence of colors.

Angela sat in a chair outside the night director's door. It was 1:10 A.M. and the corridor was empty of children. She was sitting still, watching two janitors mopping and polishing the floor. Her hands were folded peacefully and almost angelically across her lap.

The suitcase sitting at her feet looked ominous and wicked. The light beige color had been mapped over with colors of Crayon. The drawings were an overstatement of terrifying, big-eyed, bleeding and crippled rats, yellow-eyed, scowling, black cats and dogs with extensive fangs. Snakes, winged cockroaches, and other detestable bugs were fighting and chewing on the other. Faceless adults and children, some without heads, were behind bars. Their arms were extending out of their prison pleading for release. Those with heads had their mouths wide open, hollering. The entire suitcase was one merging portrait. The skin-crawling art-work was a true testament of a child passionately confused, psychologically battered about the mind. The good thing about her work, from a psychiatric point of view, was the coming through of her ability to draw the precise picture of her state of mind.

Angela's thoughts went to the foster parents that had taken her in. The Hiccups were a young, middle class, black couple with three children of their own. They were afraid for the safety of the entire family as well as relatives. Their decision to take Angela back to Auden had been made without uncertainty.

As the problems of a troubled child mounted, Thaddeus Hiccup went without sleep while his wife slept next to him under the protection of a large-silver cross. The long chain was wound around her neck. She had buried two bibles and other religious paraphernalia, such as small-wooden crosses, under their bed covers. Some of the wooden crosses were on the floor at the foot of their bed. She did the same for her own children. She had gone over the household budget to buy the religious paraphernalia. That's how serious she was about protecting her children from what she considered a demon of a different kind and not what the devil usually produces. She was determined to exorcize the special demon

148

out of Angela Walker but had failed continuously. It was the bloody incident that forced her to throw her hands up and literally scream.

After they came home from the hospital Thaddeus Hiccup unlocked a screaming, cursing, biting, and scratching Angela from the hall closet. It was close to midnight when they shoved her and her suitcase into their car. To liberate themselves quickly from their commitment, the young couple drove over the speed limit and ran several red lights. They arrived just after midnight, screeching and parking in front of the Auden Home. Thaddeus Hiccup hustled Angela out of the car. Marjorie Hiccup demanded that her husband place the evil suitcase at the child's feet. She was afraid of it, for in addition to her religious upset, Angela had drawn a green picture of a man's face with horns protruding out of his forehead. She wrote underneath it, "this is my God."

The couple did not wait for Angela to be retrieved by Miss Adams. They sped away from the Auden Home, driving at an eager and higher speed. To express how they felt they pinned a note to the lapel of Angela's jacket. It read: we will not have a child possessed by the devil's worst demon living inside our home. Damn you to hell!

Angela came out of her thoughts. The office of the night director's door opened.

Miss Adams stepped out. "Mr. Hawthorne will see you now," she told Angela.

149

Angela stood. She attempted to pick up her suitcase.

"You can leave it there," said Mrs. Adams. "I'll have it sent to your dorm."

Mrs. Adams did not want Mr. Hawthorne to see the evil drawings. She was against the continuous drugging of children to curb their behavior.

The office was not much bigger than a broom closet and was brightly lit with a desk lamp. Angela and Mrs. Adams took their seats across from the desk of Jim Hawthorne. The desk was overcrowded with papers and case files. A small fan sat on a narrow file cabinet whirring silently. It mixed up the smells of garlic, stale coffee, and the sweat that soaked through the arm pits of Mr. Hawthorne's blue shirt.

He had finished reading the report. He closed its folder and pushed it aside. "You, young lady," he said, "are on your way to becoming a permanent fixture inside this …"

"My daddy told me to …"

"Shut up about your daddy," said Mr. Hawthorne. "Your daddy was a criminal not capable of giving advice to any child. Your daddy is dead."

"Tell us what happened, Angela," said Mrs. Adams.

"I ain't tellin' you nothin'," said Angela, "on the grounds it might incriminate me."

150

Mr. Hawthorne ground his teeth. His face was red with anger and impatience. "Young monster you will tell us what happened or I will lock you up in a room that will drive you insane for the rest of your life."

Mrs. Adams hoped he didn't mean it for there was a horrible and dark place inside Auden. The most violent children were locked away there for long periods of time.

"Open your mouth, speak!" he yelled.

"Me, Carolyn, and Swig was outside playin' stick in the mud."

"Who is Carolyn and Swig?"

"The two girls across the street."

"What is stick in the mud?" asked Mr. Hawthorne.

"It's a game you play with a knife. You throw it and make it stick standing up in the mud. Who does it the most times wins."

"Go on," said Mrs. Adams.

"Jerome Hiccup came in the yard and said he wanted to play. I told him no because it was girls only playin'. I told him to get out of the yard but he wouldn't leave. He kept sayin' he wanted to play. He said if we didn't let him he was goin' to tell him his mama I took the kitchen knife out the drawer. I told him to leave us alone. After Carolyn it was my turn."

"Go on, Angela," said Mrs. Adams.

"When Carolyn gave me the knife, Jerome came and tried to snatch it out my hand. I pushed him down in the dirt. When he got up he kicked me in my stomach and I fell down. When he tried to do it again, I stood up. When he turned to leave, I stabbed him in his back with the knife."

"You stabbed him in the back?" asked Mrs. Adams, hardly believing what she was hearing.

"Yeah," Angela said, proudly, with a giggle. "He tried to run away but I grabbed him and he fell down. He kicked me again. I sat on him and punched him in the face. He turned around and bit my arm, see," she said, showing them the bite mark. "That's when I picked up the pop bottle and smashed him in the face with it. That's what happened."

"What did you do with the knife?" Mr. Hawthorne asked.

"I didn't do nothin' with it. Last time I saw it, it was stickin' out his back when his mama and daddy took him to the hospital. Before they left they locked me in the hall closet. I stayed in there till they came back and took me out. They brought me back home."

Mrs. Adams looked at Angela, trying desperately to understand her. She was tired of crying over children that were not her own. "Home," she said. "You consider this your home?"

"Everybody else in here does," Angela told her. "The food is good enough ain't it? I got a roof over my head. Grown people don't tell me what to do all the time. They don't care what I do. When I feel bad they give me pills to make me feel better."

"How many times did you smash that boy in the face with the bottle?" asked Mr. Hawthorne.

"Enough to do what I wanted," Angela said, swinging her legs back and forth under her seat. "His face was bloody and cut up. He had to stay in the hospital. It was his fault."

"Yes, he is in the hospital," Mrs. Adams confirmed. "You've hurt him badly."

"Not bad enough," Angela said, with a giggle. "He ain't dead."

"Young lady," said Mr. Hawthorne, "even though you're just a child you make it impossible for any adult to care for you. The devil has you in his grasp and loves you far more than the Lord."

"Angela," said Mrs. Adams, "your brother and sisters are with very loving families. Don't you want the same for yourself?" Angela looked at her and rolled her eyes and lowered her head.

"Well," said Mr. Hawthorne, waiting for Angela's answer.

"No," Angela said. She was thinking about Sharita. She was impatient to unpack her things and get back inside her dorm. She missed her best friend and was anxious to see her. It was Sharita who had given her the great idea about how to come back to Auden.

"You'll be here until you're eighteen," said Mr. Hawthorne.

"I don't care, I told you."

"Get her out of here," he said to Mrs. Adams.

Mrs. Adams wondered, besides seeing the murder of Jimmy Tate, what else happened to make Angela so hateful?

Her new bed assignment was on the left of the dormitory. She was closer to Sharita. She went and sat on the edge of Sharita's bunk. "Wake up, Sharita," she whispered, shaking her. "It's me, Angie Pangie, wake up."

Sharita raised on her elbows and looked at Angela. "What are you doin' back here?" she asked.

"I did it."

"Did what?"

"What you told me to do," Angela said, giggling. "I almost killed one of their kids."

"You stupid for doin' that," said Sharita, "comin' back here to this place. I'm glad I'm leavin'."

"What?"

"My Aunt and Uncle said I can come live with them. They're comin' to get me on Sunday."

"You said you didn't have family."

"I forgot all about them. Anyway, I'm glad to be gettin' out of here." Sharita yawned and lay back down. She pulled the covers up over her shoulders. "We'll say goodbye in the mornin', Angie Pangie. I'm still sleepy."

Angela's need to love someone had come full circle, and then it broke apart as quickly as it came. She walked away from Sahrita's bed feeling no anger or disappointment. Now her hatred for the world had everybody in it. When she climbed into her own bed sleep was there and she fell easily into it.

WHAT ARE BEST FRIENDS FOR

It was an early October evening and the temperature had dipped into the forties. Parker Bishop and his two best friends, Allen Sanders, and Tom McGregor, sat quietly together. They were inside the back of an old and un-kept taxi. When Allen took a break from his lamenting about the Vietnam War they participated in an awkward and brief three-way conversation. Their voices had to reach above the taxi's muffler.

Allen picked up where he left off. "It's this damn war," he said. "Our country is dying for leadership. The presidency will never be respected the way it used to be. When Kennedy went to see MacArthur he told him to never get into any kind of war with Asia."

"So," said Tom, "now you're an expert on the relationship between Kennedy and MacArthur. You're a fucking expert on everything. How can you live with yourself?"

"No," said Allen. I'm not being a smart ass. Goddamn Vietnam War has turned this country upside down. What kind of country is it that we live in? Damn kids have more love and respect for the Beatles. They're killing themselves just to get a seat to see these guys. Did you read about that kid that killed herself?"

"No," said Parker.

"Because the Beatles are breaking up some sixteen-year-old girl killed herself. When her parents found her, in bed, her record player was spinning Strawberry Fields Forever.

"Oh, Jesus Christ," said Tom. "I'm so sick of hearing about this shit."

Allen looked at Parker. "Her bed was covered with pounds of strawberries and there she lay right in the middle. Can you believe it? What makes it worse is she didn't stay true to the lyrics of the damn song.   The crazy girl had a huge bar of milk chocolate lying on her chest. The song doesn't say anything about chocolate-covered strawberries. If you're going to kill yourself at least stay true to the reason for doing it."

"Who cares about what you think about Vietnam, or the damned Beatles? Huh?" said Tom, not expecting an answer. "It's like you're on some kind of guilt trip for not getting drafted. You're scared of guns for Christ sakes. The war is not over. Join the fucking army or the marines and be their poster boy. It's not too late to get your head blown off. Maybe you'll get lucky and get yourself paralyzed from head to toe."

Tom's voice was high in pitch. It was a signal that his temper was on the edge of being out of control. Allen raised his leg and used his foot to kick down the driver's jump seat. He put his feet up on the shaky stool and crossed his legs.

To Parker the old meter sounded like a ticking time bomb. It added more friction between him and his friends. They had not seen one another for almost two years. Tom blamed Freddie Walker for the contentious divide. Until she came along the three had never gone more than a week without seeing the other.

They grew up inside the same closed and guarded society. Even the massive houses they lived in were two and three blocks apart. Their fathers, all high powered attorneys, were close friends. Once a month they came together in one or the others home for drinks and card playing. The boys were the first topic of their conversation. The older they got the more their fathers talked about sending them to attend Harvard Law at the same time.

The three rebelled against ideas about what should be done with them. After giving it thought they realized that attending Harvard together could also mean having lots of fun.

After graduation, moving back home, and while the three were in the process of taking the bar, Allen muddled inside the slowness of the State Attorney's Office. He liked working for his father who was the State Attorney of Illinois. Parker and Tom joined their father's firms.

To step back and take a good look at Tom McGregor it was best to walk around him two or three times for a wider perspective. He gave himself up for reading when he was nervous about being checked out too closely. For most of his years, as a boy, his skin was a disruption of the worst kind of acne. This gave Tom complexes about his looks. By the time he was twenty the sticking out of the bad acne was a tight sheet of noticeable scarring and the look matched the shrewdness of his character and tumultuous personality. Women who were interested in him, and liked the way he looked, also liked to be taken roughly by cold men whose faces resembled their character. Out of the three Tom was the most quarrelsome, quick to judge, and cruelest. Where his professional skills lay Parker and Allen considered him the most intelligent. He was nearer than not to having a photographic memory and could recall the particulars of any case he read. He was the one most likely to stand in front of the United States Supreme Court.

To step back and take a good look at Allen he was almost too blond, broad shouldered, and stocky. His endearing personality complimented his pretentious unsettling brown eyes. Allen was sweet and sensitive. Pretty women liked that about him because he was an easy shoulder to cry on. Where professional talents come to light Allen was remarkably tuned in to all kinds of people. He could easily detect honesty, dishonesty, or even a person's reasons for living. They believed that Allen, with his sixth sense, could read a potential client's blood line by just looking at them.

It was near 6:00 P.M. when the taxi driver pulled up and parked in front of Jack Santo's Bar and Grill. When they entered a retirement party was near its end and the attorneys were spread out in fat groups around the bar stools.

Parker led Allen and Tom through the tight conditions. There was barely enough room to get by. When they did, a circle of pretty women were at the end of the bar. Tom and Allen took their time to squeeze by them. They wanted to feel their softness and smell the fragrance of bathtub hair. They came up out of the women and went up a short flight of stairs that led inside the private room. It sat higher than the rest of the place. The layout was open and the room was connected to the bar and restaurant. At glances down, through the separation of the iron railings, cordoning off the room, they could look out over the entire restaurant and bar. Every customer was on display. The private room provided a fantastic spying position.

They sat at Robert Bishop's private table. Their waiter carried their privately stored bottles of Columbian Red Tequila, Jazenday Black Rum, and Polezenia Blue Vodka. The liquor was expensive and rare; imported from Columbia, Jamaica, and Poland. The bottles were opened quickly and the second shots of rum had been poured and drank.

Tom looked at Parker. "Do you want us to bullshit you about fucking up your life?" We haven't seen you in how long? Now all of a sudden we're buddy, buddy. You're full of it."

"He hasn't fucked up all his life," said Allen, "only some of it. Maybe his destiny has something to do with helping Negroes."

"Freddie is not a Negro," said Parker. "She has two children who are half Negro."

"Like being half Negro doesn't make them all Negro," said Tom. "The law says they're Negro. Percentage doesn't matter."

"We didn't come here to fight," said Allen. "We came here to get drunk."

"You are obsessed with this woman," said Tom. He looked at Parker. "You did something to cause this to happen. It's written all over you. When are you going to tell us?"

"I tried to help her ... to help them."

"You tried to help her, help them," Tom said. "I'm confused."

"I tried to help Freddie, Ruby, and the children." He turned away from them to think. He looked out over the railing at the bar of celebrating attorneys. He didn't want to look at his friends. He couldn't stop remembering what they did with Freddie. It was the reason he refused to see them for such a long time.

Their waiter came. He cleaned their table and left them with three stacks of clean shot glasses.

160

"You are infatuated," Tom told Parker. "Just like your ole man said. Now you want us to feel sorry for you, for falling in love with a whore who's now on her way to prison."

"Take it easy," Allen told Tom.

"You want to know your real and true problem?" Tom leaned in closer to Parker. "You have been tortured by the thrill of the hunt. It's over and there is no more chase. No more cat and mouse buddy. The lady is gone."

"Oh," said Parker. "First she's a whore. Now she's a lady."

"What about love, huh?" said Allen. "What about that King what's his name, the one that gave up his throne for that socialite?

"He's not a fucking King," said Tom. "Freddie Walker may look like some dark haired princess you see in the movies but she's no movie star. She is no socialite, okay. If she was, and had killed a man, he would be a pile of bones at the bottom of Lake Michigan and nothing about it would be read in the morning papers."

"Tom," said Allen. "You are the last piece of shit."

"Let him finish," said Parker.

"The thrill of the hunt," said Tom. "But that's not the only reason. I think you're really pissed off because you never got a chance to fuck her."

Allen did what he could to stop Parker who grabbed Tom, by the throat, choking off his words. Allen pried them apart. It took

161

more than a minute for Tom to catch his wind and regain his composure.

Allen looked at the noisy lawyers at the bar. He realized not one of them noticed the attack. He thought it was the perfect place to kill someone amidst great legal minds without the slightest detection.

"You owe him an apology you son-of-a bitch," Allen said to Tom.

"I don't owe him shit. We were supposed to be starting up our own firm. Instead of keeping his word he was out slumming, expecting us to wait until he decided to start practicing the goddamn law. You fucking bastard you hung us out to dry."

"Come on," said Allen. "You really didn't buy into all that Harvard bullshit?"

"Yeah," said Tom. "As a matter of fact I did."

They stood outside Jack Santo's Bar and Grill waiting for a taxi. Tom and Parker shook hands and re-bonded themselves. They agreed to start up their firm as soon as possible.

Allen was vomiting in the street. Through his gagging and spitting he said he couldn't drink the way he used to.

"I tried to shut Jimmy down," Parker told Tom. "I did shut him down. I paid all the right people to help me get it done."

"Does Freddie know?" asked Tom.

162

"No. She won't see me. She won't accept my calls. I've talked to Ruby once. That's about it. There's nothing we can do is there?"

"It's not looking good, buddy. A man is dead, those kids, the drugs.

"Ruby said it's a setup. She told me Jimmy was never involved in the sale of heavy drugs. I believe her."

"Hard to prove," said Tom. "If you weren't the son of Robert Bishop there would be a good chance of getting them off."

"Then fuck me for being born."

"We used to think it was great being the sons of powerful men, what it meant to have that edge. It's not so great when they work against their own sons."

Allen went to them.

"Tell him," said Tom.

"No deals were made," said Allen. "They're pleading guilty to all charges and leaving it up for a judge to decide. It's all backroom bullshit."

"Shit, shit," said Parker. "What else do you know?"

Bile had begun another rise up and into Allen's throat. He attempted to walk back and vomit in the same spot.

Parker grabbed him by the lapels of his coat, "What the fuck do you know, Allen."

Allen pulled away, leaned, and vomited onto the sidewalk. "Freddie's not going down for accomplice to murder," he told Parker. "It's the other charges. Ruby's getting the full treatment. That's all I know. I've been thrown out of my own fucking office. I'm on temporary leave of absence. No one is telling me anything else."

"Who's the D.A.?" asked Parker.

"McNeil, my ole man assigned the case to him."

"Fuck," said Tom, "McNeil is a real bastard. They have no way out."

EVERYBODY RISE

The lights that hung from the ceiling were not bright enough to see everything clear and plain. There was no gallery of spectators because there was no gallery. The room was sparse of furniture except for two tables and five chairs. The most attractive and polished piece of furniture was the judge's high-sitting bench. Even the walls were bare of legal giants looking down their noses, helping to condemn a person to their last breath taken as a free life. Overall, the room was barely passable as a court of law.

Three of the people in there were Freddie, Ruby, and their Public Defender. She was a young and perky blond with a strong southern accent.

The bailiff was a black-man. He stood with his thumbs tucked inside a belt that carried his keys, stick, gun, and cuffs. He kept rising up and down on the balls of his feet.

A grizzled and withered court reporter fiddled with her machine and the roll of paper that came with it. She blended in as though she was an integral part of her chair and equipment. The only thing noticed about her whole person was her bright-pink lipstick and curving spine that shone its boney impression under her white sweater.

Gary McNeil, the district attorney, did much of nothing at the table where he sat. A legal pad and two case files sat before him. Because he knew what was coming, the deal made, he doodled. The wood of the chair he sat in complimented the kind of stiff he was—a middle-aged man who lacked the ambition and drive to do anything other than his job. His satisfied purpose of life was derived from his success of putting people; especially Negroes, permanently behind bars.

Three doors were connected to the imposter courtroom. One led to freedom and one back to jail. The other door led to the judge's chambers. When that door opened Judge Ronald P. Schaffer came out.

The bailiff stopped his rocking up and down on the balls of his feet. "All rise," he said.

Freddie and Ruby stood up alongside their Public Defender.

165

They sat back down after the judge sat behind his bench.

Judge Schaffer was in his early seventies. He had a strained and unsociable face overran with cracks and crevices. Each line told the fate of every person, undesirable, sentenced by him into obscurity. The hostility in his eyes shone his disgust for the two women. The closeness of any Negro standing or sitting next to any white person, no matter the kind, forced him to declare himself deeper into Christianity. He labored over the papers of Freddie's case file for more than a minute. When he glanced down at her, he thought he saw the wickedness of her beauty. He lifted his eyes back onto his papers.

"Freda Eloise Walker," said Judge Schaffer.

The Perky Public Defender encouraged Freddie to stand up beside her. The judge took another look at Freddie and quickly lowered his eyes. He thought again how remarkably beautiful she was. Still, he would skip the legal deserving of legal formalities.

"I commend you and your counsel for saving the taxpayers, of the State of Illinois, the heart ship and expense of a long and publicized trial. If you had gone forth with such a trial it is my sincere belief that any jury would have found you guilty of all charges. There would have been no consideration for parole. You may have gotten life, without the possibility for parole, if you had been charged as an accomplice to murder."

Having gone over the testimony and statements given by

your children, to this court, I must say I am deeply appalled. You are not only guilty of possession of narcotics for sale, and distribution, you are guilty of the most wretched form of child abuse one can imagine. In my opinion you are the worst kind of female sore. You have destroyed four innocent lives. I don't believe your children will ever forgive you for it."

Freddie had begun to cry and the Public Defender tried to comfort her but Freddie pushed her away.

"May I remind you," the judge went on to say, "if you attempt to contact those children your chances for parole will be denied with each application."

Ruby jumped up. "What kind of judge are you to talk to a person like that?"

The bailiff went to Ruby. He reached out to grab her arm. She moved away from his touch.

"Huh?" said Ruby. "What kind of judge are you?"

Judge Schaffer pounded his gavel. "Sit down, Miss Johnson. Sit down or I will have you coupled to that Godforsaken chair."

"It's okay, Ruby," Freddie whispered. "Sit down."

The bailiff reached for Ruby's arm but she pulled away from his intended grasp and sat down. Judge Schaffer cleared his throat and shuffled around his papers. "Freda Eloise Walker," he said, "having thrown yourself on the mercy of the court this court agrees with your plea of guilty of all charges. You are hereby sentenced to

167

forty years at Gorwin Correctional Facility for Women. Eligibility for parole in twenty years, sentence to be carried out immediately." He pounded his gavel.

The Public Defender tugged Freddie's arm, urging her to sit down.

"Ruby Johnson," said Judge Schaffer. Ruby rose to her feet. The judge looked up from his papers, raised his ass a little higher, and leaned to look down deeper at her. He took off his glasses. "You were not their mother but you were their keeper. You were the one person those children looked up to for guidance and affection. They respected and listened to you. In return for their love and respect you murdered a man in front of their very eyes. If you sincerely loved those four children, the way you claimed in your statement to this court, you would have informed the appropriate authorities regarding their ungodly condition. Ruby Johnson you are a discredit to a race of disgruntled people struggling in this country while trying to find a place of acceptance. You are the worst of your kind of Negro." He raised his ass from the chair a little higher than before. He wanted to see her expression, to make sure he was hitting home. "Ruby Johnson you have been found guilty of murder in the first degree. You have also been found guilty on three counts of possession of narcotics for sale and distribution."

"What?" asked Ruby. She pointed to the District Attorney. "That liar said I would get only manslaughter. It was part of our

168

deal."

The Judge looked at his papers like he was looking for something special. He looked at Ruby and then at the District Attorney. "Mr. McNeil, did you make a deal with Miss Johnson?"

"No your honor," he replied.

"He's lyin'," said Ruby, sobbing. "He's lyin'." She sat down.

"You will stand up in my court, Miss Johnson."

The public defender tugged Ruby to standing. Judge Schaffer waited until her sobbing had subsided.

"You are hereby sentenced to life in prison without the possibility of parole. Sentence to be carried out immediately."

CHAPTER SIX
GORWIN CORECTION FACILITY FOR WOMEN

The prison was born in the spring of 1920 and completed in the winter of 1923. It was a hideous-gothic monstrosity originally designed, on paper, to perform as a maximum-security facility for six-hundred men who were classified as some of the most evil convicts in the United States. It was not a big prison. Each tier housed one hundred cells. There were fifty to the left and fifty to the right. One cell accommodated two. All six tiers were narrow with ceilings that sloped down low enough to make a tall person bend. Supposedly, it was built that way for the eyes of guards needing to see everything that moved.

The crew involved in the construction referred to the prison as a maze of messed up shit. They said it would be difficult, if not impossible, for guards to see the truth on blind spots and shadows that tricked the eye into thinking everything was okay.

The architect contracted to build the prison was a drunk that listened to the voice of his creative genius instead of reading the specifications of the plans. He worked like a frustrated director making a bad movie. He pointed his fingers, shook his fists, and cursed at the workers while telling them he didn't need to look at the plans. He said he knew what needed to be done for act one, act two, and act three. He fired those that didn't obey his orders. By the time

170

the impending disaster became known to government officials it was too late to get rid of the architect. He was the only person that knew the details of his maze of messed-up shit and what he knew wasn't on paper. The most concern centered on two underground passages than ran a good half mile outside the prison walls. If a man made it that far, after two miles, he'd find himself inside Etchings Illinois—a small country town of about seven hundred residents.

Mid construction the town found out the state was building a flawed prison. They held hot and angry pumped up meetings inside the high-school auditorium. In the heat of aggravation and senselessness, occurring over one night, the town of Etchings fashioned themselves into a sizzling vigilante committee. They were over three-hundred strong.

On a Saturday afternoon two-hundred members of the committee overstuffed their picnic baskets and loaded their vehicles with their wives, and children, and drove to the construction site. Once there they proceeded to shout obscenities at the workers. The town's women favored throwing big rocks at the men. One of the rocks, near the size of a baseball, blasted the back of the head of the foreman. He spent six months in a coma before waking up half out of his mind permanently.

Under the thrill of darkness the town's fearless men tied ropes to the prison window's and then to their tail gates. They drove

171

full speed ahead until black-steel bars and pieces of walls and windows were dragged to destruction.

The prison's construction workers had to bring their own meals to work because the two restaurants in town, and the only coffee shop, refused to serve them. After enforcing their right to eat in any facility in town they were served their meals. The waitress always presented the food with a friendly smile. When the men got through eating half of what they ordered the creepiest of insects and bugs that crawled, fluttered, and flied, were exposed. Some of the strong crawly things were still alive. One of the workers vomited from the front to the back of the coffee shop before realizing he had eaten half a rat's tail. The tainted food made a few men bed-ridden sick. Some of them quit their jobs and stayed home. They spent ample amounts of time trying to brush and gargle away the taste of some kind of bug.

After The National Guard was called in, and had left, the vigilante committee picked up where they left off and forged ahead with the same amount of venom. They gave the Governor hell through the exposure of radio and newspaper coverage. When he showed up in Etchings to take a look at the prison reporters jammed their flashing-bulb cameras in his face. They danced around him like he was a Christmas present. The Governor had to remind himself he was a politician and needed to start thinking like one.

172

The decision was made to open Gorwin for the gentle sex. Most of the women to be transferred were whores, drug addicts, robbers, and a handful of murderers that killed their husbands and boyfriends over matters of spousal abuse.

The prison was named Gorwin Correctional Facility for Women. Everybody was happy and the town relaxed back into their slow and easy lives while believing that women would not sit around plotting about breaking out, killing people, and burning down the whole damn town. But they underestimated the weaker sex. It was the perfect prison for a woman thinking about escaping.

By the year of 1926 eighteen women had escaped like ghosts through the walls of Gorwin. Only five of them were caught and brought back. One of the women had gotten married, had two children, and worked as a grocery-store clerk inside the town of Etchings. After her confession the town threatened to blow up the prison with dynamite if the State didn't fix the disaster.

By the end of 1927 blind spots and flawed spaces were torn away and ceilings were raised according to eyes needing to see everything above their head. Women imprisoned for life were kicking mad at themselves for not escaping when they had the opportunity. Over the years they told delightful stories about those that got away.

THE LAST TICK OF THE CLOCK
JULY 13, 2003

6:00 A.M.

The sound of women in Gorwin echoed off everything solid. Ruby was alone inside her cell. She sat up, swung her legs over the edge of her lower bunk, and placed her calloused feet on the cold floor in the same spot where she always placed them. She moved one foot and then the other, wanting to see their impression fixed on concrete. It was like the stamping of proof. The soles of her feet told her physical story. They said she had been prisoner in that same cell for thirty-three years.

Ruby's favorite guard, Mae, was coming down the tier in the direction of her cell. The jangling of her keys was familiar and the pants of her brown-polyester uniform made a swishing noise when the meat between her thick thighs brushed quickly together.

Mae reminded Ruby of the fall season because of her unblemished auburn skin. She seemed to float from tier to tier like a wide and stout strapping tree ... leaves drifting to the ground with content expressions. Though Mae was on the heavy side, to Ruby, she was as pretty as anything fresh in a daring new world—a strange world where people found more comfort in digital gadgetry than with one another.

When thinking about the world outside, Ruby thought the predictable times had been flipped upside down. Everything she knew about people rested without scrutiny on the back of uncertainty and people were more complex. They were no longer seen doing what they do inside their glass boxes. She couldn't read them easily like she used to when she was young. Discontent and cold disregard, or need of others, made them inaccessible.

Mae stood outside of Ruby's open cell. "Freddie wants to see you."

Freddie was very sick and inside the prison's infirmary. The doctors couldn't figure out what she was dying from, but Ruby knew she was willing herself to death over the children and even Parker Bishop. Lately Freddie was in constant need of seeing her. They had many unauthorized visits over the last three weeks. Mae was aware of the love and true friendship behind the aging black and white friends. They had nothing but troubled young lives to look back upon.

Mae left Ruby sitting in the chair at Freddie's bedside. Freddie was awake.

"I see you got a little color in your cheeks," said Ruby.

"Parker was here yesterday. He's been comin' once a week instead of every two weeks."

"I know that. We already talked about it. He's worried sick about you, same as me."

175

"He's such an unhappy man."

"We talked about that too. Don't go there."

"You and your "don't go there." The slang you've picked up in this place, Ruby Johnson, talkin' like a twenty-year old. Next thing you'll be listenin' to rap music."

"I do. Sometimes it ain't so bad. Has a real nice beat. I don't like the words. They're disrespectful about every subject known to mankind, especially women. I don't understand how black folks can create such nice music and then use it to call each other the filthiest names. It makes no sense."

"I want Parker to find some happiness. He's not too old and he's still so damn good lookin'.""

Ruby turned away when she saw the slip of tears slide down the corner of Freddie's eyes. For years she had been unable to cry with her friend. Prison had made her impenetrably tough, free of a woman's emotion. She had forgotten how to cry. "What's this talk I hear about you signin' papers?" asked Ruby.

"That's none of your business, Ruby Johnson. I know all about your spies in this place."

"Somebody's got to keep an eye on you."

Freddie sat up straighter. "Do you think about how they turned out as grown people?"

"We promised ourselves not to talk about them. You always bring them up anyway."

"Well."

"To tell the truth I do more than think about them."

"What are you sayin'."

"I do more than think about them that's what I'm sayin'.

"That's not an answer."

"I know all about them. I know how they turned out."

"Ruby Johnson, have you been lyin' to me all these years?"

"I wouldn't call it lyin'. I call it keepin' my business to myself."

"Go on."

"I've got some recent pictures of them." The color of life began its rise back into Freddie. "I've got pictures of Danny, his wife, his little boy."

"What about the others?"

"I got pictures of Angela and her two kids. I got pictures of everybody."

"How?"

"I hired me a private detective. One of the girls in here told me about him.

"What do you mean, Ruby Johnson? I don't believe a word you say. Prove it to me."

"I don't think that's a good idea. They never once came to see us."

177

"Ruby Johnson, I know what you're tryin' to do. It ain't workin'."

"Keep your voice down," whispered Ruby, shifting, looking over her shoulder. "I had to sneak these pictures in here."

She looked at Ruby's overstuffed pant pocket and pointed to it. "Is that them? Is that what's in your pocket?"

"If I get caught we're both in trouble. Remember what that judge said about stayin' away from them?" Ruby looked at the Nurse on duty behind her desk. She was busy with a tray of medicine issues. The two old women that shared the ward were sleeping.

Ruby removed the photographs from her pocket. Freddie sat up straighter and leaned in closer to Ruby.

"Ruby Johnson," Freddie whispered, "you crazy ole fool."

"I had a feelin' that one of these days we might want to see what they look like." Ruby removed the first picture from her pocket and handed it to Freddie. "That's our Neda. She ain't got no kids but she did alright with her life."

"Neda." She stared at the picture for a long time. "Like a copper penny. She's so beautiful. She's still got my eyes lookin' straight into hers."

"She didn't become a famous Puerto Rican movie star."

"What does she do?"

178

"She's a grade schoolteacher on the North Side of Chicago. Last year she won an award for teacher of the year."

"Remember how smart she was and how she taught herself to speak Spanish?"

"Yeah, she was always smart."

Freddie covered her face with her hands. "If you're tryin' somethin' tricky, I'm still intent on dyin' just to get out of this place."

"I don't want to hear no talk about dyin'," whispered Ruby, "You want to see the rest of them or don't you?"

She handed Ruby back the photograph. "Is Neda married?"

"No, but, I hear she's got a real nice man she's engaged to. You remember how independent Neda was. She's still the same way."

"Ruby pushed another photograph into her hand. "That's Danny, his wife, Pat, and their son Bobby. He's almost five years old."

"Daniel Walker," Freddie said, looking at the photograph. "He's so handsome, Ruby. Look at all that blond hair. His son looks just like him when he was that age. Don't you think so?"

"Yeah."

"What has Danny gotten his self into?"

"He's a successful businessman. He owns a book store downtown Chicago and a couple of restaurants."

179

"A businessman, how about that." She stared at the picture for a long time. "His wife looks like a real snob."

"She looks nice enough to me. This here is Betty Jean." She took the photograph and handed her another. "I couldn't get any pictures of her husband and two kids. Her son is grown. I don't know his name. Her daughter is a teenager. Her name's Rachel."

"Betty Jean is still Skinny and red as ever. Is she married?"

"To one of the wealthiest men in Atlanta Georgia. He makes a fortune sellin' real-estate."

"That bad leg of hers. I'm so glad it didn't stop a man from lovin' my little-red head."

Mae walked up to them. "You got about five minutes, Miss Ruby." She looked suspiciously at the two women and walked away, adding to the suspense. Mae knew Ruby was trying to stop her friend from willing herself to die.

Ruby leaned in closer to Freddie. "I saved the best for last." She handed Freddie the photograph. "This is Angela, her son, and her daughter. Her kids are five and seven years old."

Freddie looked at the picture longer than she did the others. "Look at that beautiful auburn skin. She's too heavy."

"Yeah, she does like to eat."

"She has the same ole-mean face. I can hardly remember a time I saw her smile."

"That's the best picture I could get. The day it was taken they were on their way to church."

"Church, that girl didn't believe God existed."

"She does now. She lives in Los Angeles and owns a successful soul-food restaurant in Hollywood. They call it South Town. People come from all over the world just to eat there."

Freddie's heart swelled with pride. Her children were not mental messes. She thought, maybe, Robert Bishop kept his word and her children were raised right. She gave Ruby back the photograph.

Ruby put it in the stack with the others. She gave all of the pictures to Freddie. "I have copies. Those are for you, for under your pillow."

Freddie leaned and put her arms around Ruby. "Thank you, Ruby Johnson. You are still the most wonderful person I've ever known."

"I wish you'd quit finalizin' everything. You ain't dead yet. She stood to leave.

"Do you know if they're in contact with each other? Is bein' two kinds of color keepin' them apart?"

"That detective told me Danny and Neda see each other all the time. Color of skin ain't made no difference in their lives."

"That's a good thing," Freddie said, tearful. "That's a real good thing."

"Yeah it is." Mae came to take her back. "I'll see you in a couple of days." She kissed Freddie's cheek and walked away from the bed.

"Ruby Johnson," Freddie called out. Ruby turned and looked at her.

"We'll always be best friends for life."

"Always best friends for life, Freddie Walker." She turned and walked quickly behind Mae. She didn't want Freddie to see her slip of tears.

Mae went with Ruby back to her cell. "You think it helped?"

"I know that woman like we were born stuck together. She just stopped willin' herself to die."

Night came quickly and the weather turned. The thunder storm made Ruby uneasy, unable to sleep. She thought about what she did and still felt good about doing it.

Freddie stayed awake looking at the photographs. Her bladder was full. She did not ask the night guard for permission to go to the bathroom. She got out of bed and attempted to go inside it alone.

The night guard saw the attempt, went to her, and grabbed her arm. "What are you doing, Miss Walker?"

"I don't need the shit and piss police every time I have to go to the toilet."

"You know the rules. Come on." The guard helped her inside the bathroom. "Go on and pull your pants down and get on the toilet."

"I got to do both. You wanna stay and smell my shit be my guest. I'd rather be alone if it won't break your heart."

"Get on the toilet, Miss Walker, or would you like for me to take you back to bed? You can do both while you're in it." She kept her eyes on Freddie.

"There ain't much to look at like there used to be," said Freddie, pulling down her panties, sitting on the toilet. "If you want to take a look at it you have to pay me first."

"Give me your arm," said the guard, removing her handcuffs. She took Freddie's arm and cuffed it to the rail beside the toilet.

"Thank God. I don't have to remind you to handcuff me to the toilet. I've got all the strength I need to break out of this place."

"You know I hate this as much as you do," said the guard, turning to leave.

"Sure you do. That's why you have that smirk on your face."

"Call out when you finish." The guard left and closed the door.

Freddie sat on the toilet longer than she should have. Over forty minutes passed. She was thinking about her children and wondering if she made a mistake regarding her last will and testament. She couldn't leave because her arm was still cuffed to the

183

toilet's rail. She called out numerous times for the guard to come and get her, but her voice was not heard. The nurse's radio was too loud. It was the gossiping hour and Freddie had been completely forgotten.

She tried extending her leg to kick the door but it was too far. If it had been closer, she was still too weak to kick it while sitting down. The only other solution to the forgotten cruelty was to stand up, extend her leg, and then kick the door as hard as she could.

She grabbed hold of the railing that cuffed her hand. She stood on wobbly legs. When she tried to kick the door, summoning the strength to do it, her head took a spin and her body followed. She fell on the concrete floor and heard the snap of her cuffed arm breaking at the elbow.

Her head slammed against the bottom bowl of the toilet. The wetness on her face, and neck, and down along her shoulder was her own blood. For what she hoped was God's forgiving reason, she felt no pain. Her eyes were drawn to the ceiling's fluorescent light. The harsh glare threw her back in time, inside a memorable Saturday afternoon in 1969. It was on a day she had taken Angela to an amusement park on the North Side of Chicago. They were sitting with their hands grasping the rollercoaster's railing, waiting for the ride to start.

The rollercoaster began its descent up the steep climb. "This is so much fun," she said to Angela, "Isn't it, Baby?"

184

"Yeah, Mama," replied Angela.

"I'm glad it's just the two of us."

Angela looked at her mother. "Mama, I'm sorry for callin' you names. I don't hate you. Really, I don't."

"I know you don't, baby."

"Sometimes, I think you love them more than me because I'm darker than even Neda."

"I love all my kids just the same. You wanna know how much I love you?"

"Yeah."

"I love you across a universe of the most brilliant and beautiful stars. I love you all the way to infinity, around the earth a billion times until I'm all the way back to you."

The rollercoaster fled down the last steep climb and was on its way back. The last thing Freddie heard was her own voice in the prison's bathroom. She told her most troubled child, "I love you, Angela Walker. I'll always love you."

At that very moment Freddie's grown daughter, Angela, had awakened. Her heart beat rapidly. Hearing her mother's voice telling her she loved her had scared the hell out of her. She looked at the old clock on her nightstand. It had suddenly broken and the last tick of the old clock read 1:33 A.M.

It was the next morning. Parker Bishop sat behind his desk at Bishop, McGregor, and Thomas. What surrounded him spoke of a man without intimacy in his life. There were no push pins of crayon-pictures pinned crookedly to something to remind a man of his children. There were no family photographs on his desk, and the stiff and dark furniture was without passion. The impressive sights were the floor to ceiling windows in back of his desk. They gave him a spectacular view of Lake Michigan. On many days he stared out at the lake watching sail boats under the height of the sun and the setting of it.

The eleven story building was located in the heart of downtown Chicago. He and Tom McGregor had built a successful law firm. There were over five-hundred associates working across the country. Most of their cases were those involving white-collar crime.

Allen had chosen not to join them. He preferred working for his father while carving out a political career. He was now Governor of the State of Illinois.

To step back and take a good look at Parker, his hair was white as a pearl except for the faint strands of blond running through it like watered down mustard. His stature held its height of six feet without any lean that comes with a tall man getting older. His weight stayed the same hundred and seventy-five pounds. His blue eyes, once flirtatious, talkative, were hardly seen doing anything interesting inside their sockets. They had lost most of their brilliance and were encased within a readable look. And the thing easily read about him was his sacrifice of giving up his need to be loved, or just cared for. These qualities were intense and showed about his person the same as that of a young man in need of the same human loving things.

Parker urgently gathered his things to leave for the day. Helen, his legal assistant, walked into his office. She had worked for him from the beginning and was near to his age. She was the mechanical part of his mind that obeyed the last of his demand without him saying it, or her hearing it. Whichever way the relationship went they were a splendid working compatibility.

While Helen stood before him she was still, delicate, worried. She never appeared to be breathing. "You look terrible," she told him, "like you haven't slept in weeks. Is there anything ..."

"No," Parker answered, gathering his briefcase and putting on his suit jacket. "I'm fine. You can leave early if you like."

"You'll need this," said Helen, handing him a manila folder.

"Yes," he said, taking the folder and putting it inside his briefcase, closing its flap, locking it.

He glanced at his watch and walked quickly out of his office and into the busy corridor. An array of associates, and legal assistants, could be seen working inside their cubicles and offices.

Rap music blared from the office of one of the young attorneys. To Parker it seemed as if all the new styles of music had nothing of substance but only rhythms of noise. He still preferred

187

the old jazz. While standing at the elevator Helen came up behind him, catching him.

"You have an urgent call," she told him.

"Tell them I'll call them later this afternoon."

"It's from the prison."

SOMETHING TO LAUGH AT

If it were not for the slopes of manicured blue grass, thick as a new carpet, or the kind of crypts and headstones that only the rich can afford, Clayton Cemetery could have been mistaken for a golf course that appeared to be sitting inside a perfect box for gardening. At every corner there were brick walls that came together, meeting at all four corners, closing everything inside. Fat and wide trees ran the length of each wall. They were tall and shady like picnic trees and did the job of blocking outside views from looking in.

Two cemetery workers left after lowering Freddie's casket into the ground. Parker stood alone beside the catholic priest. He had finished saying the heavenly things he could say about a woman he didn't know.

Parker did not know that Freddie had been raised a catholic. Ruby told him. There was still so much he didn't know about a woman he loved all of his young and growing old life. What happened to her as a child? What kind of abusive things were done to make her the kind of woman she was?   Instead of letting it all rest in peace he was more intrigued and curious about her.

After the priest left Parker revealed the grief he needed to. The tears were not all over Freddie they involved her children. None of them were present.

He glanced at the gravesite to the right of Freddie. It bare the name Robert Bishop and the date of his father's death. To the left of him was the headstone that bare his mother's name. The plot in the middle, where Freddie lay, had been his own.

Freddie once told him she didn't care where she was buried. He thought it befitting revenge, on his father, having what he referred to as "that-whore" buried right next to him. If there were any truth to spirits coming to life, rising up out of their graves, Freddie would have the pleasure of sending his father back to dead, giving him no chance to rise up and enjoy anything a cemetery gathering of ghosts had to offer.

He turned and went the short distance to where his car was parked. Burying her in his own grave gave him something to laugh at.

CHAPTER SEVEN
FURTHER THAN BLACKMAIL

Allen, now the Governor of Illinois, walked inside Jack Santos' Bar and Grill. It was after 10:00 P.M. and the place was fairly empty. Parker was sitting at his private table inside the private room. The slump and depressive disposition of a man's shadow told Allen it was him.

"Out of all the places in Chicago," said Allen, sitting down at the table, "you had to choose this place. It must be serious."

The old bartender saw Allen sneak in. He delivered a rum and soda and left.

"Freddie's gone. She's dead."

"Sorry. She was sick for a long time, right?"

"Yeah, that's not what she died from. She was handcuffed to the rail of a toilet seat, forgotten about. Freddie died saturated in her own urine, feces, and her own blood. A guard left her handcuffed to a fucking toilet."

"I'm sorry to hear that."

"I want what happened to her investigated, understand?"

"Sure," said Allen. "Full speed, you have my word."

"Good."

"How are you holding up?"

"I'm fine."

190

"Is there something you need? Anything I can do?"

"I'm not sure. I've never read the case file."

"Case file," Allen said, puzzled."

"I promised her I would look into something. It's about Ruby."

"The maid," said Allen. "Get to the point."

"I think Ruby's case should be reviewed."

"I'm not getting involved. She's gone. Leave it alone and get on with your life?"

"If justifiable homicide can be proved."

"Are you asking me for what I think you are? You, my friend, are playing with fire. You need to find yourself a twenty-year old to play with. That's a lot more fun."

"I'm serious, Allen. "You're the fucking Governor. Don't forget who helped you get there."

"I don't believe this. You are actually …"

"I gave Freddie my promise to look into Ruby's case. If I pushed for a real trial I'd get it based on our …"

"You can't prove I ever went to that house."

"Sure I can. He reached inside his jacket pocket and removed two photographs. He tossed them on the table in front of Allen. The pictures were of him, Freddie, Allen, and Tom inside Freddie and Ruby's house. Danny could be seen in the background.

"I don't believe you can do that to me or Tom. You're bluffing."

"Don't push it Allen. I'm warning you. I need all of it behind me. I'm too old to care about what happens to anybody's reputation."

"Does Tom know what you're up to?"

"Does it matter?"

"We were young men," whispered Allen. He waved his hand for the old bartender to bring him another.

"If you're not willing to consider helping Ruby you leave me no choice. I'll have to get involved."

"I can't believe what I'm hearing. We've been best friends since we were in fucking kindergarten. You're blackmailing me over some black woman nobody gives a damn about, un-fucking believable."

"I won't feed you information based on bullshit. A man like Jimmy Tate, killing that son-of-a-bitch was justifiable."

"Not if it can't be proven. You'll have to find Freddie's kids."

"I know that."

"What happens if the press gets wind of the wrong information? This could not only ruin my political career it would ruin my life. My wife would divorce me and my kids would never speak to me again."

"There will be some press. It's unavoidable."

"I believe your bluffing. It's not in you to do something like this."

"To get it over with, quickly, all I have to do is make a few statements. You'll answer some questions. Tom will ..."

"Okay, okay," Allen said, cutting him off.

"Look at it like this, remember that door you need to open in Washington."

"Sure, dangle the white house under my nose. You're no different from hundreds of opportunists doing the same thing. I hope you're not getting involved as Ruby's attorney?"

"No."

"That's a relief," said Allen, finishing his drink.

"I've got someone in mind. Black kid worked for the firm a while back. He's a hard head but he's a good attorney. I won't have to tell him too much."

The next morning Parker spent most of his day looking over the case file. Old newspaper articles and pictures of Freddie, Ruby and the kids, were spread on top his desk.

Allen didn't waste any time. He agreed to set up a special review board to look into Ruby's case. If the retired judges agreed to justifiable homicide a full pardon would be recommended. To legitimize the board, not to make Ruby's case appear special, more cases involving backroom injustice would be looked into.

193

Parker mentioned the review board and the possibility of a full pardon to Ruby. He tried to explain the details, but still depressed and grieving over the way Freddie died, Ruby told him she wasn't interested.

The signing of papers regarding Freddie's last will and testament gave Parker more excuses to visit Ruby, but on this day she asked to see him. She sat across from him inside the prison's attorney client room. He thought she looked better than the last time he seen her.

"I have those papers for you to sign," he told her.

"That's not why I asked you here," she said. "I've been thinkin' about that Governor's Review Board thing."

"Oh, that." He pretended he had forgotten.

"Tell me more about it."

He had to choose his words carefully. "As I mentioned it's not like a parole board. It's …"

"Like what then?"

"The board will consist of three judges who are retired."

"Why not four or a hundred?"

"I don't know. Three seems like a fair number to me."

"What do I have to do?"

"Well, first they have to review your case file. If they agree …"

"That I'm worth any kind of special treatment?"

194

"If they agree to the hearing there will be a series of interviews."

"You're shuffling around the subject, Parker Bishop."

"Others will need to verify your statement regarding what kind of man Jimmy was."

"How?"

"Through a series of interviews."

"I don't want her kids involved. I don't know where they are. They don't need to be dragged into this."

"What we're looking to prove is justifiable homicide. If it can be proven it could mean a full pardon, Ruby."

"I ain't doin' it if the kids are a part of this."

"I can't guarantee they won't be."

"If don't nobody know where they are they can't be in it, can they?"

"They shouldn't be that hard to find."

"Even if they say yes I can say no, right?"

"Yes you can. But if you do that you'll spend the rest of your life in here."

She was quiet for a while, thinking of how to keep them out of it. "Will I need a lawyer?"

"Yes for preparation, consulting."

"You mean someone to tell me what to say and what not to say?"

"To be honest, yes. He won't be with you during the review. This is not a process like in a court of law. It's not a trial. It's only a hearing, a series of interviews. After your case is evaluated the board will recommend to the Governor a pardon, or not."

"Are you going to be my lawyer?" Ruby asked.

"No. I have someone in mind. He's a good lawyer. You'll get along fine."

After visiting Ruby he went back to his office. He sat behind his desk looking over the case file. If he eliminated the repetition of documents, down to the plain facts, the fat file would have been thin enough for a manila folder. It was all cut and dry.

Helen stayed behind in case he needed her. She showed Billy Waller into his office and left.

"I thought you fancy lawyers spent more time in court than behind your desk," said Billy.

"Not at this age," said Parker, rising from his chair, taking Billy's handshake. "It's been a long time, Billy. How are you?" They had not seen the other since the death of Parker's father.

"Besides this bum knee and a wife that can't cook worth a damn, I'm doing fine. I can't complain more than that." He sat in the chair across from Parker's desk.

Billy was a private detective—a tall and thin black man with a neatly-cropped haircut, mustache, and trimmed-graying beard. He

196

wasn't much older than Parker. Billy had a trusting way about his character.

"Did you come up with anything?" Parker asked.

"Yep!" said Billy, tossing a manila folder onto Parker's desk. "I found all of them. Freddie's kids turned out to be a mixed bag of nuts. It's all there."

Parker glanced briefly through the folder. He wanted to hear it from Billy. "Where are they?" he asked, turning over the two glasses on his desk.

"None for me," said Billy.

Parker poured his self a drink and tasted it.

"Betty Jean lives in Atlanta. She's married, got a couple of kids. Angela is in Los Angeles. She's got a couple of kids. Danny and Neda live in Chicago. He's married with one kid. Neda lives on the North Side. She's never been married and has no children."

"Do you think they might help Ruby?"

"I don't know. I kept my distance. I didn't talk to them."

"What's your opinion?"

"Well, to be honest I think Freddie and Ruby did a lot of sacrificing for nothing. Mind?"

"Of course not."

Billy lit a cigar and relaxed into the back of the chair. "What's this all about, an appeal?"

"The Governor's review board."

"No shit. Well I'll be damned, a special pardon for killin' that bastard. I'd say that's a damn good idea. But if the wrong information gets out this thing could blow up in all the wrong directions."

"I'm not getting involved, personally. I'm too old to give a damn if I did. I've got an attorney in mind."

"You want me to keep diggin' around?"

"Yes."

He stood and took Parker's handshake. "Next time you see Ruby tell her Billy Waller said hello. Tell her I wish her the best of luck."

"I'll do that."

"Give the Governor my regards." He went to the door. Thoughts of Parker's father crossed his mind. He turned and looked at Parker. "Your old man wasn't such a bad guy. Powerful men like that are real stupid bastards when it comes to their own kids. He was just trying to protect you."

"Goodnight Billy." He didn't want to hear any pleasantries about his father.

The first time Billy met Parker, Allen, and Tom, was at Jack Santos' Bar and Grill. He was sitting at the bar when Tom called his name, waving him out of his seat and into the private room. The three young men were home on spring break from Harvard. After Billy sat down they introduced themselves. Allen made it clear, to

198

Billy, that he knew he was the black man that sometimes worked for their fathers.

When the night was over, and they stepped outside onto the sidewalk, Tom told Billy, "We would like to get with you again."

"Why?" asked Billy.

"We don't have any Negro friends," said Allen. "We think it would be interesting, nice, to have a Negro friend."

"We like Negro music," said Tom, his words stumbling. "We listen to it all the time."

"Please don't take that the wrong way," said Parker.

They took Billy's grim face to be one of a man insulted. A few seconds later Billy started laughing. They relaxed and laughed with him.

The Law Offices of John Martin were located on the South Side of Chicago on the corner of 46th and Wabash. It was a two-room operation on the second floor of a remodeled tenement. A little over a year ago, after Parker fired him, John set up his own firm but his practice was a struggling one. One room was John's office and the other was the reception area. It was overcrowded with file cabinets, his assistant's desk, and a variety of second hand tables she used to keep herself organized.

John was black, twenty-nine years old, attractive and preferred a bald head instead of hair. He believed it gave him a fearless look when dealing with those clients who were not friendly.

He was considered an arrogant egoist by his colleagues, and predicted to fall prey to his fantasies of grandeur. Regardless, he was gaining recognition as being one of the sharpest Criminal attorneys in the city of Chicago. He was known for using his legal skill and street knowledge as a lethal combination. By his hammering way of winning, in unorthodox ways, he turned some of the most outrageous criminals back onto the streets of Chicago. To ease his conscious for doing that he prayed and then reminded his self that everyone is innocent until proven guilty.

To keep his costs at a minimum John gave up his North Side apartment and moved into his mother's home—a two-story brownstone on the South Side, across from Washington Park. She kept him fed, and pampered his frustration when he came home sulking and talking about giving up his practice.

John's assistant, Nicki, was a cute-black woman. She had a face and smile that reminded one of a curious and sassy-teenage girl. Though she was single, in her early twenties, she allowed him no romancing of her because they worked too well together. He caught her mistakes and she forgave his. She did not quit like the three hired before her.

It was an early Tuesday morning when Nicki walked into his office and sat the thick file on the corner of his desk. "This just came by messenger," she told John.

He often partnered with other firms. If they had an overload of cases they were given to him.

"Who sent it?" asked John. She was hesitating. "Who sent it, Nicki?"

She sighed and said, "Parker Bishop's office."

"What?"

"Parker Bishop's office."

"You mean my ole boss. You mean that Parker Bishop. You mean the son-of-a bitch that fucked up my whole life, the man that fired me?"

"How can you be so positive and so negative all at the same time?" There it is. The man sent you some work. My new house could be at the end of that case. We need all the cases we can get. I don't give a damn where they come from." She pointed at him. "You need to get to work. Payday will be here in three days, my payday." She rolled her eyes, left his office, and closed the door.

"Is there anything," he yelled after her, "on the face of this earth that means more to you than a house and a Mercedes Benz?"

She opened the door, looked at him, and smiled. "No," she said, closing the door.

John leaned back into his chair, rocking. His arms were folded and his body pushed far away from his desk. His chair was backed up close against the wall. He stared at the thick-brown file.

201

There was a certain gleam in his eyes because his old boss had not forgotten him.

The next morning John drove to the far north end of Lake Michigan's waterfront and parked his car in a discreet place. He wasn't dressed for the long haul of jogging four miles to keep up with his old boss. He had gained weight and his blue sweats were uncomfortable and too tight around his thighs.

He could have made an appointment with Helen to see Parker. But something about the case told him Parker needed him to speak with him privately. Maybe, thought John, this was about the secret woman in prison. He heard the rumors and was sure the beautiful woman in the newspaper photographs was her.

John saw Parker running toward the bench where he was sitting. He marveled at how in shape he was for a man his age. He pretended to tie his shoe lace. Parker jogged past him.

"A man like you," said John. "People like that. What about your pristine reputation?"

Parker did not stop jogging. He saw John's bald head sitting there before John saw him. "I'll worry about my reputation. You concentrate on what you have to do. Are you interested or not, yes or no?"

John realized Parker was not going to sit down. He stood up and jogged fast behind him, catching up.

"That all depends," he told Parker. "What's in it for me?"

"Your fee. I'm hiring you to prepare Ruby Johnson's case for the review board. You'll take care of any legal complications."

"What about the other woman?"

"She passed away. Are you interested or not?"

"If I remember correctly as of one year, two months, five days, six hours and," he looked at his watch, "twenty-four seconds ago you fired me."

John was out of breath. Parker stopped his run. "You took a case I ordered you not to touch. I didn't send you a memo. I called you into a meeting, in my office, and told you specifically not to take it."

"It was personal. It was something I had to do. I explained it to you."

"I see you've learned nothing. You're still an arrogant-egotistic bastard."

"And you still can't admit you made a mistake firing me. Out of all the cases I handled for you I didn't lose one."

"Your ability to win was never an issue. You put a notorious criminal back onto the streets of this city. The man was guilty of running a narcotics operation. Admit you were wrong. Maybe we can put it behind us."

John took a few deep breaths and walked away from Parker. He looked at him. "Okay, I admit it. I was wrong."

"Go on," Parker said, waiting for the rest of it.

"Please accept my apology."

"Now that wasn't so bad, was it?"

"You never let me tell you why I took the case."

"It wouldn't have mattered. Answer the question. Are you interested or not, yes or no? I won't make the offer again."

"You know you can trust me. That's the only reason you chose me. Admit it."

"Yes," Parker said. It is personal but that's none of your business."

"Like I said, what's in it for me?"

"I told you, your fee."

"Not good enough. I want back in. Starting my own practice this early was not part of my career plan. It's too expensive. I miss all those fancy perks."

He liked John but he was hard-headed. He had the makings of a great attorney but from Parker's perspective John didn't realize an important and simple truth. He needed other great attorneys to help make him one.

"Well," John said, pushing Parker back onto the subject.

"I do have something on my mind, but if you press me …"

"Do I look like I'm pressing you? Look at this face," John said, smiling. "This is a seriously happy face. Standing here looking at you like this is making me so damned happy."

"Cut the bullshit," Parker told him, jogging away.

"It was nice to see you again," John said, playing. "I really missed you."

Parker kept jogging. John didn't know that some of the cases keeping his firm alive were referrals from Bishop, McGregor, and Thomas. Parker had not given up on John and kept an eye on him. He wanted to teach him another simple and important rule—loyalty to the firm he worked for.

Ruby sat across from John inside the prison's attorney client room. In spite of her blocking and protective stares, and pushing her real person away from the table, John was pleased to see that prison had not taken all the life out of her.

"Parker said to tell you about that night," Ruby told him. "He didn't say anything about anything else. I don't like these questions."

"Parker Bishop is not your attorney."

"Nobody said you were. You're too cocky and arrogant for me. I don't like you askin' me stuff about my life before you even get to know me."

"Look Ruby. Can I call you, Ruby?"

"Yes, you can."

"Ruby this review board is a one-time deal. I'm not here to get to know you personally. I have a mother. What you say to that review board can change your whole life unless you just love this place. If you like me, hate me, I don't care. I'm here to help you say all the right things. I'm the best at what I do."

"Back up a minute you arrogant bastard. You tell Parker Bishop I want another lawyer. You too damn full of yourself."

He stood up and gathered his legal pad and pen, putting them inside his briefcase and locking it. "If you can't talk about the past and what went on in the Walker household you will never get out of here. I came here to help you. The statement you write to that board will either convince them to look into your case, or, convince them to keep you in this place for the remaining years of your life. You don't have too many more years left. Good luck, Miss Johnson." He walked away from her.

"How old are you anyway?"

He turned around and looked at her. "Old enough."

"That ain't no answer."

"Twenty-nine." He went back to the table and stood before her.

"Is that old or young for a lawyer like you?"

"Where I am right now, in my career, it's about the right age."

"Maybe I'm just scared of all this."

"I'm a damn good lawyer, Ruby. I can help you get through it. If I wasn't good enough Parker would have never referred me."

Her eyes watered. "Do you think I have a chance? I mean a real good chance of getting out of this place?"

John held out his hand and took hers into his. He could feel her trembling. "I wouldn't be here if I didn't think so."

Three weeks went by and Ruby heard nothing from the board. On the first day, of the fourth week, Chandra, Ruby's cellmate, was reading her magazines and Ruby read her bible. She was on her way to dozing off but the swishing sound of Mae's uniform caused her to open her eyes, raise her head, and listen. It was the straight and fast walk that said Mae was headed their way.

When Mae arrived she looked inside the cell at Ruby. "I've got a letter for you." She extended the letter between the bars, waiting for Ruby to take it.

"Who's it from," asked Ruby, staring at the letter in Mae's hand.

"The Governor's Review Board."

Chandra was listening to the conversation. She stopped reading her magazine and leaned over her bunk. "Go on, Miss Ruby, take it. I'll read it to you."

"No. I'll read it." She took the letter from Mae and opened it. She read it and then laid it on her bunk. "Mae," said Ruby. "I need to call my lawyer. They'll listen to what I have to say."

Mae had to catch herself. She wanted to yell louder than Chandra.

September 29, 2003

CHAPTER EIGHT

NEDA

THE PUERTO RICAN GYRATOR

Hot Mamas was a unique gentleman's club located on the North Side of Chicago. Middle aged blue collar workers were the steady clientele. It was not the classic fashionable club where the dancers were beautiful and athletic. It was a cheap joint with a boxy-red room of rickety, unstable, chairs and tables.

The owner named the place Hot Mamas because the female dancing disasters were reminiscent of someone's aging mother, wife, lover or girlfriend. Whatever role of importance a woman of that age played in the life of a customer, be she despised, loved, wanted, or simply needed, it was this factor that drove a certain type of losing man to Hot Mamas.

Those dancers that couldn't get over their addictive craving for attention, or were unable to give up their profession, just because of age, found their selves on display there. It was the only one-of-its-kind club specializing in the sexiness, unattractiveness, or, attractiveness of dancing older women.

On special occasions a dancer dressed up to a customer's expectation and performed onstage as a design of his wife, mother, or even a sister. One night during a flying, twirling, high-legged pole performance the dancing pole became completely unhinged. One of Hot Mamas best dancers catapulted through the air like an Olympic Pole Jumper. She landed head first in the middle of the room and on top of a table seating four.

When the paramedics arrived they discovered she had broken her neck and had to spend months in physical therapy. After the aging dancer was well enough to go home she was glad to spend the rest of her life in a wheelchair on state disability. There was no more worry over how to improve her tits and ass to please a single man.

Another thing of interest, to the clientele, the roof had a hole in it the size of a quarter and was above the center of the stage. When it rained the water gathered around the bottom of the pole, and on watery nights Hot Mamas was packed with men waiting for falls to happen.

The dancers could have complained to the right authorities. Some even thought of suing the owner. Their excuse for not doing it was fear of getting fired. What really held their justice at bay were their addictive-psychological cravings for attention.

On this night a dancer finished her set without a fall. Water from heavy rain poured in from the roof's hole like an unstoppable faucet. She did her performance without shoes and stockings. The customers applauded her stamina and concentrated efforts. She made it through her set without one slip or fall.

Backstage the dancer saw Neda Walker coming toward her. She stopped and looked at Neda. "It's really wet out there," she told her. "Take off your shoes. You'll kill yourself in those things."

To step back and take a look at Neda, all grown up, she appeared younger than her early forties. Her mixture of white and black-blooded hair was still long and wavy and she wore it pulled up and away from her face. A tight band was around the high flowing tail that touched her shoulders and bounced around at the middle of her back. When her face was free from the complexities of makeup, applied to be seen from backroom distances, her ordinariness was that of a beautiful-black woman.

Her costume was a red nurse's uniform. The red hat matched her red-stiletto shoes. A red-plastic belt was pulled tight around her small waistline. The tight dress showed that the curve of her hips was spread out more than the rest of her. She was overweight in that area.

Neda rotated her ankles to make sure her shoes were secure. She told the passing dancer, "I can do this on fucking stilts if I have to." Her made up Puerto Rican accent was quick and sharp.

Her spoken introduction came out over the loud speaker. "Neda, the Puerto Rican Gyrator!" said the announcer.

When it was all over it was a performance to be pitied. Throughout her routine she fell two times and the second fall twisted her ankle. The bus boy had to help her off stage, back stage, and inside the dressing room. She sat at her vanity table crying and complaining about the pain she was in.

Three dancers were sitting at their vanity tables, preparing for their performance. They held their heads low when Mario, the owner, entered the dressing room. He was a discourteous, lumbering, bad-tempered Latino in his late fifties.

He went to Neda's vanity table and crossed his arms, looking at her. She pretended he wasn't there and continued brushing her hair.

"Look at me, Neda, he said. "Look at me, baby."

"What, Mario?"

"You're fired."

She stood up and faced him. "Why, Mario? I need this job until I can find something else."

"No." He told her. "Pack up your shit. Get your ass out of here."

"Why? Please, Mario, don't do this to me right now. I'm one of the best dancers you've got. Why?"

"I told you to lose some weight. Your ass looks like the back of a garbage truck." The dancers laughed at his comment. He left slamming the door behind him.

211

Neda looked at them. "You stupid bitches think you look any better than me, huh? That guy, the one that fixes all the broken shit around here, told me that Mario made him put a hole in the roof the size of quarter, right over the stage."

"We already know about that," said one of the dancers. "Seeing how you knew it, before any of us did, you should've been a lot more careful. Fuck off."

The bus boy opened the door and came in. He went to Neda. He cupped his mouth and whispered in her ear. "There's a man in the corridor asking for you. Mario told him to wait for you to come out."

"Did he say what he wanted?"

"No. I don't think he's a customer."

She was dressed in jeans and a blue tee shirt. She opened the door and stepped into the corridor. She stood in front of the disheveled dark-haired man.

"Neda Walker?" he said, looking at her.

"Who wants to know?" she asked, speaking fluent Spanish. The man came closer to her.

"What do you want?" asked Neda, in English.

"Are you Neda Walker?"

"Yes. So what if I am."

The man reached inside a pocket and came out of it with two envelopes in his hand. He shoved them at her. She took them without hesitation.

"You've been served."

She followed behind the man and saw him get into a grey sedan. Inside her car, she turned on the overhead light and read the front of the letters. The first one was a subpoena to testify in front of the Governor's Review Board. The second letter was from the Department of Corrections. It stated that her mother, Freda Eloise Walker, was dead. The flooding of tears came from something she did not know. Her mother had a middle name.

On the same night Ruby was awake. She knew the process of serving them had begun, and that Neda would receive the first letters. Knowing the truth about Neda, she could not tell Freddie what the made-up Puerto Rican really did for a living.

DANNY
DOUBLE LIVES

Danny's Internet Café was located in downtown Chicago. Where clientele was concerned, most of the time the place was filled to capacity. It was a two-story complex that had a touch of futuristic design. There were two large and sunny levels with glossy-hardwood floors. On the first level the chairs, sofas, and stools, were a modern sprawl of metallic legs with cushions of deep red, purple, and sunny yellow. The room was for reading and drinking fine coffees served with fine pastries.

On the upper level was a library with work tables and chairs that supported the use of many computers. Shelves of books encircled most of the walls. Skylights and abstract paintings gave one the relaxed feeling that came with being young and cool.

It was just after 5:00 P.M. Danny Walker exited his office and went toward the counter. He was dressed in dark-green slacks and a plain cream-colored shirt. His good looks were breath taking. His blond hair, shoulder length, had inherited the gloss and thickness of his mother's dark hair. What stood out most about Danny was his mother's elegant class. He went to the counter. Connie—a young brunette with intelligent brown eyes was behind it.

"I've got things to do," he told Connie. "Close up."

"Danny, I told you I have to leave early. I've got classes at six o'clock."

"That's the problem, Connie. You told me. You didn't ask."

"Okay," she said, softening, turning away from his gaze. "I'll do it this time but I can't next week. Don't forget."

"I promise. I won't forget." She reached underneath the counter, grabbed his keys, and handed them to him.

The slight touch of his hand heated her in all the right places. She always wanted him to touch her, but he never flirted with her or any woman that worked for him.

He stepped outside. It was a one block walk to the garage where his car was parked. When he arrived he handed the garage runner his keys. The runner returned driving a navy blue, convertible, BMW. The top was down. It stayed that way until the weather was too cold. Danny liked being seen and envied for having expensive things.

His penthouse condominium, overlooking Lake Michigan, was on the twenty-fifth floor of a newly built high-rise on Lake Shore Drive. The drive to it was no more than ten minutes from the café. When he arrived, he parked at the feet of the doorman and got out of the car.

"That party you were expecting is all tucked in," the doorman said, going to Danny.

Discreetly, Danny handed him a roll of cash and walked into the building to the elevator. He paid no attention to the disheveled young man standing next to him. After the elevator arrived, and Danny walked inside, he held the door from closing.

"I'll take the next one," the man told him.

The penthouse was glassy with large and opened rooms that flowed into the other. There were two levels and each one had decks that overlooked the Lake. Five bedrooms with full baths were

215

upstairs, and the living area downstairs was equipped with a full bar. The great room had been furnished to make groups of men feel comfortable while being waited on by the beautiful young call girls that lived there.

No one heard Danny enter the penthouse. It was too noisy with music and laughter. The party of Japanese businessmen that the girls were entertaining was well underway. Two of the girls were upstairs with two of the men. The other three were on their way up with the others when Danny walked in. He was not greeted in the usual manner. The girls were too busy. They could only manage a wave and a smile.

An office on the first level was along a corridor. Ginny was his full-time bookkeeper. She was white and a retired madam in her mid seventies. Danny cared for Ginny more than any woman in his life. She was nothing less than a genius with numbers and tax matters concerning his legitimate businesses and his illegal ones.

Danny entered the office. Ginny sat behind the small desk. She was preoccupied with wrapping cash in rubber bands, gathering checks, leaning and putting the money inside the safe near the desk.

"Everything's ready for the bank," said Ginny. She stood and walked from behind the desk. Her old frame had tightened up on her. She was slow putting on her sweater. Danny had to help her.

216

"My back is breaking," said Ginny. "We had a group in early this morning from that medical convention. Now we got a pack of swag bellies, noisy bunch of idiots."

"Is everybody working?"

"Yeah. That new girl you gave your card to wants to work. I interviewed her, seems alright. Smart."

"That's it?" asked Danny, sitting behind the desk.

"What more you want, huh, greedy boy? Everything is good today with lots of money in your pocket, so little in Ginny's pocket. I remember when you used to kiss me on my cheek and say, poor, poor, Ginny. I should make you throw me on the floor and fuck my brains out for my pay, so little pay it is."

"If I did that," said Danny, playing with her. "You'd die a lot sooner. What would I do without my Ginny, huh, come here." He pulled her close and kissed her cheek.

"I guess you're right. I'm already half dead, makes no sense to push it along any faster."

The buzzer sounded, signaling them to look up at the security monitors. The disheveled young man, waiting downstairs at the elevator, was standing in the corridor. He had two envelopes in his hand.

8:00 P.M. the same night.

Danny drove onto the streets of Bellagio Maria Estates. The houses inside the sub-division cost a million dollars and more.

Those homes valued at a million, or more, sat up high on man designed ground. They gave the appearance of being carved out of natural green hills. Trees and bushes gave the background of all the houses a woodsy look.

Grand terraces and decks started at the edges of kitchens and great rooms, merging outside into patios, gardens, and swimming pools. An abundance of picture windows looked out over the landscape.

Danny was king in the middle. His three-story six-bedroom home, valued at over a million, looked down on the properties to his left and right.

He parked his car in his driveway, got out, and walked to the back of it. He opened the truck. Inside were several bouquets of flowers. He chose the yellow carnations that were wilted but not as much as the others.

The turning of locks alerted Bobby. "Daddy's home," he said, running into the foyer, greeting his father.

"Hey sport," said Danny, picking Bobby up. He hugged the four-year old tighter than usual.

"You're squeezing me too hard, Daddy," said Bobby.

"That's because I'm so happy to see you," said Danny, putting the boy down.

To step back and take a look at Danny's young wife, Pat, everyday she walked throughout her home serving all the right ingredients on the table of marriage. They were together for nine years and married for seven.

Some of the neighborhood women saw Pat as a shy-perky thing. And because of her short hair, fluctuating between light brown and dishwater blond, they nicknamed her Mrs. Cute and Mrs. Dusty Beige. Those neighbors with secure incomes whose husbands were professionals saw her as an opportunist with her head bobbing for apples, tossing out the rotten ones with her teeth.

The men who shared their barbecues nicknamed her Nervous-as-a Whip. They whispered about her fabulous figure, and how her alert green eyes were always flicking the signs of a woman in denial. Some, who thought they knew Danny enough to make an assessment, said Pat was avoiding the truth about a husband of suspect character who was dazzling under the lights of false gleam.

Danny came into the kitchen and handed Pat the wilted flowers, kissing her on the cheek. He smelled the pot roast and his appetite stirred.

She looked at the flowers, puzzled. "I better put these in some water. I'm glad you're home early."

"Why?"

She had that miserable look. The one that comes at the head of an oncoming complaint of a woman never satisfied. She was always pushing him. She wanted extreme wealth. She was the kind of woman that accepted his secrets during times he could put real money on the table. When money was tight, and he couldn't put it on the table, she questioned him about the things she usually turned her eyes away from, and by doing that she urged him to make more money any way he could. Overall, if she couldn't have her vision of talked about wealth she wanted the illusion of being a rich-young wife and mother. It was an okay lie to hide behind.

He watched her choose her words carefully. She filled the vase with water and put the flowers in it.

"A black family," said Pat, "bought the house across from Carol. That makes three Black families and two Mexican families living below the hills. Remember when I asked the real estate agent about the kind of people that would buy the houses, and she said they were good people?"

"Maybe they are good people." He was getting angry. "If they didn't have somethin', goin' for themselves they wouldn't be able to live here."

"Don't use that tone of voice with me." She was on the verge of crying.

He went to her. He took the vase of flowers out of her hands and sat them on the counter. "I'm sorry. I had a really, really, tough day."

She stepped back and looked at him. "We should consider selling. It's a good time. I'm sure we'll get more than we paid."

220

The comment drove him to the end of the kitchen's island. "Pat, this is the third house in seven years. We can't keep movin' because our neighbors are not perfect. It doesn't make sense. Maybe you need to see a therapist. Talk to somebody about your inability to …"

"A therapist, I'm not a racist. I want what's best for my family. That doesn't mean I'm a racist, Danny."

"You can't keep runnin' from the Blacks and the Mexicans."

"I'll put these in the great room." She picked up the vase of flowers, leaving the kitchen.

On this same night Neda climbed over the wall of the Bellagio Maria Estates. A portion of the wall, covered with pine trees and bushes, was a blind spot for the guards patrolling that area. Once the guards drove back to the front entrance, and went back inside their booth, she crawled out from around the base of trees. She pretended to be a neighbor out for an evening stroll. After she was sure it was okay, she ran up the hill going toward Danny's house.

She knew Danny's habits. He would fix his self a drink and walk through the great room, into his office, and close the door. His chair and desk were near the window. After he sipped his drink and lit a cigarette he would open his mail.

Neda peered through the window and then tapped on it. When he didn't respond she tapped harder. Danny came out of his daze and stood. He cupped his hand over his brow, reducing the window's glare. He saw Neda and his heart raced.

"I've got an emergency at Best Seller's," he said to Pat, on his way out.

"What about dinner?"

"Keep it warm. I won't be long."

He remembered a Sunday evening when he was in his home office going over his bookkeeping. He had the feeling of being watched, but when he peered out the window he saw nothing. He walked outside and around the house where he saw a woman. She looked like the back of Neda jogging away from him. He told his self it was probably a neighbor. He didn't believe she would ever do such a thing. If she needed money she always waited for him outside the Café. Now he knew it wasn't a neighbor. It was her. She was peeking through his windows, spying on him.

He drove over the speed limit. Neda sat beside him. He couldn't look at her and couldn't say anything. The sound of her fake Puerto Rican accent would have caused him to pull over and grab her around the neck. His thoughts were of choking her to death. After leaving Kansas he thought he should have never looked for her. When he knocked on her door for the first time, and she opened it, he wanted to pretend to be someone else. It was too late. She recognized him in seconds. How was it possible he cared so deeply about her when they were kids? Now he hated her. He hated her existence and every pitiful sick thing about her. He was worn out from her sniveling, begging, and pleading for sympathy. She was always talking about the past. She was in his life too many times, ruining perfect days.

He pulled up in front of Best Sellers and parked without concern about where he was parking.

"Is this yours?" Neda asked, looking at the people waiting to get in.

"Yes," said Danny, "Don't make a big deal about it, okay. It's only been open a few weeks."

"Best Seller's" she commented, looking up, quoting the sign. "It's always about you and the books, huh Danny? It's always about word's you've never written."

He walked past the crowded bar area with her following behind him. Couples could be seen having dinner by candlelight. He liked that the servers were moving at a fast pace. It was busy, showing signs of another success. Because of his love for books, the restaurant was surrounded with shelves of them. The entrees were named after great writers. It was the perfect place for young lovers—an intimate place of dark tables.

He looked over his shoulder and Neda was on his heels. He hated being seen with her following behind him.

He walked into the busy kitchen and entered the office, closing the door. He sat behind his desk. She looked pitiful and

223

tired, looming over him like something ready to collapse. He couldn't stand it.

He kicked the step stool beside his desk. "You can sit on that." She kept standing, not wanting to sit beneath him. "It was you I saw that time. What the fuck do you think you're doin'?"

"What?"

"Lookin' through my windows," he yelled, "spyin' on my family."

"Don't yell at me like that." The Puerto Rican accent was not there. "I wasn't spyin' on you. I only did that a few times."

"A few times. You've done this more than once?"

"I was curious. I wanted to see my nephew." What's wrong with that?"

"I told you, time and again, you are not an extension of my family. Remember what the terms were? You agreed to stay out of my private life."

"You're sick, Danny, really fuckin' sick." Her accent had come back like another personality.

"I'm only gonna tell you one more time, stay …

"What are you gonna do, huh, kill me?"

"I won't have to. By the time I'm finished with you you'll do it yourself!"

"I got fired," she blurted out.

"What do you want, money?" He reached into his pocket, removing his wallet. He opened it and tossed a few hundred dollar bills on the desk.

"That's not the only reason." She reached into her jacket pocket and came out with the letters. "A man served me these letters. Our mother is dead. I have a subpoena to appear in front of some review board. It's got somethin' to do with talkin' about Ruby."

"I know about the letters," Danny said, calming down. "I got the same ones. There's nothin' to worry about. I checked into it. I called her lawyer. He wants us to talk about our relationship with Ruby. That's all."

"What about Betty Jean," she asked. "Have you talked to her? Do you know where she is?"

"No," he said. "I told you I don't know."

"You're lyin' again."

"The past and the people in it have no place in my life. That includes you, Betty Jean, and Angela. One pair of eyes lookin' through my window is enough."

"We have to talk to them, Danny?"

"Angela and Betty Jean probably got the same letters. Use your head for more than a box full of make-up."

BETTY JEAN
I KNOW SOMETHING ABOUT EVERY SUBJECT
KNOWN TO MANKIND

It was hard to tell what kind of Chevy Station Wagon it was. Besides the rusty hood, and undercarriage, the originally red car had been poorly redone with green paint. The color red could still be seen in every place the eyes could look.

Betty Jean pulled up in the old station wagon and parked in front of Scarlet's Dry Cleaning. She was not alone. Her fourteen year old daughter Rachel was in the backseat. She was a pale and overweight girl with thick-red hair like Betty Jean's, and it was easy to tell she had a depressed disposition.

Betty Jean was tall and far too thin. She looked older than her years because some of her side teeth had been removed. Her cheeks were sunken and seemed to slide away from her eyes and bone. The part of her physical self, standing out to be noticed, was the beauty of her shimmering red hair and fluorescent hazel eyes. Her limp was there but not as prevalent. She favored wearing blue jeans and tee shirts.

Betty Jean entered Scarlet's Dry Cleaning. The owner, an elderly black man, was behind the counter. He avoided looking at Betty Jean because her eyes made him nervous.

226

"Tell Howard I said come on," Betty Jean demanded. Her accent was southern.

"Howard," the owner called out. "Your wife is here."

"Howard," yelled Betty Jean, "you come on from back there."

"You know he's taking off early again," the owner told her.

"It ain't no secret. My son is up there rottin' away in Atlanta's Federal Prison. My boy needs to see his mama and his doggone daddy. Howard you come on now! Don't let me come back there and get you."

The owner walked away from the counter. He entered the steam room of laundry pressing machines and looked at Howard. He was a petite white man in his middle forties. To step back and take a good look at Howard, he was just as red and freckled as Betty Jean.

Howard was standing at the big presser, pressing down on it harder than usual. His face was angry, frozen, beat red. His eyes were in a dreamy state. His hands gripped the handle of the presser like he was an executioner and Betty Jean's head was underneath. He stayed that way with steam billowing up around his head, and when it subsided he was soaked wet and standing like a hen-pecked statue.

"Your wife is here," the owner told him.

"Yeah," said Howard, pressing down harder, steam billowing up above his head.

"Howard Purlee," Betty Jean yelled.

Howard lifted the presser and slammed it down. He imagined Betty Jean's head, unhinged, on the presser's board. It was flat as a pancake. To get her hen-pecking brain sharp, neat, creased, he pushed down harder on the presser's handle and imagined he was steaming all the stupid and wrinkled nonsense out of her head. And when he was finished, and had lifted the big presser's handle, she was the perfect wife. She was quiet, gentle, cute and subservient like she used to be. When the billows of steam went up through the ceiling's exhaust the real Betty Jean was standing before him.

"How many times do I have to call you, Howard? Come out of this steamin' snake pit, sweatin' like a red pig? You look like a man that's done lost his mind."

"Go on back outside and get in the damn car, Betty Jean. I'll be there."

Betty Jean's quiet, submissive, and shy ways were gone. She had a brash and defensive tongue. She used it to defend her unrealistic views and false knowledge of news making subjects around the entire world.

Her made-up knowledge went as far as a person could take it without their brain exploding. With evidence confirming cigarettes cause cancer, Betty Jean believed they didn't. She would argue the point with anyone brave enough to talk about it. She was hard hitting, gesticulating, and penetrating when defending the tobacco companies. She could split open the most skeptical ears with her biting and high-pitched tones that shouted cigarettes were good for the mind, body, and spirit.

With all the medical and scientific knowledge that says morphine tablets are addictive, and a derivative of the poppy plant, Betty Jean said the pills were not addictive. She said morphine was a derivative of the American backyard daisy and that the government was covering up the truth because they didn't want the American people growing yellow daisies to make their own morphine, opium, and heroin. In her opinion anyone had the right to grow yellow daisies for whatever purpose. When asked why she had not grown yellow daises in her own back yard? Betty Jean said she didn't have time to grow stupid flowers.

She had empowered herself with fantasies of her own truths, of scientific fact, while never having read or seen any television program about the subject. Her unrealistic intelligence made her feel important. She was a non-stop chatter box about the universe, the bible, heaven, God and the angels. Those who were gullible and intrigued by her feisty and defensive tongue listened intently to all she had to say. Most of them walked away believing they were dead wrong and Betty Jean was right.

Mike and Annette Cleaver, a young couple that lived in the trailer across from Betty Jean, told her she should have been a preacher. However, on a hot afternoon of unusual dry heat they changed their minds.

On the day in question Betty Jean sat on the steps of her trailer beside her daughter Rachel. They were watching Annette Cleaver water the flower garden she planted near the back end of her trailer.

"That's a damn fool," Betty Jean told Rachel, looking at Annette.

"Huh," said Rachel. "Who are you talking about mama?"

"Her." She pointed to Annette Cleaver.

"Why is she a damn fool?"

"What idiot would water flowers in this kind of dry heat?"

"I don't see anything wrong with it," said Rachel.

"That's because you don't know anything about Mother Nature. When this heat dries up that water she sprayed, on the petals of those roses, will make them dry up and die. Watch and see what happens."

"Go tell her, mama. Go tell her."

"Bring me the telephone."

Rachel went inside and came back out with the phone's receiver. Betty Jean dialed Annette's number. When her phone rang, Betty Jean watched her turn off the water hose and run inside her trailer. Annette answered the phone.

230

"Hello, this is Betty Jean. Sweetheart you are making a big mistake. You should never water flowers on hot dry days like this. When that water dries up those rose petals will be burnt to a crisp. You better find something to dry up that water. You'll regret it if you don't. You know I'm right."

She thanked Betty Jean for the pertinent information and hung up the phone. Not long after Annette came out of her trailer with a blow dryer attached to a long and orange power cord. She blow dried her flower bed. Betty Jean and Rachel watched her for more than fifteen minutes. When Annette was finished her bed of flowers shriveled up and died.

Betty Jean was hysterical with laughter. "I knew that woman was a damn fool, a real bimbo. Lord, I knew it."

When Annette Cleaver told her husband what happened to her flower bed he became frantic. He marched across the walkway to the door of Howard and Betty Jean's trailer. He banged on it as hard as he could. Howard opened the door expecting to see someone in an emergency need, but he found Mike Cleaver stuttering mad.

"Tell that crazy-ass bitch, from hell, to stay away from my wife. If she comes near us again, I might take my shot gun and shoot her like she was a rabid dog. You hear me Howard. You tell her what I said."

"I believe she already heard you," said Howard. "Whatever happened I'm sorry for it." He was used to the expected where Betty jean was concerned.

Not long after the incident another trailer park had come to the interest of the Cleaver's. He and his wife moved to it.

After they were gone Betty Jean, dressed in her night clothing with a small shovel in her hand, walked over to the empty space where the trailer had been. She dug up Annette Cleaver's neglected rose bed and then planted them in her own. That was the kind of person Betty Jean had become.

It was early evening. They were on their way back home from Atlanta's Federal Prison. All the car windows were rolled down, because Betty Jean smoked a chain of cigarettes. Her silence was a sad quiet. Their visit to see their twenty-year old son, Crawford, had depressed her.

"Pull over," Betty Jean told Howard. He ignored the request. "Pull over. Pull over right now, Howard. My brain feels like it's tryin' to break out."

Betty Jean closed her eyes and hugged her own self as tight as she could. Her expressions were those invoking pity and sympathy.

"We'll be home in a few minutes," said Howard.

"Pull over," she screamed, frantic. "Pull over, pull over. Pull over."

"Alright," said Howard. "I'm pullin' over. Don't get yourself worked up."

He made his way cautiously across the three lanes of busy traffic. He pulled over and parked close to the railing. Betty Jean could not open the door and get out of the car like she sometimes did.

"You just had a cigarette, Mama," said Rachel.

"I'm havin' another one. I need another one. Is there a law against cigarettes?"

"I'm sorry, Mama. It's okay."

Howard looked at Betty Jean and saw that her hands were shaking. She drank her coffee and lit her cigarette. "What kind of condition," asked Howard "causes somebody to walk around with a sac of water in their head? You should be dead by now."

"You'll die before me because you're a mean man. Mean men die early. One day, they just drop dead right where they're standin'. When it happens to you, Howard, I'll be right there to bury you as deep as I can."

"You shouldn't say those kinds of things," said Howard. "You know you don't mean it."

Betty Jean unrolled her cloth-pill container. All seven pouches contained a prescription vile. She removed three pills and swallowed them, washing them down with coffee.

233

"Nicotine, caffeine, morphine," said Howard, "You're addicted to everything with I.N.E. on the end of it."

He felt grief in his heart for Betty Jean. He believed it was something else beside their son that lowered her down into deep depression. He often wondered what happened to his wife when she was a child, before she was adopted. What happened to the brother she never talked about and what caused her to live in a world of made-up fantasies? Why did she make up diseases and spread them to herself?

It was dark when the old Chevy pulled up and parked next to their trailer. Betty Jean reached over the back seat and shook Rachel until she awakened, and when she looked out of the rear window she saw the man with two envelopes in his hand.

ANGELA
GOD LOVES ME BECAUSE SOMEBODY HAS TO

To step back and take a good look at Angela the total was easy to figure and the receipt gave no change. Her physical self was enriched with junk-food. She had disregard for cleanliness and wore big motherly clothes. If one didn't know she had a home, two children, and a car, she could have easily been mistaken for a malicious homeless woman. The beauty about her was her flawless auburn skin and thick wavy hair that sprung out, away from her head, wild and free. Underneath her heaviness a pretty woman could be seen, slightly.

Evergreen Church of God and Christ was in the heart of Watts California. It was a small church with a congregation of one-hundred and fifty local residents. Every Sunday Angela and her two children attended the morning and sometimes early evening services. When the plate was passed Angela contributed as much money as she could spare. God, church, and Christ were an essential part of her life.

Sunday morning services were over. Angela held on tightly to the hands of her two children as if someone wanted to steal them. She marched them toward the full parking lot where members of the congregation lingered and talked in groups around their cars.

Her six-year old daughter, Little Jimmy, stumbled along and had almost fallen many times. She could not keep up with the angry pull of her mother's hand.

Angela did not stop pulling her. "Keep up the pace, Little Jimmy," Angela told her. "Quit laggin' behind."

Abraham, Angela's eight-year old son was small for his age. He learned a musical way of keeping up with his mother. He listened to the music playing in his head and pretended to be dancing at the speed of her demanding walk.

When Angela passed by some of the members of the congregation, she looked ahead and turned up her nose. She thought

235

them to be worth no more than a day's old garbage. Under her breath she called them raw-chicken trash. Near to her parked car, she walked by a group of women. They were gathered close, whispering, looking at Angela and her two nervous children.

Knowing the women were whispering about her Angela turned her head, looked at them, and like a child she stuck her tongue out and rolled her eyes. She opened the driver's door of her car. Little Jimmy and Abraham climbed onto the backseat.

One of the whispering women broke away from the group. Her walk was confident and determined. Angela was preparing to get into her car when she felt the women's slight tap on her shoulder.

"Angela," said the young woman, sweetly. "Angela."

She turned to face the young woman and her face was awash with the type of anger that scares a person. It was a violent look, as if something along the lines of a hatchet murder was about to occur.

"What do you want?" asked Angela.

"A few members of the congregation thought it would be a great idea to get together for lunch at my home this afternoon. We would like for you to join us."

"For what reason?"

"It's for the church, to discuss the food drive. You can bring the children," she added.

"The church?" questioned Angela. She thought if God was involved it might be okay. When she looked over the young

236

woman's shoulder at the rest of the whispering women she believed them to be smiling slyly at her.

"No. I'm not gonna give you bitches more of me to laugh at. No thank you."

The young woman was shocked. She did not know Angela had the nastiest of cursing mouths. She walked away and looked back at Angela's two children. They were crouching down low on the backseat. The sorrow the young woman felt for the children caused tears to run down her cheeks.

Angela's blue Neon sped by the group of women. She looked out of her window and stuck her tongue out at them. One of the women had the courage to give her the finger.

During the drive Angela's thoughts went to her ex-husband Mark. She pulled over to the curb, leaving the engine running. She picked up her cell phone and dialed his number. Mark's pretty girlfriend answered the phone.

"Let me speak to Mark, you slutty-dumb whore."

He was shaving and getting ready for work. Mark was a compassionate and caring man. He was in his late forties. One of the city's most admired fire fighters. To step back and take a look at him, he was a handsome man who aged prematurely.

Mark's girlfriend walked into the bathroom. From the look of fear on her face he knew who was on the phone. He took the receiver from her.

237

"What Angela?" he asked, speaking into the receiver. Her indecipherable screaming had cut through and into the meat of his ear. The cruel voice broke his last nerve and he hung up on her.

Angela was enraged. Her heavy breathing fogged the front window. She forced a quick gun of the gas pedal, driving over the speed limit. Abraham and Little Jimmy held hands throughout their mother's speeding ride of fist banging and cursing terror.

She parked recklessly in front of the apartment building where Mark lived. One tire sat the car up high on the curb. She got out and slammed her door, causing the little neon to rock back and forth. Abraham's nervous hand rolled the window all the way down. Their need to hear their father's argument with their mother did not make them angry. They were happy to hear he was still alive. Their mother's violent temper had not driven her to kill him, eat him for a midnight snack, and throw his bones out to the rats and cockroaches the way she threatened.

Angela knocked on the apartment door. She could see the movement of the pretty girlfriend through the peephole. After the door opened Angela grabbed the girlfriend by the arm and snatched her into the corridor. She then pushed her to stumble, crookedly, down the stairs and to the bottom of the stairs landing. The girlfriend looked up to say something to Angela, but she was inside the apartment locking the door.

Mark came into the living room and met the crash, of a small table lamp, slamming against the side of his head. It broke into pieces and fell on the floor around him. The force, of Angela's blow, was so strong that a shard of the light bulb merged behind his ear and was sticking out. It stayed there like a strange nail.

He stumbled backward and rested against the wall. He was dazed, scared, and shaking. He thought of killing Angela, beating her until her lights went out. There would be nothing clever or accidental about it. It would be pure murder. It took great will and physical effort to stop his self from doing it. She was the mother of his children.

Angela grabbed his hair and pulled his head down in between her breast. "Do not ever hang up on me you sorry piece of shit. They will always be your children. You will pay me the money to raise your fuckin' seeds." She shoved him against the wall. She went and unlocked the door. She grabbed the pretty girlfriend, by the arm, out of the corridor, and into the apartment. She left and slammed the door behind her.

Angela sped away from the building like a race car driver gone insane. Abraham and Little Jimmy knew their father was still alive. They heard him screaming at his girlfriend. "Bring me a towel. I'm bleeding. I might need stitches."

After parking her car to cry and curse herself, groceries were bought and gas for the Neon. When she pulled into the driveway in front of her home, in Watts, she saw the disheveled-young man holding two envelopes in his hand.

October 3, 2003

CHAPTER NINE
THE MEETING PLACE

8:09 A.M.

Green-plastic chairs were scooted up to a long table that resembled thick-grey tin. There was enough room to seat the six of them tightly. The room was inside the new administrative wing of the prison and was a place for lawyers to visit more than one client.

Meeting the first two Walker siblings had given Mae odd feelings, the kind that tickle and flutter under the skin, like immature birds looking for pecking time in places where hawks fly.

"This door has to be locked," Mae told Danny and Neda.

"That's fine with me," said Neda.

"I don't see any wild and dangerous women runnin' loose," said Danny, "It might be interestin' if I did." He was flirting with Mae.

"Locking this door is for your own protection," said Mae, ignoring the pass.

"Sure," said Danny, "whatever, chief."

Mae added additional force when she slammed the steel of the door into the frame of the steel pane, rattling the room's flimsy plastic chairs and marred table. According to prison legality the door only needed locking after a prisoner's arrival, but knowing

241

some of Ruby's story, Mae wanted the Walker siblings to feel the discomfort that comes with the loss of freedom. To know what time standing still and shiftless was like in prison.

If there were any knocking on the door, caused by nervous changes of mind to leave, Mae would be on the other side of the prison. She was on her way to see Ruby, to tell her the party had started. To get there she would take intentional advantage of walking slow, pausing time, stopping to chat with inmates and guards passing by. Worry of other personnel discovering a locked door with civilians behind it was not of concern. It was Mae's click of colleagues working the prison until late afternoon.

After Mae's slow walking and chatting time was done she stood at the entrance of Ruby's opened cell. She found her pacing rapidly. Her hands were on her hips and her eyes stared out at something not there.

"If I could walk these tiers," said Mae, "as fast as you're walking back and forth inside this hole, I would lose twenty pounds a day."

Ruby stopped and looked at Mae. "Who's here, which ones?"

"Freddie didn't have but one boy, right?"

"Yes." She was anxious to hear more.

"Well, he's here with one of the girls, one of the black ones."

"What she look like?"

242

"Big pretty eyes, wavy-black hair, big boobs, small waist and wide hips. She's real pretty.

"That's my Neda." She sat on the edge of her bunk and covered her face with her hands.

"I'll be back to get you when they're all here."

A voice came through the communication device attached to the shoulder of Mae's shirt. She was given the news of another arrival.

For Danny and Neda a little over forty minutes had passed.

"Open the fuckin' door," Danny said, banging on it, yelling, looking out at the prison corridor from the door's port window. "There's no fuckin' toilet in here."

"Stop it," said Neda. "When did you become so claustrophobic?" She thought of his crooked ways. She knew the potential loss of his own freedom was making him nervous.

Danny looked out from behind the window. He saw Mae. A woman followed behind her. He moved away from the door and Mae unlocked it.

"Excuse me, chief," said Danny, "there's no toilet in here.

Mae stepped aside and Betty Jean came in. Danny's heart dropped where he couldn't catch it before it fell. The last time he saw his baby sister she was the picture of health—a quiet, shy, sweet-country girl. He thought she looked half dead and was too thin. She looked older than him and Neda. She was still so red and

243

freckled. He remembered how he used to touch the red hair and say give me some luck B.J. He wondered if she forgave him for running off and leaving her alone with the Montana's.

"Betty Jean," said Danny.

"Hello, Betty Jean," said Neda, putting her arms carefully around her sister. She was unsure if it was okay to do that.

Betty Jean returned the embrace. Danny went and put the length of his long arms around the both of them. They stayed that way for awhile with Mae looking on at them.

"You still gotta use the toilet?" Mae asked Danny.

"No," he said. "It can wait."

She stepped out of the room and again, using additional force, slammed the steel of the door into the frame of the steel pane, shaking the room to rattle the three of them and whatever else was loose inside it.

When they pulled back, to look at the other, Betty Jean wiped Neda's tears away with her fingers. "Neda, you're still so beautiful." She looked at Danny, "You too, Danny."

"Yeah, you too. You look great."

"Don't lie," said Betty Jean, "I know I look like an ugly ole thorn ridin' a broom."

When Parker got the call, from Mae, she told him she was on her way to pick up the last of the Walker sibling. He was in the small town of Etchings eating breakfast at the local coffee shop. The

244

employees buzzed with taking care of him. His large tips made the difference; especially, on days when they weren't given any. He felt no need to rush, wanting to give the siblings enough time to reacquaint themselves.

"Didn't I say walk behind me?" Mae told Angela. "I didn't say walk beside me, or in front of me." Angela stopped walking. A chill from a strange gust of wind, where there should be no draft, startled her.

"I don't see no reason for it."

"It's for your own protection," said Mae. "This is a prison. This is not a hospital or a high school. Follow directly behind me, single file." Mae continued her slow walk down the corridor. She looked over her shoulder to make sure Angela was obeying her unnecessary rule.

Arriving at the door, as if angry with her keys, Mae hit the ring on the steel door and separated the keys to fall away from the one she needed. The noise of the big keys bothered Angela.

Mae opened the door and then looked at Angela. "Inside," she told her. Angela hesitated. "I can't stand here and hold this door open, inside please."

Angela stepped inside the room. Her eyes looked at other things besides her brother and sisters. She went and sat in the chair next to Betty Jean. When she looked into Betty Jean's eyes she grunted and moved her chair.

245

"Angela," said Betty Jean. "How good it is to see you."

"Yeah, uh huh," said Angela.

"You look great," said Danny. He wanted to tell her she was too fat and looked like a crazy homeless person.

"You really do," said Neda, "look great."

"I'll be glad when this is all over with," said Angela. "I live in California. I have two kids to take care of."

"I have two kids too," said Betty Jean. "Isn't that funny?"

"No." Angela told her.

"I don't have any children," said Neda. "I've never been married."

"Oh, I'm sorry," said Betty Jean with sadness.

"Don't be," said Neda. "It was my decision."

"Angela looked at Neda. "You talk like a Mexican. You still think you're a Puerto Rican." She giggled over her comment.

"What about you, Danny?" asked Betty Jean, "Married, any children?"

He remembered how the knowledge of their existence could ruin his life. "I'd rather not discuss my personal life," said Danny. His eyes warned Neda not to say anything.

"Sure," said Betty Jean. "I completely understand. We should not talk about our personal lives unless we feel the need to purge."

"Purge what?" said Angela. "Where the hell did you get that southern accent?"

"I live in beautiful Atlanta Georgia."

"Figures," Angela replied.

"Figures what?"

"Just figures, figure it out," said Angela.

"I'm not the same ole Betty Jean, Angela."

"Good for you. I'm glad you decided to change."

"There was never anything wrong with me."

"My kids need me home," said Angela. "As soon as this crap is over with I'm leavin'."

Ruby stepped out of her cell and onto the busy tier of inmates. Some of the women passing by complimented her on hair and makeup and told her how pretty she looked. When she saw Mae, she went back inside the cell and took another look at her face in the mirror.

Mae came in. "Come on, time to go," Ruby couldn't move. "Why are you standin' there like that?"

"Do I look okay?"

"You look good enough for that brood."

"They're all here?"

"Yes. I don't know if I just met the devil's concubine or the bastard himself. I think you should consider yourself lucky. You might have been raisin' a demon."

247

"You're talkin' about Angela."

"Whatever name Satan gave her."

"I guess she hasn't changed," said Ruby, walking beside Mae, down the tier. "It could be seen if she had."

They had run out of things to say. They fitted themselves inside moments of caution by scratching where there was no itch, clearing their throat where there was no mucus, shifting needlessly.

The jangle of keys, keys in the lock, lock opening, door opening. Parker walked in with Ruby beside him. They brought with them the gust of strange wind where there was no draft.

"You still have to go to the toilet," Mae asked, looking at Danny. "You better do it now."

"No," said Danny. "I'm all good, chief." He smiled at Mae, flirting again. She rolled her eyes and looked away from him.

Mae stepped out of the room. She added additional force when she slammed the steel of the door into the frame of the steel pane, putting more emphasis on the sound of keys turning the bolt of the heavy lock.

"I'm glad to see everyone is here," said Parker. He pulled a chair out for Ruby to sit down and then sat in the chair next to her. They were across the table looking at the four siblings. No chairs were at the head of the table.

Parker glanced briefly at them. His eyes met Danny's.

248

"I remember you," said Danny, looking at Parker. Parker smiled at him.

Ruby kept her eyes on Parker's hands. She watched him open his briefcase and take out a legal pad, pencil, and the manila folder containing the information he needed.

"Parker Bishop," right, "said Danny."

"Yes. That's my name."

"Yeah," said Danny. "I remember you like it was yesterday."

"I remember you too, Danny." He looked at the four of them. "All of you."

"If you had of lived up to your part," said Danny, "maybe none of this would have happened.

"Danny," said Neda. "We didn't come here to discuss the past. Forget about it."

"You her lawyer?" asked Angela, pointing to Ruby.

"No, I'm taking care of legal matters involving your mother's estate."

"Estate," said Neda, curious.

"I do have a lawyer," said Ruby. She tossed a business card in front of Angela. "That's his card. If you need to call him, you can." Angela turned her head away from Ruby's gaze. "He's the one to talk to."

249

"You mean he wants to tell us what to say in front of that review board," said Angela. "I know what to say. I hope you rot and die in here the same way she did. That's all I have to say."

Ruby lowered her head, but not because of Angela's mean words. If she looked too much at them her heart would break. She did not want to cry over what she gradually considered lost causes. She was disappointed in herself for having failed at teaching strong-minded children to be resilient enough. What she saw were four, weak, ungrateful and sniveling human beings. They were not as smart as she believed. She thought, maybe, during the short time of raising them, she should have never pushed them to live up to the expectation of being anything else other than completely fucked up.

"What's this about the house?" asked Betty Jean.

"They should've torn the goddamn hell hole down," said Angela.

"According to your mother's last will, and testament," said Parker, while reading a piece of paper, "she left the four of you her share of the house. The other half still belongs to Ruby."

"Great," said Danny, looking at his watch. "If that's it I have to go. Ruby, it was good to see you again. If you want Jimmy Tate made out to be Frankenstein I have no problem with that. I'll do what I can to help you. My sisters can have my share of the house. I have a home. I don't need it." He stood.

"Sit down, Danny," Parker told him, "We're not finished."

250

"Please Danny, stay," said Betty Jean. "The four of us can leave together. "We can go someplace and have lunch."

"No thank you," said Angela.

"I meant the three of us," said Betty Jean. "I didn't expect you to come, Angela."

"Okay," said Danny, sitting. He looked at his watch and then at Parker. "Hurry up, pal. What are we missing? Say it and get it over with."

Parker turned the pages of the legal papers. It was time to let them know the rest of it. What their mother had done would not flow easily onto the table.

"Was there any money saved up?" asked Neda. "If there was you must agree we deserve it."

"Your mother did leave some cash and other assets," said Parker.

"What assets?" Danny asked.

"Your mother's shares in Leland Electronics."

"Shares," said Betty Jean. "Like stock-market stuff?"

"Yes," said Parker.

"Humph!" remarked Angela.

"Who did she leave it to?" asked Neda.

"I really don't care," said Angela.

"Nobody asked you to care," yelled Neda. "Shut your fat mouth."

251

"Up yours," said Angela. "You look like a bar room slut."

"Everything was left to Ruby," said Parker.

"Give me a break," said Angela. "Whores don't know the value of saving a raw penny. So what kind of fuckin' assets are you talkin' about?"

"God!" said Betty Jean, looking at Angela. "Your mouth is not just filthy it's a trash factory … a nasty ole trash factory."

The excitement of money had put them on the edges of their seat. Ruby saw their flashes of greed and selfishness.

"I can't discuss what she left Ruby without her permission," Parker said.

"Go ahead," said Ruby, "tell them."

"According to her last will and testament," said Parker, "Freddie left Ruby a fairly large sum."

"How large of a sum?" Danny asked.

"Well." He kept his eyes on the papers, reading.

"How much?" Betty Jean asked.

When Parker looked up from his papers, he wanted his eyes to meet Angela's. "Freddie left Ruby a little over sixty-million, give or take a few."

"What?"

"Dollars…"

"Are you crazy?"

"My heart's beatin' too fast," said Betty Jean. "Why isn't there any water on this table? I need a drink of water. I need to take my medication."

"Back up, back up," said Danny. "Everybody calm down, just take a deep breath and relax."

"This ain't no goddamn yoga class you idiot," said Angela.

Danny's thoughts had a ring of authority. He said to his self: These are my sisters. I am the only brother they have. I am now in charge of their entire life. Like it or not the sick bitches will listen to me, their brother. They are too fuckin' stupid to figure this out all by themselves. He looked at Parker. "You did say 'sixty million give or take a few dollars, meaning cash?"

"Like real money," said Neda, "like big-mucho dollars?"

"Yes," said Parker. "There would be more if your mother had sold her shares in Leland Electronics which was also left to Ruby."

"I remember that name," said Neda.

"Me too," said Betty Jean.

"The cell phone company?" asked Danny, looking at Parker. "Like this cell phone." He removed his phone from his pocket and tossed it on top of the table. The name read: Leland Communications. Parker picked up the phone, looked at it, and put it back on the table.

"Yes," he told Danny.

253

Danny's laughter was meant to be held inside but it poured out of him. He was thinking about Jimmy Tate. The dead bastard had been screwed out of millions. His mother was a fucking genius.

Ruby knew what was causing Danny's laughter. Why Freddie had done such a thing made her laugh many times.

"How much are the shares worth, our shares?" asked Neda, looking sternly at Ruby.

"Nothin'," Ruby said, returning Neda's cold stare. "Every piece of paper down to the last word, every penny down to the last cent of the last million dollars, belongs to me."

"The hell it does," said Danny. "He looked over at his sisters. "My family will fight you Ruby. All of it rightfully belongs to us."

"Oh, excuse me, Mr. Gold Watch," said Angela. "When did we suddenly become a family? After this day, I don't want to see anybody in this room ever again. Look at my face. Do I look excited to any of you?"

"Why don't you just shut your trash-filthy mouth," said Betty Jean.

"I don't want her dirty whore money," said Angela. "If I took one dime my children and I would burn in hell. I ain't goin' to hell over whore money."

The jangle of keys, keys in the lock, lock opening, door opening. When Mae walked into the room it had grown deadly silent.

"Excuse me, Mr. Bishop," said Mae. "Is there any assistance needed in this room?"

"We're fine, chief," said Danny, looking at Mae. There was no flirting. He wanted her to leave immediately.

Ruby wanted to laugh because she knew Mae was getting a kick out of it all. Mae knew from the expressions on their faces that they received the bad news. It looked as if the two kinds of color had all turned beat red.

"If it's okay," said Ruby, looking at Mae. Her tone of voice was soft, gentle, as if she needed time to reprimand her own unruly children for misbehaving in a grownup place. "I would like some time alone with them. No more than ten minutes."

"You've got ten minutes," Mae said, stern about it. "Would you like a cup of hot coffee, Mr. Bishop?"

"Yes," Parker replied. "I could use a cup of coffee. Thank you." He stood and left the room. Mae slammed the steel door hard into the steel frame, locking it.

There were strained moments of silence.

"I've been in here too long," said Ruby. "I don't want to die in here like your mother did."

"I understand that," said Danny.

255

"I didn't kill Jimmy Tate without good reason. It was justifiable."

"I may not remember everything," said Angela. She pointed her finger at Ruby. "I saw you, Ruby Johnson. I saw you as clear as I see you now. I saw you pick up that gun, point it, and pull the trigger. I saw that bullet slam into my father's head. It was cold-blooded murder."

"I know what you saw, Angela," said Ruby. "I'm sorry you had to witness such a thing."

"I've hated you all my life," said Angela. "I won't stop hating you to help you, not for money. I'll never forget what I saw, what you did."

"Shut up, Angela," said Danny. "Just shut up."

There were more strained moments of silence.

Ruby glanced at the four of them. "I don't know who I'm more ashamed of." She looked at Danny.

"Are you talkin' to me?"

"Yes," said Ruby. You may know how to act like an intellectual but the truth is you ain't nothin' but a liar and a loser. I'm ashamed of you Daniel Walker, runnin' whores up and down Lake Shore Drive. That cafe and that new restaurant is only a front to hide behind. I know you're mixed up in every lowdown sinful thing a person could get involved in. How long do you think you'll be able to hide your crimes without bein' put in one of these places?

Your time is runnin' out. You built yourself a family on top of deceit. You couldn't resist putting on Jimmy Tate's shoes. You broke my heart, Daniel Walker."

Danny leaned back, took a deep breath, and nearly fell out of his chair. Betty Jean was crying. Neda tried to comfort her. Angela did not take her eyes off Ruby. She knew her assessment was coming.

"And you," Ruby said, looking at Neda. "I almost took pity on you when I found out about what happened to your child. If you had been home with her instead of leaving her alone in that apartment she wouldn't have climbed up in that window. That child fell to her death because you were too busy shakin' your tits and ass all over the city of Chicago, sleepin' with every piece of scum that fell out its mama's ass, shame on you."

"You ain't got no right to judge nobody in this room," said Neda. "spyin' on people. I had to make a livin'."

"You didn't have to disrespect yourself in the process," Ruby told her. "I thought you were smarter than that."

"You start in on me," said Angela, "I will jump across this table and snap your neck like a carrot. That bitch-ass guard will have to find someplace in here to put me."

"Oh, yeah, you're good at hurtin' people" said Ruby, "even your own children. You're a big-fat bully. You back up your evil with your fist. Your trashy mouth helps you put your hot ass into

257

action. How many times you take Little Jimmy to the hospital because you beat her? Two times you broke the bones of your own child. She didn't fall down the stairs. You don't have stairs in that house you live in, in Watts. Yes I know where you live too. Naming that girl after that monster you call your daddy. You're supposed to be so religious, a real bible-totin' extremist-fool. Rollin' around on the floor of that church like a fool screamin' save me Lord. Save me from the devil. I'm surprised that church didn't fall down, on top of you, when you walked in the door. You are a hypocrite of the worst kind, Angela Walker. God has turned a deaf ear to you. He will not answer your prayers, but you can be proud of yourself about somethin'. You are just like your daddy."

"We better get this over with," said Angela, on the verge of tears. "I don't have a gun. I can't blow her head open like she did my daddy's. If she keeps on with it, one of these chairs will do the job just fine."

"Danny, we need some water," Betty Jean told him. "I'm not feeling well. I have a history of fainting spells. I need a fine drink of water."

"Little Miss Pitiful," Ruby said, looking at Betty Jean. You so sick all the time. All that morphine you're puttin' inside your body is messin' up your mind. Milkin' the government out of small change because you're afraid to go out into the world, get a job, and do somethin' constructive with your life. Your doctors told me with physical therapy you can walk without pain."

"That's not true, Miss Ruby," said Betty Jean, crying. "That's not true. My doctors are a pack of quacks. In regard to little miss pitiful, I'm no longer afraid of anything. I've rung the necks of two chickens, one in each hand, and didn't shed a tear. I'm not to be pitied by any of you ever again."

"Okay, Miss chicken killer," said Ruby. "What about that boy of yours locked up in one of these places? He ain't got sense enough to tie his own shoe. You knew he was retarded from the day he was born. They told you he would have the mind of a sixteen-year old for the rest of his life. You pushed that boy to believe he could be president of the United States. He told the police he robbed a bank, on a bicycle, because he needed money for his political campaign."

The silence that comes with the solitude of embarrassment and unwanted regret had filled the room. Angela did not look at any of them. She found her shoes an interesting sight. She thought of how the thick heels were hard enough to bash Ruby's head in.

"Over the years," said Ruby, "your mother kept sayin' I wonder what they look like all grown up. How did they turn out? What do they do for a livin'. The night before she died, handcuffed to a toilet, I told her I've been keepin' track of you. I showed her these."

259

Ruby reached inside her pocket. She tossed a photograph of Danny on the table. It landed in front of him, "I told her Daniel is a successful, respectable, businessman. He still lives in Chicago close to his favorite sister, Neda."

She tossed Betty Jean's photograph on the table in front her, "I told her this one married a rich businessman. Your Betty Jean is a real southern lady of charity. She's always helpin' the poor and needy.

And you, she said to Neda, tossing the photograph in front of her. "I said this one is a school teacher. She wins all kind of awards for the great work she does for children.

And last, but not least," Ruby said, tossing Angela's picture in front of her, "I told her you owned a successful soul-food restaurant in Hollywood. That people come from everywhere just to eat there. When your mama noticed how heavy you were I didn't tell her you're tryin' to eat away all the bad things you've done to people."

Danny stood up. He picked up the picture of himself and tossed it back on the table in front of Ruby. "You can keep that one," he told her. It'll be the last one you ever get." He stood and went to the door, banging on it. He turned and looked at his sisters. "Come on. Get your stuff. We're leavin'."

"I'm not finished." Ruby yelled at them.

260

They ignored her. They stood and went to Danny. He banged on the door.

"The money is rightfully yours," said Ruby, rising to her feet, looking at them.

Danny stopped his banging. The spoken words about money made them turn and face her.

"All I need is you to tell the truth about the kind of man he was," said Ruby. "If you don't, and I have to die in here like your mama, every penny goes to charity."

The jangle of keys, keys in the lock. Mae opened the door, setting them free. And when the strange gust of wind skirted out of the room, following behind them, it sent a chill up and down Mae's spine.

They stood together outside of Gorwin waiting for the bus to arrive and take them back down the hill. The four heads looked up at the low and blackening clouds. The sting of prison grit swirled around them and stayed stuck like glue against their skin and inside their hair. It was the same kind of grit that blew through their mother's opened window on the night Jimmy Tate was killed. The air had the same moldy and wet smell.

When Parker stepped outside Danny was waiting for him. His sisters were sitting on the bus.

"That money belongs to us," Danny told Parker.

"You have no legitimate claim, Danny."

"The hell we don't. We will fight for what rightfully belongs to us."

"I am not the enemy."

"Sure you are, Parker. That night you were supposed to take us with you. You drove away and left us there. This would not have happened if you had kept your word."

"I did keep my word. Your mother did not want to leave Angela behind."

"You know, I really don't give a fuck. I still think you're a coward. You won't get away with this."

"I understand how you feel." He walked away from Danny and toward the bus. Remembering something he stopped. He reached into his coat pocket and removed a set of keys. He tossed them to Danny. "Those are the keys to the house. Your sisters might want to stay there until this is over."

"You know what your problem is?" Danny shouted at the back of Parker, walking away. "Freddie is still controlling your dick from the grave."

Parker stopped walking and stood at the foot of the bus's steps. He kept his back to Danny. "No Danny. I never got a chance to fuck her." It was a mean and nasty thing to say. He climbed the stairs of the bus and sat down with no regrets for saying it.

Danny dropped Betty Jean and Angela off in front of the house. Betty Jean opened the door and Angela walked in behind her.

They were surprised to find the house lit up like the lights had never been shut down. The main room had been redecorated with modern and comfortable furniture except for the same old and red sofa.

Jimmy's gaming tables, they were expecting to see, were gone. The old telephones were working and the whole house was clean and free of dust. Even the hardwood floors were polished to a high shine and repaired in places where chips and blocks of wood were loose or missing. The bedroom Angela and Betty Jean shared, as children, was cleaned and their beds were made.

Nothing much had changed about the kitchen. The same table, chairs, and refrigerator were there. Where Ruby's hand-made curtains used to be there were blinds.

Someone had been taking care of the place. After looking into Miss Ruby's old room and inside the basement, calling out hello, they came to the conclusion that the caretaker had temporarily removed his or her self upon notice of their arrival.

Their mother's bedroom door was closed. They decided against opening it and looking inside, agreeing to do it on another day.

Danny took Neda to her apartment. He told her he would be back to pick her up when the time came for her interview with the board. He told his wife he was leaving town for a few days on business. Neda offered him a place to stay but he didn't feel like listening to her whine and cry over how badly he treated her.

263

Staying at the house was completely out of the question. He had no explanations for Betty Jean regarding why he left her and the Montana's without even saying goodbye.

Later that evening Danny stopped at Best Sellers and did his bookkeeping. After eating dinner he went to the penthouse and checked on his girls. He took some cash out of the safe. It was a slow night so he said nothing when he walked in and saw them lying on sofas watching television and eating pizzas. He grabbed a piece for his self and left the room. He didn't want to spend the night there because they were too talkative and whispering the way women do when they're hiding something.

While checking into a suite, at a hotel downtown, he thought about his pricy-call girls. He thought he should have questioned them about the odd glances they gave him. Under normal circumstances he would have said something.

After he shaved and showered he still couldn't relax. He walked into the living area, picked up the remote control, sat down and clicked on the television. The station was CNN. It was a repeat of Larry King's earlier broadcast. Nancy Grace was his special guest.

A caller was on the phone asking Nancy a question. "If this review board," said the Caller, "doesn't recommend a pardon who does all that money go to? Does she get to keep it? If she doesn't does it go to her kids."

Pictures of the four of them, as adults, came on the screen.

When Nancy Grace replied, "Ruby Johnson is sole heir to Freddie Walker's estate," Danny clicked off the television before she could finish the sentence. He looked like a London ghost never having seen a day of sunshine. There was no sound of anything. There was no time and no universe and his hearing had been lost. There was only a black hole filled with fear, anxiety, and the desperation to repair something immediately. There were brief and poor attempts to try and configure the perfect formula for the perfect lies he would tell his wife—a woman who was raised with the authenticity it takes to be a real racist. Now he new why his call girls were whispering. They had seen the earlier broadcast.

On this same morning, Billy Waller showed up at Parker's office. When he sat down across from Parker's desk, and lit his cigar, he had a smirk on his face. "Did you see CNN last night?"

"Yeah," Parker told him. "I don't know if leaking the story, telling the press where to find them, was a good idea. Three of them have families. Maybe they've been pushed enough."

"Well," said Billy. "Whether we leaked it, or not, all of it was bound to come out anyway. The press would've gotten hold of it because Leland Electronics is a big part of the story. Their mother was a major share holder."

Danny drove up the hill and toward his house. Out on the front lawns children played while their parents stood in groups

265

talking, whispering their curiosity about what was happening on the hill of Bellagio Maria Estates.

Reporters were gathered on Danny's lawn, waiting, speaking into their cameras. News vans were parked on side streets. Danny looked past all of them and kept driving faster than he should up the hill. When he got out of the car the attack was vicious. The cameramen and reporters encircled him within a strong huddle. Pushing his way toward the house, the double life ruining questions began.

"Mr. Walker, the Governor's review board, do you think Ruby Johnson should be pardoned?"

"Will you fight for the money?" asked another reporter.

"Will you and your sister's speak to the review board on Ruby's behalf?"

"Are you African American?"

"Have you been in contact with your sisters?"

"Will you tell the review board about the terrible abuse you suffered at the hands of Jimmy Tate?"

"Is it true your mother died on the toilet, in prison, while handcuffed to a railing?"

"Do you care what happens to Ruby Johnson?"

"Get the fuck off me," Danny told them. He pushed his way to the front door and turned the knob. It made sense that the door was locked. He saw Pat peering out from behind the curtains. Why

266

didn't she open the door for him? He stuck the house key into the lock and when the door opened he still couldn't enter because of the bolt.

"Pat. Open the goddamn door."

The door opened and he walked inside his home. The first thing he heard was crying.

"Why, Danny? Why did you lie?" Pat asked as if someone had murdered her. "You said you were an only child and that your mother, and father, had been killed in a boating accident. You said your Aunt raised you. After she died you had no family left. Is all of that a lie, Danny? Have you seen the news? Your picture is all over the television."

"When this is over," said Danny, "I'll explain everything. I can't do that right now. He was waiting for her to finish blowing her nose. Balled up pieces of Kleenex were strewn about the table like white rose petals.

"Those black women, are they really your sisters? Are you a Negro?" The word Negro had almost caused her to collapse.

"No, Pat," he told her.

"How do you know?"

"To be honest I don't, really."

"So you could be half black, right?"

267

"I guess so." He went and tried to touch her. She pulled away from him. "Look at me, Pat. Look at my eyes and hair. I don't believe I am."

"Some black people are blonder and whiter than you, Danny."

There was movement of a person, the brushing of his body against stiff and heavily starched clothing. The familiar sound rustled somewhere in the kitchen. When Danny heard the extra-slow pouring of a cup of coffee, as if pouring it that slow would make it taste better, he knew who it was.

Pat was born and raised in Arizona. Her father, Benjamin Tyler, fashioned himself as a kind of cowboy. Never having ridden the back of any kind of animal he made his cowboy ways known in the clothing he wore like the typical dark jeans, Wrangler shirt, Stetson hat, and snake-skin boots. His true person was unreadable but his surface person was seen as a tight-lipped seedy-eyed man with a snap way of talking. The stability of his racism had come from watching negative television shows in which minorities were portrayed as gang bangers, murderers, and drug dealers. His follow up of watching the late night news reflected the reality of such violent shows.

Pat was the youngest of four children. When she married Danny her father never approved of the successful, young, and handsome entrepreneur. He told his daughter that somewhere inside

268

Danny was the hiding of something serious, and that one day it would tear her world into shreds of unhappiness.

Benjamin Tyler walked out of the kitchen and into the dining room. He crept quietly behind his daughter and took a sip of his coffee.

"What are you black, white," he said in his snap way of talking, "is my grandson a Negro?"

"To be honest, I really don't know."

"Why is that?" her father asked. "A man should know what he's made of. It doesn't make any sense."

"When you don't know who your father is," said Danny, "I guess it does make sense, Ben."

"I need some time alone," Pat told Danny. "I want you to leave." After she blew her nose into the ball of Kleenex, and tossed it onto the table, he knew that money could save nothing.

Bobby heard his father's voice. He ran into the room and was lifted up and into his father's arms.

"Hi Daddy," said Bobby. He wasn't his usual happy self.

"Hey," Danny said, hugging his son as tight as he could without hurting him.

When Bobby looked up and into the tired eyes of his father he smiled. He wanted to make his father feel better. "Daddy, I don't care if I'm a Negro."

Danny had made up his mind then and there. He would fight to keep his son.

"Can I be on television too?"

"Sure you can,"

Bobby radiated warmth and great gladness, as if God had done something to give him a permanent blessing of a positive outlook on life. It was something about his son that told Danny those qualities would never change.

Pat called down the hill for security. When they came they forced the reporters, and their crews, into their vans and out of Bellagio Maria Estates. Danny said goodbye to his son and wife.

After he drove down the hill, and onto the street, he stopped and looked up at the house. Bobby was smiling, looking down at him from behind a window. It was like the boy was telling him to go, to keep driving down the hill. He was telling his father I'll be here when you come back.

He drove North in the direction of Neda's apartment. He wanted to stay there until it was all over with. He needed to talk it all out with someone, to set the rest of the lies free.

Betty Jean and Angela took a trip to the local supermarket. Angela, in charge of pushing the shopping cart, had almost filled it with items of no real nutritional value. On the other hand Betty Jean had a fondness for yogurt, fruit, and salads. She had chosen the necessary ingredients and food to make a southern breakfast and a pasta dish for their dinner.

"Do you think we should call Danny and Neda and invite them to have breakfast with us?" she asked Angela. "I wonder if Danny still likes to put grape jelly on his pancakes. Remember how he used to do that?"

"No," said Angela. "If they want to come to the house let them do it on their own. I'm not callin' them. I'm not cookin' for nobody but myself."

The butcher handed Betty Jean the pound of bacon she requested, and Angela tossed a package of peanut-butter crackers into the cart.

"For the benefit of health and fitness," said Betty Jean, "not to say that you're fat, or anything like that, but, maybe you shouldn't eat so much junk food. You'd lose weight if you didn't."

Angela came to an immediate stop, permeating with rage. The shopping cart was now her Neon, brakes slamming to a screeching halt. She turned and looked at Betty Jean. "I don't believe you have the audacity to insult me."

"Audacity, now that's a nice word and you didn't add one curse word with it."

"What I tell you, huh?" said Angela. "What did I tell you?"

"About what …?"

271

"I told you if we're gonna stay in that house, together, the best thing you can do is stay the hell out of my way. I don't want to get into with you."

"I think I better warn you, Angela. For the last ten years I've been takin' Karate and Judo lessons. I can protect myself just fine. Don't be fooled by this bad leg."

For the duration of the drive back to the house they said nothing to the other. They turned off 55th Street and onto 54th and Prairie.

"Who are all those people in front of the house," Betty Jean said, "those trucks? Is that a construction crew?"

Angela drove faster and parked in front of the house. "That ain't no goddamn construction crew. Those bastards are reporters."

"Reporters," said Betty Jean. She could see her fifteen minutes of fame coming toward their parked car with a microphone in his hand.

"Get out the car," said Angela. "Go straight into the house. Don't say nothin' to those people."

Betty Jean got of the car and three reporters with their crews and camera's approached her. She smiled into the camera and waved. "Miss Ruby, if you're watchin' this we're goin' to do all we can to help you get out of that awful prison."

272

Angela used her white-plastic purse to beat the reporters and camera crews out of her way. "Get back off me," she told them. "I don't have a damn thing to say to you. Get back."

They let her pass and went to where cooperation was being done. Betty Jean answered as many questions as she could until they got tired of her and she got tired of them.

On this same day Ruby was inside a holding cell at the courthouse. There was the sound of keys opening a door and then fast heels against concrete. After a few moments the bailiff let John inside.

"Where have you been?" Ruby asked. "You said you'd be here by 10:00 A.M. It's almost past 11:00. Some lawyer you are, always late."

"Calm down," he told her. "These things never get started on time."

"And what if they do, huh? Where would that leave me? You should have come yesterday." She started pacing. "I needed to talk to you. I told Parker to remind you that I needed to see you. I have a good mind to call this all off. The kids hate me. It was horrible. They won't say good things about me to those judges. I should just call it off and give them the money. That money doesn't belong to me anyway. As ungrateful and mean as they are the money is theirs."

273

"We've gone over this whole thing numerous times, Ruby. You know what to say. You don't need me anymore."

"Then why in the hell are you here? Go on back where you came from. She walked away and turned her back to him. "Go on, get out of here."

"I came to wish you good luck and to tell you that my prayers are with you. You know my mother isn't much younger than you. This morning when I walked into the kitchen there was nothing to eat on the table. The woman spoils me rotten and never fails to fix me breakfast. I asked her where she was going so early. Do you know what she told me?"

"No," said Ruby.

"She said I'll see you this evening, son. I'm going to the church to light a candle and say a prayer for Ruby Johnson."

Ruby turned and looked at John. "A prayer for me?"

"For you." He held his hand out. She went to him and took it. "There are people you don't even know wishing you the best. They know the story."

"Maybe I'm just scared of sayin' all the wrong things."

"You'll be fine. There's a world waiting to have someone like you back in it. I'll come see you when it's over. Keep a cool head, okay."

"Okay," she said, still not wanting him to leave.

274

After he left she sat down on the bench. When she looked down she saw a penny at the tip of her foot. It was faced down with its back looking up at her. If she stepped on a face-down penny it was bad luck. If she didn't spit on it after stepping on it the bad luck would follow her for ten years. If she did not step on it she couldn't spit on it. She didn't know what to do about the penny.

She thought that most people believed in the superstition of a fine and even equality where good and bad luck touches everyone. Like when the last day of spring is as cold as the last day of January then someone's seven years of bad luck has come to an end. Someone opens up a new bible and the middle pages never having been torn, or worn, fall to the floor then someone's good luck is coming straight from God and the angels. Or when a bird sits on the window sill of a woman's prison cell, for more than five seconds, without flying away, then the woman inside the cell is destined to spend her life in prison. She worried over the bad-luck penny until the bailiff came and got her.

CHAPTER TEN
THE GOVERNOR'S REVIEW BOARD

It was a bright and clean room of considerable size. The sun came in through long-skinny windows and added the kind of cheerful, natural, light that keeps one awake and wakes up one who is sleeping. The mural painted on the wall behind the judge's chairs was the full width, and height, of the wall and all the legal figures had been colorfully painted to merge into the other. They appeared to be young and cool representatives of a new way of handing down the law.

The three judges sat at a long and plain work table. Their just-comfortable chairs did not sit them up high to the notice of their senior legal status.

Judge Marsha Shaw—a petite black woman, in her late sixties, was dressed in a blue-slack suit and pink blouse. The long tails of the blouse were tied into a fluffy bow that relaxed onto the lapels of her jacket. She had ruled over many cases involving women who committed heinous crimes. Her eyes were penetrating and curious with an interest regarding intentions of the heart; especially, where street crimes of passion and adulterous behavior were the key factors to be looked over and considered with caution.

Judge Phillip Bennett was in his early seventies. It was easy to tell he was an alert man and not easily persuaded into thinking there was something good inside the most vicious criminal. He poured over documents and testimonies searching for the truth. And when he found what he was looking for, sure of the facts, truth and lie, he made his decisions based on a fine balance of unbiased opinion. He had ruled over a few special cases involving blacks and whites who came together with good intentions that turned sour, and criminal, and had ended with rulings that cost them their freedom. He did not let race influence his decision making. In the old days he had known other white colleagues who had. He thought often about such cases and remembered his disapproval.

Judge Mitchell Rodriguez was in his late sixties. He was a never-smiling-compact man, bunched to the appearance of balding and grumpy. He was born with tough old man qualities. He had been a family court judge. Before his retirement he ruled over the same bench for over twenty-seven years. The innocence of youth was always his grave concern. He was known for putting the fear of God into any parent, or guardian, for having abused a child. He had given the toughest sentences to those who had done so. For children that relied on him, for their well being while in states of transition, he personally saw to it that social workers did their jobs to his satisfaction.

Besides Ruby Johnson's case the list was long with those complaining of being convicted unjustly by the system's old and unfair procedures of backroom justice. Most of the complainers under review were black, older, and had been put away during the early 1960's and 1970's.

The bailiff removed Ruby's handcuffs and left the room. Across the table from where the judges were sitting was a single chair that matched theirs.

Judge Shaw looked over the rim of her glasses at Ruby. "You can sit down, Miss Johnson. That chair is for you."

Ruby walked to the table and sat in the chair. It wasn't the way Judge Shaw looked over the rim of her glasses, it was the way the judge's eyes found their way to look precisely into hers. The penetrating cold stare made Ruby feel like she was the last piece of trash to be judged and certified as a human being.

"Has your attorney made you aware of the review process?" Judge Rodriguez asked. When Ruby did not answer he stopped writing and looked across the table. "Miss Johnson, has your attorney made you aware of the review process?"

"Yes."

"Do you have any objection in regard to answering questions in descriptive detail?" asked Judge Bennett.

"No."

"Your sentence is life without the possibility of parole, is that correct?" asked Judge Bennett.

Ruby heard the question. She didn't answer. She looked from one judge to the other.

"Your sentence is life without the possibility of parole, is that correct?"

"Yes."

Judge Shaw looked across the table at Ruby. "You now believe that the homicide of Jimmy Tate was justifiable?"

"That's right."

"Please answer yes, or no."

"Yes," said Ruby. "I thought this wasn't a trial."

Judge Shaw ignored the comment. "I'd like to read a brief sentence from the statement you submitted to this board. Quote: "Maybe if I had not killed Jimmy Tate he probably would have killed me and the children too. Is that correct?"

"That's right," said Ruby. "That's what I meant."

"Miss Johnson," said Judge Shaw. "Please answer yes, or no."

"Yes."

"You used the words, "probably" and "maybe,"" said Judge Shaw. "Be clear on one thing, Miss Johnson. When a life is taken, justifiably, you don't use words like, "maybe" and "probably." There is no degree of uncertainty or questioning of judgment, regarding rather to kill or not. If there is then the person that pulled the trigger, taking a human life, will find their selves sitting where you're sitting now. When one is protecting their person, or others such as children, as you claim you were, there can be no hesitation. There can be no doubt."

"Jimmy Tate," said Judge Rodriguez, "and Freddie Walker had a history of domestic violence. Their fighting never ended in murder. Wasn't that your choice?"

"You don't know what it meant for a man like him to lose a woman like her," said Ruby.

"When did you meet Freddie Walker?" asked Judge Shaw.

"August, or July, 1957. I don't remember the date."

"What age were you?" asked Judge Bennett.

"Well," Ruby said. "I guess I must've been about fourteen years old."

JULY 1, 1957

The night was humid and the ground wet after a hard and brief rain. Every existing star shone as bright and clear as the full and low sitting moon. The offering of natural light guided young Freddie down a dirt road that was winding, and was inside the middle of an expansive apple orchard. Trees were in full bloom on either side. Spurts of quick wind came out of the trees and carried the smell of fresh apples.

To step back and take a look at young Freddie, she wore a white low cut blouse and a tight-fitting blue-knit skirt that showed the ample curves of her figure. The skirt stopped just below her knees and the back of her legs, sharp and quick, pushed out of the back slit. One of honesty, or average intuition, could see that something was not right about the look. Behind the makeup, and well developed figure, a child was seen pretending to look like a woman.

She held her high-heeled shoes and a brown paper shopping bag in one hand. Inside the bag were three dresses, two blouses, two skirts, a pink slip, another pair of high heeled shoes, two pair of brown and black flat shoes, a new pair of panties, a size 36C bra, three pairs of black-silk stockings and two garter belts. The bag swayed in rhythm alongside her legs, and kept up with the confident way her bare legs and feet stepped out far and gripped the road.

In the other hand she held a pink leather make up case. Inside it were bottles of red and pink nail polish, tubes of Max Factor Pancake Makeup, a variety of lipsticks and brown eye-liner pencils.

At the end of the road, sitting directly on the edge of it, was the town's only country store and gas station. It had the rarity of having two pumps. The owner, Thornton Willis, was a young man in his late twenties. He had an adolescent lively face and submitting demeanor of customer service.

Freddie put her shoes on and walked up the steps of the store's front porch. Behind a stack of empty crates, lined against the porch wall, she noticed a foot in a boy's black boot sliding out of view. She ignored the foot and entered the store.

When she walked in Thornton snapped to attention. The first thing he noticed was the shopping bag and make-up case she sat on the wooden floor.

He looked across the counter. "Hi, Freddie. Where you off to? Going someplace special?"

She glided from one aisle to the next and ignored his questions in the nonchalant way she ignored all men and all questions. "How much you want for a carton of cigarettes, Thornton Willis?"

"Gee, I don't know. How much you want to pay?"

She was gathering items of canned food, snacks, and lunch meats from the store's refrigerator.

"How much you want to pay? I didn't know you smoked cigarettes."

"There's a lot you don't know about me, Thornton Willis." She walked up to the counter and placed her items onto it. Taking notice of the rack of newspapers, she lifted the one she wanted. "Why Thornton Willis, when did you start carryin' the Wall Street Journal?"

"Since I found out you like reading it. How much you want to pay for that carton of cigarettes? I've got some Camels on sale. Everybody's smoking them. They're real popular right now."

"Oh, I don't know." She walked up closer to the counter. "My panties and everything else, under this old skirt, is soaked through. I just love walkin' in the rain." She traced her hands over her body and pretended to straighten out her clothing.

"Yeah, I can see that. They look a little damp. Not all that wet. I think you'll survive."

His thoughts were focused on the reality of the rare occasion. Would he be the grown man to watch her pale hands peel and slip off the damp clothing? If this was the night Freddie Walker was leaving town for good, and he was the one, he could speak the unspoken words about her freely to the other men. There would be no repercussions from her jealous father.

Freddie looked up at the brand new suitcase sitting on the shelf above the counter. "Where's that pretty wife of yours?"

"Visiting her mother. She won't be back until tomorrow night. Why you ask?"

Thirty minutes later she had a Wall Street Journal tucked under her arm, a new suitcase, and a paper bag overflowing with groceries. She walked out of the store, onto its front porch, and sat the suitcase and bag of groceries against the porch banister. She sat on the steps, removed a Camel cigarette, and lit it. The sound of a muffled sneeze came out from behind the crates.

"Bless you," said Freddie. "You better come out from behind those crates. You can be sure rats are back there with you, big ones."

Fourteen-year old Ruby Johnson emerged. The hopsack green dress she wore was wet from the rain that pooled around the crates and under the back of her. To hide her crying face, she held her head down and turned it away from Freddie's gaze.

"If I was you," said Freddie, "I'd take that old-ugly hat off and throw it in the trash. It does nothin' for you."

"It's not old," said Ruby. "It's brand new, ain't been worn but twice."

"What you doin' back there behind those crates? You ain't from around here. I know all the colored families this part of Indiana. And with that crazy southern accent, like the one you got, I'd say you from some place deep in the south. Someplace that ain't even on the map."

"I'm from Jackson Mississippi," said Ruby, still holding her head down, eyes away from Freddie. "It's on the map, probably bigger than this whole place. I'll be leavin' here soon. I just got caught in the rain."

"It ain't rainin' no more." Freddie held out the palm of her hand just to make sure. "Looks like we both poor and broke with no place to go in any direction."

"I know which direction I'm goin'," said Ruby, defensive. "And I ain't poor and I ain't broke. You talk like you from someplace south as much as me."

"That's because I'm originally from Tampa Florida. That's where I was born. I lived there until I was ten years old then my daddy moved us to this dead doggone town. "What's your name?"

"Ruby ..."

"Does Ruby have a last name?"

"Johnson."

"I'm Freddie Walker, pleased to meet you Ruby Johnson." She extended a hand for Ruby to shake. After a few moments of hesitation Ruby walked closer and placed her hand into Freddie's and shook it. "Sit down and take a load off." She made room for Ruby to sit on the step next to her.

"Freddie is a boy's name," said Ruby.

"Yep, sure is. Everybody always kid me about it especially boys. I hate the little bastards ... Cigarette?"

"No thanks." Ruby scooted closer to the edge of the step. She did not want to sit too close.

"So, Ruby Johnson, what's the story behind you and those crates?"

THE SAME NIGHT
KEEP GOIN'

Everything a poor and desperate family owned was tied to the back, sides, and roof of an old gray and rusty truck that had been salvaged from a Mississippi junk yard. The bed of the truck, its back windows, and metal framing had been removed and then converted into an enclosed compartment for Ruby and her three younger brothers. It was just past 9:00 P.M. when the truck pulled up and parked in front of Thornton's store. The stop had occurred because of Ruby's need to pee.

"You hurry up, girl," said Ruby's father, "we losin' time."

Ruby climbed over the front seat and onto her mother's lap. When she got out of the truck she turned and looked at it. She ran up the steps of the store's front porch and opened the screen door. "Hey, Mr.," she said to Thornton. "You got a toilet I can use?"

"Not for no colored folks," said Thornton, noticing that the raggedy looking black girl was bouncing up and down on the balls of her feet. She was desperate to pee but not on herself. "You can use those bushes out back."

Inside the truck Ruby's mother did not cry. She was too worn down to know the difference of what was right, or wrong, where Ruby was concerned.

286

"Mississippi wasn't the place to leave her behind," said Ruby's father. She'll be fine here in the North."

"How will she find her way to her own kind?" asked Ruby's mother.

"This Brian Indiana," said her father. "They say lots of colored folks live here. I put that twenty dollar bill in her boot. Somebody will take her in and put her to work."

Ruby found the bushes. After relief she pulled up her panties and straightened out her clothing. When she stepped out from behind the bushes she saw the old truck driving fast, away from the store. She had a brief thought to chase behind it. Another brief thought told her it would do no good.

"That's pure cold blooded," said Freddie.

"My mama and daddy was wrong. I got the feelin' colored people treated worse here in the North."

"Colored people treated bad everywhere. That's just the way the world is right now."

"What about you?" asked Ruby.

"See that big ole apple orchard down the road? My daddy owns more apple trees than that. He grows watermelons and cantaloupes too."

"You must be rich."

"Not like the fancy people you read about in magazines. Not like those New Yorkers that live on Park Avenue. My daddy's pretty well off but he's a real cheap man. In the morning when he walks into my room he won't find nothin' but them old dolls in my bed."

"What about your mama?"

"She died when I was three. By the time I was eleven my daddy couldn't take his eyes off me, then he couldn't take his hands off me, then he got real mad when somebody else put their hands on me. Now, my affection for more hands than his is something I can't shake."

"No brothers and sisters?"

"No. My mama wasn't around long enough. It was just me, my daddy, and Miss Miller the housekeeper."

Ruby noticed the newspaper lying on Freddie's lap. "You read the Wall Street Journal?"

"Yep!" If I make more than a penny in this world, I'll know what to do with it. This paper teaches me about the value of a dollar and a whole lot of other things. How old are you, Ruby Johnson?"

"Thirteen. Be fourteen in a couple of months."

"I'm fifteen already. Be sixteen soon."

"You sure look older than that."

"That's gonna help me survive in this old world. What's your plan?"

"Ain't made one yet."

"What about relatives?"

"I don't want to be the soul on nobody's shoe."

"I know what you mean." Freddie tossed her cigarette butt onto the ground. When she stood she gathered her things. She extended her hand for Ruby to shake. "Good luck to you, Ruby Johnson."

Ruby returned the handshake. "Good luck to you, Freddie Walker. Where you headed?"

"Bus stop ain't too far from here." She walked away from Ruby. "I'm bound to catch one that'll take me half way to Chicago. I don't wanna spend too much of what I got. After that I'll probably hitch a ride."

"I've never been to any big cities before," said Ruby. Freddie had gone further into the darkness.

"Me either," said Freddie. "You can tag along if you want."

Ruby watched Freddie disappear out of her sight. She turned and looked at Thornton. He was looking at her through the closed screen door. She stood up and ran down the steps. "I'm comin'," she shouted. "Wait for me."

Within the next hour they swore themselves into the kind of commitment it takes for two-teenage girls to survive, together, without a mother or a father. As they walked they told the other stories about the bad things that happened to them.

The next morning when they got off the bus they were somewhere in the State of Illinois. Nothing around them flourished as a welcomed greeting. To Freddie the people that scattered off with waiting relatives were just as cold, plain, and country as those in Indiana. To her Indiana had merged into Illinois with no change at all. There was no sweet smell of fruit. The farmland on either side of the road had taken up with the boredom of corn and endless rows of soy-bean.

They walked along the side of a paved road. An occasional car whizzed by. Once a driver got a good look at Freddie, and thought of stopping, his mind was changed after seeing the skinny colored girl wearing a green dress made of hopsack curtains with white paisley designs. Some drove away faster than others.

It was late afternoon when Freddie stopped walking, slipped off her shoes, sat on her suitcase and lit a cigarette. Ruby sat on the ground beside her. The cushion of weeds and crabgrass felt good underneath the heavy dress—a remedy that helped take away some of the cramps in her legs.

"Now what do we do?" asked Ruby.

"The right car will come along. Whoever's drivin' it will take us all the way into Chicago." Freddie balanced herself on top of the locking part of the suitcase. When she stretched out her legs, and arms, looking up at a full run of blue sky, she did not tilt her body in any way that would make her fall. Where her body sat, or lay, was a comfortable place to be. To her the new suitcase was as comfortable as any chair.

290

"I wish it wasn't so darn hot," said Ruby. This is a different kind of hot than in Mississippi. Smell different. Feel different too."

"It's that darn dress you're wearin'. That thing must weigh a ton. For a body to behave, you've got to wear the right clothes Ruby Johnson."

A car slowed and then sped away.

"Another one seen the color of me," said Ruby.

"Forget it. That's a hard case. Nothin' but trouble drivin' that beat up old thing." She flicked her cigarette butt onto a patch of weeds and looked at it until the smoke died out. A part of her wanted to see the smoke come back to life, to see something catch fire and burn.

She picked up her suitcase. "Come on, Ruby Johnson."

After walking for more than two hours, a young man, in his late twenties, driving a white Chevy, drove by them and skidded to a stop at the sight of Freddie.

She walked to the car and bent down, looking into the open window. "How far you goin' mister?"

"Where you girls headed?" he asked.

"Chicago," Freddie told him.

"Well," said the man. "I'm not going that far. I can take you a few miles in that general direction. Get in if you want."

"Come on, Ruby Johnson."

Ruby opened the back door and slid onto the back seat. During the drive, while Freddie made small talk with the driver, Ruby read a child's book. It was the story about a dog chasing a cat. Reading the book had done the opposite of keeping her awake. She had no choice but to lay down. The old heavy dress felt like a warm blanket urging her into dreaming about happiness instead of tragedy.

Freddie never liked boys and men that talked too much, demanding attention. She thought the young man was a chatter box. She stole moments to look out the window, watching the last rays of the sun go down behind the earth. When the first grey layers of dusk were there to take the rest of the day's light, a full yellow moon shone bright in the sky. When nothing else of interest was seen she gave the young man all of her attention. She knew what he wanted. She didn't want him to do something crazy to get it.

Ruby was awakened by a persistent and gentle rocking of the car. It wasn't the deep groaning of the man's voice that woke her up. It was the moaning of Freddie's voice. It sounded, to Ruby, like the kind of moaning a woman does when she's lying about something that's supposed to feel good.

She heard this same kind of disinterested moaning during her Father's business on top of her mother. For a moment she thought she had awakened in her bed, but quickly realized her bed was the backseat of a stranger's car.

It was the rush of people and the sound of so many cars that prompted Ruby to sit up fast. When she looked out the car's window it was late in the evening. She had never seen so many street lights, tall buildings, cars, and people walking and gathered in one place. She had never been anywhere other than Jackson Mississippi.

"We here, Ruby Johnson." said Freddie, opening the door, getting out of the car.

Ruby opened the back door as fast as she could and jumped out. The young man leaned, looking out of the passenger's window. He shoved three twenty dollar bills at Freddie. She stared at the money, realizing it was payment for the good time she gave him. Most boys gave her a dime while men bought her something pretty like lipstick or silk stockings.

"Go on," said the young man. "Take it. Big city like this you girls will need some extra cash."

"You've done so much for us already," said Freddie, looking at the money as if it would burn her hand.

"Take it before I change my mind."

She took the money. Her hesitation was strong, but not strong enough. She did not recognize a woman's intuition trying to catch up to a girl, to tell the girl to listen to the woman's voice and not the child's.

"All I have to say is I'm a friend of Ralph Pitney, and show him this card?" She looked at the business card in her hand. One week was written on the back of it.

"That's it," the young man told her. "Just ask for Woody. He's the owner. If he isn't there he hasn't gone far. Wait for him. Show him the back of the card. Leave your friend outside until you get the room. You take care little lady."

They stood across the street from Pitney's Motel and looked at its shabby two-story appearance.

"I think we might be somewhere near Lake Michigan," Freddie said. "I can smell it." She closed her eyes, took a deep breath, and nudged Ruby. "Smell that Ruby Johnson. Take it all in, girl."

Ruby closed her eyes and imitated what Freddie was doing with her breathing. "All I smell is a lot of food."

Freddie picked up her suitcase and nudged Ruby. "Come on. I got myself a big idea—a big plan for tomorrow."

Woody suited the motel owner's name. He looked like the fat pieces of wood paneled unevenly on the wall behind the desk. He wasn't much interested in anything about the young and beautiful girl standing before him. He could not see much without placing a magnifying glass over the left eye of the pair of glasses he wore. After he read the writing on back of the business card he gave her the key to a room.

294

"Your check out time is one week from today, twelve noon," he told Freddie.

"That long," said Freddie.

Woody walked away without answering. He disappeared behind the discreet door he came out of when she rang the clerk's bell.

Freddie picked up her suitcase and went outside. She came around the corner of the motel's staircase. Ruby was hiding behind it. She was shifting from one foot to the other.

"What's the matter with you?" asked Freddie.

"I've got to pee real bad."

"One of these days you'll have to learn how to hold your water. Guess what?"

"What?"

"We can stay in this ole motel for a whole week straight."

After Freddie opened the door the surprise of twin beds caused them to yelp girlishly. A poorly painted water color of the Chicago skyline was between the two beds. It seemed to be there to remind them of where they were. The room was relentless with industrial colors like dark brown and dark brown. The smell of cigarette and cigar smoke was embedded like a permanent personality. The little there was of white color made the room standout more than it should have. Regardless of its monotony and grownup smells it was clean.

295

Ruby sat down on the edge of the bed she had chosen. "I'm so hungry, starvin'."

While they ate the rest of Thornton's snack food, Freddie gazed at the water color. Ruby talked of taking the hot bath she never had, and how it felt to use the second toilet she had ever seen. She pretended to be okay with all that happened to her, but Freddie saw how nervous and scared she was. It wasn't easy to hide the type of nervous breakdown a child has when a loved mother and father are dead or just gone.

Freddie gave Ruby a pink slip to wear and told her she could have it. When Ruby came out of the bathroom, wearing the slip, it looked more like a long-party dress.

Freddie laughed. "You look like you playin' dress up in your mama's slip, girl. We really have to get you some clothes."

"I was gonna wash that ole dress," said Ruby, climbing onto her bed and under the covers. "But it's so thick it won't be dry in the mornin'." She looked at the crumpled bills and coins spread out on Freddie's bed. "What are you doin'?"

"Countin' the little money we got. Including your twenty, we have one-hundred dollars and seventy-three cents. That'll keep us alive for about two weeks.

"What are we goin' to do tomorrow?"

"Get ourselves some identification. We can't get jobs without it."

296

"But we ain't old enough."

"You sure ain't old enough with those pigtails and no makeup. That dress makes you look like you ten years old, girl."

"I do?"

She heard the worry in Ruby's voice. "I'm just kiddin'. You can pass for eighteen easy."

While Ruby slept Freddie couldn't. She thought of how elated she would have been to see the shock on her father's face after finding her room empty. If he had caught her he would have tried to bribe her with promises to buy her pretty dresses, handbags, and pairs of shoes seen in the pages of her favorite catalogues.

It was after 4:00 A.M. when sleep found Freddie, but shortly after that the sound of muffled crying awakened her. She got out of bed, walked to the window, and opened the curtains. It was still dark outside and the once empty parking lot was half full. Blue patches of light behind a dark sky told her the hour was before dawn. She looked at the twin bed and saw that Ruby was not in it.

She knocked on the closed bathroom door but Ruby would not open it. When she turned the knob, opening the door, she found Ruby curled up and crying inside the empty bathtub.

"I know why my daddy put twenty dollars in my boot when he thought I was sleepin'. How could they do that to me? They my mama and daddy, how could they do it?"

Freddie came into the bathroom and sat on the toilet's top. She pulled her legs up and rested her chin on her knees. "You mean how could they leave you to hide behind ole dirty crates?"

"It's like you said, I need to learn how to hold my water. If I had waited they would've needed an excuse to throw me out the truck. They just couldn't tell me to get out. I should've peed on myself. That's what I should've done."

"You ain't the kind of girl that pees on herself. Only babies piss their pants, you too big to be a baby."

"Why did they do it?"

"I read about what goes on with colored people, especially in the south. What I didn't know my colored friends told me. I think every colored person in the whole world is scared of everything right now. Scared to walk, scared to talk, scared to smile, scared to laugh, they even scared to cry. What's the worst thing your mama ever told you that hurt you? I mean the really bad and worse thing."

"I don't know."

"Come on. There must be somethin' you remember that stuck in your head."

Ruby thought about a day of hanging laundry out on the clothesline, helping her mother. "One time she told me the white man is king. The white woman is his queen. The black man, who ain't worth a beat-up nickel, will always have a hard way to go. She said the black woman is last on everybody's list because nobody cares about a woman that's invisible. Maybe it's true. Sometimes I feel like everybody can see right through me."

"I'll be right back," Freddie told her. She stood up and left the bathroom. When she returned she had her cigarettes and a book of matches.

"It's time for you to have a cigarette," she said, lighting two and giving one to Ruby. She climbed into the bathtub and sat at the opposite end. "Hearin' somethin' like that I would give you a shot of whiskey but I ain't got none. If you inhale that smoke it'll calm you down and make you dizzy."

"I know how to smoke. My brother taught me. I just don't like the taste."

"That worse thing your mother told you has a whole lotta meanin' behind it."

"Like what?"

"She's a woman without any hope. She's been told all her life that colored women are worthless pieces of trash. If she ever had any likes, for herself, it's been ripped away the same as rippin' out her heart. If she really believes a colored woman ain't worth nothin', in this world, then, how she ever gonna believe you were worth keepin'. Her boys are that beat-up nickel with a hard way to go and that's enough for her. To make it easier for them to be worth five cents, findin' their hard way, somethin' had to be sacrificed and that was you." Freddie lifted the toilet lid and tossed her cigarette butt inside. She took Ruby's and did the same. She climbed out of the tub, and extended her opened hand to Ruby. "Come on, Ruby Johnson. Get out of that ole tub unless you just like sleepin' and cryin' in cramped places."

"After tonight I'm through cryin' over stupid things lost." She took Freddie's hand and climbed out of the tub. When they got back into bed the light of dawn had found places on the walls and carpet.

Later that morning Freddie wore the same clothing. She did not want Ruby to continue having a nervous breakdown after seeing her in a new change of clothes when she had none.

Ruby watched attentively while Freddie oiled and brushed her hair into a high shine. She stretched and pulled it up tight, braided it, and wrapped it into a tight bun. She then pinned it to stay to perfection. This gave her the look of being taller, sophisticated, and older.

"Girl, you look older than you did yesterday," said Ruby.

"That's my intention."

CHAPTER ELEVEN
GROWING UP FASTER

The two lines inside the Department of Motor Vehicle were not longer than twenty people in each one. An array of ceiling fans did nothing to cool down the heat, and dry the sweat that came from overheated and frustrated bodies waiting their turn.

The employees, sitting at desks, behind the surrounding counter, were beside themselves with trying to figure out ways to stay cool. The most popular solution was to fan themselves with sheets of paper.

Looking up and down one of the lines, at those standing out to be noticed, were three black men. They could have been mistaken for downtown executives with a touch of flair.

The three black women, standing at their side, wore the tight sexiness of suited apparel which included strict and wide-brimmed hats, silk stockings, and high heeled shoes with handbags to match. The looks of the women had inadvertently given up the secret of what the three black men did for a living. When standing together as a group it was clear they were all hustlers.

Freddie wondered why the black men were not gawking at her. Searching for reasons why, she saw the hustlers were focused on accomplishing something. They were passing something to the head of the line to one of their women, standing in front of the clerk.

301

Freddie's heart skipped a beat when she saw the woman pass a folded up bill to the clerk—a squat, balding, overworked white man with a high degree of nervousness.

The clerk pointed to a booth and the hustler's woman walked to it and sat. A driver's test was placed in front of her. Freddie's heart skipped another beat, for she saw opportunity before it knocked on the door. She knew the woman was taking the test for one of the men.

"Ruby," Freddie whispered, "we're in the right place at the right time, but we're in the wrong line. Come on." She took hold of Ruby's arm, pulling her to the end of the second line of the clerk who had been bribed. "Keep our place. I've got to get something."

Without questioning her motives, Ruby watched Freddie walk over to the snack machines. When she came back she had a bag of potato chips and a bottle of Coca Cola in her hand.

She handed them to Ruby. "Drink and eat this as fast as you can."

When her turn came Freddie walked up to the counter and smiled at the clerk. "This is the hottest most frustrating place," she told him. Her hands caressed and wiped away the sweat on her neck and the barest part of her breast.

The clerk was unable to take his eyes away from what her hands were doing. "How can I help you?"

Ruby looked at Freddie. "Miss Walker, I don't feel so good. My stomach is so upset."

"Well, just hold on," Freddie told her. "I'll be done soon."

"Okay."

"New girl," Freddie told the clerk. "My mama just hired her. Her whole family came all the way down from Jackson Mississippi. You know how they can be."

"Miss," said the clerk, "what is it I can help you with?"

"I'm here to get myself an identification card. Not a driver's license. My daddy won't let me drive any kind of car."

"I'll need to see your birth certificate, or, previous identification card," the clerk told her.

"I don't feel so good, Miss Walker," said Ruby, leaning over on the counter. And like a fast river of mashed potatoes, mixed up with Coca Cola, Ruby sent her vomit flying over the counter and onto the clerk's face and his clothes. The expression on the faces of the pool of employees, and the customers standing in line, was one of disgust and surprise.

"I'm so sorry," Freddie told the clerk, "My daddy will pay to have your clothes cleaned. Sir, I'm so sorry. Is there someplace I can take her—a room where she can lay down for a minute or two?"

The office was separated from public view but not too far from the public restrooms. Ruby stood outside the office and next to the pay telephone.

303

A woman came into the area looking to use the phone. Ruby put the receiver up to her ear and pretended to have a conversation. "I'll be done in about five minutes," she told the woman. When the woman left Ruby went back to the kind of shaking that comes with a child having a nervous breakdown. She thought that the clerk in the office with Freddie was grunting and moaning too loud.

When he came out of the office he looked back at Freddie. "Give me about twenty minutes," he told her and then walked away.

Freddie stepped out and into the corridor.

A half hour passed before the clerk tapped on the restroom door. Freddie reached her hand out and took the identification cards.

She finished cleaning herself up and they were alone when Ruby came out of the stall. Freddie stood in front of the mirror, washed her hands, and groomed her beauty back into place. Ruby was trying to figure out how to live up to the expectations of her identification card.

"If I ever get married," said Ruby, "I'm puttin' chains on my husband to keep him away from women like you, Freddie Walker. I didn't know a man could be made to do somethin' he shouldn't so easily, especially, when they know you pretendin' to be all grown up. They should be in jail."

"Well," said Freddie. "If somebody put all the greedy and stupid men, crossing my path, in jail then where would that leave us?"

304

"This card say I'm eighteen-years old. I'm old enough to get a job."

"Sure are."

"Mine say I'm twenty one. I'm old enough to buy myself a drink. We old enough to do just about anything we want."

"Look at me," said Ruby. "I can't pass for no eighteen."

"When I'm finished fixin' you up you'll beg God to make you young again. Come on, Ruby Johnson. Let's get outta this place.

Later that day Ruby's appearance changed. Her hair had been pulled up and stretched away from her face. One neat braid stopped at the base of her neck. The used clothing she wore appeared as if a bucket of pink paint had been thrown to splash clothing on a milk chocolate bar. The paddle pushers, knee length tight pants, were pink cotton with a matching pink and sleeveless-cotton blouse. The front tails of the blouse were tied tightly around her waist.

To compensate for what Ruby was lacking, Freddie had chosen a 32a bra. She stuffed its cup's with toilet paper until a supple and natural look had been achieved. The stubby heeled black shoes did not match the style of the pink outfit and were too big. The heels took Ruby's height up from a childish five-foot three. The rose colored earring clips, red lipstick, and eye pencil helped to bring

305

her up in age. But it was not enough to make her appear older than a girl in her early teens.

Ruby's slender figure, long neck, and keen features reminded Freddie of the pictures she had seen of Egyptian girls that lived long time ago. She told Ruby that one day she would look like a queen from Egypt and Ruby blushed. She did not know how pretty she was. No one ever complimented her on her looks. She didn't even know that queens from Egypt were black women until Freddie told her.

Their stay at the motel had been extended for two more weeks. Freddie's experience with Woody was the worst she had with men. She cried like a child for two nights and was depressed during the day. Ruby did not know what to say, or do, so she chose to do and say nothing. Freddie was her old self again on the third day. Ruby knew she made the right decision to ignore the crying.

Their money was running out and they were desperate to find jobs. Ruby suggested their chances would be better in an all black neighborhood, because Freddie would be something like a novelty.

Three days later, at the end of their three week stay at the motel, their worries were over. They found jobs at Remy's Soul Food. It was a black owned restaurant on the Southside of Chicago's black ghettos, on 47th and Calumet. The black people, especially the women that frequented the restaurant, were unpleasant and rude to Freddie. Ruby earned more tips while Freddie struggled to make hers. The male customers couldn't figure out why the owner hired such a distraction. Every time Freddie swayed by their tables she interrupted their eating. Most of Freddie's tips came from gawkers and dignified hustlers interested in adding something rare to their line of women.

Freddie was aware of what the black hustlers did for a living. They reminded her of the three black men at the Motor Vehicle Department. When offers were made, and invitations extended, her resistance was sturdy and her words firm. She told them no thank you. The words had become part of her job.

In regard to the giving of money the hustlers didn't under tip her. The amount was more or the same.

The owner of South Town could tell that the young girls had been thrown together behind something bad happening to them. He was an older black man with a kind and friendly disposition and wanted to help them. He told them about an apartment building with a vacancy. He said the building's manager would be reasonable with the cost to move in.

On the last day of their stay at the motel they moved out and into their cold-water flat. The building was on the South Side, on 43rd and Calumet. The restaurant where they worked was only four blocks away. When they rented the one-room flat with a bed, sofa, two tables, tiny bathroom, and an area to use a hot plate for cooking meals, the landlord did not ask too many questions.

By the end of August, the same year of 1957, they settled into their daily routine of living comfortably on their own. Friday was the only day they wanted off work. On this Friday they awakened early. They counted their money and set aside what was needed for rent and food. Ruby saved enough to buy herself some new work shoes, personal clothing, and something to wear under them.

There was an unpleasant chill, a touch of winter. Ruby was not used to hearing talk about weather that dipped, unexpectedly, below zero. Sometimes, at the slightest breeze, giving her a chill, she felt sick with a cold she never caught. The preparation of what to do to contend with the brutality, of the oncoming winter, was often thought of during slow times at work. But more than anything she daydreamed about girlish things that would never happen to her like going to high school.

While on the train, taking them into the underground subway stations, the rhythm of expectation that comes with girls, going shopping, had sat down with them like a separate energy. Getting off the train, pushing through the crowds, going up the steps, and then outside, they pointed at the tall buildings and whatever else attracted them and made them laugh.

As morning turned into late afternoon they ate their hamburgers and French fries in a crowded place of noisy conversations, grease, and smoke that stuck to everything and lingered in their hair and clothes. The smell of the stock yards and the shoving and pushing of so many people did not bother them. The wholesomeness of the experience was mixed up into big-city rush. Being in the middle of it all was far more exciting than deciding what kind of dresses Ruby Johnson should buy. By early evening the soft and cool breezes that came in from Lake Michigan made the downtown experience better than what it was.

The two dresses Ruby bought at Woolworth's Department Store were conservative autumn colors. The printed and feminine design brought out the compliment of a pretty-young girl on her way to becoming a very-pretty woman. Freddie renewed two of her lipsticks with the latest in Max Factor's fall colors.

On the hour before the look of darkness tells one of its coming, they got on a subway train heading back to the Southside. The separate energy they brought with them had chosen to stay downtown, but it left them with the sweet tiredness that comes about children after spending the whole day and part of the evening at an amusement park.

Freddie took off her high heels letting the cold floor and vibration of the train caress and massage her feet. Ruby looked inside her shopping bag of new clothes. She wanted to see and feel the material of dresses made by someone other than her mother. Some of the people on the train liked that the colored and white girl acted like best friends with no difference in color. The others, racists on both sides of the aisle, did not.

They talked about the truth again and the too many bad things that happened to them. Still, it was a fine situation of not knowing or even caring about what to do with the rest of their lives. They were young and free of adult authority.

When they got off the train it was early dark. They worked their way out of the shoving, squeezing, crowd of black downtown workers. Ruby noticed the platform's sign telling her where they were.

"We got off at the wrong stop," said Ruby. "We're on 55th Street and Garfield Boulevard. We should've got off on 47th Street. It's gettin' dark already."

"We'll walk back," Freddie said.

"No. We already paid. Let's go on the other side and get the train back the other way. It's a short ride."

"I ain't gettin' on no more trains," said Freddie. "All those people pushin' and shovin' and lookin' at us makes me jump around. I feel like walkin' anyway."

"We been walkin' all day."

"My feet ain't hurtin' yet. Come on, Ruby Johnson. We might as well see what kind of trouble we can get ourselves into."

55th STREET

When stepping onto 55th Street one is confronted with the smoke and smells that come from soul food restaurants, coal-burning barbecue pits, and indoor and outdoor hamburger joints. The most popular places included a pool hall. All the specialty shops, restaurants, bars, and lounges were on either side of wide streets. A grassy strip of unattended knoll with fat spreading oak trees divided the four lanes of car traffic, two on either side that traveled north and south. There were also benches that sat near the trees and close to the walkways that led to pedestrian crossings.

Those unemployed black men, who were not hustlers of women or even small-time gamblers, spent their days and nights shooting pool and making bets for twenty-five cents a game. When bets were won, and the money used for sharing ten cent cups of beer, the pool games continued on for fun.

The variety of live music that came from the bars and lounges seemed to flow onto the streets from every hole. Most of it was fast-jazz with deafening horns that were heard high above all other instruments. The old and new sounds of jazz, mixed in with bebop, filtered onto the street from car radios of young people driving by.

On weekends the place to be was on the grassy strip of knoll. Many people packed their picnic baskets and spread out their blankets to reach out far around them, under the oak trees. This gave them a close-up view of all the happenings on both sides of 55th Street.

Many of the cars that cruised along slowly, on the edges of the right lanes, were filled with teenage boys. They blew their car horns and yelled sexually suggestive things to the young welfare mothers who were sitting in groups, on the concrete steps, of the tenements that faced the main drag. This was where they lived. One of the reasons why the mothers sat there was because their children were in arms reach of discipline. It was hard to pry a mother away from the front steps on weekends. When she saw and heard the gossip of what 55th Street's hustler's and their whore's were up to it was reality entertainment supplied for free.

Most of the mothers were hardly over the age of eighteen. Many lost their finer qualities to the welfare ways of unstable, unstoppable, womanhood derived from having children too early. They had been caught by the slickest of men and young boys that pounced on them after hearing, or seeing, the urgent news that a menstrual flow had begun or that a chest was in need of a bra.

For those older mothers preferring the comfort of home at their backs, they leaned out of their windows that also faced the main drag. It was from there that they socialized, smoked cigarettes, and shared bottles of Schlitz Beer that was hidden inside brown paper bags.

For all the onlookers of 55th Street, additional excitement came when the police showed up and raided hidden gambling places. When the questioning was over they hauled all the occupants up the two steps that led inside paddy wagons and then off to jail.

It was chilling entertainment when one of the dignified hustlers cut up one of his women, or another hustler with his razor. The young-welfare mothers paid close attention to all of it and made mental notes of what they saw and heard. The next day's gossip about who did what to who floated throughout the neighborhood as a kind of aftermath.

On any given day if a stranger of any color were walking along 55th Street, unaware of the brutality of their surroundings, it was easy to gain the impression that every man, woman, child, dog, and cat were thinking about doing something horrible to somebody.

Like fire under the feet, to keep them hopping along, any white person or groups of white people brave enough to stop and go sightseeing, as if 55th street were a zoo of wild animals, left the area immediately on anything that would take them back into the safety of their own world. In the midst of their tours, of slumming, they were exceptionally lucky if they were driving a car for their speedy departure. If they did not leave 55th Street after several visible signs of warning, some verbal, nine times out of ten they were hauled off to Cook County Hospital in the physical state of being beaten, half dead, or dead.

To Chicago's elite, black and white, or any educated outsider, the residents of the neighboring ghettos of 55th Street were a disgusting black people going no place but poorer faster. Some believed they were incapable of understanding the hard work it would take to pull their selves up, even though there were little or no jobs available.

Many blamed the black churches and its preachers. Believing that the preacher's heated lamentations about poverty, injustice, and racial discrimination were responsible for holding an entire race back from being prosperous. From their one sided point of view, the preachers were only interested in lining their own pockets while telling their congregation to pray to God and the angels for help.

As a result, of this kind of ignorance, it was believed that the neighboring ghettos of 55th Street would stay the same until the cities powerful ran them off to someplace else like Rockford Illinois. It was the second largest city and not that far.

The loud racket of fast jazz, coming from the bars, and lounges, excited Freddie and worried Ruby. Freddie claimed Jazz as her favorite music. Hearing it played live took over all her senses of caution. She was propelled to get closer to the places where the music was coming from.

They walked into the heart of 55th Street. Suddenly, as if it manifested itself at the sound of God's growling, a strong gust of

314

wind stirred up from the ground and down from the sky. Swift onslaughts of churning, whips of wind, came out of nowhere from every direction. They were like mini tornadoes, spinning up soil mixed with tiny pieces of street glass. The rush of the wind pushed onto Ruby's chest and shoulders, shoving her to walk backward, giving her a deeper feeling of something bad coming, something ominous, something bad moving her legs to walk forward against their will. The crazy wind sent fine gravel up and inside billowing skirts. It dirtied up the hair and clothes of all the people walking, trying to brace themselves steady enough to lean into the crazy wind or away from it.

Ruby believed when sign's of a pending storm come up from the ground, and down from the sky, with such fury, and nearly at the same time, that God and the devil were clashing. They were heated, infuriated, in disagreement along the lines of saving someone's soul from the fiery pits of hell.

"God sent some kind of crazy wind down this street as a warnin'," said Ruby. "We ain't supposed to be here. We should turn around and go back."

"You are so scared of everything and far too superstitious," Freddie told her. "I've got to see where all that nice music is comin' from. I want to look through a window then we can go on home."

"What if they ain't got no window?"

315

"I'll just have to go inside. I've got an identification card that says I'm old enough to drink myself crazy." Ruby stopped walking. Freddie looked over her shoulder at her. "I'm just kiddin'," she said, laughing at the shock on Ruby's face. "Come on, Ruby Johnson."

The young black men, who were up and coming hustlers, dressed in suits, ties, and silk shirts, lingered on the sidewalks and in front of the doorway of bars and lounges. Yet to discover their own style, they copied the looks and ways of the older hustlers. The big floppy fur hats, sweeping fur coats, and in-your-face-big jewelry had not come yet.

Beautiful, bare shouldered, black women, sold out in the open on 55th Street, who did their business inside the small rooms above the taverns and lounges, sat inside convertible parked cars that sported the look of all shiny and new. They drank from tall bottles of spiked Coca Cola, smoked cigarettes, and chatted boisterously about the night's experience. Their young and handsome hustlers stood in groups near the cars they owned, and some sat on the hoods and on the tails.

At first sight of Freddie swaying the perfect hips their way, jaws hung low and mouths gapped opened with expressions of stunned. She had confused them. A woman, to them, worth no more than the charge of her price, had tossed them into the midst of feeling like they were living inside a paralyzing dream. Even the color of skin was something she didn't have.

The closer Freddie and Ruby walked their way the stronger the crazy wind whipped and churned. The hustler's hats, cocked to the side, tilted up, pulled down over one eye, were loosening and losing their style. The crazy wind blew some of the expensive hats clean off their heads, sending them up into flight and down the length of the sidewalk.

The thick-dark hair, bouncing around her shoulders, blowing across a classic-looking face, could have been the thing about her that held them in a state of unexplainable awe. They were not sure which part of her cast them spellbound. It was like watching a young movie star strutting by while on her quest to go slumming.

Some thought she was a movie star preparing for a new role. Maybe it was Elizabeth Taylor or some kind of Grace Kelly in disguise. Whoever she was she had borrowed the slender side of Monroe's figure without losing a single, luscious, curve.

The hustlers blotted out the sights of Ruby like she was a ghost trying to keep up under the shadow of a rare diamond. Some of them thought the pretty-black girl hovering fast, like a pest or a pet, could have also been her maid.

The black women sitting inside the cars, showing their own God given awes of beauty, looked hard and strict at the woman that cast their men into a state of warmth and concern. For some of the women it was the first time they felt the power of hate that comes with feeling the highest percentage of female jealousy. Color of skin had nothing to do with it for again she had no color. It was about the beautiful girl, or woman, and the natural grace and heightened femaleness that came with her. It was about pure, naturally born, unadulterated class. Her looks went deeper than just physical.

Later that night one of the women said God was the culprit … God must have been drunk the night He made her … He was feeling too free with His Self.

As quickly as the storm came it was gone. Not a drop of rain fell. The heaven and hell fighting that came up so furiously from the ground, and down from the sky, had settled back to being discussed.

"Feel that," said Ruby.

"What?" Freddie asked.

"Stop." She grabbed Freddie's arm, forcing her to stop walking.

"What?"

"It's gone. No rain. No lightin'. Nothin'." Ruby put her hand against her chest, feeling the fast pounding of her heart. "God may have lost."

"God lost what? What's the matter with you?"

"The devil is trying to move my feet forward and God is trying to move my feet backward. If you don't come with me, right now, I'm goin' home without you."

"Will you stop this nonsense?" She was frustrated with Ruby. A part of her wanted Ruby to turn around and go home by herself. "The devil ain't nothin' but the bad people have inside themselves. I ain't scared of nobody's devil. He ain't no match for God anyway."

The lounge where the fast jazz came from was 229, a few feet away from where they stood. Freddie walked away from Ruby and stood at the picture window. She cupped her hands over her eyes and looked inside at the band on the stage.

"Come here," she told Ruby. "I can almost see everything."

Ruby was reluctant. She stood beside Freddie and looked through the window but nothing of clarity could be seen. Cigarette smoke lingered in front of everything.

The people inside did not pay much attention to the two young women trying to peer in at them. The film of nicotine, and fog from an insensitive chill, distorted what kind of young women they were. From those that caught glimpses of Freddie, she could have been a light-skinned colored girl.

"Now," said Ruby. "You saw. Let's go home."

Freddie lifted her foot out of her shoe. "My feet hurt."

319

"High heels and concrete don't go together. You should know that by now."

DREAMS DO COME TRUE

Mimi's Dress Shop provided clothing for the women who belonged to 55th Street's hustlers. The most successful had a credit line. Though the shop catered exclusively to a certain class of women, they were rarely seen inside Mimi's shopping for themselves. Their men went there and picked out their clothing and lingerie. For those hustlers that had no taste for style of hat, dress, suit, or lingerie, their women exercised their right to do their own shopping.

Jimmy Tate was the only customer inside Mimi's Dress Shop. He had become frustrated with the store's clerk. He was having trouble choosing a dress for a young black girl—a new recruit. It had taken him many months to stop her from working for free at the Salvation Army.

The store's clerk was a fragile, sensitive, middle-aged black woman. She was at her wits end. Jimmy's aggressive and frustrating behavior made her anxious. When telling her of the type of woman's clothing he wanted to buy, he often described something he saw on television or inside a magazine. This time he had no idea of what he really wanted.

She disappeared into the back of the store and returned with a presentation similar to his request. She held the dress up in front of him. "I think this is the one, Mr. Tate. She'll love it."

"That ain't the goddamn dress. Here you come again with some goddamn black dress. It looks like a goddamn nun's habit. She ain't no goddamn nun. I ain't runnin' no goddamn convent."

"I'm sorry, Mr. Tate. Let me see what else we have."

"Forget about her favorite color. She don't know what it is. Bring me somethin' fire-engine red, low cut, tight, and with ..."

"Class," said the dress clerk, finishing the sentence.

"Yeah, that's it, class."

Jimmy twirled his hat in his hand, pacing, anxious to leave the store. He walked up to the store front window and looked out onto 55th Street. He saw Freddie standing at the window. She was admiring a deep-lavender dress with a discreet-white bow on the chest.

Though he tried many times he failed to recruit a white girl. He dreamed constantly of having one. Freddie was none like he'd ever seen. Breaking a slight sweat over the possibility, his mind started clicking like the second hands of a clock that achieved high noon. He immediately noticed that clothing for her would be inexpensive. She could make a potato sack look like it came from Sax Fifth Avenue.

Jimmy took off his suit jacket, put it on the seat of a chair, and rolled up the sleeves of his shirt. He wore his dark gray silk suit. It was his most expensive and showed off his flat stomach and slender waist line. He opened the door and stepped outside. The skinny-black girl standing beside Freddie had been blotted out of sight like a disappearing ghost. He looked and smiled at Freddie. "Can I help you, Miss?"

"No," said Ruby.

"I wasn't talkin' to you," said Jimmy, without looking at the reappearing ghost.

"That dress sure is pretty," said Freddie.

"What a nice southern accent you have." He walked closer to them.

"I'm from Tampa Florida. A lot of people don't know that people from Florida are from the south. We have our own southern accent too. It just has a different kind of flavor." She went into her flirtation mode. It was the kind she used to make someone else pay for what she wanted.

"Come on, we better go," Ruby told Freddie. She tugged at her sleeve.

Freddie pulled away from Ruby's tug and looked at the dress. "I couldn't afford it anyway."

"Sure you can. We're havin' a holiday sale, ninety-percent off."

322

"Today is not a holiday," said Ruby.

He knew she already hated him. "Young lady, you're right. Today is not a holiday. We're makin' up for the one that just passed."

"Oh, yeah," said Ruby. "Which one was that?"

Freddie had no interest in the war that begun between Ruby and Jimmy Tate. "Ninety-percent off, are you sure mister? Are you tellin' me I can have that dress for almost a dime?"

"Sold," said Jimmy. "Everything is on sale. You can try on anything you like."

"Sounds to me like you goin' out of business," said Ruby, "puttin' everything on sale for a dime."

He ignored Ruby. She was a ghost again. He took small baby steps toward the entrance of the store, coaxing Freddie to come with him. "I bet you're a perfect size six."

"No. I'm a perfect size seven."

They were inside the store. He closed its door and inspected her closely. How in the hell did she make it through the gauntlet of other bastards trying to take his place?

Ruby's arms were folded. She had summoned her short lifetime's worth of self protection.

Freddie was about to ask the price of a hat that matched the dress when the distressed clerk appeared with a red dress in her hand.

323

"Mr. Tate," said the clerk, "I believe I've found the perfect dress."

Jimmy spun around and glared at the clerk. "Excuse me," he said, smiling at Freddie. He grabbed the clerk by the arm, rushed her around the counter, and pulled her quickly into the back of the store. "Shut up with that," he whispered. "Keep your ass back here. I'm makin' you some money. Where's that purple dress with the white bow between the tits, the one in the window?"

"That man is no good," Ruby told Freddie. "There's somethin' funny goin' on. He is no dress salesman. He's like them men that come where we work, tryin' to mess around with you."

"Be quiet. He'll hear you. Keep your voice down."

"You ain't listenin' to me."

"I know he ain't no dress salesman. I don't care. If I can buy a dress like that and a hat to go with it for nearly a dime …"

"If you don't walk out that door, right now, Freddie Walker, you gonna get yourself into a whole heap of trouble. I'm talkin' about the kind of trouble that only God can get you out of. Mr. Grapes and Mr. Books ain't too happy with us right now."

"Who's Mr. Grapes and Mr. Books?"

"God."

"You sure have funny names for God. I'm just dyin' to hear what else you named Him."

324

The clerk had a size seven in the dress. The price of the dress, hat, and matching leather purse, was never discussed. All of it was wrapped, packaged, and given to her without money exchanging hands.

"This is a gift out of the kindness of my heart," he told Freddie. He then smiled, lifted her hand, and kissed it like it was fine and fragile porcelain.

"Why thank you so much," said Freddie.

Seeing the obvious and deceitful counterfeiting of a real gentleman raised up the little food Ruby had in her stomach. She had to hold herself back from vomiting.

The dress clerk did not question the transaction. Jimmy secretly gave her a twenty-dollar bill. She put the real price of the dress, hat, and purse on his account. The clerk couldn't understand the importance the bastards put into buying sophisticated clothing when all the whores did was take them off after they were bought. The ruin of the expensive dresses would be caused by the excreting stains of the first sin.

Ruby wanted to say something. She wanted to call him a lying snake, a parasite, a vampire, but fear of Jimmy Tate held her words at bay. She sensed him to be the kind of man that could kill somebody. She did not want to be one of his victims. No one would know what happened to her. It was the first time she had seen

325

a nearly all black-eyed man. From a short distance he even looked like a demon.

It was full darkness of night and from a long distance the parade of blinking neon signs, glare of traffic lights, reflection of cars whizzing by, made 55th Street appear as normal and prosperous as any other big-city strip. Jimmy walked with them toward the train's station. He offered them a ride but Ruby refused and Freddie went along with her.

When they were near enough, Ruby noticed that the bare-shouldered women were no longer sitting inside the line of convertibles. The closer they got to the group of young hustlers Jimmy slowed the pace of his walk and ignored their surprised stare over what he had, seemingly, captured when the rest of them made no effort at all. Jimmy turned his head, looked at them, and smiled slyly. They tipped their hats and bowed their heads slightly. If there were any after thoughts:

You're the man, Jimmy Tate. You saw the potential when we all fell down, blinded, hypnotized by the beauty of the woman—a passing movie star. Good luck to you, Mr. Tate. Catch it. Jail it. Remember to make love with her just one time. Make her wish you'd make it with her again. As you go along making all that white-girl money take this as a reminder, remember to heed the rule: If you let a wild stallion out of its gate too many times, eventually, it will find out how fast it can run. If you let it run too far, too fast, and too

326

soon, it will run all the way to the finish line and never look back—gone baby gone. If that happens in the middle of riding that wave of big money, if you didn't take caution, if you didn't set aside that old-man pimp-security, then, your winning ticket wasn't worth the paper she was printed on. If you live rich, die poor, die poor ass broke, your tombstone will read the same as all the sweet daddy pimps before you ....

"A Fool and Their Money Are Soon Parted.

Amen."

Ruby trailed in back of them. She knew what type of man he was. More of it came to light when she realized the slowness of his walking was for showing off his prize.

"Now that you know all about me," said Freddie, "where are you from, Jimmy Tate?"

"Who said I know all about you?"

"Believe me, in this here short time you know more about me than a lot of people do. At least tell me where you're from?"

"Fabulous New York City."

"Did you hear that Ruby?" Ruby did not answer. Freddie looked at her. "Did you hear where he's from?"

"Yeah," said Ruby. "I heard it."

"I've always wanted to go to New York," said Freddie.

Another group of hustlers, Jimmy's age, those he referred to as his business associates, were standing in a group while socializing in front of Smitty's Pool Hall.

Jimmy took Freddie's hand and hooked her arm around his. When he passed by his associates he looked over his shoulder and bobbed his head up and down, pointing out Ruby. Through his silent language he was telling them she was a possible recruit.

His associates ignored the silent plea for help. Ruby looked far too young to be considered as any kind of recruit. Even with all the makeup and poor attempt at a grown-up hairdo they figured Ruby to be no more than fifteen. The age of the white girl, if she was close to being a woman, was also questionable.

"Your slave back there," said Jimmy, "ain't too happy about …"

"What you call me?" Ruby stopped walking and stomped her foot hard on the ground. "I ain't anybody's doggone slave. Slavery is over, mister. The reason why you don't know that is because you still one yourself."

Jimmy's group of associates walked closer to where Ruby was standing. They wanted to hear what the sharp tongue had to say. It was a rare occasion when anyone had the guts to stand up to Jimmy.

Freddie looked at the top of Jimmy's height and leaned into the tallness off him. "Don't talk about my best friend like that," she said. "We've been through a whole lot together. We've been treated bad by people claimin' to care about us. You owe my friend an apology."

"You shut up, Freddie Walker. I don't need you to defend me."

"I'm sorry, young lady," said Jimmy. "Please accept my apology."

"I don't need no apology from some crook like you." She had begun to cry. She was tired in the way a kid gets angry for getting sleepy.

"Ruby this ain't nothin' to cry over," Freddie told her.

"You're a fool if you believe he's from some New York. I know where he's from." Ruby put her hands on her hips and looked up at Jimmy. "You from deep Mississippi just like me. All us good slaves come right out of good-ole Mississippi."

"Young lady, I think you better watch what you say."

"No," cried Ruby, "I ain't scared of you. I'm gonna say my piece. You wanna know how I know where you from? Cause folks like us, from good-ole Mississippi, can't get rid of the smell. I ain't ashamed of bein' from Mississippi, it's just as bad as any good place to be." She rolled her eyes. "Goodbye ole black Bubba that's probably your name. I hope I never see your ugly face again."

329

Jimmy's associates laughed out loud and repeated ole black Bubba over and over again. The train station was a block away and Ruby was heading toward it.

"Ruby," Freddie called out.

"Shut up!" Ruby told her. "If you stay here they gonna find you dead in some alley."

A shock of reality came over Freddie when she looked around and into the eyes of the sophisticated older hustlers. She thought about the possibility of danger.

She grabbed Jimmy's hand and shook it fast, up and down. "Thanks, Mr. Tate. It was nice meetin' you. I have to go now. Thanks for the nice presents."

"Where you live?" asked Jimmy, watching her run away from him.

For his associates it was pure joy to see Jimmy's eyes bulging out of the skin of their narrow slits, rolling quickly from left to right. A nervous hand was inside his pant pocket, jingling coins. For that final indication of a man thinking about big money, escaping, Jimmy reached inside his breast pocket and removed his cosmetic sponge. He mopped the shine off his face. The showing of his popular vanity told his associates that nothing, short of the end of the world, could stop him from pursuing the hot-impetuous thing running away on cheap high heels.

Parked in front, of the row of convertible cars, was a black 1957 Cadillac. The top was down. From the way the car was parked, at an arrogant slant and too far away from the curb, made a clear statement. It had the right to be at the head of the line. It was Jimmy's car. His cars had been at the head of the line for almost eleven years.

The fast and crazy wind had kicked up again, coming up from the ground and down from the sky. Jimmy held onto his hat and ran toward his car. His associates broke out into more fits of outrageous laughter while watching Jimmy fumble, and struggle, with pulling up the hood of his Cadillac.

"This is like a goddamn funny-ass cartoon," said one of the hustlers.

"Hey you goddamn fool," another one shouted. "If you stick the key in the ignition, push the right goddamn button, the hood should go up automatically."

"Unless you done already broke that motherfucker," said another hustler.

The train had just arrived and was there waiting at the platform. The doors were open and only a few seconds from locking Freddie out. She managed to get onto the same train, but Ruby was in a different car.

She sat down in back of the train's car, trembling, feeling afraid of nothing in particular. She looked around at the people. All

331

their faces were black, silent, and staring at her. Some turned away like it disgusted them to look at her.

Some of the children stared at her for long periods of time, their eyes fixed on her face with curious fascination. It made her feel much better when one of the children smiled at her. She returned the smile and gave the girl a wink.

Jimmy remembered Freddie told him they lived near 47th Street. He was sure they would get off at the 47th Street platform. He thought about finding a short cut and drove fast into the alley, catching up with the train they were on.

As he drove faster fine charcoal, broken glass, and days-old garbage kicked up from the ground and was mixed up inside the swirls of crazy wind. Debris blew in circles around and above his car. Some of the heavier trash landed on the hood, and roof, before bouncing back down onto the alley's ground.

Ruby stood at the bottom steps of the 47th Street Station. Her arms were folded across her chest, eyes looking up at the top step like a mother waiting to reprimand her child for lagging behind. Freddie appeared holding her shoes in her hand.

"I'm so glad you found some sense," she told Freddie. "If you had of stayed back there, with them men, they would've took you someplace. Nobody would've been able to find you."

"Oh, be quiet, Ruby Johnson," said Freddie, walking down the stairs, joining Ruby. "My feet are so swelled up I can't put my shoes back on. I think these feet of mine grew a couple of inches overnight. I might have to change the size of my shoes."

"You gotta put those shoes on. If you don't, your feet will be cut up and bloody in the mornin'. We still got a few blocks to walk."

"I'm sorry about what that man said to you." She held onto Ruby's shoulder, putting her shoes on.

"You ain't got nothin' to be sorry about. He ain't nobody important. Looks like some kind of colored gangster to me."

Ruby noticed Freddie's limping. She put her arm around her waist. "Take one shoe off and walk tip-toe on that foot. That'll help. You can lean on me for the weight. Come on."

Jimmy parked across the street and away from the front of the station. When he saw them walk the rest of the block, he put his car in drive and followed behind them. He thought he had to get to her before 47th Street's hustlers did. Most of the women they ran were notorious heroin users. They acquired the women through the use of addicting them to drugs. New recruits were held in dark rooms until they were delirious and singing the happy songs of needle high. He hated unhealthy women and got rid of those that used drugs. After they were gone, they wound up in the clutches of 47th Street. For his own self rewarding reasons, he didn't want that to happen to Freddie.

333

The next morning the rush of being late for work pushed them quickly out of bed, into a minute's shower of cold water, and then inside the rust colored waitress uniforms with green aprons and black shoes.

Parked at a good distance, Jimmy watched them leave their apartment building and secretly followed them to work. He did that for two days. When they got off work they went straight home and stayed there. He appreciated that. It eased his tension and worry of losing her to 47th Street.

On the third day before their shift was over, Jimmy slipped into the restaurant and sat at the empty counter. Freddie was behind it, filling salt and pepper shakers.

"Miss," he said, while her back was turned, "can I get a cup of coffee?"

Freddie picked up the coffee pot and went to him. He lifted his head and took off his hat.

She took the opportunity to play with him. "Why, Mr. Tate, you must be followin' me around."

"Do I look like the type of man that would do such a thing?"

"As a matter a fact you do." She turned on her charm. "If you ain't followin' me around then how did you find me?"

"When I heard about the beautiful girl that worked at one of my favorite eatin' places, I had to see what all the fuss was about."

"I don't believe you. That's just too coincidental. Anyway, I'm long past bein' a girl."

"I did all my side work. I guess we can go on home now," said Ruby. She walked from the center of the restaurant and then behind the counter. When she saw the man Freddie was smiling at, flirting with, the feel of creeping trouble was there. It was like a dreaded person growing bigger and bigger, oozing inside of her with no warmth that helps a person like another.

"Hello, young lady."

"Hello," said Ruby.

"You still mad at me, huh?"

"I don't know what you talkin' about, mister."

Jimmy extended his hand to Ruby. "Please accept my very serious apology. Call me Jimmy. Can we shake on bein' friends?"

Freddie nudged Ruby with her hip, urging her to take Jimmy's hand. "Go on Ruby. We ain't got no friends in this town. It's time we made a few."

Ruby took Jimmy's hand and gave it one shake before pulling out of his grasp. His hand was softer than hers. She knew he had never worked a hard day in his life.

"Apology accepted," she said, her head down. She didn't want him to see her lie over the acceptance of his friendship. She still saw the danger behind the eyes of a mentally unstable man and he still frightened her.

335

"Can I offer you ladies a ride home?" he asked, looking at Freddie.

"No thanks," said Ruby, giving him back the cold shoulder. "We can walk."

"Ruby Johnson," said Freddie, "what in the world is the matter with you? My feet are tellin' me a ride home ain't no bad idea."

They left the restaurant and went across the street. Jimmy pointed to his car. "That's my ride. I call her Sheba."

"You must have a big ole wad of money in your pocket," Freddie told him. "I know exactly how much that car is worth. I even know how much it cost when you bought it brand new."

"You do. And how do you know all that?"

"Oh, I read the Wall Street Journal. That's my favorite newspaper. It teaches me all about the value of a dollar. If I ever make more than a penny in this crazy world, I'll know exactly what to do with it."

His laughter over what she said was genuine. He thought it cute. On the truthful side of things, she knew the price right down to the penny which included the cost of his insurance plan.

During the drive Ruby sat on the backseat and looked around at the details of the immaculate Cadillac. The white-leather interior was hard, pristine, not worn. It was like no one had ever sat there but her. Before she got out of the car she intentionally ran the rubber

336

sides of her work shoes on the bottom edge of the seat, leaving behind the black slide of a deep mark. Freddie did not get out of the car. She stayed behind and talked with Jimmy.

REVIEW BOARD

The judges looked across the conference table at Ruby. They waited until she finished the glass of water and cleared her throat.

"Miss Johnson," said Judge Shaw, "did you try to convince your friend not to have anything to do with a man like Jimmy Tate? The two of you claimed yourselves to be best friends. Don't best friends listen to one another? Isn't that one of the most important ingredients that makes a relationship viable?"

"We were not grown women," said Ruby. "We were still children, teenagers. Children need their mothers and fathers. We did not have that. To Freddie, in many ways, Jimmy was like a father figure."

"Fathers that love their children don't turn them into prostitutes," said Judge Bennett. "Miss Walker did become aware of what kind of man Mr. Tate was, didn't she? She did know what he did for a living?"

"Yes," answered Ruby.

"Had Miss Walker given up her job as a waitress?" asked Judge Rodriguez.

"No, not right away, not until after that night."

"What night was that?"

"The first time she slept with him. After he left the next morning, she didn't do nothin' the rest of the day. She stayed in her room and cried a lot. I tried to talk to her but she just kept saying I'm alright, I got a bad case of the blues."

"How long was it before Jimmy convinced Miss Walker to work as a prostitute?"

"I guess it was only a few months, or so. If I remember right, it was around the end of December 1957. Yes, it was around that time. Right after we moved into a bigger apartment in the same building. Jimmy paid for the move. I had my own room and Freddie had hers. We had a living room and a real big kitchen and bathroom. He even went out of his way to decorate the place for us. He bought us a lot of new furniture."

"And how did their working relationship begin?" asked Judge Shaw.

"When he brought them."

"Them who?"

"Barbara and Juanita.

"Who were these women?" asked Judge Rodriguez, making note.

"I don't know their last names. They worked for Jimmy. They were more in love with each other than they were with anything else. They didn't say much and did whatever Jimmy told them to. I never heard them question his authority.

December 23, 1957

CHAPTER TWELVE
THE MONEY

Barbara and Juanita were young black women in their early twenties. They were with Jimmy and Freddie inside her bedroom, packing Freddie's things inside an array of suitcases. Though not strictly elegant they were sleek, graceful, beautiful women. Starting at the ages of seventeen, and nineteen, both began working for Jimmy. They were now in their mid twenties.

Freddie sat at her vanity table in front of the mirror while Jimmy stood in back of her. He was brushing her hair slowly, gentle, as if she were a rare doll easily broken into pieces with the wrong stroke. His body heaved slightly, breathing sighs of content. She thought the strange breathing orgasmic and creepy. The crazy way he thought of her was almost making her change her mind about his way of getting rich.

Her way of thinking, earning real money, was more interesting being read about and accomplished in ways done by those on Wall Street. She didn't know why making money that way appeared to be so much fun. There was a real satisfaction about buying and selling stocks and bonds—a person using their mind to be clever enough to make a fortune. She dreamed of being able to do that someday.

When Ruby had awakened the same morning, she climbed out of bed and went to her window. She pulled back the curtain and saw the brightness of the sun spread out equal to a pure blue sky, but the ball of the sun was not seen anywhere.

She looked up to the left of the sky and saw a full moon and its pretense of being the sun. A full daylight moon, for the one having seen it, meant bad luck coming soon and nothing could be done about it.

Older black women in the South who were in their eighties, and nineties, always made meaning out of the sky and the strangeness of weather. When groups of them sat with Ruby's grandmother in their chairs, under the shade of magnolia trees, and Ruby was playing nearby, she listened to their superstitious comments about the temperament of Mother Nature. She knew that no matter the season the day would be considered a bad one for anyone searching for the ball of the sun only to find a full-daylight moon.

To get through the bad luck coming, and to keep her faith strong, she promised the heavens she would stay on the right side of God. She also promised not to call upon the Virgin Mary, the one she called Big Mama, unless she had no other choice.

She remembered the words of one of the old women. They once told her when the Lord's too busy Big Mama is his backup plan. She's the one that won't deny help to any life that's female. They said if you ain't caught up in a life and death situation, and you don't have children, do all you can to solve your own problems. The old superstitious women believed that the Virgin Mary's most important work lay with answering prayers of needy women and children.

"I've got to say goodbye to Ruby," Freddie told him. Jimmy continued brushing her hair. He had not heard her. "Jimmy, I have to say goodbye to Ruby."

Snapping out of his daze, he laid the brush on the table and stepped away from her. "Yeah, go on. It's gettin' late."

Ruby was in her room, cleaning it vigorously. It was sparse of furniture with only a small dresser, night table, and twin bed. Freddie knocked more than twice on the door before Ruby told her to come in.

"How long are you gonna be mad at me?" said Freddie, entering the room. She sat on the edge of Ruby's bed.

Ruby stopped polishing of her dresser. "That man will ruin you," she told Freddie. "He's the worst kind of vulture, a parasite. He makes his livin' off women. You ain't even no woman yet. I still can't believe you doin' this. You are crazy out of your mind."

342

"You know it ain't never been no secret how I got my hands on money when we needed it."

"No. Don't you try to make me feel bad. I ain't never approved of all the bad stuff you do. Shame on you for sayin' such a thing."

"I didn't mean it like that. You always take things the wrong way."

"Those two women in your room get paid for doin' it," Ruby whispered. "I heard them talkin'. They takin' you to work in some house in Indiana. Indiana. Does that ring a bell"?

"I know, Ruby. I know exactly where I'm goin'."

"Oh! My God! She knows. Dear Lord, God in heaven." Ruby sat on the bed next to her. "What if your father sees you? Think about that."

"I'll just have to make him pay for it. No more feelin' his way around the main idea. After we do it he'll go home and shoot his self in the head so he can go to hell a lot faster."

"I don't believe what I'm hearin'."

"The only one worked up about this is you."

"Why do you do it, Freddie? Look at you. You are so smart and beautiful. You can marry any man you want. You don't have to do this kind of stuff. He will hurt you. He's a beater. I know it."

"Christ Ruby. I ain't in love with him."

343

"Why would you do somethin' so bad, so wrong in the eyes of God?"

Freddie looked sadly at her, "I don't know."

"It's okay," said Ruby. "Just take care of yourself. Come back here safe. You're the best friend I ever had."

"Me too, Ruby Johnson. Promise you won't move out when I'm gone. You don't make enough money to get a place of your own."

"Why would I do that? God put us together for a reason. Maybe it's somethin' more important than the both of us."

There was a strong knock on Ruby's door. Jimmy opened it. He ignored Ruby's irate gaze and looked at Freddie. "Come on, baby. It's a long drive."

Ruby looked at Jimmy. "I'll take Freddie's keys until she gets back. This is our place. Not yours."

"Sure thing, Miss Ruby," said Jimmy, "even though I pay the rent."

"You don't pay my half of nothin'. I pay my own way," Ruby told him.

He sneered at her. "One of these days you might want to look under your mattress." He reached inside his pocket, removed the keys and tossed them onto Ruby's bed. They did not know he had been standing outside the door listening to their conversation.

344

He wanted to kill Ruby Johnson for every bad thing he heard her say about him.

Ruby stood at her window and watched Barbara and Juanita escort Freddie to the car they were driving. It was Jimmy's second car. After they drove out of eyesight, Ruby watched Jimmy walk to his Cadillac. He knew she was watching him. He raised his middle finger and gave her the fuck-you sign.

Ruby opened her window and stuck her head out and yelled. "You goin' to hell ole black Bubba."

She stomped to her bed and grabbed the edges of her mattress, flipping it onto the floor. She saw the money, picked it up, counted it, and realized it was her share of the rent. At the first opportunity she thought of throwing the money in his face. She was smart enough to know what it meant to owe a penny to a man like that. She wanted to burn the new furniture he bought for her room. But after thinking twice about dragging it into some alley and pouring kerosene on it, watching it burn, she changed her mind. It was too cold to sleep on a hard floor.

Jimmy's farm house in Terra Haute Indiana was a two story, wide, wooden box. The previous owner had gone bankrupt and Jimmy purchased the property for far less than its value. To conceal what went on inside, especially in spring and summer, overgrown trees flourished around the house and went up tall to the top of windows on the second floor. The walls had been reinforced with insulation, acting as a sound barrier against the loud music and strong voices of men and women having a celebrated time.

There was nothing to admire about the furnishings. As with most houses like that it was cheap, soft, worn, colorful and accessorized to enhance the beauty of women while they sat or lay underneath yellow and red lights. The specialty was the irresistible supply of seven beautiful and sensuous black women. Most were of light complexion with more mixtures of white than black.

After a few days the word had gotten out about Freddie. This increased the number of black customers putting their names on the list. Her room stayed busy, and after the end of the second week she was tired and worn out. She was near to deciding a change of mind about being a full-time prostitute, but as weeks turned into a month she eventually settled in. The consistency of the work gave her the experience she needed to give a man early withdrawals. The skill kept her pain free and off her back.

Barbara and Juanita made note of every customer that came in and out of Freddie's room. The women hated it when they worked the house because they were Jimmy's snitches, his spies.

Zip, the old black woman that ran the house, was known to the women as the old crow. She was bad when it came to keeping Jimmy's books. Jimmy had no mind, no patience, for numbers except when it came to counting money in his hand.

346

Because Zip spent her days, and nights, nipping bottles of gin the women were able to doctor her books while she was sleeping. The stealing of their own money gave them more than just a pinch of their share.

One night Freddie caught one of the women coming out of Zip's room. The accounting books were in her hand.

The woman was startled, afraid. "If you say anything you'll regret it," she told Freddie.

This did not faze Freddie. "If you ain't doin' it right he'll find out."

"Do what right?" the girl whispered.

"What else," said Freddie, "steal your own money."

The woman went back to her room and when she went inside some of the women were waiting for her. "I think she might be okay," the woman told them. She stepped aside and let Freddie into the room.

"I know how we can do it perfect," Freddie told them.

That night Freddie showed them how to steal more of what they made. She could even duplicate the old crow's handwriting down to the dollar sign. They were pleased to meet a young white girl living in a color blind area. She also believed that being a whore does not mean a woman has to be stupid where her own money is concerned.

To keep Barbara and Juanita from finding out two of the women pretended to be sick. This kept Barbara and Juanita on their backs making the money the two women did not. Freddie, with more freedom, took charge of cooking the books a lot faster.

On the 15th of February, 1958, Juanita put in a phone call to Jimmy. "You better get down here quick," she told him. "You got yourself a big problem."

He did not hesitate, leaving directly after the call. His two spies were never wrong about a big problem being a big problem. During his drive he thought about Freddie. He was not able to get her off of him, out his skin. The scent of her perfume trailed him like it was her ghost, never giving him a moment's peace. Showers and baths couldn't get the scent off because it wasn't there. It was him, his imagination, his wanting to have her again and again. He knew he crossed the line. He made it with her more than once because he wanted to. It unnerved him when visualizing flashes of other men touching her. He drove recklessly faster after thinking that maybe he loved her.

When Jimmy arrived it was past 2:00 A.M. The house was closed for the night. Barbara and Juanita were waiting for him. The rest of the women were in their rooms. Those that could eaves drop listened to the conversation.

"What's the problem?" Jimmy asked, looking at Barbara.

"Don't you go blamin' me," said Barbara. "I showed her how to use the damn rubbers. Juanita showed her too."

"We both kept our eye on her just like you told us to do," said Juanita.

"What you expect for us to do?" asked Barbara. "Two of the girls are sick. We been workin' their time and our time. We can't keep an eye on every John that comes in and out of her room."

"Shut up." Jimmy told them. "I'm askin' you one more time, what is the fuckin' problem? Get to the point."

"She's knocked up," said Juanita.

"What?"

"She missed her period. She's knocked up, pregnant, havin' a damn baby."

"I told you she was too young," said Juanita. White girls like her ain't nothin' but trouble. You'll be sorry you ever met her. She'll ruin everything."

Jimmy took off his hat and sat down. He didn't see the problem as a real problem. He knew what had to be done. "Tell Zip to get in touch with that quack doctor. He don't live too far from here."

"We already did that," said Juanita. "He's been here two times. She locked herself in her room. She told him ain't nobody killin' her baby.

"Where is she?"

349

"She's locked in her room."

"Come on," Jimmy said, "both of you. Get her shit together. She's leavin'."

He banged on Freddie's door. "Come on, baby. It's okay. Open the door." When he got tired of pleading with her he kicked it open. Freddie did not flinch when they came inside.

"Ain't nobody killin' my baby Jimmy Tate. I'm goin' back home to my daddy."

He stood there looking at her while Barbara, and Juanita, threw her things inside the suitcases. "You doin' what?" Jimmy asked.

"You heard me." She looked at him and pretended she had no fear. "I'm goin' home to my daddy. Ain't nobody killin' my baby."

"You think you just gonna get up and run?" asked Jimmy. "You think I'll let you run? You owe me." He raised his hand and pretended to hit her. She cowered low and stayed that way. "You keepin' your baby," he laughed. "You keepin' your baby. Besides bein' a financial genius you didn't tell me you was a comedian too." He grabbed her by the hair and pulled her head upright. "Look at me." She ignored him. "Look at me." She looked at him. "I'm not goin' to hit you no more. I'm waitin' until we get to Chicago, to your place, then I'm goin' to beat the shit out of you and kill that

350

mistake you call your baby." He grabbed her by the hair and dragged her onto the floor, down the corridor, and down the steps.

Listening from behind their doors the women could do nothing. Some of them felt responsible for the disaster. After finding out how old Freddie was they kept at her until they convinced her to go back to her daddy. They wanted to help her best friend, the one she called Ruby Johnson, find a suitable family she could live with in Georgia. They even gave Freddie several contact phone numbers. They wanted to help and succeed at taking the two girls away from Jimmy Tate.

THE FIRST BEATING

Bam! Upside the head! Kick her again in the stomach to make sure you kill it. You like her hair a lot. You like the feel of it trying to pull away from your hand. Rip out some more of her hair. That'll make her scream louder and beg for more mercy. Don't give her any. After you hit her in the back of the head, bend her over and rape her, grab her hair and hold her down until you're finished. Put a bunch of her hair in your pocket for the witches to work with. Maybe they can get her to behave under a dark spell. Her eye is black. Her mouth is swollen. Her lips are bleeding. Punch her again in the face. Stand her up. Punch her in the stomach. Good, that should do it. That should kill the got-damn thing; the unwanted, harassing thing trying to take her away from you. Kill it! Kill it! Kill it!

Ruby had come home from work. Jimmy's Cadillac was parked outside. She knew they were back early. She was sure her friend hated the experience.

Ruby knocked on Freddie's door. "Freddie, is that you?"

"Ruby," Freddie said.

"Don't come in here," Jimmy told her. "Do it and you'll get the same treatment."

Ruby opened the door. Jimmy was standing over Freddie. His feet and chest were bare. The only clothes he had on were his pants. Freddie was naked, cowering under him on the floor. Ruby looked at her and swallowed hard because there were so many bruises.

"Ooops," said Ruby. "I'm sorry for interruptin'." She stood still, looking at Freddie, thinking.

"Get your black ass out of here and close the goddamn door," said Jimmy.

Ruby did not budge. She felt as if her feet were glued to the floor. She wanted God, anything, any one to tell her what to do.

"Get the fuck out of here, Mississippi. Don't let me repeat myself. Understand?"

"Sorry, Jimmy. I understand." She left and closed the door behind her. Jimmy continued his beating.

352

A minute had not passed before Ruby returned and opened Freddie's bedroom door. She had come out of her coat and her shoes. Her feet were bare, gripping the floor steady and firm. In her hand she held a long and fat stick, broken off from the head of a janitor's mop.

She did not hesitate. As soon as she entered the room she started beating him across the head with it, landing blow after blow, as hard as she could. The last of her blows was across his face, putting a deep and bloody cut above his eye. Freddie had crawled from under him and into a corner.

Ruby held the mop handle up and over her right shoulder. She had both hands on the stick, ready to swing it like a baseball bat. "Get out of here. You get out. I'm callin' the cops."

Jimmy was stunned. When he lunged at Ruby she swung the mop handle back, and up, as far as she could, and brought it down on top of his head. She had landed the worst of her blows. Ruby raised the mop handle again.

"If you hit me again," Jimmy said, "I'll shove that stick up your ass."

"I ain't scared of you. I ain't."

"Okay, okay," said Jimmy. "Just let me get my stuff."

"No! Get out," she told him.

Jimmy stumbled out of the room. Ruby slammed the door behind him and grabbed Freddie's vanity chair. She stuck the back

353

of the chair under the door's knob. She wasn't afraid of him and was calm. It was as if someone else had beaten him.

"Give me my shit out of there," Jimmy called out to Ruby.

"I ain't openin' this door. I'll throw your stuff out the window."

"You do that, Mississippi Ruby." When he felt the cut above his eye he knew he would need stitches.

Ruby heard the front door close and his footsteps going down the stairs. She pulled back the curtains and waited until she saw him walk out of the building and onto the sidewalk. She picked up his clothes, spit on them, and said a quiet curse of revenge. She opened the window and sent hat, shirt, suit jacket and tie sailing out and down into the sleet of melting snow.

"I need my ...."

His keys sailed out of the window, landing further than the rest of his things. Out came a shoe and then the other shoe.

"Hey!" he called out to Ruby, "Hey, young lady, Mississippi Ruby."

She wanted to hear all he had to say. The more she knew about the deranged, psychotic hustler, the better her strategy for war. She inched to the window and stood where he could see her.

"I'm sorry, Mississippi Ruby," he said, looking up at her, using his handkerchief to wipe the blood from his face. "Things just got out of hand. I'll make it up to the both of you."

"You goin' to jail. That's where trash like you belong in jail forever." Ruby slammed the window shut and locked it, closing the curtains.

His nerves were pulsating. The fear of losing his prize was a reality. After getting into his car he thought about putting his lawyer on standby.

Freddie was laughing.

"Why you laughin' like that?" asked Ruby. "What's the matter with you?" She kneeled beside Freddie. "He almost beat you to die. I'm callin' the cops."

"No, Ruby." She was crying again. "You can't do that."

"Yes, I can. I'm not listenin' to you. Can you stand up?"

"I'm havin' a baby. He tried so hard to kill it, but I know he didn't. I can feel my baby is still alive. That's why I was laughin'."

Ruby ignored the importance behind another tragedy coming. She saw many babies come to life inside dark rooms and sheds.

"I gotta go to the store and get some stuff." She helped Freddie onto her feet and into bed. "If he comes back, you call the cops. Promise me."

"He won't come back. His tail is tucked between his legs like a mean-ole-mangy dog lookin' for someplace to hide. I know that much about him."

"I'll be back before you can count to ten. I hope he didn't break anything I can't fix."

She cried the whole way of running to Walgreens. The bad luck started with a grand show of brutality.

Freddie was in and out of sleep when Ruby got back. Her face was hardly recognized and both eyes were red, black, and swollen from the force of his punches. She cleaned her friend up and cried silently while doing it.

In Mississippi Ruby remembered a low walking, shy, woman that stopped occasionally to stand at the foot of their front porch to talk to her mother. The woman was always battered and bruised. Her mother told her the woman was the type of female who was not content unless her man beat her up as bad as he could.

When Ruby asked her mother, why? She said that being beaten gave the woman the desire of feeling as worthless as anything crawling low on the ground. She said the woman had no respect for herself because of something terrible that may have happened to her.

Ruby couldn't shake the feeling that Freddie was like that woman. Maybe she was punishing herself for something tragic, deep, and hidden that was not her fault. She thought that maybe Freddie's father had something to do with her desire to be abused by men. Freddie said she had never bedded with her own father, but Ruby was keen at recognizing when her friend was not telling the truth.

Regardless of the psychology behind the behavior of having no true self respect, Ruby was puzzled. How could any kind of woman, with or without self respect, be attracted to a cowardly-vicious man like Jimmy Tate? It had to be trickery. He had to be the devil. Ruby prayed the baby was not his. She thought it would be a cursed and devilish thing that caused people to run for their very lives.

Some of the spring and summer of 1958 was easy on their lives. Ruby was proud that Freddie had kept her word. She turned up her nose and ignored Jimmy Tate's begging, pleading, and stalking.

He drove slowly behind them when they walked home from work. He sat inside his car outside their apartment building. Sometimes he slept in his car. He sat inside the restaurant for long hours until the owner told him to leave. The flowers he sent, to the both of them, with a card begging for their forgiveness, were thrown in the trash. They pawned his begging gifts of jewelry that were laden with gold, diamonds, and silver. They threw away the cheap stuff. The extra money was used to pay the rent. A lot of it went to pay Freddie's medical expenses at the local clinic.

Ruby kept her job at the restaurant and worked a lot of overtime. Freddie worked until the swelling of her belly and feet forced her to stay home. When the beginning of November came she was in her ninth month.

November 3, 1958

HERE COMES THE FIRST ONE

Freddie shivered and coughed while standing in line at the crowded supermarket. When she exited with a bag of groceries Jimmy was standing there.

"Looks like you could use ride home, baby."

"Not from the likes of you, Jimmy Tate. She did not look at him. She kept going.

"Let me carry that bag for you," he called out. She ignored him.

The sick look of her worried him. The coat she wore was too small and it had no buttons to close up her big stomach. Her dress was not just thin it was flimsy. He thought about her dying on him. All that money, his money machine dead, buried somewhere in Potter's Field. He promised his self if he got her back he would never hit her again. He would slam his fist into a wall or into Mississippi Ruby.

When Freddie got home she went into the kitchen and began putting away the groceries. The first pain came from the strong kick of the baby. The second pain was caused by the baby twisting inside of her. After a few more kicks her water broke and spilled out from between her legs and onto the kitchen floor. The knock on the door startled her.

Jimmy knocked louder. "Freddie, baby, is there anything I can do for you?"

"Go get Ruby."

He did not hear her. He knocked louder on the door. "What, baby? Open the door."

"I can't," she cried. Go get Ruby."

"Okay, baby," he said. "Okay." He heard the distress in her voice.

The second Ruby saw Jimmy she knew it was time. On the drive to the apartment her head was filled with thoughts of what to do. She remembered Mississippi and the old mid-wives. She remembered her mother's pain and visualized what her grandmother did during the birth of her youngest brother. Cold rags, hot water, scissors, sanitizing the area, clean sheets and clean towels were needed. She had most all of it ready.

Later that evening the manager of the apartment building knocked on their door for the second time because Freddie's screams could be heard throughout the building. They echoed out into the corridor, down the stairs, and onto the street.

Jimmy was a wreck. He opened the door and saw the apartment manager standing there again. He walked into the corridor, grabbed the man by his throat, squeezing it. "If you knock on this goddamn door one more fuckin' time, I will snap your fuckin' neck." He shoved the man aside and kicked him. "Get your ass on back down the goddamn hall, motherfucker. If the police knock on this door I'm blamin' you for it."

The manager got on his feet and did as he was told. Jimmy went into the apartment and into the kitchen where two iron pots sat on the stove's gas burners. Throughout the process he found comfort being un-kept, barefoot, and shirtless. It was something about it. He felt normal and homely, like a hardworking man at home with his wife having a baby.

He stood in front of Freddie's locked door. He yelled at Ruby. "What you doin', killin' her?"

Ruby opened the door with a bang. Jimmy saw Freddie in bed twisting and turning. Her hands were tied to the iron railings of the bed. A chair and table was at the foot of the bed.

"What the hell you doin'?" he asked Ruby.

"I'm doin' what I'm supposed to do." She was scared, nervous. She looked at Freddie. "I'll be right back. Don't go anywhere."

"How in the hell is she goin' anywhere," said Jimmy. "You got her tied up in a goddamn straight jacket."

Ruby closed Freddie's door and went past Jimmy. She entered the kitchen. She enjoyed seeing Jimmy Tate sweating, nerves frying, processed hair dripping and stuck to his forehead like a wet rag. Still, he found time to beautify his vanity by mopping the sweat from his face with his sponge.

Ruby looked at the stove. No steam was rising from the pots.

"That water ain't ready yet?" she asked Jimmy. She went to the stove and turned up the gas burners. "It won't get hot if it ain't got no real heat. A fool would know that."

He crossed his arms and watched Ruby opening kitchen drawers, searching for things. He thought about how much he hated her and how he should have beaten the bloody shit out of her instead of his money machine. He should have killed her black-country ass, chopped her up into tiny pieces, and then sealed her up in concrete and ghetto brick. And to put an end to the hated country girl he would have thrown her despised remains into the stormiest, blackest, and deepest part of Lake Michigan. Ruby opened another kitchen drawer and removed some utensils.

"What you lookin' for doctor a spoon, a goddamn fork? You ain't no goddamn doctor. We need to take her to a hospital."

Ruby gnashed her teeth together and ground them back and forth. "What did you say?"

"This ain't Mississippi you dumb-country bitch. And you ain't no goddamn doctor. We need to take her to the fuckin' hospital."

Ruby remembered the story she read in the day's newspaper. The paper was still lying on the kitchen's table. She reached out and snatched the paper, ripping it apart, throwing pages onto the floor until she had the section she wanted.

She stomped over to Jimmy and stood enraged under his tall frame. "I know you can't read, Jimmy Tate. Know how I know? I saw you tryin' to read the newspaper upside down. I'll read it for you." She looked at the paper, reading the quote: *"Black man castrated, hung from tree in Washington Park for dating a white woman. Sergeant Kowalski said that the body had also been tarred and ..."*

"Shut up!" he told Ruby. "You made your goddamn point."

"Sure, we can take her to the hospital. But what if that baby comes out as black as you? The word will get around about a white baby havin' a black baby. White folks will hunt you down and hang you from the biggest tree they can find in Washington Park."

The fear of being hung from a tree did not bother him. It was the possibility of the baby being his that made him smile, calming him down. "Maybe you right." His eyes were dreamy over thoughts of the baby being his. It would tie her to him forever. "I didn't think about that. You're right. It could be mine."

"Bring me that water when it's ready."

Freddie was screaming, calling her name.

"You better get in there," he told Ruby. "Stick a goddamn sock in her mouth. Stop her from screamin' like that."

Ruby ignored his request to suffocate her friend with a sock. When she entered the room she went to Freddie's bedside and picked up the rag on the table, dipping it into the bowl of cold-ice water. She laid the rag on Freddie's stomach.

"Pretty soon," she told Freddie, "that baby will crawl away from that cold rag so he can be in his mama's arms."

It was past 2:00 A.M. The baby was born at 1:28 A.M. Ruby made note of it. After Freddie was asleep and the baby bathed, powdered, and wrapped inside the expectance of a girl's pink blanket, Ruby left the bedroom with the baby in her arms. She made no mistakes. She even cut the baby's cord the right way.

She went into the living room with the baby in her arms. She saw that Jimmy pieced his vain self back together. He was fully clothed and sleeping, snoring inside the stillness of his practiced way of sleeping while sitting up and staying wrinkle free. His hat was even carefully positioned in his hand.

Ruby walked over to the sofa. "Jimmy, wake up. Jimmy." She kicked his foot hard. "Wake up." He opened his eyes and looked at her. She was smiling down at him, holding the pink bundle in her arms, "Don't you want to hold your son?"

She offered the baby to Jimmy. He did not hesitate to take it. When he pulled the cover away, exposing Danny's white face and wisps of golden hair, he plopped him down on the uncomfortable end of the sofa.

"What's the matter, Jimmy Tate? Don't you recognize your own son?" She was not able to stop herself from laughing. "Should I go buy some cigars, daddy, so we can celebrate?"

Jimmy got up from the sofa. His tall frame loomed over Ruby like a building ready to crush her. He put his hat on, cocking it to the famous tilt. He mopped the shine from his face and put the sponge back inside his breast pocket. "One day. You'll pay for that." He walked out. The jolt of the slamming door scared Danny awake.

Ruby picked him up from where Jimmy plopped him. She held him in her arms, close to her small breast, and rocked him back to sleep.

Freddie rejected Danny, refusing to cuddle him. On the next day Ruby wrapped him in his blanket and went into her room, waking her up.

"You have to take care of the baby," she told Freddie. "I have to work this afternoon. I need some more sleep. Freddie reluctantly took the baby from Ruby's arms and into her own. "Don't forget to feed him. When Ruby left them alone they were cooing and smiling at one another.

She went back to her room for a much needed sleep. The night of the baby's birth had aged her. She felt tossed and carelessly bolted into the unwanted realizations of grown-up life. She was forced into the growth of being an enraged and cursing woman. The southern and polite young-girl charm was gone.

REVIEW BOARD

Judge Shaw stopped writing. She looked at Ruby. "How did Mr. Tate feel about the two of you owning property?"

"At that time he didn't complain about her doing much of anything on her own. He was afraid of losing her because of the beating."

"You didn't answer the question," said Judge Shaw. "How did he feel about the two of you owning property?"

"He hated it until she convinced him that it was a good idea, especially, for his gambling."

"And the prostitution …"

"Not much of that went on in the house. Once, sometimes twice a month, two of the girls came down from Indiana to work on weekends. It was done in the basement. The house was mainly for Jimmy's gambling."

"Didn't Miss Walker work as a prostitute inside the home?" Judge Rodriguez asked.

"Yes, sometimes for special customers. Her work was also done in the basement."

"Didn't the children see this?

"When that kind of work went on inside the basement the kids couldn't get down there. The door was always locked. Freddie spent most her time working his houses in Indiana. Jimmy didn't like to see the way men drooled over her."

The judges looked at their notes and did some writing on their pads. "When did you and Miss Walker purchase the property on 54th Street and Prairie Avenue?"

April 15, 1959

CHAPTER THIRTEEN

EVERYBODY'S HOUSE

From its outward appearance the house looked like an oversized, dumpy, two-story brownstone. The conditions inside were deplorable. It was as beat up and rundown as any old firewood house. It could have easily been imagined sitting in the forested parts of the rural south. The rooms had been walked heavily around in and the walls had been damaged by destructive renters. But the frame was solid, an indication that the big house would stand up to the drills of tough repairs.

It was the only house that sat on the corner of 54th Street and Prairie Avenue. Like the back porches of tenements, lining the same side of the street, the back of the house and its stairs sat inside a long narrow strip of alley. And on either side of the alley every tenement had a back porch that owned a good deal of the alley's height and ground. At a glance the back porches appeared uneven and only just secure. The whole of the three story porches and their staircases were constructed with the kind of lumber that was easy to rot.

The bed of the alley's ground was made up of dirt, busted bits of charcoal, and thousands of pieces of shattered beer, wine, and whiskey bottles. It was easy to dig holes in the alley and bury things. It was where people laid their dead dogs and cats to rest. If one dug deep enough, into the alley's belly, it was rumored they'd find human beings buried there too.

Predominantly, the alley was a garbage stop where tenants dumped their trash inside steel garbage cans. In harsh winters, for those that didn't live on the first floor, they slung their trash over their banisters and onto the alley's belly.

In hot summers, for whatever reason behind the immovable waste stuck to the lowest bowels of poverty, the city's garbage keepers detested cleaning it up. They considered the unpackaged slim as the squalid result, laziness, of slum people. The stuck on remains of decomposing animals; raw, left-over food had to be pulled up by hand. Putting off the clean up, the garbage keepers waited until people called in and complained about the smell of something dead or dying.

For the sake of existence flourishing the alley was a place of plentiful meals. Cockroaches and rats grew stronger and more resistant to the products meant to kill. Their babies increased in abnormal droves and took up residence inside every flat. A kitchen light could not be turned on without seeing armies of running roaches. For many of the poorest children, to avoid unleashing baby roaches and lice inside classrooms and school cafeterias, their hair had to be washed with lye soap.

The alley was also a desired place for street whores, alcoholics, and heroin addicts, to accommodate their work and addictions privately. If you were not identified as a person of the street you didn't dare take the alley as a short cut unless you were brave and fearless like young Ruby Johnson.

Every fifteen to thirty minutes a city train stopped at the 55th Street Station. Upon arriving over 55th Street's neighboring ghettos—the section in question over the infamous alley—the trains had to slow their speed on a portion of rickety tracks. Knowing the unstable track spanning over the alley and away from the 55th Street Station, was in need of repair, the city took its time doing the work necessary to keep the trains accidental free.

Behind the bold neglect it was sensational entertainment when a train sped too fast around the curve and jumped the track. Seeing the industrial misfortune happen, for a few tenants, was like watching the opening of a grand-theatrical show.

Soon after a barrage of wailing fire trucks, police cars, and ambulances arrived. If any of the cars fell completely off the track, dangling just above the alley's ground, and if they were badly mangled, it took the fire department hours to rescue the passengers.

For many of 55th Street's neighboring residents the accident brought about memorable and exciting times. The theatrics of the rescue would sometimes last until daybreak. Back-porch parties could go on all night long.

When the heroic maneuvers unfolded, under the seal of darkness, it was hard for the city's heroes to see anything under the

369

dim streetlamps. For better sights on cries and pleas for help, and where they were coming from, the city brought out its tallest, brightest, and most powerful spotlights.

For the alley's back-porch people the fixed stare and brilliance of the huge lights transported them into a happy and agitated state. The heads of the powerful lights beaming up and down on the disaster, making monstrous shadows, finalized the unveiling of a long and spectacular event.

If there was catastrophic misfortune, people having met the fate of death, reporters and their crews arrived. They parked their vehicles askew anywhere they could. The most ambitious of them went from back porch to back porch asking questions, and paying special attention to those who saw it all happen.

As word of mouth traveled from ear to ear, throughout all the neighboring ghettos, crowds gathered at the edges of the alley. They marveled at the brave fire fighters transporting passengers onto the tracks, down ropes, ladders, and onto the alley's bed where ambulances and paramedics awaited them.

Those back-porch spectators, in it for the long haul, joined with friendly neighbors that had balcony seats with a good view. The men hurried off to Mr. Clark's store. They bought liquor, hamburger meat, hot dogs, and beans. They fired up grills and took over the cooking. Children stayed up past their bedtime and the young-welfare mothers took full advantage of the free food. If in summer they served every child ample portions chased back with cups of ice cold Cherry Kool-Aid.

While the men became intoxicated their interest went elsewhere. They danced and crooned in perfect harmony to the New Motown Sound that cut loose from loud radios and record players.

For those aging, in the middle of changing times, the sound of jazz with strings and horns could be heard. The voice of Billie Holiday did not hide from the threat of becoming lost recognition.

Some of the attentive people on the train could see the poor-black people having their back porch parties. They saw some of them dancing, eating, and drinking. Those on the train that couldn't see them could hear their laughing, cursing, music, and singing.

Passengers who never crossed the line, on foot, into the ghettos on the South Side of Chicago, believed that the fanatical-black people were somehow responsible for the disaster. They did not understand the reason behind having a big party at the expense of their fear and misery.

After it was over and the last person rescued, stand-up, back porch ovations of yells, rooting, cheers, applauds, and whistles were directed at the rescuers for a job well done. Smirks of appreciation and pride were seen on the faces of the white and black heroes.

The young-welfare mothers ran the excess of neighbors off their back porches. Motown crooning intoxicated men, and teenage boys, lingering in search of a hot time to make more babies, were run off too.

The young welfare mothers cleaned up the debris and threw the empty whiskey bottles into the alley's garbage cans. They cursed their stubborn children inside and into bed.

Most every child fell asleep to the dreams of being fearless firefighters, life-saving paramedics, and the toughest of police officers. The true heroes of all the neighboring ghettos of 55th Street, and its back alley ways, had set a good example from something bad happening. As depressive and exciting as it was the alley was part of everybody's house.

All the buildings on either side of 54th Street and Prairie were built in the early 1900's and late 1920's. Inside each were six apartments, two on each floor. They were referred to as coldwater flats because in winter when the pipes were frozen there was no hot water. In below zero weather, just short of most of the time, no heat came from the tubular iron radiators. And throughout the duration of humid summers, ninety-degrees in the shade, the only cool air came from electric fans. Overall the main subject of immediate environment was about unwanted cold or needed cold. Hot and cold was responsible for the definition of a cold-water flat.

A concrete-vacant lot separated the Walker house from the tenements on the same side of the street. The emptiness of nothing, next to the house gave it a false sense of privacy.

For neighborhood children the vacant lot was a fine concrete playground. During the week's end, throughout the hottest and most humid days of summer, they played softball and baseball games. The noise of their aggressive and hard playing fun floated inside every open window. The young welfare mothers, while cooling off and relaxing behind the blades of electric fans, sipping icy glasses of Orange Crush, felt good about having children without the anxiety of feeling burdened.

When the annoying heat of the sun slid behind everything tall, and the children's playtime neared its end, sheets of summer breezes wrapped up with cool wind, spun and cracked like a whip between the tenements. When the whole of the sheets unraveled the cool wind traveled in rushes and went inside all the open windows. The young welfare mothers then took their baths inside porcelain tubs without sweating too much.

Any time of year, at the beginning of darkness, for customers visiting the Walker house, the empty lot served as a place to park their cars. During exceptionally good times when money was an endless stream, the lot filled up with cars parked nearly on top of the other. The children, of other mothers, stayed awake past their bedtime just to listen to all the laughter and music that poured in through their bedroom windows.

Though Ruby had not contributed enough money to pay for her half of the house Freddie added her name, on the deed, alongside

373

her own. The agreement Freddie made with the slumlord, owner of the property, included the adjacent garage apartment across the alley. The entire purchase had been one of cash and flesh. The deal was made while Jimmy was out of town.

On the day of the move Jimmy was on his way to pick them up. During the drive he thought about his mistakes. He should have never agreed to let Freddie keep ten percent of the money she made. He knew she was keeping more than that. It was another thing done out of the beating guilt. Still, he thought, no matter her ownership of anything he owned her and anything she owned was automatically his.

Baby Danny was a year old. He was strong for his age and learned to walk early. While driving to the house Jimmy looked into his rearview mirror at Ruby playing with the blond baby. He hated how she treated the boy like she was his mama. He hated that her salary, one-hundred and fifty dollars a week, came out of his pocket. He felt she was overpaid.

"Pull over, Jimmy," Freddie said. "That's the house." She pointed to it.

"I can't fuckin' believe it," said Jimmy, parking his car. "You bought that big ugly ass house. It's been sittin' there empty for years. Nobody ever wanted the fuckin' thing. It's a bad-luck house."

"You don't see the whole picture," Freddie told him.

374

"Oh, I see the fuckin' picture in big fuckin' color."

Ruby got out of the car with Danny in her arms and went inside the house.

"You really wanna know why I bought this particular house?"

"Sure. I just love surprises."

"Look at it. It's practically a doggone mansion—a real bargain. There ain't nothin' next to it. People won't know what goes on inside unless they're lookin' through the windows. There's this really big room. You can set up some of those gamblin' tables."

"Not interested."

"Jimmy Tate, when are you goin to use your head for more than a lamp post?"

"Get out my fuckin' car," he told her. "That's it. Just get out."

"Now there you go gettin' mad at me for nothin'."

"You, that kid, and that country-ass slave can live in it without me."

Eventually Jimmy came around and the entire house began the process of being refurbished. A long corridor of rooms was off limits to those that didn't belong to the Walker Household. At the end and very center of the corridor was a sixth door that led up a short flight of stairs. The attic had been gutted out and remodeled to include a small apartment for Jimmy to use when he was there.

To create more space, for his gambling tables, the walls of the dining room had been knocked out and when it was joined, to include the living area, the huge room gave the illusion of being from one end of the house to the other.

A crap table took up the center of the floor. To the left of it a round table, with five chairs, sat in a corner and was used for black jack and poker games. Two worn sofas were up against the walls and had two matching easy chairs. A small bar was against a mirrored wall and mirrored shelves were embedded into it. All kinds of liquor bottles sat there. Four stools stood on the other side of the bar. Most of the time they seated restless women waiting for their men to quit gambling.

On Friday and Saturday nights, when the crap table was full, the kitchen table was removed and put in the basement. Customers rolled their dice on the kitchen's clean and even linoleum floor. Ruby served many plates of food alongside her feet. It was impossible to cook meals without floor gamblers getting hungry from the smell of real southern cooking right under their nose.

January 5, 1960

HERE COMES THE SECOND ONE

On January 5, 1960, late afternoon, Ruby delivered Neda into the world. After her birth, mother and daughter resting quietly, Ruby stood at the kitchen sink to wash her hands after putting the big pots away. Jimmy sat at the kitchen table with a deck of cards, playing solitaire.

"What color is it?" he asked.

"Lighter than you," she told him. "Pretty thing with a head full of beautiful black hair. It'll be thick like her mama's with more wave to it."

"A girl, huh?"

"Yeah, but, it's hard to tell."

"How in the hell is it hard to tell if it's a girl, or a boy?"

"I'm not talkin' about that. What I'm tryin' to say is it looks a little like you, but on the other hand."

Jimmy bolted up from his chair and left the kitchen. Ruby smiled quietly to herself.

Freddie was in bed and had stopped marveling over Neda when Jimmy opened her door, came in, and went to them. He leaned and stared at the baby's face. He looked hard, questioning.

377

"She ain't mine," he told Freddie. She looks like a got damn Mexican."

Ruby often wondered if the children were really mistakes of carelessness, or was her friend having the children she didn't know she wanted?

A few weeks after Neda's birth Freddie was up on her feet. It was late afternoon when Jimmy arrived with plans to take her to a matinee at the Michigan Theater on 55th Street. The movie was Breakfast at Tiffany's. He knew how badly she wanted to see it.

After it was over, and on the way of walking back to the house, she was surprised to find out he liked the movie as much as she did. They laughed and talked about bits and pieces of their favorite parts.

"I've been thinkin'," he told her.

"What's on your mind, Jimmy Tate?"

"About you and the kids." She stopped walking and looked at him.

"I ain't gettin' any younger. Maybe it's time I settle down. It's time for you to stop workin'. I never liked you doin' that anyway. You were never cut out for it."

"What are you sayin'?"

"I want you to rest for awhile. Stay home."

"Sure. "Any girl would like a rest off her back." She continued walking.

378

He stopped walking and looked at her. "I mean it. I'm thinkin' about changin' how we operate."

She thought something was not right. Besides gambling, the fattest part of the money in his pocket came from her. Was it possible he really cared for her? Maybe he even loved her. How many times had she tried to see something inside of him to love? Nothing ever showed itself.

He touched her cheek and kissed her hand. It was like the first time they met. "I mean it, Freddie. It's time to change things." He pulled her closer to him and kissed her intimately. She was surprised at the tenderness of it. "Promise me something."

"What is it?"

"Don't discuss what we just talked about with Ruby. I owe her so much for looking after you. I've got some making up to do. Something I want to surprise her with. Okay?"

"Sure. I've never seen you so secretive, Jimmy Tate. I wonder what's really on your mind."

He spent the night with her. Where sex and men come together, within her bed, he was the same roll over as all the others. If love was an existing thing that came from him she didn't feel any of it.

By the end of April she was sick of him hovering around her all the time, spending the night, having mindless and stupid sex with her. He was always there. He didn't go to Indiana and rarely checked on the girls working 55th Street. He made phone calls all the time to tell people what needed to be done.

He was always inside her room, lying on her bed, eating all the time and laughing at silly television programs. He played with Danny in a way a man plays with a child he hates.

Ruby was sick of him too. She said he was pretending to be sweet and that he was up to something strange. She said there was something more to it than sex and love.

December 9, 1962

HERE COMES THE THIRD ONE

It was the night of a blizzard. Smooth and clean sheets of snow covered the house and all its windows. Streets were shut down and no cars were able to drive in and around 55th Street, or into its neighboring ghettos. Ruby thought God was using the freezing cold and hard weather to stop something from happening. He was trying to kill it dead, or keep it frozen in time, never coming forth to join hands with demons.

It was bad and more than too much blood. Maybe the baby was turned in the wrong direction. Ruby didn't know what to do. If it got any worse there would be no choice. Even with traffic stalled dead in its tracks she'd have to find a way to get her to a hospital.

While Freddie was giving birth, Jimmy sat on the sofa staring out and into nothing. When he wasn't doing that he was sleeping, eating, or shuffling decks of cards and playing solitaire.

Freddie screamed loud from the pain of the baby's twisting and turning, trying to find its way out. Ruby breathed a sigh of relief when she saw the baby's scalp. She didn't see much more than that. It was a big child with a big head.

"Push hard, goddamn you, Freddie Walker," Ruby yelled. "Push it out of there."

When she pushed the baby's large head split some more of her open and there was more blood. More stitching needed to be done.

"Come on out of there," Ruby screamed at the baby. "You're killin' your mama. I said come out of there."

As if by Ruby's command the baby slid its way out. Ruby looked at it and shivers went up and down her spine. She took a step back. The baby didn't need help to holler. It cried out loud on its own—a wailing abnormal and ear-piercing sound. Cutting the cord was not easy. It was a hard and tough cord like a hundred rubber bands tied all together.

Ruby wrapped the baby in the blue blanket and handed it to Freddie. She stayed longer than she wanted. She had to clean up the mess, sew the stitches, bandage and comfort until mother and child were sleeping.

381

She left the room after 11:00 P.M. She had written the day of birth and time inside her black book along with the others.

Jimmy was sitting on the sofa waiting for Ruby. He was anxious, alert, looking as if he'd eaten all the slickness of the devil's smile. He saw the grim and sour look on Ruby's face.

He pointed his finger at Ruby and laughed. "I told you, Mississippi Ruby, doctor, one day you would pay for that remember? How you like your surprise. Is it a girl or a boy?"

Ruby said nothing. She stomped past Jimmy, into her room, and slammed the door shut.

Freddie was asleep and the baby lay beside her. Jimmy walked in. He gathered the baby up from the bed and took her into the kitchen. He removed the blanket and laid the naked baby on the kitchen table. He turned on the lights and began inspecting every inch of the baby.

A deep gasp came up and stayed in his throat. The sight of something, seen on the baby, had taken his breath away. He touched the deep-red splash, the cap-size birthmark on the left side of his neck. He turned the baby's head and was careful touching the same deep-red splash. His birthmark was in the same place on her neck. He went into the bathroom, off to the side of the kitchen, turned on the light and looked into the mirror. He pulled his collar down so he could see his mark. He went back into the kitchen and over to the baby, turning her head, looking at the mark.

"Yeah, you mine alright," he told the baby, picking her up, rocking her in his arms. "You came to me with a goddamn identification card. You'll know who your daddy is, angel baby. I think I'll call you Angela, short for angel, daddy's little angel. Don't ever forget it."

Ruby listened a little harder at her door. She couldn't believe it. The bastard had the nerve to be humming the devil child a sweet lullaby. Ruby was singing her own pissed-off song. She called it rock-a-bye-baby-my ass. She was angry at Mr. Grapes and Mr. Books for letting the evil deed come to life. She now knew why Jimmy was hovering around the house like a saucer with no place to land, always watching Freddie. He wanted her to have his child. It would tie her to him forever. He wanted to be sure the baby was his by keeping guard over her. Pushing aside her anger at God, Ruby picked her bible up from the table and knelt beside her bed. She prayed for the kind of help that would make it easy to love and raise the child.

383

September 21, 1963

HERE COMES THE LAST ONE

Ruby thought the afternoon was filled with melancholy and discontent. Leaves did not just separate and fall from the big oak trees, drifting to the ground, they stayed floating high on currents of wind as if they wanted to reattach to the trees they fell from. She believed she felt God's sadness over the last Walker sibling to be born.

It was just after 3:00 P.M. and Freddie's water broke too early. She was only in the middle of her seventh month. Jimmy argued against taking her to the hospital. Ruby ignored him. She knew the baby would not survive if she tried to deliver it herself.

Looking at Jimmy, arguing the facts behind Freddie's hospitalization, she saw it in his eyes. He wanted the baby to die and knowing that made Ruby more determined to see it live.

The taxi driver that picked them up was a quick-witted man that knew the back alleys, and streets, of the Southside like none she had ever met. Ruby told him to fly to Cook County Hospital if he could. They arrived in record time. Betty Jean was born right after they got there.

Outside the nursery's glass window, looking in at Betty Jean, she was a tiny and premature-incubator baby that could easily fit into the palm of a man's hand. She was hooked up to tubes and machinery.

Ruby looked at Freddie, sitting in the wheelchair, looking through the glass at her baby. She cried quietly and looked at Ruby.

"No more, Ruby," she said. "Sometimes girls, even women, make the kind of big plans they don't talk about. Not even to best friends. Big plans can mean taking risk. Sometimes, things can't change without following through with a plan. If I don't mess up my plans will all work out. Just don't stop bein' my friend."

Ruby leaned and hugged her. "I can never stop bein' your friend, Freddie Walker. We all the other's got besides those children."

"How will a child with one leg shorter than the other be treated in this world?" She asked Ruby.

"That doctor said it won't be noticed too much. A good-heavy brace will help stretch that leg out a bit. She'll be okay."

"I think I'll call her, Betty Jean," she told Ruby.

"Yes. She looks like a B.J."

"They said I couldn't have any more kids, Ruby. That's a good thing isn't it?"

385

REVIEW BOARD

"After the birth of Betty Jean our lives became routine. The kids were growing up fast. I relaxed into being more than partly responsible for raising them. I guess there was comfort in knowing she couldn't have any more babies."

Judge Bennett looked across the table at Ruby. "Betty Jean was the only child born in a hospital?"

"Yes," answered Ruby.

"Miss Johnson," Judge Bennett said, "Do you realize you took it upon yourself to bring three children, into the world, without the system knowing they existed? In essence you stole their identity. You denied them the right to be noticed, legally, as American Citizens."

"I told you why she chose to have those children at home?"

"If she cared nothing for them," said Judge Rodriguez, "wouldn't it have been best to see them adopted into loving homes?"

"No."

"Why is that?"

"She loved them," Ruby said. Maybe she didn't know it at first. Freddie was a complicated girl the same as she was a complicated woman."

"I don't understand what you're trying to tell us," said Judge Shaw.

386

"She could have planned the whole thing," said Ruby. "She was always thinking ahead. Maybe she mapped out her whole life the way she wanted. Maybe it included having children."

The bailiff entered the room. The questioning was over for the day.

That evening Betty Jean invited Danny and Neda to the house for one of her pasta dishes. After dinner they admitted the food was good and complimented her. Betty Jean cleared the kitchen table and the four of them sat together to finish the two bottles of red wine Danny brought with him.

"I think I saw a light inside that old garage apartment," said Betty Jean. I wonder if what's his name is still alive."

"Spits," said Danny.

"Yeah, him," said Betty Jean. "Do you think he still lives in that ole-dirty place?"

"No," said Danny. "He's probably dead."

"Or in prison," said Angela, "Where he should be."

"He wasn't such a bad person," said Neda.

"By the way," said Angela, "I know what this cozy little dinner is all about."

"Everything doesn't have a motive, Angela," said Danny.

"I don't care what you say," Angela told him. She looked at all of them. "You can forget it. Don't try to influence what I say to

387

that review board. I'm tellin' them every bad thing she ever did to me."

"It would be a pack of lies," said Neda. "Miss Ruby never did anything bad to any of us. She took care of us when nobody else gave a damn. Get over it, Angela."

"You and that stupid Puerto Rican accent," said Angela. "She didn't take care of me. My father did."

"Oh, give me a break," said Danny. "My father, my daddy, I'm so sick of hearing you glorify that monster you called your father. He was an evil son-of-a bitch."

"I wish you would quit blamin' me," said Angela.

"Blamin' you for what?" Danny asked.

"It ain't my fault you don't know who your fathers are." She looked at all of them. "Maybe if you knew who he was you wouldn't be so anxious to kiss Ruby's ass."

"What the hell does a father have to do with tellin' the truth?" asked Neda.

"You are so screwed up, Angela," said Betty Jean. "You're goin' to die alone. Nobody will be there for you. Your own kids will grow up to hate you."

"Yeah," said Angela. "That's not original. Think of somethin' else Miss creativity."

"If we don't at least get some of that money," said Neda, "it'll be because you screwed up everything.

"No, shit," said Danny. "You need to have your head examined. The three of us will contradict everything you say to that board. You think ..."

Betty Jean interrupted Danny by saying one of her poems. *"Be nice to the birds and the bees and the frogs. Be nice to the little baby cats and dogs. Be nice to the little baby roaches and rats. Be nice to the people so big and fat. Be nice to the little cripples don't be mean. Be nice to the little cripple girl Betty Jean. Be nice to Danny, Angela, and Neda. Give them lots of candy they love mashed potatoes. I'm the crippled girl that wrote this poem but don't worry about me because I'll get along."*

They were silent, looking at Betty Jean. Danny's laughter turned into a roar and his sisters laughed with him. "I remember that stupid poem," said Danny.

"Me too," said Neda, laughing, taking her brother's hand.

Betty Jean threw her head back and laughed just like her mother. She reached out and took Angela's hand and for a few moments the house shook with all their laughter. After realizing they were holding hands they stopped.

Angela got up from the table. "I have to get some sleep. It's my turn, remember?" She went out of the kitchen and it saddened Betty Jean.

"I know all about her now," said Betty Jean. "One of these days, just like Miss Ruby said, she'll be alright."

"That money is ours," said Neda. "I won't let her ruin it for us."

"You know somethin'," said Danny. "I don't believe Ruby gives a damn about the money."

"She's not so old," said Betty Jean. "She can still have a good life."

Danny got up from the table and walked out of the kitchen, through the old gaming room, and into the corridor of bedrooms. He opened the door to Freddie's room and went inside. He thought he could smell her perfume.

He went to the window where she liked to stand. He looked out from behind the curtains, toward 55th Street and saw the neon lights. He turned and looked at the room, still sparse of furniture. He remembered how she had taken great care to arrange her room to what he thought made her feel ordinary. She didn't like things crowding her in. The one old dresser was still there. Her many perfume bottles and makeup were gone. The top sat empty of everything except a new lamp. Jimmy's wall length mirror had been removed. There was still the one night stand, and on top of it was nothing. The Wall Street Journal's and books about finances were gone. He sat down in the same chair where he always sat with Neda beside him. Being in the room brought back a flood of memories.

HIDING UNDER BEDS

On days when Jimmy wasn't there Danny sometimes hid under Freddie's bed playing with his toys. He believed he was quiet enough and that his mother did not know he was under there.

When she was sleeping and he was under her bed, reading one of his comic books, trying not to disturb her, he thought the way she snored was nice. It wasn't loud. It was breezy and pretty and she made an odd whistling sound that was cute and funny. To him it sounded like some kind of melody to a song.

Hiding under her bed was his way of being close to her. It was his way of getting to know more about his mother. Her presence made him feel safe, sheltered and loved.

On Wednesday and Thursday until late afternoon he often wondered what she did alone in her room for so many hours. He learned she read books about finances. She had a library card and was always checking out books, reading them quickly, and taking them back the same day.

When her telephone conversations were spoken through whispers he took the liberty of playing louder than usual with his toys. Because his mother was on the phone he figured she wasn't paying attention to small details.

One day after she hung up the telephone she leaned quietly over the edge of the bed and her head was upside down. Her hair was loose and sweeping the floor. She looked at Danny. "What are you doing under there, Daniel?"

"Visitin' you."

She smiled at him. "How long have you been doin' this?"

"I don't know."

"You can play louder than that if you want." You're not botherin' me."

Danny's eyes swelled with tears and his voice was weak. "You mean you don't want me to leave, Mama?"

"No," she said, still smiling at him. "I don't want you to leave. You can stay under two conditions."

"What?"

"I don't want you under there when Jimmy is here. Promise me."

"Promise. What else?"

"Well," Freddie said, thinking hard about the second promise. "You have to promise me, Daniel."

"What, mama? Whatever it is I promise. Cross my heart." He made the sign of the cross.

"Promise me you will always, always, leave some of your comic books for me to read. Especially Archie, those are my favorite." Danny started to giggle and laugh and so did his mother.

"I promise."

392

Through the happiness of knowing she knew he was there, and didn't want him to leave, Danny cried quietly to himself and played with his toys louder than he ever did.

He kept his promises starting on the day they were made. He gathered all his Archie Comic Books and left them in a stack on the right side under her bed. When she was finished with them she left them under her bed on the left side. Sometimes she left him some change to buy new ones. If it was too much money he went to Mr. Clark's store and bought some candy underneath the glass-counter top.

Long after Danny quit hiding under his mother's bed Jimmy took revenge anyway. He saw signs that Freddie was starting to care about her children. She was spending time with them.

Danny remembered a noisy and crowded night of gambling and drinking was over. Ruby came inside their rooms to tell them it was okay to take their baths and go to bed. She did not allow them in any part of the house on nights of gambling or basement prostitution.

Jimmy, Spits, Freddie, Big Sadie, Spit's girlfriend, sat on the sofa inside the gaming room. The house was empty of clients. The music was loud and they were drinking.

Spits, in charge of playing the music, played a song by James Brown, "Say it Loud I'm Black and I'm Proud."

393

Jimmy stood up, went to the center of the room, and began to dance.

"Mr. Jimmy Tate," said Freddie, joking, "You cannot dance a lick."

"Back in New York," he said, "when I was a real young man, I won all kinds of money when my feet hit the dance floor."

"Yeah," said Spits. "Soon as your feet hit the dance floor somebody was tryin' to trip your ass."

Spits and Sadie broke up with hysterical laughter and pointed their finger at Jimmy. Freddie tried to hold back her laughter, knowing it would make him upset.

"Show me your moves Jimmy," said Freddie.

The more stilted and stiff his dancing became the louder they laughed.

"I'm sorry," said Freddie, "looks like all black folks don't have rhythm." Their laughter became louder.

Jimmy stopped dancing. He looked angrily at the three of them, laughing at him. He glared at Freddie. "What the fuck did you say? You white motherfuckers ain't got no rhythm."

"Man," said Spits, "you blowin' everybody's high."

"Fuck you," said Jimmy. "That's the got-damn truth. I can prove it. Danny!"

"Leave him alone, Jimmy," said Freddie. She was no longer laughing.

394

"No," he said. "I'm provin' the shit. Danny."

After yelling his name a few more times Danny appeared. He stood in the corridor's doorway.

He looked at Jimmy. "What?"

"Come here for a minute, white boy," said Jimmy.

"Don't do this, Jimmy," said Big Sadie.

"Shut your fat-fuckin' mouth," said Jimmy. "You ain't part of this family."

"Come here," he told Danny who went to him.

Jimmy put his arm around Danny's shoulder as if he were on display. "This here white boy has been around black folks all his life. I will prove that rhythm is in the blood. Not in the fuckin' feet." He walked over to the stereo, picked up the record player's arm, and restarted the record. "Dance" he told Danny.

"I don't want to," said Danny, looking at his mother. She lowered her head.

"I said dance goddammit and sing the song with Mr. James Brown. I know you know it. Dance and sing the goddamn song."

Danny knew if he didn't do what he was told the cruelty would go on longer. He looked around for sights of Ruby.

"She ain't here," said Jimmy. "Dance white boy. Sing the song." He went to the sofa and sat beside Freddie. "Do it. Let's see what you got."

Danny danced and sang with the record. And each time he sung, "I'm black and I'm proud," spits and Jimmy laughed hysterically.

Big Sadie, disgusted with all of it, got up and left. Freddie went searching the house for Ruby who had finished bathing Betty Jean.

Freddie entered the bathroom, "Danny needs you."

Ruby went into the gaming room. She looked at Spits and Jimmy pointing and laughing at Danny. She lifted the record player's arm. "Go to your room," she told Danny, shoving him in that direction. "Take your ass home, party's over," she told Spits. She went into Danny's room and found him sulking, near to tears. "He ain't worth the salt." She lifted his head, making him look at her. "What are we made of?"

"Steel," said Danny.

"You damn straight."

Jimmy opened the door and walked into Danny's room. He looked at the two of them. "Hey, white boy, I'm sorry. Okay? Okay?"

"Yeah Jimmy," said Danny.

"You and me," said Jimmy, "we'll do somethin' tomorrow, somethin' special. I'll make it up to you. Okay?"

"Sure Jimmy," said Danny.

Jimmy looked around at the posters on Danny's wall. "How come you ain't got no black folks on your wall, white boy?"

"Get out of here," Ruby told him. When he left, slamming the door, Ruby saw the huge poster of Martin Luther King. It covered Danny's door.

Danny tried to come out of his memories but couldn't. He didn't like that the past was flooding every inch of him. He looked on his mother's wall at the blue ribbon he won in school. He was first place in the class spelling bee. He thought how hard it was to attend an all black school.

He remembered a time during his second year. The demoralizing happened during a full class. Thelma Brown, his teacher at the time, came near the desk where he sat. "Daniel," she said, "what date and year did Rosa Parks refuse to give up her seat to a white passenger?"

"December 1, 1955," answered Danny.

With no praise for the correct answer she asked another question. "What year, and date, did Dr. King have his first meeting with a United States President?"

Danny was anxious for her praise and approval. "June 23, 1958,"

"No, Daniel. The date was June 24, 1958."

"Somebody's got there dates screwed up," said Danny. "It ain't me."

397

The children laughed and pointed fingers at Thelma Brown. She went to her desk and picked up her ruler. "Come with me, Daniel." She took him inside the boy's bathroom. With each strike of the ruler onto the palms of his hands tears streamed down his cheeks. "In my classroom you are invisible."

On the same day Ruby noticed he had trouble holding a cup of milk in his hand. Knowing that the school's corporal punishment was either on the back of the legs, buttocks, or hands, she took Danny's hand into hers. Her heart skipped a beat at the sight of the blistering red palms and fingers.

"I don't want to go to that doggone school," said Danny. "I ain't right even when I'm right, Miss Ruby."

She checked the facts of the question. Danny was right. It was after school hours but she knew some of the teachers stayed late marking their papers.

Ruby and Danny entered Thelma Brown's classroom and found her erasing the blackboard. The room was empty.

"He's the only white child in this school you drunken fool," said Ruby. "Do you know how hard it is for him to be accepted?"

Thelma continued erasing her blackboard. "Maybe it would have been best if none of the Walker children had ever been born."

Ruby could not stop the release of her own corporal punishment. She went to Thelma and slapped her across the face.

Thelma squealed from the sting of the slap. She tried to walk away from Ruby who grabbed her and pushed against the blackboard.

"If you ever hurt one of my children again," said Ruby, "I'll beat the hell out of you."

"Who do you think you are marching into my classroom and attacking me? I'm going to report you to the police. Get out of my way."

She tried to work her way past Ruby who pushed her harder against the blackboard. "You ain't reportin' on nothin' you ignorant-racist fool."

Thelma Brown's fear of Ruby had left her. "There's a movement going on in this country. An educated-black woman, such as me, will never devote any sincere time educating Freddie Walker's white trash."

Ruby stepped closer to her. "If you hurt any one of my children again with words, or rulers, I'll kill you on a dark night when I don't have a thing else to do. I'll get you when you're walkin' down the alley with that dirty dog, goin' to buy your whiskey. I'll be waitin' for you in the shawdows, hidin' behind somethin' you can't see."

Neda knocked on the door, breaking up Danny's memories. She walked in and looked around Freddie's room.

"It hasn't changed that much," said Neda.

"No, it hasn't," said Danny. "Let's get out of here."

After they left Betty Jean cleared the dishes. Her leg was bothering her and for some reason her limping was more prevalent than before. She went into the old gaming room and while cleaning up behind Angela, wedged underneath one of the legs of the sofa, she found the old doll that caused so much trouble between them.

She remembered the hot summer night when the house reverberated with fast jazz and the gaming room overflowed with customers. The kitchen table was full and Ruby was busy feeding the men that sat there. Angela chased Betty Jean into the kitchen.

"Go back to your room," Ruby told them.

"Give it to me," Angela said, snatching the doll out of Betty Jean's hand. Angela's pulling of the doll, and the heaviness of the steel brace on Betty Jean's bad leg, caused her to stumble and fall.

Ruby helped her stand. "Go get ready to take your bath, baby. I'll be there in a minute."

Betty Jean limped out of the kitchen. She cried over the taking of her favorite doll.

Ruby grabbed hold of Angela and shook her. "When are you goin' to stop beatin' up on your own sister?"

"She wants people to feel sorry for her because she's a cripple," said Angela. "I'm gonna beat her up every chance I get. Ain't nothin' you can do about it."

Jimmy came into the kitchen and looked at Angela. "What's all the fuss about?"

400

"I just wanted to play with it," she told him, hugging the doll.

"That white doll don't belong to you," said Jimmy. "Where's that black doll your mama bought you?"

"It's ugly," she said. "I don't want it. I'm white and black. I can have both. I want this one."

On the same night Ruby was finished bathing Betty Jean. It was time to button the child inside the tight pajamas she made for her.

"Why I have to wear so many clothes to bed?" Betty Jean asked.

"If anybody makes a wrong turn into the wrong room," said Ruby, "I'll have time to kill them."

"I know why Angela is mad. She wanted a white doll and …"

"I know," said Ruby. "Your sister doesn't want a doll that looks like a Negro. Your mother bought her that doll for a reason. She wants to help her understand who she is."

"She should have given the doll to Neda. She tells everybody she's a Puerto Rican. Sometimes, she even talks like one. She hates being a nigger more than Angela."

Ruby had never hit the children. She did not believe in punishing children with pain. She grabbed Betty Jean harder than she should have. "Don't you ever use that word," she demanded. "Look at me, girl." Betty Jean, crying, raised her head and looked at

401

Ruby. "All of you have the same mother. You may be two kinds of color but color ain't more important than your own blood. That word has no business comin' out of your mouth. You understand?"

"Yes, mam. I'm sorry, Miss Ruby."

Ruby softened her tone and pulled Betty Jean into her arms. "Promise me you'll never say that word as long as you live. Promise me, Betty Jean."

"I promise," she told Ruby.

"I'm sorry your sister is so mean to you. She's mad at the world because she doesn't like bein' in it. Color of skin has nothin' to do with it. She'll change one day. You'll see."

The next day Jimmy gave Angela a five dollar bill to purchase the kind of doll she wanted. Instead, Angela went to Mr. Clark's store to buy candy underneath the glass countertop. Mr. Clark was busy waiting on another child buying candy. Angela hated that he took so much time with the girl who was around the same age.

Once outside, Angela walked behind the girl while she ate her candy. "I like your red sweater with all those flowers on it," said Angela. "It sure is pretty. Can I walk with you?"

"No," the girl said.

Angela got angry. "Why?"

"My mama told me to stay away from you. She said you're evil and that your mother is white. She sleeps with men for money."

402

She followed the girl to the building where she lived. She beat the girl badly.

That same day Jimmy arrived at the police station in a panic. He entered the room where Angela was being held. He looked at the red sweater on the table. He picked it up and threw it back onto the table. "What you cryin' for?" he asked her. He looked down at her swinging her feet back and forth. "What the hell are you cryin' for?"

"To make myself feel better that's why. I thought you were goin' to leave me here."

"You nearly put that girl in the hospital. What you have to say for yourself?"

"I ain't sorry and I'd do it again."

He shook his head and turned away from her gaze. He was smiling at her comment. "When are you goin' to learn to be nice to people? Your sister is still hurt behind that beatin' you gave her."

"She deserved it. I hate her. She's a stinkin' cripple."

He cupped her chin, forcing her to look up at him. "When you do something bad to people, especially white people, they make you pay for it. From now on try to be nice to your mother, sister, and brother. But don't ever trust them."

"Why not?"

"Besides Miss Puerto Rico they're white people. So what if they're your own blood. They will stab you in the back whenever they get the chance.

"Trust nobody," she said, crying.

"That's right, baby. Trust nobody." He picked her up. Her head was laid on his shoulder and her arms around his neck.

"No matter what people say about you I love you so much, Daddy."

"You better not stop. Let's go buy you a red sweater. That one is too small anyway."

The closer Jimmy came to losing Freddie the more he influenced Angela to be cruel to her brother and sisters but more to her mother. The first time Freddie confronted him about Angela's behavior she was standing in back of him, looking at him in the mirror while he was shaving.

"Why do you teach her to hate her own flesh and blood?" Freddie asked.

"Is that what this conference is about?"

"Don't you realize what you're doin' to her. How mean and hateful she is?"

He looked at her looking at him in the mirror. "Angela is mine. I'm her daddy. I'll teach her how to survive in this fucked-up world."

"I'm her mother. I gave birth to her."

He laughed. "Yeah. That's too bad."

"Jimmy."

"What?"

404

"Before I got pregnant with Angela remember those few days I was not under your guard? Maybe, she isn't your child."

He laughed. "Fuck you," he said. "Don't try it. My baby came into this world with a goddamn identification card." He pointed to the red splash of birthmark on his neck. He laughed again until she left him alone.

Betty Jean came out of her memories. She finished cleaning Angela's messes around the coffee table. It pleased her that the old red sofa with its fringes on the pillows was still there. If it had been changed to something new, she wouldn't have found the doll. She would take the doll back home with her.

REVIEW BOARD

The next day the judges were more specific with their questions. Ruby knew it would not be long before she lied about what she didn't want them to know.

"You said that Mr. Tate supplied the children, except for Betty Jean, with fraudulent birth certificates and social security cards. Is that correct?" Judge Bennett asked.

"Yes," said Ruby. "The school wouldn't accept them without it."

"You said Jimmy increased his cruelty toward the children as they got older?" asked Judge Shaw, making her notes.

"Yes," said Ruby, "except Angela. He knew Freddie was starting to act differently. It was like she was growin' up in front of the eyes of everybody. I guess he knew change was comin'."

"Who was the other man?" Judge Bennett asked.

Ruby shifted left, right, showing that the question made her uncomfortable. "I don't remember his name?"

Judge Shaw stopped writing and looked at her. "The statement from one of the children at the time of the arrest said the man was Caucasian."

"Yes, he was."

"It also stated that their mother was taking them to live with this man?"

"Not to my knowledge," said Ruby. "I know he was not a customer of hers. Their relationship, from the little she told me, was a personal one. They were friends. Jimmy knew about it. She didn't hide it. I did know he was trying to help her get out of prostitution."

"How often did they see each other?" asked Judge Rodriguez.

"Maybe once a week. He came to the house but never inside. He waited in his car until she came out."

"Come on, Ruby," said Judge Shaw. "You and Miss Walker were best friends. She must have told you more about this man. Best friends tell each other private things, very private things."

406

"Not us. Not all the time."

"Have you ever heard the name, Robert Bishop?"

"No."

"Have you ever heard the name, Parker Bishop?"

She thought the lie would not win her any points if they knew about Parker's ongoing visits to the prison. "Yes, I have," she answered. "Freddie hired him as an attorney to handle her money while she was in prison. He came there to see her once in awhile."

"Mr. Bishop's visits were more than once in awhile," said Judge Rodriguez.

"I guess that's true. She made all that money while she was locked up. Somebody had to help her look after it."

"What is your relationship with Mr. Bishop?"

"I don't have one. He referred me to an attorney to help me with this review. He's the one that told me Freddie left me everything. I signed some papers for him."

"Is he this man?" asked Judge Bennett.

"You mean her friend from long time ago? Not that I know of. If he was I'm sure I'd recognize him."

"That was a long time ago," said Judge Bennett. "Maybe you wouldn't."

"Maybe," said Ruby.

"When did Freddie Walker meet this man?" asked Judge Bennett. Do you remember when the relationship began?"

407

Remembering the time Freddie met Parker was easy. Ruby would never forget how animated she was when she came home and told her about the sweet young man she met at the park.

September 22, 1967

CHAPTER FOURTEEN

AN ANGEL UNDER A TREE

Early on Saturday morning's Freddie went to Mr. Clark's store, picked up her Wall Street Journal, and headed toward Washington Park. She didn't like the edge of the park closest to home. She walked through to the other side where her favorite oak tree waited for her to come and lay underneath it. A short distance from where she lay was a bench. She hardly paid much attention to anyone sitting there.

On this Saturday morning after she stretched out her blanket and lay down, opening her paper, she heard the rustle of someone near. She continued to read.

"Not many women read the Wall Street Journal," she heard someone say.

"Well," she said, "if I ever make a penny in this world I'll know exactly what to do with it." She looked up from her paper at the young man sitting on the bench. "All I ever see are colored people in this park."

"I love this park," he said. "Did you know some of these trees are over a hundred years old?"

"Not really," she said. "I never gave it much thought." She looked at her paper and read something. She sighed with frustration. "If I don't get my hands on more pennies than I got, I'm gonna miss out on somethin' big."

"Oh, yeah," said Parker. "Like what?"

"This here Leland Electronics," she said, pointing to a section in the paper.

Parker stood up and took a few steps toward her. "Mind if I …"

She looked at him. "Not unless you tell me your name first."

"Parker," he said, "Bishop."

"You don't look like a Bishop. As a matter a fact you don't look like the religious type."

"Bishop is my last name."

She hesitated, looking at him. "Well, have a seat Mr. Parker Bishop."

She scooted aside and he knew it was okay to sit on her blanket beside her.

"See here," she said, showing him the section inside the paper. He leaned and read some of the print. "When the time is right that stock will hit the roof."

He wanted to see if she knew much of anything else about stocks and bonds. "What about that Maverick stock? It looks like a winner."

"No," she told him. "That'll fizzle out soon enough."

"What's your name?"

"Freddie," she said.

"A guy's name, I like it."

"Yep, everybody always kid me about it. You ain't no serial rapist or anything real bad?"

"No," he said seriously, "not at all."

She looked at his expression and laughed. "I was just kiddin'. My full name is Freddie Walker."

Parker extended his hand and she took it. "I'm very pleased to meet you."

"Likewise, Parker Bishop."

The thing he hated like nothing else was the slipping away of the sun and the chill it left behind. It was like they had known each other all their lives. If there was perfection of pure beauty, and grace, inside and outside of a woman she had it all. It was not only her sensuality but the unexplainable that came with it, like the warmth and kindness she generated. As she went on talking he didn't hear her. He just wanted to look at her and smell the discreet scent of her perfume.

"One day," she said, "everybody will be walkin' around talkin' on little telephones."

"Really."

"Sure. Think about it. Just imagine. Here I am in some fancy restaurant. I reach into my purse, take out my little telephone, and call my best friend Ruby, "Hello Ruby. This is Freddie." She pretended to hold a phone close to her ear. "I won't be home until this afternoon."

"Yeah, I can see that. I can."

"Electronics is the wave of the future." She looked around and up at the darkening sky. What time is it?"

"Why don't you buy some shares? They probably don't cost much because it's a new company? I can take care of it for you. Buy all the shares ..."

"Hey," she said, "wait uh minute."

"No, not like that. You wouldn't owe me a thing. I mean you can pay me back."

"What's your callin' card, Parker Bishop?"

He thought about what she said. "Oh! You mean what I do for a living?"

"Somethin' like that?"

"Promise you won't hold it against me?"

"Of course not."

"I'm an attorney. I might start my own practice or work my way up in my ole man's firm. "

"So, you're a lawyer."

"Sometimes I don't think so."

She stood and he helped her gather and fold the blanket. "Well, I'm truly honored to have you as my friend. You never know when you might need a good lawyer. It was a pleasure to meet you, Parker Bishop."

She extended her hand and he took it, not wanting to let go.

"See you around she said," walking away from him.

"Hey! I'd like to see you again."

"Woolworths Department store has the best hamburgers in town. You can find me there every Sunday at Noon."

"Which Woolworths," he said, calling out to her.

"47th Street, this side of town." She turned around and walked backwards, smiling, waving bye to him.

"See you tomorrow," he said, watching God's perfect creation walk away from him.

THE BADNESS OF MEN

By the end of winter, 1967, Parker learned many things about her, the children, Ruby and even Jimmy Tate. He knew what she did for a living. With each word, hearing it first hand from her, the nasty tale chipped at his heart until it was completely broken. He was left to realize that he may never have her as his wife or his woman. He wished she had lied, allowing him to continue to live inside his fantasies of there being something wholesome and virgin about her. But she hid nothing from him. She wasn't a liar.

She was in need of friendship from a man who wanted nothing else. So he gave into the kind of childish loyalty said and done by children which included hooking together their little finger, promising themselves as friends forever. It was that or being left to love memories.

The night he fell drunkenly into bed upset with the men that had raided her body his thoughts were screaming murder. He thought he would have to find out more about Jimmy Tate. Having him killed would be the right thing to do. After the rest of his dizzy drunkenness had been fed to the toilet he fell back into bed. Before sleep took hold he thought about the badness of men. No matter the status. No matter the color. No matter the man. The infection of cruelty to women was within all men. Some were just more infected than others.

Every Sunday afternoon he parked in front of the house and waited for her to come out. On four different occasions he ignored the black man looking down through the curtains at him sitting inside his car, engine running. When she came outside the house she was always on time and happy to see him.

They never shared late night dinners together. Their time together was on Sunday afternoon. They spent two hours sitting inside a warm booth at Woolworth's. There they proceeded with their ritual of eating hamburgers, French fries, and drinking Lipton Tea.

After their plates were cleared they read the Wall Street Journal and had more tea before discussing the financial section. With his support she purchased an abundance of stock in the small company Leland Electronics. She was their largest share holder. She even paid him back the loan. It was not only Leland Electronics she invested in but other companies which were doing well. She was making real money. She even had a secret bank account.

He loved it when she looked up over the top of her paper and smiled at him. The simplest of things made her so happy, like seeing him smile at her.

"You know what you are," he said, folding and laying his paper to the side.

"I don't like where this is heading, Parker Bishop," she said, looking over her paper at him.

He reached and took her paper, folding it, placing it on top of his. "I'm not kidding. Know what you are?"

"No. Maybe I don't care."

"You are a naturally gifted stock broker," he said, loving the way she threw her head back and laughed.

"You are a naturally gifted maniac."

"People like you only come along every fifty or so years. They call them financial geniuses. They have this ability to sniff

415

trends, where things are headed. They can read the market and feel where it's going. It's a gift, a talent. Just like any other. Like a Van Gogh, a Mozart. They not only hear the music they can see it. You can paint the true making of money. I mean real money, not dimes and nickels." She sighed and he knew she didn't want to talk about having that kind of ability.

"I feel like walking over by the Lake," she said.

"It's too cold. We'll freeze are asses."

"Just for a little while. We can drive over there." She stood, put her coat on and walked away from the table toward the exit.

The coldest and thickest clouds of cold wind had risen and stayed still just above the Lake. When it was too foggy the Lake cleared the clouds and sent them rushing and pushing hard onto shore. The cold air of clouds separated and blew around them, pushing against them when they tried to walk. While they leaned into the strong wind he told her about his two childhood friends, Allen and Tom. He tried to put her at ease about meeting them.

"Just because they're rich like you, Parker Bishop, doesn't mean they ain't bad. There's always a side of people nobody knows about. Sometimes that side is just as mean as an old devil."

"Not these, guys." His tone of voice defended them.

"I don't know, Parker. You shouldn't have told anybody about me. Our friendship is private, between us. What if I give

416

them bad advice? I'll be responsible for some rich guys losin' money. Forget about it."

"No, you won't give them bad advice," he said, trying to convince her. He wanted to show her off to his friends. "Every stock you've picked is doing great."

"No. I can't do it. Every time I get a bad feeling about something the back of my neck starts itchin'. Just like now." She scratched the back of her neck. "Do they know I'm a woman?"

"No. They think Freddie is a guy. It'll be a surprise. It'll be fun." He walked backward in front of her, making her smile.

"Jimmy doesn't know I do more than read the journal. If he finds out I'm playin' the stock market ..."

"He won't. Come on. It'll be more like a small cocktail party. You can even wear something fabulous."

"It sounds to me like you're tryin' to show off somethin', Parker Bishop."

On the evening she agreed to meet his friends, the dress she chose to wear was a stunning red evening gown that showed her bare shoulders and cleavage. The deep brown and black fox wrap, keeping her warm, could have been mistaken for something more expensive.

Seeing her dressed so classically beautiful took Parker's breath away. After getting into the car, without saying a word, he

417

reached over and gently removed her glittering earrings. He unhooked her necklace. He put the jewelry on top of his dashboard.

"Hey," she said. "What'd you do that for? A girl's jewelry is her security blanket especially when it just might be real, Parker Bishop."

"You don't need any enhancement. It's already there. You were born wearing diamonds."

"Now that sounds real crazy. I'm startin' to worry about you. Come on. Drive this ole car before I change my mind."

While driving toward his side of the city they were quiet. He kept his eyes on the icy road. Along the stretch of curving drive that led to the house where Allen lived, he heard her gasp.

"Who in the heck lives in a mansion like this?"

"Allen Sanders, the State Attorney's son."

"He's one of those best friends?"

"Yep," he said. "I live a few blocks away. My house, my dad's house, where I grew up is larger than that one."

Allen, Tom, and a young Billy Waller were waiting for them when she stepped down the stairs and into the great room. She did not look around at the luxury of the room with any kind of awe, for she thought it best to appear unimpressed. Parker did not like the way that Tom looked at her.

"Gentlemen," said Parker, "this is my broker, Freddie Walker."

"Wow," Tom said, taking the long gloved hand, kissing it. "I believe you have yourself a couple of new clients."

"Tell me about it," said Allen, taking her hand, kissing it. Though he was not as wealthy as the three white men, she extended a hand to Billy who took it and kissed it.

"And what might your name be?" she asked Billy.

"Billy Waller. I do all the dirty work for their daddy's when they need a good-private dick."

"Well," said Freddie, "that must be a real exciting profession."

"I'm here because these guys think it's cool to have a Negro as a friend."

Parker, Allen, and Tom exchanged looks behind the comment. When Billy started laughing they did the same.

Tom crossed to the bar and behind it. Freddie took it as a cue to sit on one of the bars stools. She took off her gloves.

"What is the lady drinking?" Tom asked.

"A very dry Martini with three fat olives ..."

"At your service," he said.

Parker sat on the stool beside her. Allen and Billy stood at the bar near them. Parker saw Tom give her the kind of look he didn't like.

As the night went on they moved the party into the den where there was a desk and Freddie sat behind it. The Wall Street Journal

419

lay on the desk in front of her. When she talked about some of what she read Tom put his head close, over her shoulder, reading with her. He had far too much to drink and whatever it was that he whispered in her ear affected her negatively and Parker knew it. He wanted her to suggest they leave and gave her certain signs but she ignored them.

She got up from the desk and looked at Allen. "Is there a ladies room in this ole house?"

"I'd be more than happy to point you in the right direction," said Allen. His words were slurred.

When she left the room Allen slapped Parker on his shoulder, "You lucky bastard. She's not only fucking gorgeous she's got a brain. When's the wedding?"

She entered the bathroom and went to the sink. The look she gave herself, in the mirror, was one of loathing. The glint of tears shone that she was hurt by what Tom whispered in her ear. She felt disgusted with herself. She felt there was no escaping what she was.

Parker picked up a bottle of scotch. He opened the French doors and stepped outside onto the cold terrace. Billy was with him. Through the windows, left of them, he could see her sitting at the bar flirting with his friends. He hated her for doing that. Why didn't she follow his signals to leave?"

Billy looked at his watch. It was too cold to stand on the terrace. He had work to do for Parker's father and needed to leave.

420

"She knows more about the stock market than any man or woman I ever met," said Billy. "Where did you meet her?"

"At the park," Parker said, sipping from the bottle.

"Where's her office, downtown?"

"She's a whore," Parker told him, blatant about it. "She has four kids and none of them have the same father. I meet the woman I love, the woman of my dreams, and she's a whore."

"I'm sorry to hear that. Sometimes the best people can get caught up in all the wrong things. Sometimes all it takes is the right person to come along and pull them out."

"Yeah."

"She's something special. I ain't seen beauty and grace like that in a woman in a long time. Matter fact, I don't think I've ever seen it in any woman. There's something about her, something without answers or explanations. Race has nothing to do with it. I don't know if I pity you or envy you." He looked at his watch. "I've got a big day tomorrow. Tell everybody I said goodnight."

"Yeah," Parker said.

Billy left and Parker went back inside the den. The scotch had gotten the best of him and he fell asleep in the chair where he sat. More than an hour passed before he awakened. The clock on the desk read 2:23 A.M.

421

He walked into the great room and saw it empty. He heard her somewhere in the house, upstairs. "Hey." he called out. "Where is everybody?"

He climbed the last stair. At the end of the corridor of bedrooms and baths he saw a door slightly ajar. He heard her again, laughing. Arriving at the room he pushed the door open and saw the three of them. Tom and Allen were in bed with her. Their shirts were off and the rest of their clothes unraveling. Her dress was on the floor and she lay between them. Their eyes met. Her look at him was cold and distant. It was the only time she appeared to be ugly and cheap. He said nothing and left. He was under the impression she was trying to hurt him intentionally.

A few days later he left the city and went to his father's house in Florida. He stayed there for months. When he came back he and Freddie picked up their friendship as if nothing ever happened. Where Allen and Tom were concerned he ignored their phone calls and refused to see them.

By the beginning of summer, 1970, Jimmy's gambling houses and his whore houses in Indiana and Michigan were doing worse. The police he had on his payroll shut down all but two of his houses.

Many of the women left him. Even Freddie wasn't bringing in the kind of money he was used to. She refused to work out of town under the poor and insecure conditions the houses fell under.

That same summer Parker began the process of working for his father's firm. While Robert Bishop was on vacation he worked out of his personal office. On the day Jimmy came to visit Parker he was seated behind his father's desk. The assistant working with him had gone to lunch.

When Jimmy walked into the office Parker just looked him. For some odd reason, he was not surprised to see the hustler standing there with his hat in his hand. He was smiling like they knew each other.

"I understand you have interest in some property that belongs to me," said Jimmy, going deeper into the office.

"Property as in a piece of furniture?" asked Parker. "Do you mean like a car, or a house?"

"Mind," said Jimmy, nodding toward the chair across from the desk.

"No. Please do."

"Think about like this," said Jimmy, sitting in the chair. "Property falls under the category as being just another material possession. Eventually material things perish, gets thrown out in the trash ... gets worn out ... dies. People perish. They get worn out and eventually die."

The threat of hurting her caused Parker to tremble without it being noticed. He smiled at Jimmy. "You made your point."

"I'm a businessman. I'm here to extend you an invitation."

423

"To what?"

"My place. You've been pickin' her up there every Sunday, for the last two or three years?" He looked around at the notice of wealth.

"I get it. This is like a business arrangement between us?"

"Yeah. You can call it that." He stood and put his hat on. "I run the best crap game on the Southside. I book it by the days. Friday nights is wide open. Bring some of those rich friends with you. Drinks are on the house."

Parker took a deep breath and relaxed in his chair. He picked up the phone and dialed her number. When Freddie was on the line he told her what happened.

"Don't worry," she told him. "Please do what he says. I told him I'm leavin' him."

"You mean it?" asked Parker. "I can help you."

REVIEW BOARD

"This invitation Mr. Tate extended to her friend, did he take him up on it?" Judge Shaw asked while writing her notes.

"Yes," but he only came inside the house a couple of times."

"Did he bring friends with him?" Judge Rodriguez asked.

"Yes."

"Is there anything else you want to tell us?" asked Judge Bennett.

"When she came home that morning from that cocktail party she was different," Ruby told them.

"And you still don't remember where this party took place and with whom?"

"No," she answered, eyes shifting. "It was such a long time ago. All I know is that she told me the men were very rich."

"I find it hard to believe that you cannot remember any of their names," said Judge Shaw.

"It was so long ago. I just can't remember."

"Go on," said Judge Bennett.

"Like I was sayin' she was sad but in a different way. It was the kind of sad that comes after something loved has died. It was like all the girl in her was dead, gone, and the woman had emerged and wasn't leavin'. She started payin' attention to her children. She took them places like museums and amusement parks. I saw it happen."

"You saw what happen?" asked Judge Bennett.

I saw her fall in love with her children and the young man she was seeing."

"And Angela?" asked Judge Rodriguez.

"Jimmy hated the new Freddie, the woman. Every time she tried to take Angela with her to the park or something like that he

425

found a reason to pick the girl up. Sometimes he didn't bring her back for more than a few days."

The judges looked at their notes and whispered the last of what they needed to say to each other.

Judge Shaw looked across the table. "Ruby, do you sincerely believe, with all honesty, you were justified in killing Jimmy Tate?"

"Yes," Ruby answered. There was no hesitation.

The Bailiff opened the door and Judge Bennett motioned for him to enter. He went to Ruby. She stood and put her hands in back of her.

"Thank you for coming," said Judge Bennett.

The Bailiff took her arm. "Is that all," asked Ruby.

"Yes," said Judge Shaw without looking at her. "For now it is."

The Bailiff led her toward the way of leaving the room.

"Miss Johnson," said Judge Shaw. "Why didn't you just leave?"

Ruby smiled and tears filled her eyes. "I'm not a selfish woman."

The bus ride back to the prison was a rattling relief. She thought about them. No matter how things turned out she had no right to keep all that money. It was theirs. Parker would help her figure up how to divide it between them. With all their faults she still loved them more than her own self.

426

CHAPTER FIFTEEN
TRUTH THAT COMES TO LIGHT

The judges knew that Angela was a frightening woman with an angry temperament. They knew that questioning her to get straight answers would not be easy. Angela cocked her head from side to side while glaring hatred at the judges. Her hands were clasped together tightly on the table.

"What do you want from me?" she asked them. "I don't remember a whole lot about that night."

Judge Shaw looked at her papers. "Not according to this," she said. Your statement is fifteen pages."

"That was a long time ago. I was a child. All I have to say has been said. It's in my statement. I have nothin' else to tell you. I do know that Ruby Johnson killed my father. It was not justifiable homicide. It was cold-blooded murder."

"Are you referring to Jimmy Tate as your father?" asked Judge Bennett without looking at Angela. He continued writing his notes.

"Who in the hell else would I be talkin' about?"

"How can you be sure that Mr. Tate was your legitimate father?" Judge Rodriguez asked.

"How do you know he wasn't? We share the same kind of birth mark. I know he was my father. Everybody knew it."

427

"Angela do you mind if I call you by your first name?" asked Judge Rodriguez. His tone of voice had softened because he saw that Angela was in serious need of help.

"I don't care what you call me."

"Very, well," said Judge Rodriguez. "Angela are you sure you have nothing to tell us about the night your father was killed?"

"No. How many times do I have to repeat myself? Can I go now?" Angela had become agitated and her whole self appeared to be trembling.

Judge Shaw leaned and whispered something to the judges. She cleared her throat. "Since you have nothing you'd like to tell this board, at this time, you are hereby ordered to remain within the city limits of Chicago Illinois until you can. You can leave now."

"You can't do that."

"You will remain as ordered until something jogs your memory," said Judge Bennett. "If you do not remain you will be arrested and brought back to the State of Illinois."

"I have two children that need me home."

"Then I suggest you cooperate," said Judge Rodriguez.

Angela jumped up from her chair and it tilted over and slammed to the floor, causing the judges to move around in their seats. "Take me away if you want."

"Why would we want to do that?" asked Judge Bennett.

Angela balled up her fist and glared at them.

"We're only trying to get at the truth, Angela," said Judge Shaw.

"The truth," said Angela.

"Yes," said Judge Shaw. "Please sit down." Angela kept standing and tears were sliding down her cheeks. Judge Shaw got up and walked around from the table. She picked up the box of tissues and passed them to Angela who took one. She put Angela's chair upright and she sat down. Judge Shaw returned to her seat.

"I know this is hard," said Judge Rodriguez. "But we need your help. We have to be sure we're making the right decision."

"On the night Jimmy Tate was killed your mother had been brutally beaten and hospitalized," said Judge Bennett. "Did you witness this brutality?"

"Yes," Angela cried. "But he wouldn't stop kickin' her and hittin' her. She didn't even try to defend herself. She hardly even cried. She just let him do whatever he wanted to. I had no choice. Some of her blood was on my clothes. There was blood all over the floor."

"What are you trying to tell us?" Judge Shaw asked.

"After Neda ran out of the room and Ruby came and he hit her I had no choice."

The judges sat quietly until Angela stopped crying. She pulled several Kleenex from the box and blew her nose.

"Take your time," said Judge Shaw.

"I remember I was so cold. It was a storm but there was no rain. But after my daddy had been shot it was strange. It started raining. When the lights came on I remember I was sitting on the floor, in the corner, and he was lying there in front of me, dead."

June 23, 1970

I LOVED YOU MORE THAN ANYONE

The room was still dark but Ruby could see the gun in Angela's hand. She took it and put it inside her dress pocket and got up from the floor. She stumbled to the wall and flipped on the ceiling light. Jimmy was slumped over on top of Freddie.

Ruby went to them. "Freddie," she said, shoving her. Freddie moaned and Ruby looked at Danny. He was sitting on the floor with his back against the wall, looking at Jimmy's body. "Where's Betty Jean?" Danny pointed under the bed. Ruby looked and saw that Betty Jean was awake and crying.

"Help me get him off your mama," Ruby told Danny. "Danny." He had not heard her. "Danny," she yelled. "Help me." Danny stood and helped her push Jimmy over and onto the floor. "Go get Neda. She's with the twins." Danny ran out of the room.

Ruby went over and knelt beside Angela. "Sweetheart," she said, "I want you to go to your room for right now."

"No. You shot my daddy. You killed him."

"Go to your room," said Ruby, tearing up. "For once do what I say."

"No! I'm staying with my daddy."

"Do what I tell you," Ruby yelled. "Do it now."

Angela got up and left the room.

Ruby did the best she could to help Freddie. She knew she would have to go to the hospital. She put a blanket over her and a pillow under her head and left the room, closing the door.

Danny and Neda sat on the sofa watching Ruby pace, thinking about what to do. Betty Jean was asleep and her head rested on Danny's knee.

"What are we goin' to do, Miss Ruby?" asked Danny.

"I don't know, Danny. I just don't know. We can wait much longer to get your mother to the hospital."

"I'm glad he's dead," Danny told her. "I'm glad you killed him." Ruby breathed a sigh of relief. She was happy the boy did not see much in the dark. He didn't know his sister had killed her father. No one knew it but her.

"Maybe he's not dead," said Neda.

"We should shoot him again," said Danny.

"The bastard is dead," Ruby told them. She went to the bar, removed a bottle of whiskey, poured some into the glass and drank it.

431

"You killed my daddy," Angela was standing at the edge of the gaming room looking at Ruby. "You killed my daddy. I saw you do it."

"You're nuts," said Neda. "He shot his self in the head. When the police come that's what I'm tellin' them."

"I'm goin' to tell the truth," said Angela.

"You will go to your room and stay there until we figure out what to do." Ruby yelled at her.

Angela had become hysterical. "You killed my daddy."

She screamed it over and over again until Ruby went to her, grabbed her, and put her hand over her mouth. "Danny," said Ruby. "Get the clothes line."

Ruby forced Angela inside the bedroom she shared with Betty Jean. When Danny walked in he helped Ruby tie her up with the clothesline. It broke Ruby's heart. She had to tie a rag around Angela's mouth. She was just too hysterical.

When they were back inside the gaming room Ruby turned to Danny. "We've got to work fast, Danny," she said.

"Let's bury him in the alley," said Danny.

Neda stood up from the sofa, "I can help."

"No," Ruby told her, "we'll manage. You keep an eye on your sisters. A loud noise came from Angela and Betty Jean's bedroom. "Go check on Angela," Ruby told Danny.

432

Danny went inside the room. He did not see Angela. He looked at the window. It was wide open and the dresser was pulled up close to it. Angela had untied herself. She made a rope out her sheets and had tied them to the leg of the dresser. All Danny saw was the top of her head outside the window. He ran to the window and looked at her climbing down the sheets.

"I'm tellin'," said Angela. "I'm goin' to the police."

Danny bolted out of the room and ran into the gaming room. "She got loose," he told Ruby. "She went out the window."

"Go after her Danny." Danny was out the kitchen door before she could finish her sentence. Ruby followed behind him.

Those looking at the black girl running down 55th Street might have wondered if she was in some kind of training. Her legs were like the fast grinding, churning, wheels of some kind of awesome machine; strength drawn from someplace not of the earth.

It could have easily been declared that a child flying on feet that fast was destined to be an Olympic Sprinter … the fastest girl in the world with her neck full of medals. When her running days were over she would become a famous doctor, lawyer, or even a politician making her people so proud. The supremacy of a ghetto super girl was being looked at with hopes.

Then the white boy came running after her. He looked crazed, running nearly just as fast. The people were amazed that the white boy stayed on his feet.

Then the black woman came running behind the white boy but by the time she reached the next street she stopped, out of breath. She fell to her knees and screamed, "God no. Please no."

All the people watching recognized her as Freddie Walker's best friend. She was the one Jimmy called Mississippi Ruby. She was the woman he hated. They then knew who the runners were and that trouble was headed toward that house of ill-repute. Some of the people were happy about it. They believed that Jimmy Tate's crime against women and children was on its way of being looked at under a spot light.

Danny was only a few feet behind Angela. "Angela wait." he cried. "Angela, Angela, Angela." When he reached out, touching the back of her blouse, almost grabbing it, she dodged him and ran up the steps and into the police station.

Angela shoved open the door with a bang. She had the attention of the police officers. "Miss Ruby killed my daddy," she screamed. "They're goin' to bury him in the alley."

Outside the station Danny heard what she said. He turned and ran back the other way. When he saw Miss Ruby he ran into her arms.

"It will be okay," Ruby told him. "Remember what I said, say nothin'. Promise me, Daniel."

She only called him Daniel when there was nothing she could do about something bad. "I promise, Miss Ruby. I promise."

REVIEW BOARD

"Angela," said Judge Shaw. "Did you kill Jimmy Tate?"

Her silence was long. "Yes. I killed him. I didn't remember for a long time." She looked at the judges. "I had to kill him. He was killing her. You see I did love her. I loved my mother more than anyone."

Ruby was allowed to have John with her. She stood in front of the judges because she was too nervous to sit down.

Judge Bennett cleared his throat and read his papers. "Based on the testimony given to this review board, regarding case number: 1645-67-78916, the State of Illinois Versus Ruby Johnson, this board ..." He stopped reading and looked at Ruby. "This board of retired old judges find you not guilty of the murder of James Nathaniel Tate. You have been granted a full pardon. You are a free woman."

The heaviness of her tears weighed her down and John held her up. "Thank you," said Ruby. "Thank you."

"Good luck, Miss Johnson," said Judge Shaw. "I hope you find some happiness in what's left of your life."

Inside the judges break room Judge Shaw could not hold back her tears. "How is it that a woman can sacrifice her life, for so long, for those she loved without ever saying a word? I envy Freddie Walker for having a friend like Ruby Johnson."

Danny arrived at his home and saw that the grass had not been cut. His wife was meticulous about their lawn. The front of their house was always nicer than any other. He parked in the driveway and knocked on the door. There was no answer and the curtains were closed. He stuck his key in the lock and opened the door to any empty house. The outcome of everything was all over the news and his wife knew what it was. He walked into the great room. Over the fireplace was an envelope. He picked it up and pulled out the letter inside, reading it quickly.

He tossed the letter onto the floor and sprinted out of the house and down the street, looking at neighbors addresses. He saw the right one. He rang the bell and a young black woman opened the door.

"Oh, hi," she said. "Your wife said …"

Before she could finish Bobby came up beside her. "Hi, Daddy."

Danny couldn't believe what he was seeing. Was the boy his imagination? "Hi, sport," he said, picking Bobby up, squeezing him and putting him down. "Go get your things."

Betty Jean stood in the doorway of their old bedroom. She was watching Angela pack her things. "I have something for you."

"What …?"

"It's what you tore the house apart looking for." Betty Jean went and handed it to her.

Angela looked at the silver identification bracelet that read "Jimmy Tate's Little Girl." She shoved it into her pocket.

"Take care," said Betty Jean. She hugged Angela before she could push her away.

Parker arrived at his office early that morning. He wanted to see how John was getting along. John was sitting behind his desk, hands folded in back of his head, with his feet up.

Parker looked surprised. "Just because this is temporarily your office, while I'm away, doesn't mean you can put your feet on my desk."

John took his feet down. He looked at Parker and smiled. "Hey boss. It's good to be back. Back in the fold." Nicki came in and handed John a message. She smiled at Parker and left.

Parker went to a window and looked out at the Lake. "Ruby is going home today."

"Yes. I know," said John. "The Walkers are very rich people, Ruby too."

"Go on and say what you have to."

John got up and went to his side, looking out at the lake. "That review board, Ruby, the Walkers, lots of unanswered questions.

437

"Sometimes it takes a three-ring circus to give people justice."

"Maybe," said John, "that review board was some kind of therapy session you created for Ruby and the Walkers."

"Maybe you should concentrate on what you have to do while I'm away."

"The Governor has announced his intention to run for President. I heard you were friends since you were kids."

"Well, if he's elected, I'm sure he'll do a fantastic job."

"Yep," said John. "Power and money can make a serious dent when it's used to manipulate the law."

Parker turned and smiled at him. "I knew you were a fast learner."

Angela passed through the metal detectors at the airport, sending off the buzzers. She took the silver identification bracelet out of her pocket and placed it on the conveyer. Once back through, she was allowed to pass.

She picked up the bracelet and shoved it back inside her pocket. As she prepared to board the plane she passed a trash can. She stopped walking and turned around to look at it. She took the bracelet out of her pocket, went back to the trash can, and tossed it inside.

Later that day Mae came to process Ruby out of the system. When it was done they hugged and Mae cried.

"I'm so happy for you, Miss Ruby," said Mae. "You take real good care of yourself. I'll miss you."

"It's been real nice knowin' you Mae," said Ruby. "Thanks for lookin' after me and my friend. I have something for you." She gave Mae an envelope. "Don't open it until I'm gone."

"I won't," said Mae.

Ruby watched Mae walk away and thought about how much she would miss her.

Mae wondered what was inside the envelope. She opened it, pulled out the check, and screamed.

The gates were opened and Ruby stepped out from behind them. She was surprised to see all four of them waiting for her. Danny had Bobby with him.

Angela went to Ruby. She reached and took Ruby's bag. "We thought you could use a ride home, Miss Ruby."

"Why thank you, Angela. I guess I could use a ride home.

Made in the USA
Charleston, SC
05 January 2012